ININDU

CHAD MICHAEL COX

Note: If you purchased this book without a cover, you should be aware that this book is stolen property. It was reported as "unsold and destroyed" to the publisher, and neither the author nor the publisher has received any payment for this "stripped book."

Inindu

Cover Painting: Eric Wilkerson
Map and Interior Artwork: Chad Michael Cox

ISBN 978-1-7356718-5-7

For Mom——a survivor, and the definition of strength;

and to my other mother
who believed I could write

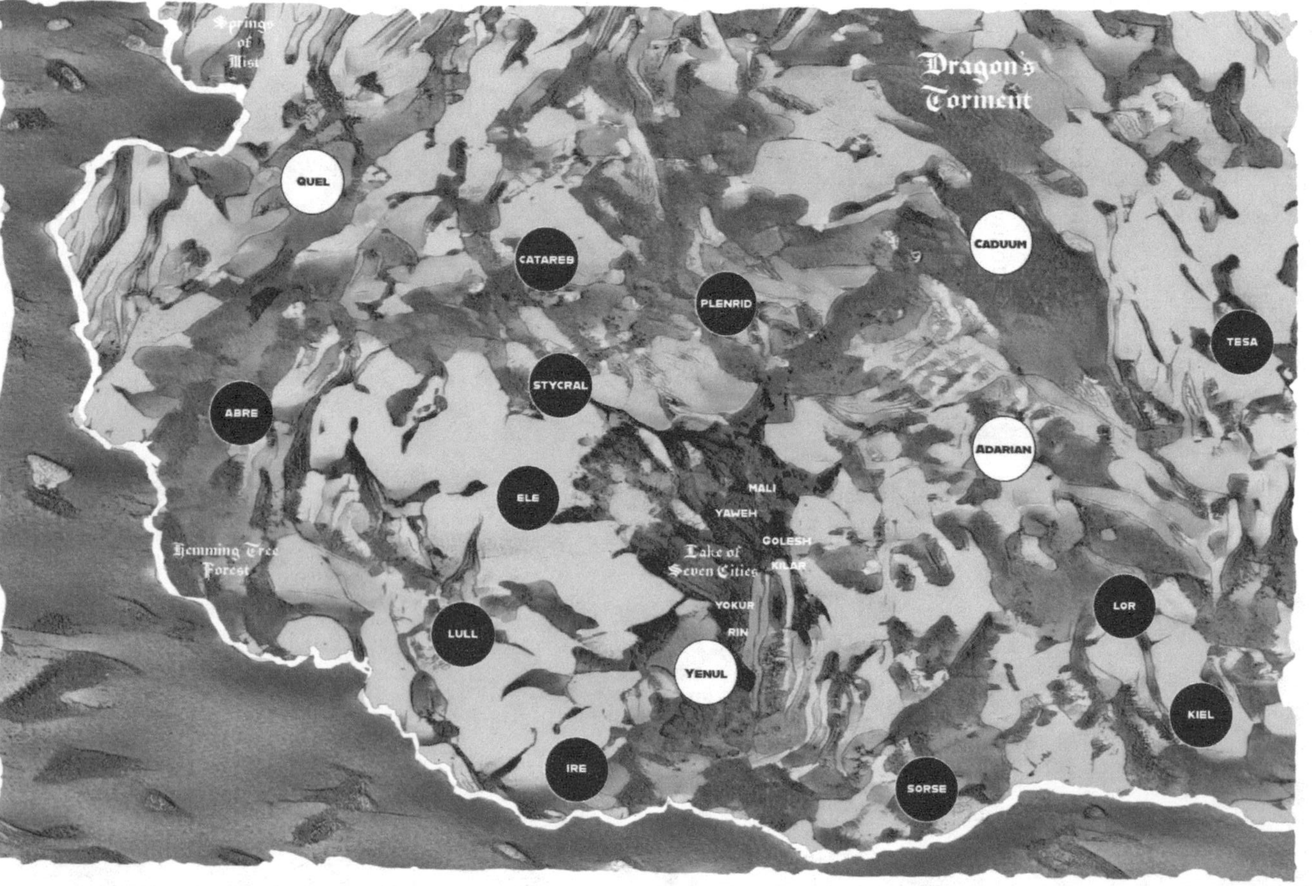

Dragon's Torment
Springs of Mist
QUEL
CADUUM
CATARES
PLENRID
TESA
STYCRAL
ABRE
ADARIAN
ELE
MALI
YAWEH
GOLESH
Lake of Seven Cities
KILAR
Hemming Tree Forest
YOKUR
RIN
LOR
LULL
YENUL
KIEL
IRE
SORSE

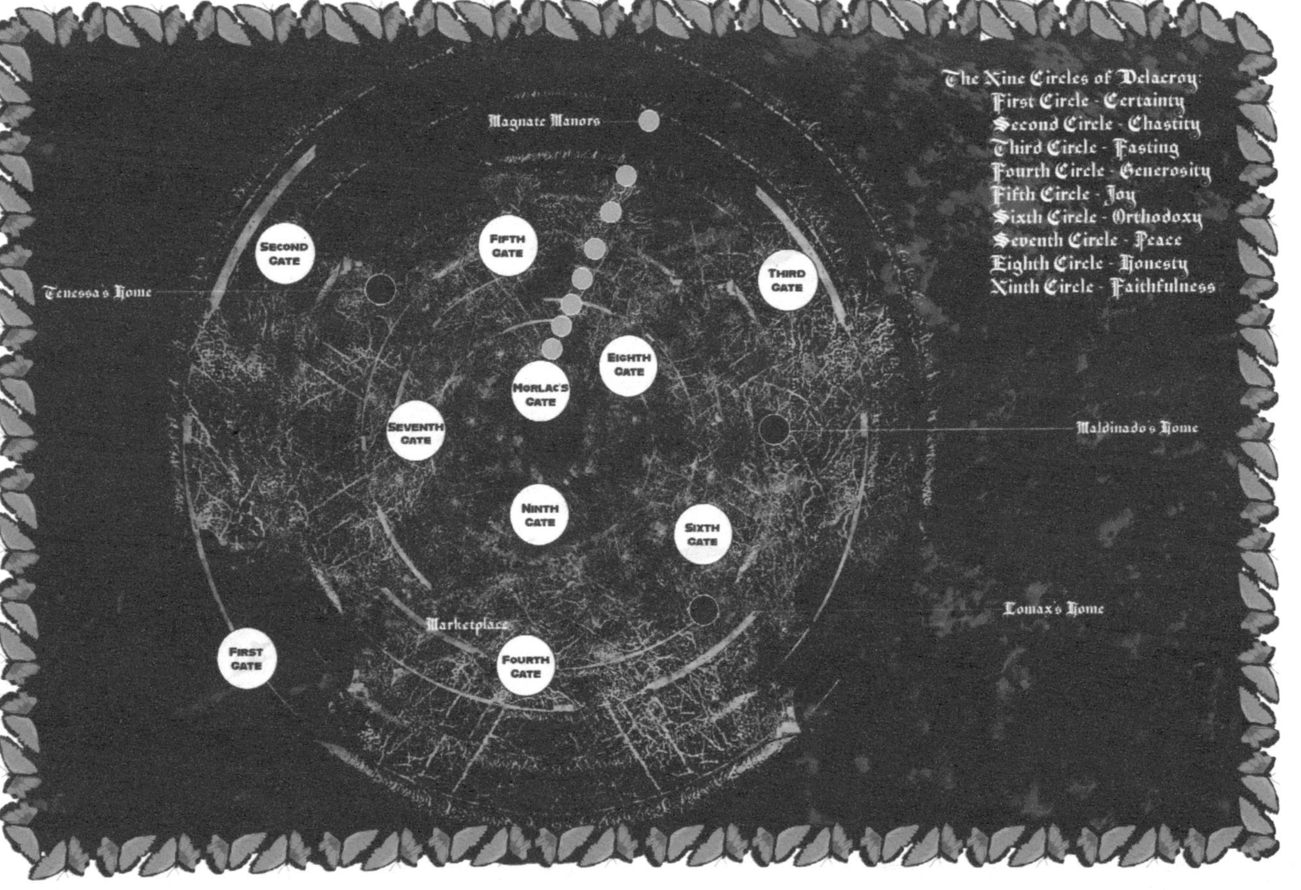

The Nine Circles of Delacroy:
First Circle - Certainty
Second Circle - Chastity
Third Circle - Fasting
Fourth Circle - Generosity
Fifth Circle - Joy
Sixth Circle - Orthodoxy
Seventh Circle - Peace
Eighth Circle - Honesty
Ninth Circle - Faithfulness
Magnate Manors
Tenessa's Home
Maldinado's Home
Lomax's Home
Marketplace
First Gate
Second Gate
Third Gate
Fourth Gate
Fifth Gate
Sixth Gate
Seventh Gate
Eighth Gate
Ninth Gate
Morlac's Gate

BEFORE

aunride and Teyo stood beside massive double doors leading to the Daughter of the Adow's sleeping quarters; each of the twelve painted door panels combining to depict the final moments of a First Etabli's life as he lay dying in the arms of his Adow. Adarian, hero of Ire. Portrayed in swirling magenta and gradually darkening shades of gray. Leading up to the majestic door, several torches lined the corridor in either direction, but aside from their own shifting shadows Faunride and Teyo found no cause for concern. War raged far from these doors. Indeed, the Adowian Army had marched toward Quel three years prior, yet both guards felt uneasy. Faunride paced to the opposite side of the curved corridor. He looked to his left and then to his right, finally returning to his position beside the doorpost and to the right of Teyo.

"I saw it, too," Teyo cleared his throat as he spoke. They hadn't uttered a word since assuming their posts.

"That flicker?"

Teyo nodded.

Faunride carefully opened one of the heavy doors to the Daughter of the Adow's room—oddly severing Adarian's painted head from where his body lay portrayed upon the opposing door—and stepped inside long enough for his eyes to adjust to the darkness. He saw Troq holding the Daughter of the Adow against his chest; warrior and yearling lay asleep in the bed. Nothing else moved.

Morlac, god of another world, entered the room unseen by either guard.

Faunride closed the door and returned to his post.

Inside the room, Morlac moved to the bedside and waited. Troq's breathing appeared much more laborious than that of the yearling whose chest rose only slightly, imperceptible if not for the black hair that fell from her shoulder and gently shifted with each breath. She nuzzled against the ancient warrior who slept on his back, his white bearded chin resting comfortably upon her head.

Morlac waited, the rhythm of his breath matching that of Troq's. He stepped closer. The warrior's bushy white eyebrows began twitching. Troq's eyes moved wildly—frantically attempting to escape from beneath fully sealed and unrelenting black eyelids. His right hand gripped the decorated quilt that covered his body, his left hand calmly cradling the yearling. Troq turned from her as though wishing to speak with Morlac, but his eyes never opened. His neck arched momentarily even as Morlac snatched Troq's soul—his light essence—at the moment of death, inhaling the ethereal streams of yellow light with a single, deep draw of life-extending breath. Thus, Morlac prevented the warrior from rejoining the Sphere. Troq's body fell and slunk in a lifeless heap.

The yearling slept unaware.

Morlac opened his mouth and exhaled the captured light essence—streams of yellow turned red. The kiss of Morlac. He pulled dust from the moth and wind from the sea, churning them together with the glowing red light. He drew milk-like tears from his ivory-white eyes and tossed them into the whirling mix of suspended life. The torrent solidified into the shape of a body and, a moment later, Troq awakened within the space between life and death. The dream world. Illusion.

"What is your name, pilgrim?" Morlac asked.

Troq opened his eyes, "I am Troq."

"I am your god, Troq," Morlac placed his arm around the dead man's shoulders.

"Where are you taking me?"

"To another world."

Troq followed his new master across the room toward the massive double doors, but they did not open to the hallway beyond. Instead, Morlac opened them to reveal a red dirt road leading toward the city of Delacroy.

"What is to become of her?" Troq looked back at the still sleeping yearling.

"She is no longer your concern," Morlac stopped walking, but indicated Troq should continue.

"You're not coming?"

"We must part, for a time, but I will soon return." Morlac pointed toward Delacroy, "Worship me faithfully, Troq, and I will invite you to live inside my palace, at the center of the city. Forever."

The chosen one passed over the threshold to Delacroy.

Morlac seemed to fade from existence, slightly—a flutter—before hastily closing the doors to another world.

He waited. Then he opened the doors again to reveal an altogether different world. On his left, a graveyard of beasts spread into the distance. Towering bones crumbled like glaciers into a cloud of dust that covered the land. On his right, lush, green gardens filled with a dozen varieties of green foliage. And a path of white sand between. This time, Morlac himself passed through before closing the door.

Back in the Daughter of the Adow's room, following Morlac's departure, a small glowing sphere rose from Troq's docile remains. It shone a brilliant yellow, hovering momentarily before diminishing into darkness, leaving the Daughter of the Adow where she slept. A moment later, a blacksmith's forge roared to life in Caduum. Hiate's thickened fingers wrapped around a long-abandoned hammer, and he breathed the stale air of a long-forgotten town. Hiate. The Sphere incarnate. Brother of Troq.

The red-bearded blacksmith turned to his apprentice, Edran, "Fetch more Dragon's Ore, yearling. 'Tis the ping of my hammer be waking the town this morning. The rooster be damned."

THE SORTING

Let those who worship, gather for a Sorting. Leave fields and sea and hilltop. Seek after me, alone. Come to my city that you may gain entrance and live in my presence. Show yourself worthy and I will grant you favor and boon.

Delcrean Proverb, Sixth Circle

ressed in wool tunic, dyed orange using snarble extract, and with a silver scarf around his neck, one end suspended from his teeth, Phinx stood perplexed. The painter held a hastily assembled plate of food in his paint splattered hand: noodles stuffed with goat cheese; pickled obian dates; and sour amber grain rolls. A neglected knife dangled off the edge while he studied his latest work of art. He leaned forward, causing wrung-out, shoulder-length hair to spill out from behind his ears. Suddenly convinced into action, he carelessly shoved his plate onto a small wooden table already cluttered to the point of collapsing; sending iron knife careening to the red dirt floor of Fourth Gate.

Ignoring the utensil in favor of a brush, Phinx hastily mixed yellow and blue and a touch of red, forming a pool of wet brown.

He added several quick strokes to canvas. The painting depicted a crowd gathered near two guillotine platforms: A gray-haired prisoner knelt upon one of the platforms, his bearded head positioned expectantly into cradle. Upon the other stood a despondent child, still in chains, awaiting his own execution. Numerous wide-mouthed, blood-stained reed baskets surrounded the platforms, overflowing with severed heads. A dozen swads stood guard; three of them shown sorting a group of condemned prisoners: One line led toward the child—premature death. The other toward the elderly man—death delayed. Either line, death.

Phinx pulled scarf from mouth and reached for a date even as he stepped back to study his sharply outlined painting, "Let those who worship, gather…"

a taggle's painting

Maldinado

Maldinado stirred from slumber. White whiskers scraped against a flattened, feather-filled pillow as the tailor closed his mouth and opened gray eyes, scratching once black hair turned mound of white. It drooped over his indented head and beyond his fading ears like the belly of a pig. He snorted at morning mucus which threatened to choke him and coughed as he swallowed. He kicked with fickle interest at wool blankets until his rangy legs lay free. Several minutes passed before he finally sat up and swung them over the edge of a wooden bed padded with the blankets and animal skins Maldinado inherited from his father who died, passing beyond Ninth Circle, nearly eleven years prior.

Placing wrinkled hands atop his legs, Maldinado leaned forward and pushed himself upward, groaning against an ever-present pain in his right hip. It tormented him and grew worse with each passing year, but he managed to cope; usually sleeping on his back to keep from putting too much pressure on the hip. It helped. He felt certain the small adjustment to his sleep position would even allow him to sleep through the night if not for the seemingly constant need to relieve his swollen bladder.

The tailor stood momentarily beside the bed, allowing blood to flow downward. He tugged at the white linen gown he wore until the fabric dutifully mimicked the folds of skin which hung loosely around and about his gaunt frame. The oldest resident in Fourth Circle. His dream of reaching Ninth Circle faded years prior, along with his health. Nevertheless, Morlac favored Maldinado with a good business and new friends on a seemingly daily basis. Indeed, his network of friends extended throughout the city—and every circle. In his youth, he sought them out. As he grew in age and purported generosity, others sought to align themselves with him.

The old tailor moved slowly toward a red stone wall, opposite his bed, and relieved himself, watching the sour smelling dark yellow fluid circle a beveled hole in the red stone floor until it disappeared into the sewers beneath Delacroy. Rumors suggested people dared live in those sewers, but the gossipy tailor questioned whether anyone actually lived in such conditions. Mostly, he believed rumors existed in order to turn curiosity to fear, though he could not imagine why anyone would possess enough curiosity to explore the sewer system. Even in his youth, Maldinado never felt that adventurous.

He pulled his gown over frail shoulders and bent head and stuffed it into a tall basket near the bed: sturdy and well-crafted by Lomax, one of Maldinado's favorite merchant peers. The tailor often displayed his goods next to the ill-tempered basket weaver in the Fourth Circle marketplace. They started each day with whispers, sharing idle city chatter, fully aware Delcrean gold more often exchanged hands under tables and shadow than it did under sun. Babble then gave way to gregarious laughter, drawing the attention of prospective consumers, providing tailor and weaver ample opportunity for a playful ruse—or the more advantageous manipulation. At times, when bored or otherwise bothered, they prodded one another:

"I think I'll purchase a new robe from Topher?" Lomax said at one point, recalling a time when Maldinado purchased a basket from Denam instead of Lomax. It fell apart within a month.

"Topher sells rags! Maldinado sells robes," Maldinado responded. "Here, see for yourself. This is a robe. Take it home and store it in your denam-basket."

"I would sooner store it in a camel's mouth," Lomax spat.

Maldinado smiled at the memory while he rummaged through the replacement lomax-basket he had diffidently purchased as a result, choosing a bright-yellow robe he draped over a brown linen shirt and matching trousers. His father worked as a stone mason. His father's father, a fisherman, spent his days at sea. They tried to teach Maldinado their respective trades, but the boy inherited his mother's hands…and her affinity for cloth. Sewing came naturally to the tailor. Residents throughout Delacroy wore his robes, including those living within the prestigious and most favored Ninth Circle. But Maldinado could claim nothing greater, for Morlac had yet to wear one of the tailor's robes. Thus, Maldinado remained a resident of the overpopulated, though less favored, Fourth Circle.

Perhaps, whilst Maldinado's fingers remained nimble, Morlac would don a maldinado-robe instead of his customary yiddick-shawl. What I would give for such favor and boon; for a chance to prance in front of Lomax on my way to Ninth Circle? All of his contrived fame and amassed wealth paled in comparison to what awaited him—what awaited anyone invited to live in Ninth Circle. But his hope faded with age and whispers. The adherent reserved Ninth Circle for the young. Maldinado, resigned to his fate, would pass beyond Ninth Circle and join his father at the bottom of the sea, a Delcrean burial custom for the less favored.

But not before Lomax. Living to see his friend's death served as Maldinado's only true remaining desire.

Replacing lid on basket, Maldinado left the scant room. He walked down a narrow hall past an equally meager guest room. Often occupied, it sat empty that morning—Maldinado's impetus for his annual journey to First Circle where he would offer the room to another pilgrim.

Thousands traveled to Delacroy with hopes of escaping the outer lands. An act of faithfulness, perhaps. A spiritual quest, some professed. Maldinado grinned at the thought. An act of desperation, more likely. Self-preservation. He knew the tales and horrors of the outer lands all too well, for his house guests shared a common past and regularly disclosed their private terrors during dinner conversation: Inindu. The name seized every heart. A creature of the Sphere. His assassin. Tales suggested Inindu hunted in the outer lands and slay all she encountered, but Maldinado suspected Inindu less a creature and more personified myth. Tiger attack: Inindu. Death in shadow: Inindu. Rampant disease: Inindu. Real or not, however, Delacroy provided its residents protection from Inindu…from death.

Perceived protection. Maldinado rubbed at his still attached neck. Death most certainly existed in Delacroy. It simply took a different form.

The tailor crossed the main room of his home, large enough to comfortably seat three around a small wooden table. He took a deformed potato and spotted knife from a long shelf mounted above the table. Long ago, bacon also comprised a portion of his morning meal—a time when his stomach welcomed such things. He slid the knife and potato into a small leather pouch pulled from a hook next to the shelf, and reached for a wine skin, placing it to his lips to rinse away the bitterness in his mouth.

Then he left his home, pulling aside a rugged canvas which covered the doorway, and entered the already overcrowded street. Hundreds of travelers moved in a dozen directions; all shoulder-to-shoulder. Maldinado heard greetings immediately and often. Despite his inability to break into the inner circles, Maldinado ranked as the most prominent resident of Fourth Circle. His fellow residents, therefore, believed it in their best interest to befriend the tailor; or, at a minimum, thought him an ally in their quest for favor and boon. And Maldinado found no reason to disparage his own reputation. In truth, he relished the fame. If the roads of Delacroy end at Morlac's palace, his friends frequently boasted, usually after consuming much wine, those same roads begin at Maldinado's doorstep.

"Morlac's boon upon thee, Maldinado," a woman waved to him over the crowd, her brown velvet sleeve sliding downward to expose a heavily freckled arm. She arrived for the Sorting along with her young son and though the governing magnates called her name, thus inviting her to enter Delacroy, they never called her son's name. When he heard of their sudden separation, Maldinado offered the boy shelter.

"Favor and boon," Maldinado nodded in response, eyes focused elsewhere, as though talking to himself.

"I spoke with Camen last night." The tall, young man walking alongside him waited for Maldinado to register his meaning, "Maldinado! Are you even listening to me?"

The tailor started and, at first, forgot his courtesies. Then he stopped walking, wrapped his left hand around the young man's head and pulled him closer until their foreheads touched. Maldinado's forehead displayed a tattoo of four circles, one inside the other, representing the outer circles of Delacroy. The young man displayed eight circles. As least favored, therefore, it fell to Maldinado to initiate the traditional Delcrean bow, an act of both greeting and humility.

"Sosiid, what news do you bring?" Maldinado released Sosiid's head.

"I spoke with Camen last night," Sosiid repeated. He wore a light orange yiddick-shawl which hung loosely from his shoulders.

Maldinado lowered his gaze, expecting the worst, "And…what did Magnate Camen decide?"

"He said Penrem already answered enough questions."

The tailor nodded in resignation, "A fleeting hope from the tailor of Fourth Circle. Tell Magnate Camen I bow to his authority."

Sosiid departed as quickly as he appeared, leaving Maldinado to his journey. Few residents within Fourth Circle claimed Sosiid as an acquaintance let alone engaged him in conversation, and the Eighth Circle Post, chosen carrier of messages from Magnate Camen, owed Maldinado nothing. He came. He went. Another scheme. Another failure. Maldinado possessed no greater leverage than before.

"Morlac's boon upon thee, Maldinado," a bare-chested man muttered as they passed, carrying a dulcimer under his muscular arm; his dark skin a smooth sheen under the sun. The aspiring musician served as apprentice to a master musician, and while Maldinado, based on rumors, considered the apprentice an adept learner, the tailor frequently wondered aloud as to the master's ability to teach. He believed many of her students focused solely on the rhythms of a particular piece without fully grasping the necessary elements of entertainment, thus they consistently struggled to command the stage…any stage—large or small.

"Favor and boon," Maldinado nodded in response, though their opposite journeys took the aspiring musician well beyond earshot.

"You're still alive?"

"For at least another day," Maldinado greeted his friend who sat impatiently beside the dirt road with his arms crossed. He leaned back against a short stone pillar—one of two pillars which formed the gateless entrance to his one-story home. "Morlac's boon upon thee, Lomax."

"Favor and boon," Lomax stood and walked ahead of the tailor, "Denam's probably already there!"

Maldinado nodded, "Denam has to start early or no one would buy his baskets."

Lomax led the way through the crowd. Long gray hair brushed against his faded, light brown maldinado-robe while he walked; hair braided in the Delcrean style: Four scarlet beads, corresponding to his level of favor, held the braid tightly in place. He, too, displayed a tattoo of four circles upon his forehead, but same-circle residents did not, in most circles, exchange courtesies.

"I trust Muriel is well?" Maldinado forced his way past three bleating goats inexplicably stopped in the middle of the crowded street, the smallest of them attempting to nurse.

"She bemoans her blackened teeth as always, and fears I'll divorce her…" Suddenly distracted, Lomax placed the palm of his hand over the shoulder of a middle-aged man who emerged from the crowd to walk beside the two merchants; four circles upon his forehead; wearing a red yiddick-shawl, "Morlac's boon upon thee, Fanzir. I hear your daughter is lately attracting the attention of a certain Sixth Circle resident"

"Favor and boon…yes, I suspect he seeks a bride," Fanzir beamed.

Maldinado placed a cupped palm upon Fanzir's other shoulder, the three of them walking stoutly if not briskly, "Shame their union should happen now. I've heard rumor this same resident is fallen out of Morlac's favor."

Deep wrinkles underscored the worry in Fanzir's widening eyes, "Surely, not."

"Surely, not," Maldinado nodded absently. "I suppose rumors are only rumors, aren't they? Hard to believe, really. Hard to imagine someone from Sixth Circle falling out of favor."

"May we all find such disfavor," Lomax muttered.

"Still, rumors are rumors," Maldinado tightened his grip upon Fanzir's shoulder. "Damn nuisance, some of them. Delcreans tend to lose their heads over rumors. A damn nuisance…Hate to see such a lovely daughter lose her head."

"Maldinado," Lomax started. "The orphanage! Didn't you say your friend wants to build an orphanage?"

"Yes, yes, the orphanage…but he needs more gold. I was thinking of making a journey to see him week after next."

"Making a donation of gold?"

Maldinado patted Fanzir's shoulder, "Ideally, but I'm afraid I gave away all my gold last week."

"Pity, you'll have to postpone your journey," Lomax also patted Fanzir's shoulder.

"Do…do you think I could make a donation?" Fanzir asked, "I have some gold…would you…would you take some to your friend. Tell him it's a gift from my daughter and her suitor. Morlac's favor upon them." He reached into the pocket of his red trousers to retrieve two gold pieces.

Maldinado accepted the gold coins and coyly slid them into his own pocket, "Your generosity is your charm, Fanzir. Yes, I'll speak to my friend. Though, I fear the rumors are true. Your daughter's suitor has indeed fallen out of favor."

Lomax pulled Fanzir's head closer, speaking softly, "Guard your daughter well, friend, lest you fall out of Morlac's favor." Then, the two merchants released the horrified father to the crowd.

A group of women, on their way to the marketplace, passed by and carried Fanzir along with them. Maldinado watched after them for a time, and then pulled two coins from his pocket…and three more which Fanzir unknowingly donated. Lomax flashed three additional gold pieces, gently lifted with gifted fingers, "Fanzir seemed overly generous this morning."

"I fear his gift is not enough to build a new orphanage, though, nor will it gain him Morlac's favor," Maldinado jingled the gold pieces in his hand. "But now his daughter is free to marry her much younger lover."

"Free to marry him once she delivers the rest of the gold, you mean. Rumors aren't cheap."

"Rumors are cheap enough. We are not," Maldinado stashed the morning's earnings in his pocket. "I leave the matter of collection to you, old friend. Though I suspect it will cost me half my share. "

"Probably more," Lomax scraped yellowed fingernails against his beard. "So, you still intend to make for First Circle, then?"

"I never miss a Sorting," Maldinado nodded a greeting in response to a large woman who wore a strand of orange beads wrapped tightly above her left elbow, "Favor and boon."

"That hip of yours will likely shatter along the way," Lomax patted Maldinado's shoulder, "The better for me. I'll sell your cart and your goods to a proper merchant; someone who knows how to sew a decent seam."

The tailor patted Lomax's shoulder, "I've already made arrangements with Denam. My cart is his, should I die. Think of how many baskets he will sell with two carts in the marketplace."

"You're a foul friend," Lomax waved him be gone. "Go, find your hopeless pilgrim. Collect your rent and give it to the poor. The damned Adherent will never notice," he turned into the crowd and disappeared, but not before he held two coins out long enough for Maldinado to see.

The tailor considered the two coins in his own hand and smiled.

He continued along his path toward First Circle.

"Favor and boon, Maldinado," Harian, an all too round woman, and cousin of Maldinado's long-deceased spouse, waved with vivacious enthusiasm. She struggled to cross the street, however, and ultimately the crowd kept them separated.

"Favor and boon," He responded, grateful they were heading in opposite directions. Even better, his journey to First Circle would consume the better portion of two days, sparing Maldinado from Harian's weekly visit to the marketplace. Her obstreperous demeanor and piercing voice proved more than he could endure most mornings.

The tailor approached a tunnel: Fourth Gate. The giant, round wooden gate swung outward and hung from reinforced iron hinges. Three swads stood guard on either side of the massive entrance. The tunnel served as home to a collection of taggles, unique artisans who filled each city tunnel with various booths, platforms, and fire pits—creating a festive atmosphere and a welcome distraction for most travelers. The taggles included painters, sculptors, and weavers. They danced, played a multitude of instruments, and performed in skits and plays. And, often, they told the most fantastic of tales.

Maldinado passed into tunnel shadows and soon encountered a small platform, positioned in the middle of the crowd, high enough to attract the attention of passersby. He recognized Vitrec, a taggle storyteller who stood comfortably atop his platform despite the dearth of performance space. He wore a close-cropped beard, vibrant blue and orange scarf wrapped tightly around his neck, and a wool tunic dyed yellow using birmly weed; he displayed no tattoo upon his forehead, a taggle custom. The dark-haired, rugged-featured taggle spoke confidently, announcing, "This tale originated in Fourth Circle."

Maldinado shifted off his bad hip and settled in for the tale; travelers nearby grew silent.

"Listen to these warnings," the taggle continued, "and may Dsal guide you on your journey."

The taggle took a deep, calming breath. Then his face and eyes—his whole body erupted with practiced emotion and wild delight. His tale began:

No one travels the streets of Delacroy. It is late in the evening, and Dsal Tiger lingers in deep shadow under the circular gate. He stalks those who wander through the streets alone. He hunts those who wander from their home.

He sniffs the air and smells the scent of an approaching stranger. Dsal Tiger lowers his ears and licks the whiskers around his nose. He settles onto his paws…then leaps into the light of the street.

Vitrec leapt toward the crowd with stunning control, landing inches from the edge of his platform. Maldinado and others jumped then chuckled at their own seemingly unified reaction.

"Who are you?" Dsal Tiger asks the stranger.

"A boy with a goat."

"What do you seek?" Dsal Tiger circles the boy and his goat.

"I seek a pool of water for my goat. He is thirsty."

Dsal Tiger whispers into the boy's ear, "Your goat is thirsty, but it is not water he shall drink."

The boy attempts to flee, but Dsal Tiger bites—ripping into neck and shoulder. He devours the boy's body. All that remains is a pool of blood from which the goat begins to sip.

"Return home," Dsal Tiger tells the goat. "Tell your brothers what you saw."

The goat leaves, and Dsal Tiger withdraws into shadow.

He sniffs the air and smells the scent of an approaching stranger. Dsal Tiger lowers his ears and licks the whiskers around his nose. He settles onto his paws…then leaps into the light of the street.

Again, Vitrec deftly navigated the tiny platform. Again, the crowd jumped.

Maldinado did not.

"Who are you?" Dsal Tiger asks the stranger.

"A girl with a camel."

"What do you seek?" Dsal Tiger circles the girl and her camel.

"I seek a pool of water for my camel. He is thirsty."

Dsal Tiger whispers into the girl's ear, "Your camel is thirsty, but it is not water he shall drink."

The girl attempts to flee, but Dsal Tiger bites into her neck and shoulder. He devours the girl's body. All that remains is a pool of blood from which the camel begins to sip.

"Return home," Dsal Tiger tells the camel. "Tell your sisters what you saw."

The camel leaves, and Dsal Tiger withdraws into shadow.

He sniffs the air and smells the scent of an approaching stranger. Dsal Tiger lowers his ears and licks the whiskers around his nose. He settles onto his paws... then leaps into the light of the street.

"Who are you?" Dsal Tiger asks the magenta-haired stranger.

"A woman and a horse. I am Inindu"

"What do you seek?" Dsal Tiger circles the woman and her magenta horse.

"I seek a pool of water for my horse. She is thirsty."

Dsal Tiger whispers into the woman's ear, "Your horse is thirsty, but it is not water she shall drink."

The woman turns on Dsal Tiger. She buries her sword in the belly of the beast. Dsal Tiger collapses in death, and a pool of blood flows from his body. The magenta horse begins to sip.

"Return to your homes," Vitrec implored with voice altered force, successfully achieving a stunned silence. "Inindu enters the city."

Maldinado grinned with admiration at the storyteller's expert manipulation of the crowd, and clapped while Vitrec took several ceremonial bows, "Favor and boon, Vitrec!"

The tailor's voice merged with three dozen others. A chorus of well-wishers followed, sending a shower of coins raining down upon the stage, all of them aiming at the dallic—a small, reed basket which Vitrec held forth with a simple plea. Maldinado, too, threw a coin—one of the pieces lifted from Lomax.

"Yes, taggle," Maldinado muttered as he resumed his journey. "Inindu enters the city, and I must greet her."

Delcreans believed Inindu slipped into the city whenever First Gate opened. But they trusted the Sorting kept her from any of the inner circles as though the calling of names somehow sequestered her to the outer lands. Maldinado smiled at the idea, and wondered how he might persuade one of the magnates to call out Inindu's name during the Sorting; quickly dismissing the thought upon realizing such a riotous act would likely lead to his beheading.

Leaving Lomax the victor.

His old friend would certainly attend the beheading and position himself in the front row to ensure Maldinado saw his smug grin even as the blade fell.

Foul friend, indeed.

His attention veered toward an out-of-place taggle whom he recognized from various journeys through Eighth Gate. Maldinado hobbled over to the painter, "Phinx, I've never known you to leave Eighth Gate."

The blonde-haired taggle turned from his mostly finished painting, still holding a paintbrush coated with light-yellow oil, and dangling a silver scarf from his teeth. He let the scarf drop, "Favor and boon, Maldinado."

"Favor and boon," the tailor motioned toward the painting, a brutal depiction of a beheading, "A dire scene."

"Dire times," Phinx pulled a pickled obian date from a side table.

"You mean Penrem? What news do you bring from Eighth Circle?" Maldinado moved closer, placing a gold coin, this one donated by Fanzir, into Phinx' palm. "Sosiid is silent on the topic, and Magnate Camen refuses to let anyone question his prized prisoner."

Phinx lowered his voice, "They fear what he may say. Eighth Circle worships Morlac with honest words, but its residents are not without certain secrets. And secrets in the mouths of the condemned have a habit of turning into whispers..."

"And whispers into shouts." He pushed another coin, generously gifted by Fanzir, into the painter's hand.

"Some believe Penrem is more than a simple resident of Eighth Circle."

Maldinado stepped back to consider the idea, "Camen's lover? Yes, I have heard as much, though it is not widely known. No doubt, Camen spends an exorbitant amount of gold squelching the rumor, but then why the woman?" He did not pay for the answer, however, doubting even the taggle knew for certain.

"We may never know," Phinx raised scarf to lip and stepped toward his painting with a sudden focus that suggested an end to their conversation.

But Maldinado lingered. Something felt odd. He sensed a deeper corruption and salivated at the thought, "Why are you really here in Fourth Gate, Phinx?"

Most Delcreans understood the taggles practiced both creative arts and those of a darker nature. Yet Maldinado knew few could afford to enlist them in even the simplest scheme; let alone pay a taggle from Eighth Gate. Need a thief? Hire a taggle from the lower gates. But extortion? Murder? Such shady dealings required much gold and the exquisite talents of a more skilled taggle. A taggle from Eighth Gate appearing in Fourth Gate suggested a maneuver of grand proportion. And presented a tantalizing opportunity for Maldinado.

"Do you know Nebon? He commissioned me and insisted I paint here instead of Eighth Gate, so he could more easily track my progress," Phinx carefully dabbed a dot of color onto the canvas.

Elusive. Not surprising. Real information required gold, but Maldinado, already down two coins—and a third donated to Vitrec, felt compelled to continue his inquest without the traditional recompense, "Yes, Nebon runs a food trade in Third Circle." He nimbly, somewhat childishly, swiped the last remaining pickled obian date from the side table. Free information. Free food. The tailor felt emboldened. "He passes through here all the time," he found the thought genuinely amusing. "Dire times, indeed. The honest harbor secrets, and bed a chaste woman from Second Circle; while a resident from Third Circle, known for his fasting, runs a prosperous food trade."

"And the most generous resident in Fourth Circle steals from the less fortunate," Phinx pointed to the empty plate of dates.

Maldinado laughed, still unwilling to pay the expected fee, "Would you have me believe a taggle could ever fall out of Morlac's favor? The pure born of Delacroy. Descended from the First Taggle. A life without scars," he pointed to the taggle's unmarked forehead. "A taggle, fall out of favor? Vitrec tells one story and receives more gold than I can manage after a week selling robes in the marketplace. And how much is Nebon paying you for that painting? No, between the two of us, I am the less fortunate." And the less informed.

"Pay a taggle, earn Morlac's favor," Phinx returned to his painting.

"So, they say," Maldinado relented and dropped a gold coin on the taggle's plate. The second of three coins lifted from Lomax rattled around the empty dish for several seconds. "Morlac's boon upon thee, Phinx. Not that you need it."

"Favor and boon," Phinx replied dutifully, yet offered nothing further.

Maldinado, after several moments of silence, and soundly beaten, dropped his last coin, lifted from Lomax, onto the plate. Payment for a stolen date.

"Maldinado," the taggle spoke without the slightest hint of pity. He pointed the end of his brush toward the painting. "Do you recognize the condemned?"

He did, and wondered how he missed such an accurate depiction, "Magnate Boltmar? You mean to suggest..."

Another coin on the plate. He felt a sense of deep shame using his own gold.

"Some say he worships the Sphere."

"I've not heard this rumor," Maldinado considered the impact of such an accusation. Magnate Boltmar ruled over Fourth Circle. If true, the most populated circle in Delacroy would fall into chaos. And chaos brought opportunity—an opportunity of which he knew about, and Lomax did not. "Are you certain?"

"As I said, there are many secrets in Delacroy," Phinx turned to his palette. "Beware your journey, tailor. Today is the Sorting. Inindu enters the city."

"Perhaps," Maldinado hobbled onward through the crowded tunnel, his pockets much lighter than when he entered Fourth Gate. "Perhaps, Inindu is already here."

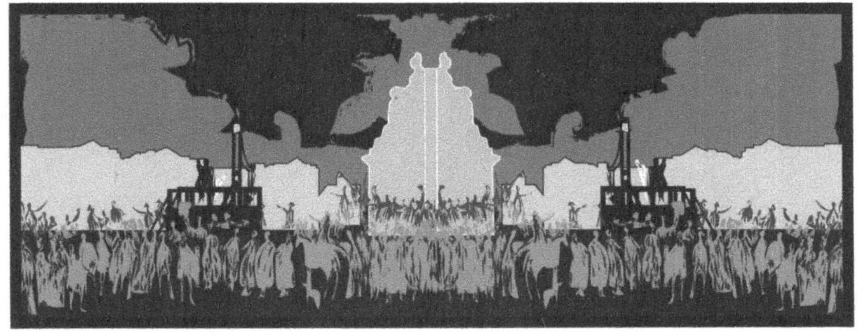

The Sorting

Inindu

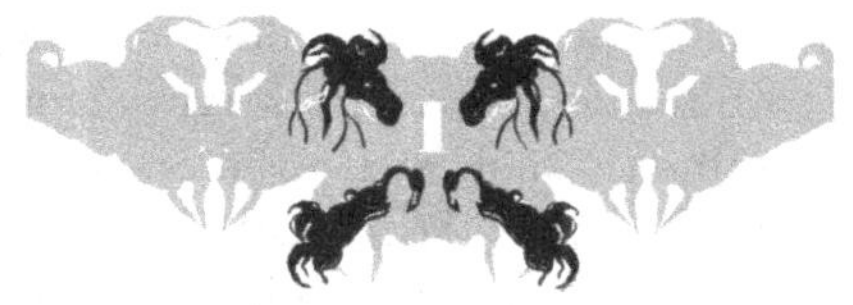

I'm always shocked by its size," Murdin says. He walks slightly ahead of us carrying a rope-bound bundle of possessions upon his back.

"And the number of people," his son, Albie, has a full beard and could pass for Murdin's brother. His real brother, Bontlevier, with rounded jaw and receding hair line, bears little resemblance. All three men walk to our left...

Another world. A world created by Morlac.

We journey in silence in this world, this illusion, forced to write words on a black slate board using blocks of chalk. This world fears us, so we hide our magenta beauty; disguised as a black-haired mute and a plain, ordinary black horse. *What would Adarian think of us, now?* We wander a red dirt road—descending toward the stone city of Delacroy—one of several thousand pilgrims who journey toward Morlac's city. These pilgrims see us as two separate creatures: Horse and rider. But we are *not* separate.

We are Inindu.

Once, we were loved by Adarian.

In the Sphere's world, we entered the creature of fire, the Kul. We emerged inside a cave in the farthest mountain of the outer lands of Morlac's world...alone. We found no trace of Maldinado. Perchance, he made it to Delacroy; more likely he died.

Or he is good as dead.

Adarian is dead.

We are one of several thousand pilgrims who journey toward Delacroy. All of them dead. Taken from our father's world. They believe themselves born in the outer lands. They tell stories of the lives they live and the farming towns from whence they journey. But when we traveled down from the mountain, we saw no town, or farm, or any sign of shelter. We discovered only the dead. They stood motionless in fields and forests; one stood in the middle of a lake atop the water. Another appeared quite suddenly, as though stepping through an unseen doorway. They did not breathe or blink or react to our presence...even after striking them... several times.

We wandered amidst the dead for a time, traveling the seemingly endless outer lands in a fruitless search for Morlac. Storms brought rain, but the dead never shifted. Wind. Sun. Even Snow. Nothing bothered them or caused any of them to stir. We lived off grasses and shrubs and the occasional berry, but the lack of animal life left us starving. After months of vegetation, we wrapped our magenta hair around one of the dead and devoured all of her. Despite the tinge of rot and decay, we feasted on two more. Later, another. In this manner, we survived for several months.

But the dead see what they do not speak. After a time, we noticed disturbing changes whenever we approached: Pupils widened until only a sliver of color remained. Black eyes. And lips parted and mouths fell open in a silent scream. The dead grew to fear us. However improbable, they clearly felt uneasy around the eater of the dead. Or rather, Morlac fears us, and instilled this same panic in his creatures to warn him should we ever enter his land. Thus, whatever path we chose to travel, we encountered black eyes and silent screams. We found ourselves surrounded by fear instead of beauty; but we are a creature of beauty, so we changed our color. We continued to devour our prey while adorned in magenta, lest they fear any other color. Otherwise, we wore black while traveling in their midst, or whenever we spoke to them, though they never replied. In this manner, we fostered both terror and kinship with the dead.

Then, our new companions stirred. We followed.

Soon afterward, the dead began to speak. They asked us to join them on their journey to Delacroy—a city we feel certain, after traveling the land so extensively, does not exist. Just as odd, and though they all walk afoot, these pilgrims speak of wagons and horses. Though plainly attired in simple, mostly weather-worn linens, they discuss robes and scarves. Whatever this illusion Morlac has created seems real enough in their minds. To the point, and even now, they make no mention of their former lives and retain no memory of the Sphere's world. Rather, they appear convinced of a new life with an extended family and an alternate home.

Curiously, they cling to their former names. A last shard of truth, perhaps. We know many of them—recognize the identities to which they clung in the Sphere's world; those whom we encountered in our father's world, or those who traveled to the city of Adarian, named after our lost lover, to glimpse our beauty. *Yes, Morlac, we recognize them—the soul within.* And we remember our own identity. Horse and topi. We are Inindu. Once, we were loved by Adarian.

One of the dead speaks. We wrap our black hair around his head and over his eyes and enter Morlac's grand illusion. *Let us see what lies Morlac feeds these creatures.*

"I'm always shocked by its size," Murdin says. He walks slightly ahead of us carrying a rope bound bundle of possessions upon his back.

"And the number of people," his son, Albie, has a full beard and could pass for Murdin's brother. His real brother, Bontlevier, with rounded jaw and receding hair line, bears little resemblance. All three men walk to our left.

It is only an illusion. We search Murdin's soul: In our father's world he ran a spice trade from Abre to Sorse. And Albie was only a boy when Morlac took him. Bontlevier worked at a log mill. We are Inindu. Once, we were loved by Adarian.

"There before?" We write our half-question on the thin slate board which hangs from our calloused neck. The written words blend with what remains of previous words hastily wiped into a chalky cloud with our long, black sleeve. It is a plain linen gown belted with bailing rope at our waist.

Bontlevier nods. "More times than I can count."

"Twenty-fourth Sorting, I think. Only the third one for Albie, though." Murdin says. "My sister and her family live in Fourth Circle, so it makes it easy for us to come every year."

We wipe and write, "Describe inside."

Bontlevier places the palm of his hand on our shoulder, "Do you have relatives in the city?"

We shake our head.

"You want to live here then?"

We nod. *Oh, yes, we seek Morlac.*

"That's the problem," Murdin barks with laughter. "Look around you, mute. All of these people want to live in the same house where you hope to reside."

"Trust me," Bontlevier says. "You're better off returning home."

Albie shakes his head, "Don't listen to them. You were right to come. Life in the city offers better conditions than the mud pits we farm in the outer lands. Like everyone else, my father and uncle hope to hear their names called during the Sorting."

"Sorting?" We write.

"I only want to visit your Aunt," Murdin mutters.

"You want her pastries," Bontlevier removes his hand from our shoulder to adjust his pack, also rope-bound.

"And why not? We give the city half of everything we manage to grow. Why shouldn't they feed us?"

"We give our food as an offering to Morlac," Albie reminds his father.

"Offering," Bontlevier spits, "the swads take what they want whether we offer it to them or not. And still we do not hear our names called in the Sorting."

"Sorting?" We tap our slate this time, effectively drawing Albie's attention.

"That's where they decide if you're allowed to stay in the city. My father used to bring the entire family, my mother and three sisters, but they turned us away so often that it's just the three of us who make the journey, now. My Aunt made it through the Sorting about nine years ago."

"How many get in?" Chalk dust coats our right sleeve which measures out beyond our fingertips, tailored longer than the left side for wiping purposes.

"Not enough!" Murdin replies.

"It varies. Depends on how many Delcreans died the previous year," Albie says.

Bontlevier shakes his head, "Death has nothing to do with it. If you offer enough gold, they'll let you in."

"Or if you know somebody," Murdin adds.

"Your sister?" We write.

"You would think so!" Murdin responds.

"Delcrean politics are not so easily navigated, mute," Bontlevier says. "I'm afraid you are in for a bit of a shock. Even if you make it through the Sorting there is no guarantee you will make it to Ninth Circle."

"Paradise," Murdin closes his eyes with a sigh.

Albie explains, "Morlac reserves Ninth Circle for his most faithful servants. Most are chosen to reside in other circles where they learn to worship Morlac according to the laws of each circle."

"The Nine Circles of Delacroy," Bontlevier recites, "First Circle: Certainty. Second Circle: Chastity. Third: Fasting. Fourth: Generosity. Hmm…Happiness. Orthodoxy. Peace. Honesty. And Ninth Circle: Faithfulness."

Murdin shakes his head, "Fifth Circle: Joy. Not Happiness."

Albie nods, "So if they sort you into Fifth Circle, you must discover the secret of Joy. If Second Circle, you must remain chaste; and so on. Only then will they move you into Ninth Circle."

"Why Ninth?" We write.

Albie responds, "Any of the circles offer a better life than the farms from which we all journey. It means no more empty stomachs. No more forced labor. No more beatings. That food your family grows…all of our families—the swads take our food to Delacroy. My aunt says you still have to work, though, depending upon the circle. That's why everyone wants to live in Ninth Circle. Prove yourself worthy, and Morlac will reward your faithfulness. And it doesn't even matter where you begin, or rather, the circle where you reside. You just have to make it through the Sorting. Then prove yourself faithful to Morlac by obeying the laws of your chosen circle and the Adherent is certain to appear at your door and invite you to live in Ninth Circle: Paradise."

"Barrels of wine…" Murdin continues, "Streets filled with food. Servants from Eighth Circle everywhere you turn waiting to feed you, bathe you…"

"Love on you," Bontlevier turns a barbaric eye toward us, navigating our every curve.

"Ignore my uncle," Albie quickly apologizes. "Favor and boon, mute," He wraps his arms around the other two men and, slightly embarrassed, hurries them along.

We pull back our hair to emerge from the illusion.

The dead still slowly pass on either side. Extremely slow. Barely moving. They wear only linens. No horses. No wagons. No purpose.

After so much time in stasis, why stir now? Why call forth the dead, Morlac?

Something feels…different. In the distance we find a city rising out of the ground: Delacroy. Massive, red stone walls conceal everything within except for a towering ruby palace which strikes at the sky from the heart of the city. Thousands of dead pilgrims walk along a dirt road leading to a single, circular gate.

We extend our hair and return to the illusion.

"You're tasty good lookin'."

Beside us, a tall, toothless man grins.

We are not amused. He could use a bath…and someone to lead him far away. Lust is one thing; and mostly welcomed. Filth is another. His breath smells like the back half of a cow.

This is only an illusion. He once served as a herald in Quel. We are Inindu. Once, we were loved by Adarian.

"Mute," we write.

"I don't mind."

We consider wrapping him in our hair and removing his body from our presence…his unwashed body. Ugh. Perhaps a *long* sword, instead.

The crowd disperses, marginally, as we reach a large wooden table surrounded by three of Morlac's swads, guardian warriors of Delacroy. All three stare at us, one of whom sits with elbows on table. We allow them to stare. Illusion or no illusion, it feels good to draw their attention as though we are a goddess. They see us as beautiful. We are Inindu. Once, Adarian looked upon us with similar wonder.

The seated swad finally remembers his duty, "Name?"

"She's mute," our toothless fiend calls out from behind us even as he helps himself to a casual handful of our topi's ass. Our horse steps onto his foot, causing him to recall the vocal range of his youth. We ignore him and write, "No name."

"Mute: with black hair and possessing a horse," the swad speaks the words while he scribbles our name. He folds the slip of paper and places it into a basket kept under table, "Proceed through the gate."

We move to the right of the table, away from the head of one crowd into the back of another.

We emerge from the illusion. Still, we travel amidst the dead. City walls surround us, mirroring what we saw within the dream-like world. The air feels cool and damp, here, and while the open air previously cloaked death's odor the city offers little relief. It reeks of decay. Indeed, the dead appear more blighted. Seeking to escape the foul stench, we wrap the eyes of another nearby lifeless form and re-enter the illusion.

Exchanging one smell for another.

There is much filth, both in the air and upon those against whom we brush. *Damn your illusion, Morlac. You think us pigs?* We join together, rider mounting horse, eager to move more swiftly through the crowd. Unfortunately, the toothless herald, his beard and neck dripping in sweat, also attempts to mount. We can feel his sweaty palms upon our horse's croup. We swat him away with our tail, flinging him back into the crowd with enough force to send five more pilgrims to the ground.

Did the dead just try to mount our horse? Only Adarian has ever shared our horse.

There is little room to maneuver within First Gate, but the commotion creates enough of a stir that we manage to finally leave the toothless herald behind. Our horse squeezes past body after body, as though a slick rat escaping the rain through a hole in the wall. Filthy flesh slides against our beautiful flesh and wondrous horsehair. *Cold flesh? It feels cold. Is this all an illusion?* Fingers grab and twist our flank and thighs, causing pain. Something scratches our skin on the near side; deep enough to draw a streak of blood. *Are we bleeding?*

We suddenly remember our father, the Sphere, sent us to this world. May the Sphere be with us…oh, silly daughter, our father stayed behind. Safe within his world. Useless.

We spot several more horses scattered throughout the tunnel gate, unfortunately, mounted or not, all the pilgrims move at the same pace. The crowd pushes us closer to a torch-lit wall where a series of booths and stages serve to focus our attention away from our general lack of progress and toward a wooden stage where three boisterous performers enact a scene involving the throwing of a knife at a tied-up goat.

"Blind Goat," an excited yearling points toward the stage, "I know that game."

The performance slowly blends with another stage and another performance. Commotion exists everywhere in the tunnel. Stages lay in rows on either side of the flow of pilgrims. The amount of people in this tunnel rivals anything we ever experienced in our father's world. Even Yenul, during its first year, didn't pack so many travelers into one area, though our sister, the Adow, certainly tried—issuing a decree that everyone in the known land make the journey.

"Your name, fair creature?" The performer wears a magenta scarf; the color of beauty.

"No name."

"Morlac's boon upon thee, mute," he bows and draws the attention of someone else in the crowd.

Finally, the tunnel exit appears. Light flows inward through a circular gate, overpowering the torchlight. Pilgrims flood past the exit into a courtyard beyond. We follow, anxiously.

"The Sorting has begun," a frantic and shrill-voiced woman says, "The swads in the tunnel still have my name. How can they start if they don't have all the names?"

You cannot keep us away, Morlac. We found your city . . . this illusion.

We exit the tunnel onto a ramp, descending to walk along the edge of an outer wall; the only available path amidst the crowd.

We've come to kill you, Morlac. We are Inindu. Once, we were loved by Adarian.

The Sorting

Delcrean Council

Are we certain Penrem ever entered her home?" Maldinado asked the taller magnate.

Simiad noted, and not for the first time, the lack of gold in exchange for information. A conversation with the Fourth Circle tailor included certain expectations and, in accordance, Simiad nodded, "Three witnesses saw him leave her home on more than one occasion, Maldinado. Not to mention Penrem's own admission." He wore a brown maldinado-robe which appeared a shade lighter than the long beard which covered his otherwise irregular face. The ruby ring on his left thumb designated him magnate. The wine bottle in his hand designated him Second Circle Magnate, lowest ranking and most miserable of all magnates.

"He's hiding something," Maldinado spoke without looking at Simiad, a habit of more than one Delcrean, and held his thumb and forefinger to his lips as he whispered, "and I don't mean his affair with Magnate Camen."

Simiad snickered at the remark. Despite his best efforts, and several bags of gold, Camen had failed to fully suppress his rumored preference for young men. Simiad knew the truth: The young men attended to the needs of Camen's wife while the magnate watched, longingly. Age, it seems, affects one's ability to satisfy their lover. Not that Simiad would know. As magnate of Second Circle, he faithfully maintained his chastity; perchance the reason Camen spoke so freely to Simiad about his displaced love life.

"You suggest Penrem speaks falsely?" Simiad raised the bottle to his lips, the only relationship he actively maintained. "Would you have him beheaded twice?"

"No, Penrem would never lie. But truth and honesty are not always bound with the same thread. Surely you've been magnate long enough to discover that much."

"I admit honesty has its uses," Simiad agreed. The best lies remained unspoken.

"It's almost as though he *wants* to die."

The two men stood amidst the crowd. Intended as a gathering area,

First Circle boasted none of the typical Delcrean structures. Rather, Simiad thought, it resembled a holding pen for goats with only eight large stone platforms, evenly spaced around the circle, suggesting otherwise. These platforms, one for each of the eight magnates, served as central focus for the annual Sorting. Pilgrims stood tightly packed around the base of these towering platforms—causing Simiad and Maldinado to pause in their travel while several brutish looking swads cleared a path. Numerous temporary shelters made the task all the more difficult.

Tents, blankets, and other makeshift shelters covered the entire circle, an unpaved dirt ring, leaving most of the gathered pilgrims coated in varying amounts of red dust. The ring of dirt, more liken to a ravine, sunk further each year; so much, in fact, the Adherent finally ordered two stone ramps constructed: One leading up to Second Gate. The other descended from First Gate.

"It's too obvious a crime," Maldinado continued, "If Penrem was so in love with the girl why didn't she visit him in Eighth Circle? Why not marry the girl? Why consummate their love in the only circle where the act is expressly forbidden?"

Simiad resumed his walk, and his drinking, escorted by thirty swads who held their swords at the ready. This, too, amused the magnate. Only during the Sorting, surrounded by desperate pilgrims from the outer lands, would anyone assume the Second Circle magnate held any influence or power; enough to provoke an attack. "Perhaps you would like to question the girl, yourself?"

Maldinado kept pace, "Yes, I would like that opportunity. Magnate Camen refuses to let me speak with Penrem."

You hold no leverage over Magnate Camen? Simiad realized in that moment he possessed more sway over Camen than did the tailor and shuddered to think what vile manipulations Maldinado would pursue should he discover the truth about Camen. Equally disturbing, Simiad discovered he lacked the initiative to properly exploit such knowledge. Wine, it seemed, muted his sense of ambition. Subsequently, he lost his train of thought.

Simiad paused to grip the back of Maldinado's head, bringing him closer until their foreheads touched. Two circles meeting four circles—a gesture of honor Maldinado did not resist, though Simiad's rank as magnate repudiated such formal acts of greeting. Yet, the expectation lingered between them, for Simiad knew the tailor's reputation; best yield to the tailor's more favored standing than risk falling prey to the well-liked and well-informed rumor monger. He failed in his attempts with Camen, so naturally, Maldinado turned to Simiad; and not for the last time, he suspected.

The magnate detected a faint musty smell emanating from Maldinado's beard, "I will leave word with Mathay you wish to meet with the prisoner," he released the tailor's head and, somewhat wobbly, climbed a wooden ladder to the top of his designated stone platform.

Maldinado followed without asking. Another unspoken expectation.

Atop the Second Circle Sorting Tower, Simiad took a seat upon an undecorated, red stone bench. Despite his long, thick beard, and the perception of age it provided, this represented only the third Sorting for the chaste Magnate, fewest amongst his peers. Still, he knew the sequence of rites and, more importantly, he understood the role he must play during the ceremony...and in life. In the distance to his left, he found Third Circle Sorting Tower and his fellow Magnate, Honcherub, overseeing his 41st Sorting. A lifetime of fasting left him uncommonly thin. The heavy-set Simiad struggled to imagine a lifetime with so little food, though he supposed others felt the same about his vow of chastity. Regardless, it fell to Simiad to keep Honcherub's cup filled with wine, so he dutifully sent weekly shipments from his personal cellar. To his right stood the tower of Ninth Circle—representative of Morlac's most faithful worshipers. Honored Magnate Galeab served as magnate of Ninth Circle ever since his father received an invitation to enter Morlac's palace. And though Galeab drank with passion, he demanded a higher quality wine than any Simiad possessed. Nevertheless, Simiad served Galeab's tastes by frequently and secretly supplying him with virgins hand-selected from the unassuming residents of Second Circle, for no resident would dare refuse an invitation to Ninth Circle, regardless the intent. These residents went willingly, leaving quietly after nightfall during the darkest hours...and then went missing, shortly afterward.

It fell to Simiad to replace them each year during the Sorting.

Yes, he knew his role.

Morlac chose the original magnates, and the title passed from father to son with one exception: The childless magnates of Second Circle. Upon death, the Adherent appointed a faithful disciple from Second Circle to serve as the new, hopeless, powerless magnate. Unlike the other magnates, Morlac did not choose Simiad. His god could not be bothered with such menial tasks. Still, Simiad did not represent the only break from tradition. Galeab held distinction as the only *resident* not chosen by Morlac to reside in Ninth Circle; or at least, not chosen as the result of his displayed faithfulness. In that sense, Simiad felt himself better than Galeab, but quickly squelched the thought lest someone find reason to drop a dose of poison in his next bottle of wine.

He took a drink, half wondering if such a tasteless death already coated his lips; and if he cared.

With a lingering pensiveness, he returned to his conversation with Maldinado, who sat to his right, "This is a good thing you do, tailor. We turn too many pilgrims away." Simiad glanced again at the Ninth Circle tower. *They* turned everyone away. Truly, Galeab's presence upon the tower served only to inspire those below, a symbol of the home for which everyone longed; a promise of what lay as reward if they faithfully followed the tenants of each Delcrean circle.

Morlac's greatest deception: A happy life.

No, Galeab did not participate in the Sorting. Delcreans believed and, actually, despite his grumblings, Simiad agreed: Strangers from the outer lands did not belong in Ninth Circle. *Let us all fully experience the curse of Delacroy.*

Maldinado grabbed both lapels of his robe, "I do what I can, but I wish I had more to give."

"You are the most generous resident in Fourth Circle. Everyone knows it is only a matter of time before you are chosen to join Ninth Circle."

"Then may I be chosen after you, honored magnate," Maldinado gave a slight bow of his head, white hair flopping over his brow with casual flair.

Simiad marveled at the ease with which the tailor navigated political matters. Though he felt certain Maldinado considered himself of higher rank than the magnate, and in truth did hold greater sway with those in power, he nevertheless spoke with a polished tongue; absent any pride. Simiad once spoke similar enchantments, but when he ascended to magnate, he discovered truths…and lies…and soon enough drank himself to silence.

"Let the Sorting commence," Galeab announced from his tower. *His lone task. Bastard!*

"Duty beckons," Simiad excused himself from the conversation with Maldinado and walked over to a wide-mouthed denam-basket. He hesitated before opening the lid as though expecting to find a snake inside. Instead, he found parchment slips containing the names of those found most appealing and attractive. The best of the pilgrims from the outer lands; mostly female, but not exclusively. Simiad's name once made its way into a similar basket. He pondered his fate: Sorted into Second Circle and allowed to thrive rather than traded for a night of pleasure. His body disposed of in secret; his name forgotten.

The magnate still possessed handsome features, though he kept them well hidden behind his beard and a gut which extended outward beyond his toes.

As predicted, Simiad found three leather pouches inside his basket, each open at the top where a single piece of parchment lay. Special requests from Galeab and other residents of Ninth Circle. A beauty spotted from afar and "sorted" into the city with bartered gold. He felt oddly disappointed. His second Sorting proved far more prosperous— eleven pouches. Eleven names. All of them later found missing. *Gone*, he told the people, *back to the outer lands. Unfaithful disciples.* Too easily, they believed the same lies he once believed. And why not? He served as their magnate. Why should he lie? Why, indeed?

In truth, Simiad did not know how the bribes made their way to his basket, or if the other magnates received similar bribes. The magnates never discussed such matters; at least, not with him. Nor did Simiad know who, in fact, handled the exchange. He suspected the other magnates better acquainted themselves with the particulars. Such secrets, no doubt, passed more easily through bloodlines. Regardless, they chose to keep Simiad in the dark, ignorant if not guiltless, for he played his part and he played it well. Better, perhaps, than even the politically savvy Maldinado could manage.

Still, he reached for one of the loose names first, his way of acknowledging the universal hope and intended spirit of the Sorting ritual—his way of protesting his own disillusionment.

He slowly stroked his long beard and called out in a well-practiced, booming pitch, "Henrit: possessing a black mole on his left ear." The swads who collected names at First Gate carefully noted some unique identifying mark or possession. Simiad wondered how many Henrit's actually stood in the crowd below, for it did not seem the most popular of names, but he decided the precaution of including physical features certainly discouraged any impostor. *We wouldn't want the uncomely living in Second Circle.* Kome, Second Circle Post, carrier of Simiad's messages, recorded the selected name and respective description upon his scroll. Later that evening, the swads would match names on the scroll with those wishing to enter the city.

Simiad reached for another name, choosing the first of three unsuspecting pilgrims who would most certainly make it through the Sorting.

Boltmar, a stout eighty-nine years old and presiding over his seventy-sixth Sorting as Fourth Circle Magnate, reached for another piece of parchment. "Lewhit: in possession of a ram's horn," his voice trembled around the fringes, but he maintained the forceful bark he developed in his youth after struggling mightily during his first few ceremonies. Uncommonly soft-spoken in conversation, his training required the aide of several taggles familiar with various voice inflections used in performance pieces. Once a source of embarrassment, Boltmar's voice eventually carried further than any magnate, and resonated off the outer wall of First Circle.

Remni, Fourth Circle Post and Boltmar's faithful lover, recorded the pilgrim's name and description upon her scroll. The magnate noted her jagged handwriting, and how her words appeared overly spaced at first, yet tended to clump together as she reached the edge of the parchment. Lewhit's addition to the list of thirty-six names forced her to adjust the scroll downward. The sun reflected lightly upon her smooth, dark hands, evidence of the care she took to preserve the softness of her skin despite the consistently harsh conditions found throughout the city. For this, he loved her.

He waited for Remni to finish writing. The adherent, Shale, asked her to serve as Fourth Circle Post at the elder magnate's urging, for Boltmar desired her beauty long before he knew her name: Remni. At twenty-three years old, some held the opinion she remained a child, including Valun, his son—older than Remni by twenty-two years. Boltmar saw only her beauty. She looked up from her scroll and waited for him to speak a different, meaningless name; her black skin highlighting the white of her eyes—a dark rind, like the deepest shadow around the moon on a clear night.

Reluctantly, the left-handed Magnate turned from his lover to draw another slip. He pulled it from atop a large, open pouch of gold. Then his heart fell with violent force, as though the tower beneath his feet suddenly collapsed. He stared at the revealed name. The *only* name. *Her* name.

Remni: worships the god of another world.

An accusation rather than the name of an expectant pilgrim. An indictment of his lover.

Long accustomed to political improvisation, however, Boltmar calmly, forcefully announced, "Albie: wears a full red beard." Albie, the nephew of a woman in Fourth Circle, a resident who previously made several rather indiscreet attempts to bribe the magnate, proved a fortunate recall.

He felt Remni take the torn parchment from his wrinkled, suddenly weakened hand. Oldest of the Magnates, his hands often shook, a recent sign of his ever-increasing age, yet they hung motionless at his side when she parted his fingers with her own. The passing of parchment…a passing of death. Boltmar saw little distinction. Let Valun pull the magnate ring from his father's thumb. It made no difference. Boltmar no longer wished to rule over Fourth Circle. Never did he imagine the remainder of his life without Remni, certain he would pass beyond Ninth Circle well in advance of his much younger lover.

Remni opened the parchment. Though he knew what she would find, he did not avoid her eyes. Her look of sudden shock and terror seared the flanks of his soul. *No, my love, it does not list Albie's name.* Rather, it bore an accusation written in a most elegant script.

Remni: worships the god of another world.

Death. And, per his duty as magnate, Boltmar would issue the sentence for all to hear.

Anyone found or accused of worshiping another god soon lay under a falling guillotine blade. Remni looked up from the slip of parchment, if only for a moment, her eyes filled with terror. A wave of warmth flooded Boltmar's chest and throat. He forced himself to swallow, resisting the urge to look around for her accuser, and willed Remni to focus on her scroll. If someone watched from a distance or nearby…if someone saw her. He prayed she not give them any further reaction. Responding to his silent urging, Remni lowered her gaze and proceeded to write Albie's name upon her scroll using overly great care. Each word far too evenly spaced.

How much do they know? If they know about Remni…

Boltmar brushed the implications aside and forced himself to return to the denam-basket. One untouched bag of gold remained—one more name specifically routed to the Fourth Circle magnate. He feared the name he would find. Despite his outward calm, he needed a moment to recover. He drew another random name, and read it aloud.

"Phain: wears three silver earrings in his left ear."

Boltmar handed the parchment to Remni. This time, he avoided her direct gaze lest he betray her…betray himself. Her accuser…*their* accuser would not know for certain if Boltmar found the name atop the pouch of gold so long as the magnate remained poised. But even as he birthed the thought it floated helplessly within the confines of his mind. He could not hide. Someone knew. Someone knew *enough.*

What have we done, my love?

Thirty-eight bags of gold littered the sorting basket. He drew the first thirty-seven names from atop those bags; starting with the smallest bribe, a favorite and long-standing custom of Fourth Circle magnates. As the ruler of a circle known for generosity, he reasoned, it made sense to reward the least wealthy before reaching for larger bribes. Yes, someone knew. The placement of names meant his accuser, or accusers, need only listen and count.

The last pouch—the largest pouch—remained. His name remained.

With the ruse ended, therefore, Boltmar gathered a deep breath. He embraced the full extent of their denunciation, reaching into the basket to withdraw the final slip.

Boltmar: worships the god of another world

If Remni, then also Boltmar.

The magnate dropped his name back into the basket. Private accusations meant nothing.

"How many names do you list, Remni?" He spoke only loud enough for the honored guests to hear, those gathered atop the tower, although few of them paid any attention. Boltmar realized, in fact, he barely recognized a third of those assembled—and few of the rest actually resided within Fourth Circle.

Have you gathered to mock me?

Remni hesitated, and then had to count twice before responding, "Thirty-eight names sorted into Fourth Circle, Magnate Boltmar."

"I fear I miscounted," he bellowed to the crowd below. "We have room for thirty-eight, and no more. If you heard your name called, I invite you to enter Delacroy. This concludes the Sorting of Fourth Circle."

He spoke truthfully. Fourth Circle provided its residents much freedom, demanding only that they give to others generously. No vows of chastity or weeks of fasting. As such, every opening within Fourth Circle commanded a large bag of gold. He imagined other magnates received fewer bribes, but Boltmar never found reason to draw a random name… until he read Remni's name.

The magnate placed lid on denam-basket and passed it to a pair of nearby swads. Whether by their hands, or those of someone else, Boltmar knew the bags of gold would arrive discretely at his manor within a week; and the unselected names burned. His name, burned. The accusation forever lost.

Accuse me publicly, or not at all.

He calmly reached for Remni's perfect hand, bringing it to his lips before escorting her forward. In her other hand she carried a pouch containing her scroll and the chosen slips of parchment. Somering,

Appointed Recorder of Delacroy, had need of the scroll. And they would dutifully hand it to her as they passed through Second Gate, for no one passed through unless their name appeared on Somering's ruby scroll, official record of all the residents in Delacroy. Boltmar planned to burn the slips of parchment, however, leaving no evidence anything out of the ordinary ever occurred.

Together they descended Fourth Circle tower, Boltmar firmly grasping each rung of the ladder to keep from falling. Remni followed. A legion of swads cleared a path through the crowd, as magnate and post made their way toward Second Gate where a carriage awaited.

Boltmar's carriage sat unmoving within Second Gate; unmoving but properly aligned with the carriages of the other magnates. In this manner, Galeab, Honored Magnate of Ninth Circle, departed first—and, over the course of several hours, allotting enough time between carriages so as to prevent one magnate from overtaking their higher-ranking peers, Magnates Camen, Exchure, Morunon, and Jethrome followed. This left Boltmar at the head of the remaining procession with Honcherub and Simiad bringing up the rear. Thus, Galeab would likely reach Fifth Gate before Boltmar and Remni ever started their journey. The magnates, the only residents of Delacroy allowed to pass through the city gates at night, would continue traveling until sunrise, each of them arriving at their respective manors at roughly the same moment as when Galeab reached his manor in Ninth Circle.

Previous magnates, those who ruled prior to Boltmar and his peers, spent a great deal of time and energy ensuring the proper timing of the annual procession. He suspected it led them to close the gates at night, though Second Gate remained open once a year following the Sorting; and ardently discourage travel after sunset in hopes of achieving a more consistent result. Regardless, the delayed departure eventually led to another tradition requiring the magnates to celebrate the arrival of newly sorted pilgrims, a frolic enthusiastically led by the taggles. Boltmar typically left Second Gate delightfully inebriated, but that night he found nothing delightful about the celebration. He kept close to Remni and offered perfunctory greetings. By the time he entered his ornately decorated carriage, escorted by ten mounted and armored swads, Boltmar had yet to finish his first cup of wine. The gold-lined doors closed behind them, and together they closed all four sets of cream velvet curtains, two on either side.

Boltmar held Remni's thin, smooth fingers between his pale, gnarled hands as the carriage finally departed Second Gate. He felt the tremor in her hand and felt certain his own hand betrayed the outward calm he displayed upon an aged countenance. Someone knew their secret, someone who possessed both leverage and gold—enough to plant their accusation inside the denam-basket.

Why such an extreme measure?

Did their accuser wish to play with them, or merely watch them suffer…or, perhaps, not an accuser but a friendly warning? A message sent from a Son or Daughter of Oblation. But whether friend or foe, they remained well hidden. Identity unknown, and no known method of discovery. The magnates had long ago disengaged from and turned a blind eye to the exchange of bribes which preceded each Sorting.

Remni leaned her uncovered head against his shoulder, nestled her tear-streaked, deep ebony nose under his ear, and kissed the crenelated skin of his neck with the hopelessness of the elderly releasing their final breath. He knew the sound. The sound his father made at the end; and his mother…so many of his family and friends. Not the last breath, but the final release of life—the moment when a soul departs and nothing remains but an empty, barely functioning body. Age had muffled most of his senses but, strangely, heightened the sound of a life resigned to fate.

We may yet survive, my love.

He rested a bearded cheek on her braided hair and squeezed her fingers, anew. The silver magnate's ring he wore around his thumb slipped forward, weighing heavily upon his knuckle. The ring held a square cut ruby within a dragon's talon setting—representing the magnate's heart as clenched by Morlac, a god whom neither he nor Remni worshiped.

"May the Sphere protect us," she whispered.

"And keep us in his light."

Designed by Auriferous, a talented goldsmith from Fifth Circle, the carriage offered guests a reasonable level of comfort and luxury. Lined with cream velvet, the interior boasted two well-cushioned benches—hollow underneath to allow for storage; typically, Boltmar stored a change of clothing, two wine skins, and a selection of parchment paper and ink. But Boltmar did not want wine, and he found no comfort in his surroundings. Indeed, he felt every lurch and surge of the journey as four black stallions, one horse with a cataract in its left eye, jerked and pulled the carriage through Second Circle, wheels cutting grooves into a worn dirt path more accustomed to bare feet and sandals.

"Shale!" Boltmar reasoned.

"No," Remni replied, "Not Shale. The fact we still live serves as proof."

"Not Shale," Boltmar agreed.

She slowly traced the yellow stitching on his clothing with her free hand, a jagged design which ran the length of his sleeveless, brown half-robe.

They both knew their accuser: Valun, Boltmar's son. His beardless heir.

But Boltmar refused to believe his son would stoop to such levels. Those accused of worshiping the god of another world did not die alone. Behead the father, and also the son lest he go astray, in accordance with Delcrean laws. Yet Boltmar could not deny Valun possessed both the means and motivation. Adept politically, and powerfully connected in ways Boltmar struggled to admit, his son ruled in his place, if not from his seat. Valun despised him, loudly lamenting the fact Boltmar still lived—though only in private. Boltmar took pride in his son's sense of discretion, for Valun never shouted at him in the presence of others, and never without reason.

"Valun..."

"No!" Boltmar ended the discussion.

She stopped tracing the yellow stitching but did not pull her fingers out of his hand. Rather, Boltmar released *his* grip. He sat forward and moved window curtains to the side, staring absently into the night.

Not Valun. Not my son.

"So many Sortings..." Boltmar allowed the curtains to fall back into place, but he continued staring through them, "...still unaccustomed to traveling in darkness." Boltmar picked at his eyebrow, "Not Valun."

Remni crossed her arms, fingers fidgeting with a wide, silky ribbon which laced white linen sleeves together from wrist to shoulder. Boltmar liked her dress...he wanted to tell her the color of silk, dyed purple using tacia wood, a dye more commonly used in Seventh Circle, highlighted the blue undertones of her skin.

But he sat in silence.

"Not Valun," she said, at last.

Maldinado

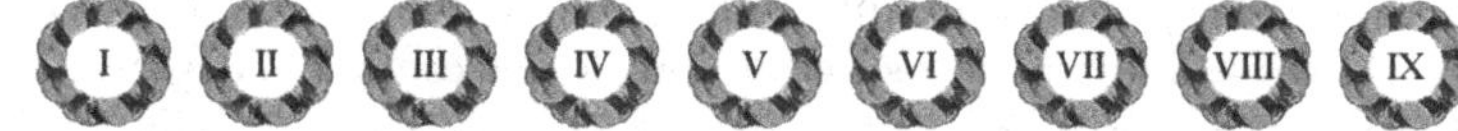

Hobbled by his aching hip, Maldinado walked without concern or haste through the visibly bitter crowd which filled First Circle. The magnates hastily retreated back to the city, along with every other Delcrean who made the journey, for they feared what may occur if they dared stay—and with good reason. Instead of life in the city, the gathered pilgrims faced an unwelcome return to their back-breaking servitude on distant farms.

Maldinado understood what it meant to hold status, to walk among them, as a resident of Fourth Circle—a resident of Delacroy. Given enough wine, and knowledge of said status, even the tamest of pilgrims would quickly turn on the tailor, resulting in several, violently inflicted injuries or a gruesome death—certainly not the first attack to ever occur after a Sorting. And for their part, the swads encouraged, or at a minimum ignored, such behavior. They left First Circle unguarded except for a short period of time immediately following the Sorting when they posted a legion of swads to guard the entrance of Second Gate; which they did until sunrise. At which point the swads sealed the gate. Aside from entering the city, therefore, the pilgrims could act in whatever manner they saw fit, for as long as they desired.

Yes, Maldinado knew the risks.

News of his death would, no doubt, leave Lomax singing a sweet tune, but the tailor stubbornly refused to provide him so pleasant a gift. Nor did Maldinado, in fact, plan to die that night—and certainly not in First Circle. Those who *did* die there, on the night of the Sorting, of all nights—*Morlac's boon upon their wretched souls*—would lay neglected for an entire year. Abandoned. Forgotten. Their bodies left to rot under sun and moon while the wind sifted dirt over their dislodged bones.

No, Maldinado would not die in such a manner.

He had survived every other Sorting to that point…though, not without incident.

Maldinado, in his youth, once convinced Lomax to travel with him to the Sorting. When night fell, they wandered into a random tent and stole enough clothes to disguise themselves as pilgrims, then proceeded to drink all the ale given them even as they lifted a small fortune from the unsuspecting drunkards. But after a time, the strong drink made them clumsy enough to attract attention, if not capture. They ran, and Maldinado soon found himself separated from Lomax. Abandoning his friend to whatever fate awaited, he continued running until he reached the other side of Second Gate and seemingly all the way to Third Gate—forced to finally stop until sunrise when it re-opened.

He smiled at the memory. His only regret lay in the fact Lomax beat him to the closed gate.

Though age had not dulled his appetite for gold, his faulty hip would hardly allow him to run any longer—though he felt certain his older, more experienced, self would avoid detection all together given the same scenario. Regardless, other matters held his attention at that moment. He searched for a sojourner, one suitably desperate yet not without promise. Beyond the political advantages he may gain, should his chosen lodger catch the eye of the Adherent, he had also to consider the practical matters associated with inviting someone into his home. Too loud a voice would give him a daily headache. Too honest a face and he dare not trust them. Most pilgrims grew up on farms but knowing how to plant seeds proved a useless talent inside the city walls. Maldinado needed someone with actual talent—something he could leverage. Did they know how to sew? Could they sing, or play an instrument?

Of course, some he avoided altogether.

Those who gathered their belongings to leave immediately after the Sorting didn't concern him. They lacked faith. And he refused to chase them down. Those with relatives already living in the city didn't need him. *Let family concern themselves with family.* As for the ones who planned to stay in First Circle long after the Sorting—and some stayed for days or weeks afterward, according to rumors—Maldinado wondered if they would not also stay too long in his guest room.

"Morlac's boon upon thee, traveler," he greeted a young, scruffy-haired pilgrim who sat just outside a makeshift tent. The shelter, a red-striped blanket hopelessly stretched over a piece of short rope suspended between two large sticks, provided only a sliver of privacy; yet the yearling retreated into the tent without responding.

"Is this your first Sorting?" Maldinado leaned down to better engage the reclusive pilgrim. Torches and fire pits, several hundred burning throughout First Circle, provided enough light for the tailor to catch a glimpse of the boy then seated with his head between raised knees. "What is your name, yearling?"

No response.

Maldinado waited a moment longer before standing to leave. Whether mute or dumb, neither quality enticed the tailor. He did not travel far, however, before encountering another lost soul. Young and alone, a blonde-haired woman sat crying atop red canvas—either it recently collapsed, or at one point she sought to erect the canvas and failed. "Morlac's boon upon thee, traveler."

"They took my mother," she cried. "I don't understand. She's lived her life. She begged them to take me instead, but they wouldn't listen."

"They never do," Maldinado hurried along.

He searched for someone with more discernment—someone more aware of Morlac's boon. *Not everyone can claim a connection in Delacroy, pilgrim.* Connections meant everything in a city filled with circles, political or otherwise, and Maldinado's next house guest would either increase or decimate his sphere of influence. He held no doubts as to the damage the sniveling fool would cause him.

The tailor gripped the lapels of his yellow robe and moved past Third Circle Sorting Tower. He walked with purpose but, unfortunately, he found no one in need of his assistance. Most of the pilgrims, apparently having experienced the letdown of more than one Sorting, gathered together in small or larger groups to raise a joyful toast to their foul luck. With wine and cynicism, they extended an invitation to any and all passersby. Maldinado continued on his way, politely declining several offers to join the mock celebrations.

A sure way to die.

He remained all too aware of his physical limitations—his inability to escape should the need arise. Best he stayed away from too much firelight and the curious eye. The rabble need only look closely at his robe to raise suspicion. Morlac greatly favored him in matters of corruption but, forced to defend himself in a fight, or worse, wield a sword, and even Maldinado would place a wager on whomever he fought.

Lomax would then collect all the winnings.

On second thought, he decided to place the hypothetical wager on himself lest Lomax find reason to celebrate both Maldinado's death *and* his share of the gold.

"Hey, you're the tailor from Fourth Circle," a rat-faced traveler yelled. He stood amidst a group of three much larger, noticeably chubby, pilgrims. The speaker continued with puckered lips, seemingly extending his already elongated jaw line and pointed nose, "I've heard about you… you've been to every Sorting. Hey, you can get me into the city, can't you?"

"I'm no one," Maldinado responded. "Just a pilgrim, same as you—same as everyone."

"No, your clothing suggests, otherwise. It tells me you're from the city."

"An embarrassment, really, I thought it would bring me fortune during the Sorting," Maldinado fell into a familiar verbal cantor, "Yet here I stand."

"You're lying," chubby on the left accused, his mouth all but hidden behind a swollen and splotchy double chin. He stepped forward and away from the group, "Why are you lying?"

"Yes, I'm lying," Maldinado almost pitied them. But, left with no other defense, he pressed his advantage. First, a disparaging remark, "If you live long enough, you'll discover the old are quite accustomed to hearing and telling lies." Then he turned his attention toward rat-face, seizing his only opportunity to escape, "Yes, it seems I *am* quite able to take you with me into the city, but I observe there are four of you…and I only have room for *one* pilgrim. So then, who shall it be? Maybe you should take a moment to discuss the matter and let me know?"

Without further coaxing, chubby buried an enormously large fist into rat-face's nose which sent the yearling flopping to the ground. It served as the first punch thrown in what quickly became an all-out brawl. Vastly ill-equipped in matters of manipulation, the four travelers completely forgot about Maldinado, so he slipped quietly away.

Someone followed.

Not rat-face, or chubby. Rather, a mounted rider.

The petite woman sat calmly atop her horse—a powerful, towering black mare. She rode without saddle or bridle—neither did she grasp the mane—yet appeared in complete control of the elegant beast. Her black hair flowed about her shoulders like a bed of reeds above the water, unmistakably, if somewhat oddly, mimicking each movement of the horse's tail.

He paused to wait, finding her presence of little threat. And also, out of curiosity. She clearly possessed the confidence needed to attract the Adherent's attention, and if not, then certainly he would notice her beauty. Yes, unquestionably, her beauty. Maldinado found he stared at her timeless face; struggling to guess her age, but if Remni loved Boltmar, then perhaps this woman could learn to love the tailor. In that moment, completely infatuated, he knew his quest ended. How could he ever find a more perfect creature?

The rider wrote something in white chalk upon a slate board which hung about her neck, "Maldinado?"

He stared stupidly at the letters of his name...and at the horse...and again at the rider.

"Also mute?" She wrote.

"No...um, no," Maldinado emerged from his momentary trance, "I can speak. Your name...what...what is your...beautiful. I mean, Morlac's boon upon thee."

The rider shook her head, placing a hand to her mouth. Then she slid down from the horse and pointed to her slate board, "Also mute?" She stood much shorter than the tailor, several inches below his shoulders, in fact; yet she walked with fierce aplomb, quickly closing the gap between them. Again, she pointed to the slate board.

"Also mute?" She circled the last portion, repeatedly pointing at the board, "Mute. Mute. Mute."

"Mute? You're mute?" Maldinado considered the notion, still unable to pull his gaze from the woman, "I'm comfortable with silence. My friend Lomax, his wife has black teeth. Terribly self-conscious about it, but Lomax loves her despite her teeth. So, you're mute? But you're speaking to me in so many other ways." *What am I saying?* He felt helpless in her presence. And words continued to fall from his mouth, "Do you want to live with me? I mean, no...what I meant to say, I'm looking for someone to live with me."

Well, that sounded even worse.

"I'm Maldinado...wait, you already know my name," he felt a surge of clarity. Suspicion followed, "How do you know my name?" He looked past her into the crowd, half expecting to find Lomax bent over with laughter.

She moved toward him more quickly than Maldinado could react, reaching up to hold his face between powerful hands. Her savage grip surprised him, and he wondered how such a petite creature managed to so completely immobilize him. Then an overwhelming panic displaced all thought when, somehow grown longer, she wrapped her black hair around him.

Black turned to magenta.

A soft magenta glow encompassed him, filling his senses.

Her hair smelled like warm apples layered in butter...fresh lilacs in the morning air...the cool spray of a salty sea. All of it. None of it. Terror faded from his thoughts, and he nuzzled deeper into her hair. He felt completely insulated, yet wonderfully helpless.

An old, familiar image filled his mind, and then another—images of Adarian, both the warrior of old and the city of his youth. Not where Maldinado the tailor was born. Someone else. A different version of himself: Maldinado the warrior—young and strong and confident. Images of Breline and Nataline surfaced. His father's body, slain by Adarian warriors while he slept. The Battle at Quel where Maldinado fought alongside Hintor. He saw the face of the Adow…*I love her*…and the Toast of Sark where they first kissed. He rode with the Adow into Dragon's Torment and fought against the Rorne. He saw her on a distant cliff while he, Maldinado, the warrior, rode with Inindu into the Kul.

Inindu…

"Maldinado," Inindu released her grip, gently withdrawing hair and hand.

He opened his eyes to discover a much different world than the one he knew. He still stood in First Circle, or a version of First Circle, but he stood as a warrior, rather than a tailor. He stood as Maldinado, Madar of the Adarian 45th. Minus the vitality of his youth.

He collapsed in exhaustion, "Tasa Ro! What just happened?"

"I brought you out of Morlac's illusion."

"Inindu," he struggled to sort through thoughts which oscillated between the world of his past and that…that of his other past. *Inindu enters the city.* "Inindu," he leaned forward, grasping for the land and his fleeting mind.

"Not exactly the warrior I remember," Inindu said. "Try not to vomit all over yourself."

"Inindu," he smiled despite feeling sick, and slowly leaned back on his heels. "I don't suppose you have any ale?"

"No ale, and no food," she helped the Madar to his feet.

"We survived the Kul?" Maldinado asked. And then realized, "We survived the Kul! Tasa Ro! That deserves some kind of toast. Broth and beer? Wine?"

"Look around, Madar. Then tell me we survived."

Darkness hindered his vision, but the moon provided enough light. Hundreds of shadows…maybe thousands of them stood throughout First Circle. Unmoving figures. Deteriorating forms. Instinctively, he looked out across the landscape in search of torch or campfire, but the dead offered no sign of life. No makeshift shelters or blankets. All merriment gone, replaced by silence.

"What happened to them?" Maldinado took a cautious step forward, reaching for his sword only to discover the white linen gown he wore. *Great, no sword.* It seemed nothing remained of the armor he proudly donned as they entered the Kul.

"I thought them dead until I found you," Inindu replied. "I *refer* to them as the dead, though I suppose I'll need to find a new name for them, now."

He slowly turned in place, tracking the outer wall along the starlit sky, and catching a glimpse of one of the sorting towers in the distance, "I don't understand..."

"It helps if you think in terms of layers," topi-Inindu mounted Inindu-horse, and then offered a hand to Maldinado who clamored up to sit behind her. "When we passed through the Kul, we breached one layer of existence; the one which conceals this land from my father."

"So, this is Morlac's world?"

Inindu navigated her way through the dead, and in the direction of First Gate, "No, I don't believe we ever left the Sphere's world, not that I haven't tried a time or two. But it seems I cannot escape my father, no matter how hard I try." She maneuvered around a cluster of the dead, "The terrain beyond the wall looks similar to what we saw in Dragon's Torment, so maybe we stepped through to the other side of the mountain range. No doubt my father knows this land exists, but for some reason he can't see it—like you can't see the back of your head."

"Wait, are you implying you *can* see the back of your head?"

"Of course."

Maldinado shifted uncomfortably behind her, suddenly uncertain where to look.

"Anyway, think of the Kul as the first layer of existence, and where we are now is another layer. The illusion from which I pulled you out, works as yet another layer."

"Like three shields stacked together?"

"Probably more than three, but yes, at least three shields. All of them protecting Morlac."

"He definitely takes precautions. Kind of impressive, in a way."

As they entered First Gate, darkness filled the tunnel to the point Maldinado could no longer see Inindu, either in front of him or beneath him, yet she never faltered, "I can't see a thing."

"That's because you're not a horse."

He wondered if that meant she could see *him*—uncertain, however, if that meant she watched him with her real eyes, or those in the back of her head. But then, he also wondered if he unwittingly stepped into a dream world. Tailor. Warrior. Delacroy. Adarian. All of it left his head spinning. Similar to how the tailor felt when he first encountered Inindu.

Oh, no.

"Inindu," Maldinado searched for the proper words. "When I saw you just now…I mean, in Delacroy…the illusion, as you call it…"

"Are you going to ask me if I'll move in with you, again?"

He cringed, "Yes, about that…"

"Yes."

"I sounded like a fool."

"Yes, I'll move in with you."

"What?" His attempt at an apology suddenly went missing in the darkness.

"Don't worry, I won't tell the Adow," she shifted closer to him, her hair caressing his ear.

Maldinado scooted further away, "Yes, well…" He moved his hands up off her hips, and then down again—and then away from her altogether—unsure where to hold her.

She flashed a mischievous grin.

Then, finally aware of her ruse, he laughed at his own foolishness.

Moments later, Maldinado noticed subtle changes in the level of light and, when at last they emerged from First Gate and his vision returned, the lingering night seemed bright as day. The dead stood all around them, littering the landscape for as far as he could see in the moonlight. He studied their faces in hopes of recognizing one of them, but no one looked familiar.

But then, the tailor only knew those who lived in the city.

Inindu came to a stop, "The outer lands extend for many leagues in every direction, but you won't find a single farm or town out there. The grass never grows. Water never flows. Rain and snow fall from cloudless skies, but the trees never change color. I traveled every path I could find through field and forest, but never encountered another living creature. Only the dead."

"How long have we been in this world?" Maldinado wondered aloud.

"Years…minutes…a day," Inindu started forward at a cantor. "Time only tracks the passage of life. We are surrounded by death."

Maldinado watched as the land passed underfoot with increasing speed. Soon, everything seemed a blur. The wind chilled his skin, for the linen gown offered little in the way of protection. Inindu appeared unaffected, however. Her hair floated mysteriously above her shoulders like always; untouched by the wind.

"Shouldn't you have magenta hair?"

"You really are blind, aren't you?" Inindu ran gentle fingers through her hair, and then over her mane, "The dead fear me. I can see it in their eyes. But it's more than that—I think the dead serve Morlac. Like sentries, they keep watch, and whenever I display my magenta beauty, they seemingly track my movements. So, I travel in black, for now. Nice of you to notice, though."

"Sorry," he said sincerely. It felt odd to see her in black once he finally noticed the change in color.

Inindu slowed to a trot, and then a walk, eventually stopping beside a small lake, "You wanted to toast our victory over the Kul?"

"I wanted ale, not water," Maldinado moaned.

"Drink. And be merry."

She lowered her head even as he slid down from her back. He knelt and drank his fill of the lukewarm water; slowly, at first, then in large gulps.

"He funnels the dead toward Delacroy," Inindu raised her head. The moon shone brightly upon her dark form, creating a soft glow which reflected on the water's surface. "When they move, they travel toward the city."

"The Sorting?"

"Both here and within the illusion," she nodded. "Another layer, maybe, but I can't get past First Circle. Only one way in, and one way out."

Maldinado shook his head, "But I live in…I mean, Maldinado the tailor…Morlac's illusion, or whatever. He lives in Fourth Circle." He suddenly laughed, "Tasa Ro! Is any of this even real? I must be dreaming." He stood and shouted up into the sky, "Wake me up, Hintor!"

"Are you finished?"

Maldinado nodded, slightly embarrassed.

"This is no dream, Madar," she motioned for him to mount. "Show me the way to Fourth Circle."

They left the lake at a cantor, slowly gaining speed until the land blurred all around them.

"What does Morlac need with the dead? How did they get here?" Maldinado looked anew at the linen gown he wore, "Is that how you found me, dead like them?"

"Yes."

He shuddered at the thought. And again, realizing he held no memory of his time in stasis.

"I recognize many of them, but I don't know why they populate this land," Inindu continued. "Or why Morlac funnels them toward the city.

They appear out of thin air as though stepping through a breach in the layer of existence. From what I can tell, they serve no purpose."

He rubbed at his bearded face, and ran a hand through a full head of long, black hair; surprised to discover how thick it felt compared to that of the tailor, "How did you escape a similar fate?"

"I'm Inindu. My own father has yet to gain control over me, let alone the schemes of a lesser god."

The moon gave way to darkness as they entered First Gate, but reappeared moments later above First Circle.

"That direction," Maldinado pointed to his left and toward the inner wall. But as they journeyed, mostly following a circular path, occasionally forced to alter their course due to a sporadic grouping of the dead, he grew concerned. "We should have reached it by now..." Maldinado turned to the closest sorting tower, searching for the symbol carved into its base, thus designating the circle: Ninth Circle. Honored Magnate Galeab's tower. It stood directly across from Second Gate, yet he could find no passageway into the city.

"It's gone," Maldinado admitted.

Inindu stopped walking, "Then we must return to the illusion."

His attention shifted to the dead, "The old man...the tailor...he traveled here in search of someone to live with him."

"So, you said."

"Yes," he slid down from the horse. "So, he...or *I*... can return to Fourth Circle and bring you with me." He stepped around her to study the unblemished inner wall, "I think."

"It's worth trying. Oh, and don't worry," he felt her hair wrap around him, "I won't eat you."

He felt a moment of panic, wondering what she meant, before his thoughts shifted and Morlac's illusion returned—along with a lingering pain in his hip.

Maldinado slid through a gaggle of women. They wore leather skirts and white shirts with lace around each wrist. He noticed their hair curled fully around the right ear, worn in the fashion of several eastern provinces—based on what he knew of the outer lands. He thought it odd he would notice their hair. Mostly, the tailor thought women a needless bother.

Hair.

He turned instinctively to find the mute woman leading her horse. Somehow, he had known she followed.

"What happened?"

She stared up at him, blankly.

He recalled meeting her, inviting her to his home, and then...

Inindu.

She motioned him forward, and he continued. He stopped, again, after a few feet, only to feel her hands pushing him onward. He walked, and then ducked under the twirling arms of a bald pilgrim who's badly burned right arm displayed a wrinkled and weathered scar. The grinning drunk attempted to pull Maldinado into a whirl, but Inindu walked between them, effectively pushing the drunk aside. The pilgrim shrugged and pulled someone else into the dance.

A haunting image filled his mind.

The same pilgrim, unmoving. Unresponsive. Standing with the dead in First Circle.

He shook the thought and squeezed behind a stringy-haired traveler. His broad shoulders and sun worn skin identified him as a craftsman from the southern provinces, further identified by the intricately carved wooden bracelet which the pilgrim wore on his wrist, popular in the Tessel region.

The Adow. Dragon's Torment.

Maldinado stopped as memories of another life flooded his mind.

"...that's when I told her I would *never* sell my goat." The craftsman with the wooden bracelet had drawn quite a crowd. "Hey, I'd grown up with that goat and I wasn't about to sell it to her just so she could cut him up and use his parts in her bubbling concoctions. She left, alright, but I could tell she wasn't really happy.

'I wasn't happy, either. She'd gone and left me in a horrid fit, and to make matters worse she was a *witch*. Well, I'd never fought against magic before, but I didn't wait around. I got my sword and marched right on after her. Way I figure, if you're gonna fight a witch you'd better do it before she can go and brew something.

'And it's a good thing I did. When I reached her hovel, she was drinking some kind of green liquid—thick as tree sap. She didn't finish it, though. I made sure of that when I took my sword and cut off her head. That's the only way to kill a witch, you know. Hate to think what she would've done to that poor goat if I'da sold him to her."

"Witches tend to *milk* goats," Inindu spoke loud enough to be heard.

Maldinado searched the crowd, but no one seemed to realize the horse had spoken, rather than the woman. Her comment drew a snort and a few snickers. Soon after, everyone stood laughing—even the storyteller who, though momentarily deflated by Inindu's comment, recovered enough to join in on the joke.

"You're no taggle, Caig," someone yelled, "but it's a good tale all the same."

Maldinado stared at Inindu who simply shrugged. He led her away from the gathering before she said anything further, and just as Caig raised a toast in the goat's honor. The tailor's mind started to filter through memories: His own, and the vaguer images of a young warrior from Adarian.

"It's dangerous to speak like that," Maldinado drew near the black mare. "Delcreans will curse you as a creature of the Sphere—call you Inindu. And not in any manner you desire. In Delacroy, *Inindu* means death. They will kill you if they find you can talk. And if I recall correctly, you're eternal not immortal."

Inindu pointed innocently to her slate, "Mute."

"Yes, and I'm an old man," he sneered.

A tall, dark-skinned pilgrim emerged from the crowd a few feet ahead of them. Thick with muscle, he had rolled the sleeves of his gray linen shirt tightly around both biceps, effectively accentuating the curve in each arm. And both forearms displayed a large, ivory bone which pierced the skin to emerge on the other side. His hair resembled a short-cropped tangled bush and skimmed the top of his ears, but a split lower lip served to truly define his freshly bloodied face.

"I hear you have a room available," he spoke in a garble of deep vibrations, his pronunciation almost indistinguishable between words.

"Morlac's boon upon thee," Maldinado looked past him to find a pile of at least twenty badly beaten pilgrims, including rat-face and chubby whom he recognized from his earlier encounter. *I only remember there being four of them.* "Yes, well, the room. Recently lent, I'm afraid..." He motioned toward Inindu, "But if you feel compelled to add her to your pile of bodies over there, then by all means."

Maldinado couldn't help but notice how quickly the man turned toward Inindu, obviously intent on striking her down, closing the gap between them in a few quick steps. Jagged front teeth slid down over his cracked bottom lip, biting deeply into the wound. He inhaled loudly and rolled his shoulders back.

Though the brute towered over the diminutive mute, Inindu stood firm. Her hair swayed perceptibly, and Maldinado silently wondered if he had not, in fact, made a deadly miscalculation.

Finally, the man simply turned and walked away, "Morlac's boon upon thee."

"Favor and boon," Maldinado exhaled, relieved nothing more occurred.

Inindu raised her slate board, "Necessary?"

"A calculated risk," he started forward. "He didn't look the sort to fight a woman, though I honestly didn't know what *you* would do to him."

Maldinado led her to Second Gate without further episode. The well-guarded entrance, wholly and thankfully intact, located precisely where he thought, boasted seven swads on foot and another five on horseback. The tailor noticed at least twenty more on the wall above. Not archers. Flints. *So, the rumors are true.* He dipped his head, slightly, looking back toward Inindu. She saw them, too. He wondered how she would fair if she encountered them in battle. Regardless, he could not offer her any aide. Though he shared a mind with the warrior, his body remained that of the tailor.

"Morlac's boon upon thee, Maldinado."

He turned to find Somering, Appointed Recorder of Delacroy, resident of Ninth Circle, sitting behind a weather-beaten wooden table which appeared decidedly uncluttered despite several piles of leather-bound books, loose parchment paper, and a large scroll containing an embedded ruby on either end of dark-stained handles. Somering had served as recorder since before Maldinado's father passed beyond Ninth Circle, but her face remained a source of particular amusement to the tailor. He felt it resembled a chicken. Narrow eyes nearly linked together beneath the bridge of her nose, and a boneless chin fell steeply away from her mouth. But her nose struck him the most. He imagined she could dig a large trench using only her beak.

"Favor and boon, Somering," Maldinado navigated his way around her nose to touch her forehead in greeting: four circles meeting nine.

She unfurled her scroll and promptly buried said beak, as though pecking at the carefully written text. Maldinado sat on the table and leaned forward, unable to resist a casual peak at potentially useful information. Somering shot him an evil eye in warning, and without ever raising her head.

"You'll find my name listed in Fourth Circle," he chided.

"Still?" Somering ran two fingers along the text to help her focus.

"Feel free to take the matter up with our Adherent."

"I never speak to Shale," her fingers stopped at a name. "Maldinado, Fourth Circle. You may enter."

Maldinado motioned toward Inindu, "I've invited a house guest to live with me in the city."

"Naturally," Somering reached for pen and parchment, "Name?"

"She's a woman," he smiled. "Beautiful and suitably mute."

Somering looked up, "She's still a girl. I'd rather kiss the horse."

"Interesting," Maldinado leaned closer, "I thought that just a rumor, but I can certainly make arrangements." His eyes wandered to one of the names on her list: *Albie, wears a full red beard.* But she pulled the scroll away before he could gather more information, useful or otherwise.

"If I want to kiss a horse, I will simply purchase one. I do not need the services of a Fourth Circle tailor."

"Unless, of course, that tailor *is* the horse," Maldinado watched her smile. It broke along the edge of her mouth, and quickly disappeared. An annual tradition. To his knowledge, Somering would not smile again until the next Sorting occurred, or until he saw her next.

The last, uncorrupted soul in all of Delacroy. Yet, Maldinado found the means to bribe her.

He backed away in delight.

"Name?" Somering returned to her scroll.

"No name," Inindu wrote.

Somering recorded *mute girl with black horse* on her sheet, and then motioned them proceed forward to the marking station. "One circle on the forehead for the girl," she announced.

"She's clearly a woman," Maldinado rose from the table.

"And one circle for the horse," Somering quietly quipped.

"That's just mean."

He led Inindu away so the mute could receive her identifying tattoo, a necessary step for any pilgrim wishing to enter the city. The marking station displayed a set of needles and various bottles of black dye atop a long wooden table. On one side sat an unmarked taggle wearing yellow and white. On the other side, sat a swad from Second Circle.

"Pay the taggle and get a circle," Maldinado pointed. "Don't pay and you take your chances with the swad. Most of the pilgrims pay, but I've seen more than a few oddly shaped marks." He handed Inindu three gold pieces, again lamenting his earlier losses, "Trust me, you want to pay the taggle."

Inindu pulled on the robe of his sleeve. When he turned around, she pulled back her hair to reveal a mark already tattooed on her forehead.

"When did..." Maldinado scratched at his beard, "Well, that saves me a few coins. I think I'm going to like having you live with me."

At last, Maldinado entered the city. And Inindu followed.

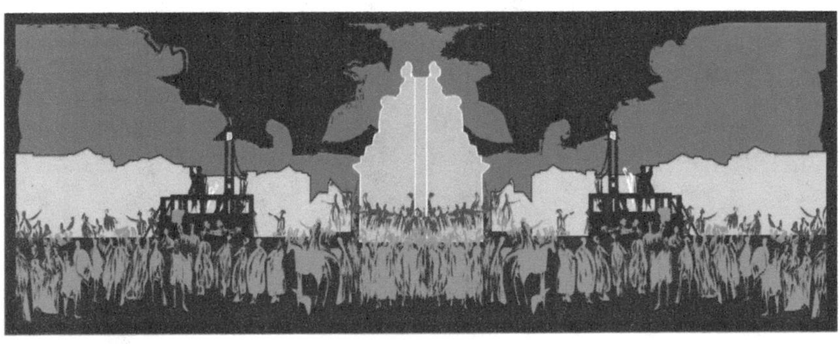

The Sorting

Delcrean Council

Certainty | Chastity | Fasting | Generosity | Joy | Orthodoxy | Peace | Honesty | Faithfulness

(before)

Troq slid gleaming knife through peeled carrot, cutting a series of small orange spheres that fell against one another at an angle. Remni watched his practiced motion, perfected after serving in the magnate's kitchen for almost thirty-nine years, three years prior to the day Boltmar received the magnate ring from his father's thumb. Troq's own thumb, she observed, held against the unsliced portion of the dwindling carrot, showcased several scars from calloused tip to interphalangeal crease; and a cracked nail which pushed under a hardened knot of skin like a rusty shovel lifting drought-stricken earth. She watched him scoop the carrots between cupped palm and knife's edge, dropping them into a cold cast-iron skillet with careless grace; and continued to follow his hands when he grabbed another peeled carrot from the pile of carrots Remni had cast aside.

She stood on the other side of the table, peeling with only casual interest. She did not feel like eating, but Troq would not let her leave with an empty stomach no matter how full she felt.

"I wish it was cooler, this evening," she continued. "It seems like it should be cooler if we are going to have a fire. Will it be a large fire?"

"The Fires of the Sphere are symbolic, proselyte. There are no bonfires," he smiled. "We prefer candlelight."

"And everyone wears a mask? They won't know who I am?"

Troq nodded, slightly. His black eyelids drooped down over dark brown eyes as though collapsing. Wrinkles crossed his nose and dug deep beneath his cheeks, and deeper still under the short white beard he wore in stark contrast to his bushy eyebrows. "They won't know you, and you won't know them. We worship in secret; safer for us all." He pointed at her with his blade, "That's enough carrots."

Remni set the paring knife down and retrieved a metal slop bucket from underneath the wooden tabletop where it hung on a hook. She grabbed a handful of slick peelings and dropped them into the bucket, already full of brown and white potato peelings from the evening dinner, "Agatha will be happy."

"Pigs are always happy. They eat whatever you throw into their trough."

"Not apples, I hope?" Remni dropped more peelings into the bucket, "It seems like they shouldn't eat apples…only dead pigs should eat apples."

"It is their last meal, yes. But I've yet to see a cooked pig that actually *ate* the apple," Troq reached for the last remaining carrot. "You don't have to come with me."

"I know."

She watched him wipe his hands on the white apron tied around his waist, and then followed them as he placed the skillet on an iron rack above the fire pit, dipped his hand into a small burlap sack, and sprinkled salt over the carrots. She handed him a mortar and pestle and he sifted black pepper flakes over the pan, speckling the simmering orange vegetables until pepper looked like ash freshly fallen from a pipe. He shook the skillet to separate the carrots while she added butter, evoking an immediate and sizzling response.

"Does the Sphere really exist?" Remni walked over to a large, undecorated wooden cabinet. It stood against the wall like a swad standing guard. Inside the cabinet was an assortment of metal place settings, wooden bowls, and glass pitchers. At the very top lay a stack of five wooden plates.

"That is a question you must answer for yourself, proselyte."

"Morlac exists. I have seen him. But I cannot worship him," she set a polished wooden plate, one for each of them.

"You don't believe what you see with your own eyes?" Troq removed the skillet from the fire pit, holding it over her plate while he shoveled the carrots with a spoon.

"No, I guess I don't."

"That is why we wear masks. We believe what we cannot see because what we *can* see, we cannot believe."

She stabbed dutifully at a small orange sphere near the edge of her steaming plate and took her first crunchy bite. Butter coated her lips as she withdrew the fork.

The carriage slowed to a stop while one of the swads opened Fourth Gate. Remni let the curtain fall and straightened her back against the padded interior wall. Boltmar stretched his legs, toes reaching out to touch the opposite bench. She rubbed at her knees, and then her calves.

It seemed to her their journey would never end. Whenever they reached the manor, however, she would head to the kitchen and speak with Troq. He would know what to do.

"A warning?" Boltmar spoke as though pleading with her, still unwilling to admit his son's betrayal. "A Son or Daughter of Oblation telling us to be careful?"

Remni felt her chest compress as the carriage resumed its journey.

The Sons and Daughters of Oblation gathered in secret and adorned themselves in black robe and gold mask—including Remni and Boltmar. Aside from Boltmar, Remni knew only one of the other worshipers—Troq, her friend. For good or ill, therefore, everyone's identity remained hidden and unknown.

We believe what we cannot see.

"No, not a warning," She concluded.

"No," he agreed.

Remni leaned her head against his shoulder but offered no words of comfort. Their friendship, their love, did not extend into matters involving Valun. She knew better than to have accused Boltmar's son aloud, but such knowledge did not usurp her conviction. Valun had long hated her—and Boltmar, as a result. Jealousy, most likely, caused the friction between them. He once commanded his father's ear, but she unwittingly stole that from him, along with his heart.

"Who can I trust?" Boltmar asked. "A magnate worships the Sphere...I have doomed us both."

I trust Troq. He'll know what to do.

The carriage lurched forward.

Why are we stopping?

Remni pulled velvet curtain aside as they slowed to a stop inside the oddly quiet and empty Fourth Gate; abandoned by travelers and taggles alike, after sunset. Several paintings sat out on display and in front of a taggle's booth not far from the carriage—a vivid and balanced contrast of light and dark, an effect eerily enhanced by the torchlight cast in several directions by their escort of swads. The painted figures seemed to lift out and away from each canvas in an artistic style unique to Fourth Gate, and it may have brought her comfort if not for the grotesqueness of the compositions. Every painting seemingly depicted the dead, their highlighted bodies strewn across canvas in twisted, unnatural angles.

She hated the artwork in Fourth Gate.

Boltmar leaned into her, perhaps also intending to look out her window, or kiss her, but someone ripped open the carriage door and grabbed the magnate by his clothing. Remni watched as their attacker pulled Boltmar from the carriage and threw him to the ground all in the same motion. Their attacker wore a red maldinado-robe, cowl raised, and a red porcelain mask that hid his face. But she did not need to see his face to know Valun stood over his father. She dove for her lover, but another cloaked figure slammed the carriage door, sliding a long-knife through the latch to prevent her escape.

She screamed, "Valun, no!"

A tilt of the head confirmed her suspicions, but he did not pause in his actions. Valun slid a knife under the white beard of her lover, pulling his head back by a handful of hair. Then she watched the son of Boltmar as he cut into the neck of his father, nearly severing head from body. Neither father nor son uttered a word. Boltmar died with his left-hand grasping at the foot of his killer, body arched outward and away from a fractured right arm; his legs folded inward like a spider.

My love!

But she could no longer speak. He worshiped the Sphere because she asked him to, and now he lay dead.

What have I done?

The attack shifted to her.

They shoved torches through the windows on both sides, promptly igniting the velvet interior. Remni coiled away from the flames, desperately kicking at the carriage door. The resulting heat overwhelmed her senses as smokeless flames arched from curtain to velvet covered wall. The finely woven material, comprised of silk fibers, curled away from the fire, revealing dry wood beneath.

"Valun!" She finally screamed.

She grabbed a wine skin from beneath the bench across from her, pulled the cork, and doused her clothing with red wine. She poured the wine over her hair and her face and hands. But pain struck her mercilessly. It soared through her right foot where it lay hovering over a flame. It burned the back of her thighs where she hadn't poured the wine. She flung herself at the door and reached her arm through the window, grasping for the latch, frantically trying to escape. Her sleeve ignited, searing her face. She kicked again at the door, and pounded both fists into the carriage floor, but nothing brought freedom from the suffocating flames. Her body burned.

Troq!

She watched as three black stallions, out of the four tasked with pulling the carriage, ran from the fire. Only the stallion with a cataract lingered to watch the carriage burn——and Remni within. Flames roared upward. Ivory carvings, fastened along the exterior, charred and fell with grand bursts of flame. Burning chunks of wood popped loudly and frequently, sending sparks flying toward nearby stages and the oil paintings which promptly ignited.

May the Sphere be with us...

But Remni prayed no more.

Inindu

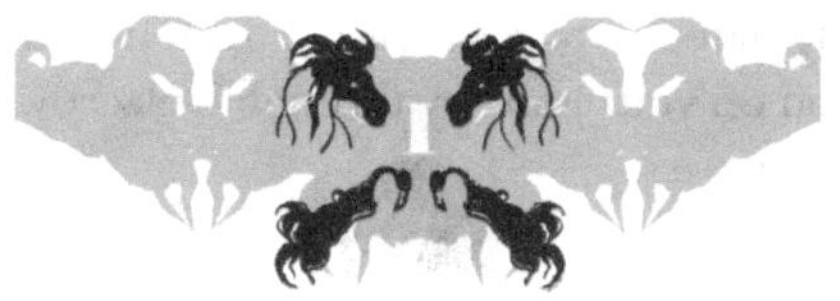

Somering thought to brand our forehead, but we refuse to wear Morlac's mark—even in this illusion. Instead, we present a trick of the eye. The circular key grants us entrance to the city, and we follow Maldinado through Second Gate. Despite the late hour, the tunnel appears overcrowded, filled with merchants selling their wears and myriad goods to pilgrims. We allow our attention to wander freely and often: Leather sandals, silver jewelry, and clay pottery. The random placement of items and booths, combined with several colorfully adorned performers, serves to create a festive flair we find pleasing.

Maldinado carves a disjointed path through and around various pinch points as the crowd ebbs and flows, mostly dictated, we notice, by the quality of goods on display; or whenever they gather below the stage of a particularly talented performer. We pause to watch three jugglers toss torches at one another. They add more torches with every toss, creating an endless and wonderful flow of fire between them.

"There's nothing quite like a taggle celebration," Maldinado says. "I'm sure they do this every night inside their gates, but we only get to walk their tunnels at night one time a year—and only in Second Gate."

The taggles display no identifying mark upon their ears as they do in our father's world, nor do they appear enslaved. Rather, we discover artisans, entertainers, and...

"Storytellers?"

Maldinado motions for us to follow, "We'll find Beah further ahead. He's my favorite storyteller in Second Gate," he pauses, "I remember him...from the old world, I mean."

Moments later, Beah emerges onto an elevated wooden stage, presenting a visual spectacle we rather quite enjoy. His leggings display a checkered pattern of three vibrant colors: purple, yellow, and orange. A green scarf hangs from his throat, allowing each end to fall loosely down his rigid back. Hair, black and long, frames his clean-shaven face. But we linger on his exposed torso—delightfully hardened and grooved in all the right places—seemingly strong enough to tame a horse.

Beah begins:

"This tale originated in Second Circle. Listen to these warnings and may Dsal guide you on your journey through Delacroy."

Atop the home of a young servant, on the flat rooftop of his home, lies Dsal Tiger. Each day, the young servant presents Dsal Tiger with a visitor from the city below. They come with offerings and a single request. One such visitor, a collector of fine oils, bows before Dsal Tiger, offering him a wrap of gray, course wool.

Dutifully, the young servant declares, "A gift! The collector desires your favor."

"What use do I have for wool?" Dsal Tiger asks.

The collector bows lower, "Please, in exchange for a carafe of fine oil, for what need have you for oil? Is wool not equally useless?"

Dsal Tiger licks his paws and considers the request, "Take my oil, leave your wool, and worship me as payment."

"Will you worship Dsal Tiger?" The young servant asks the collector.

"Yes, of course. I will worship the tiger until my death."

The young servant exchanges wool for oil and the collector departs on her merry way. Afterward, the young servant makes his own request. "Is my debt now repaid?"

Dsal Tiger sprawls sleepily upon several large cushions, "I saved your home in exchange for your service. When my worshipers no longer worship me, only then will I forgive your debt."

The young servant leaves in silence, excusing himself with a slight bow. He descends to an empty home and falls asleep in the corner of an empty room. Next day the young servant presents another visitor from the city below, a maker of goat cheese who grovels with practiced form, extending his arms to the edge of the plush, red rug where Dsal Tiger lounges. The cheese maker holds a corkscrew in his hand.

Dutifully, the young servant declares, "A gift! The cheese maker desires your favor."

"What use do I have for a corkscrew?" Dsal Tiger asks.

The maker of goat cheese stretches further, "Please, in exchange for a drink of black wine, for what need have you for a corked bottle? Is not an empty bottle equally useless?"

Dsal Tiger bites into a ripe cantaloupe; seeds hanging from the fur around his mouth. "Drink my black wine, leave the empty bottle, and worship me as payment."

"Will you worship Dsal Tiger?" The young servant asks.

"Yes, of course. I will worship the tiger until my death."

The cheese maker drinks black wine until the bottle lies empty and then departs on his merry way. Afterward, the young servant makes his own request. "Is my debt now repaid?"

Dsal Tiger paws playfully at the braided cords that hang from his cushions. "I saved your home in exchange for your service. When my worshipers no longer worship me, only then will I forgive your debt."

The young servant leaves in silence, excusing himself with a slight bow. He descends to an empty home and falls asleep in the corner of an empty room. The next day the young servant presents another visitor from the city below, a scrounger with hair as brown as the dirt on her face. She kneels and extends a wooden bowl, and the water within, as offering.

Dutifully, the young servant declares, "A gift from the scrounger!"

"What use do I have for a wooden bowl?" Dsal Tiger asks.

The scrounger woman raises her head, "You would refuse my gift?"

Dsal Tiger rises and approaches the scrounger, "What favor do you seek?"

"I ask for nothing in return," the scrounger woman bows her head.

"Then I will favor you above all my worshipers," Dsal Tiger lowers his head to the water and laps with savage haste.

"What use do I have for favor?" The scrounger woman asks, "Is an empty bowl not equally useless?"

The young servant, standing unusually close to the scrounger woman, reveals a sword from behind his back. He strikes while Dsal Tiger yet drinks. The beast falls beside the overturned wooden bowl.

Dutifully, the young servant says, "Take your treasure, leave your bowl, and worship me as payment."

"Yes, of course. I will worship you until my death." She skins Dsal Tiger and departs on her merry way.

Beah ends his tale with a bow and a dallic, raising the latter to catch several coins thrown in his direction.

"I told you he was good," Maldinado throws a coin at the taggle's stage.

"Need him," we point at the taggle, and then write, "He's young. You're old."

"Yes, but only in this world," Maldinado starts forward, "I'll make the arrangements. No doubt, it will cost me more than a few gold pieces."

We turn our attention to a nearby collection of paintings, each image depicting man, beast, or landscape using shapes to create a fractured pictorial space. One of the paintings, depicting a magenta horse, stands out from the rest. Despite the cubist portrayal, the horse's identity remains clear.

Only a few feet away, another rendering shows a magenta horse and her magenta haired caretaker.

"Inindu," a taggle steps forward, presumably the painter. We notice her body mimics the inverted triangles in her work: Tiny legs supporting wide hips and an even larger bust line.

How does she know our name?

She points to our forehead, "First Circle, eh? I'm sorry to see you didn't make it through the Sorting, but at least you get to visit."

"Mute."

"I can tell. The slate board around your neck gives it away."

Tell that to Maldinado.

She folds one arm under breast, using it to support the other arm which points back toward her paintings, "In Delacroy we ward against Inindu by displaying her image. Usually, she sits on a shelf or table or, if you prefer, on a wall. And if you pay a taggle, let's say for one of those paintings, you will earn Morlac's favor."

"Keeps Inindu away?" We hastily scrawl, unable to resist.

"I give you my pledge as a taggle."

We consider showing her our true color but decide against the idea— uncertain how Morlac would respond. Instead, we write, "No gold."

"I can tell," she points again at our forehead, "No one enters Delacroy with gold, pilgrim. Especially someone bearing only the mark of First Circle. No, I spoke of the horse. I can use her as a model. Any three paintings in exchange for the horse. You're bound to find it difficult to travel in the city, mounted or otherwise."

We allow her to look at our horse a moment longer and raise our head so she may see our full beauty. But we grow bored with this verbal banter, "No deal."

She flashes a sour grin, "You'll soon learn. Pay the taggles or risk Morlac's favor."

We find no need for Morlac's favor. We are Inindu. Once, we were loved by Adarian.

Moving away from the booth, we discover another painting from a different taggle which depicts the same magenta image. In fact, our fractured image is everywhere: paintings, pottery, and mosaics. Clumsy renderings, though. The shapes mostly elongate our nose and definitely widen our hips.

Maldinado returns with Beah, "What's wrong?"

We point at a mosaic bowl. It shows a magenta horse in the middle of a white circle.

"Inindu? Oh, right…I guess that would bother you."

Beah furrows his brow, confused.

It's about to get even more confusing, taggle.

We reach out to grab him, a hand on either side of his temples. He struggles against our grip, lacking the strength to resist, though we enjoy the resulting tremor in his muscles. Indeed, we draw him closer as we attempt to pull him out of Morlac's illusion. Something feels wrong, however. Second Gate grows silent. The dead appear sporadically throughout the crowd, but their images flutter. Beah and the rest of the taggles still linger in their bright colors. Maldinado his robe. Torchlight flickers along the red walls and across works of art.

We cannot escape the illusion. We…cannot…

Beah looks horrified, unable to comprehend this half-world, as though we stand here torturing him, filling his head with broken memories and a lost identity, rather than saving him from Morlac's grasp. Yet we persist. His face slackens—eyes turn moribund. Tattered white linen clothing surfaces over his checkered yellow leggings and then, just as quickly disappears. Nothing remains of the world of the dead beyond. Second Gate stirs, once more.

We release Beah from our grip.

We cannot save him.

He looks at Maldinado with terror-stricken eyes, and again to us— gazing not at our beauty, but at a monster. No doubt, he sees the evil against which this city wards: Inindu. If Beah carried a sword he would certainly draw and attack. Instead, he turns and flees.

Maldinado hobbles after him, but the younger taggle quickly disappears into the crowd. The tailor returns a minute later with arms raised in bewilderment, "What was that?"

"No escape."

"You mean…" He points back toward First Circle, "Out there. The dead?"

It means we have finally entered Morlac's world.

CONDEMNED

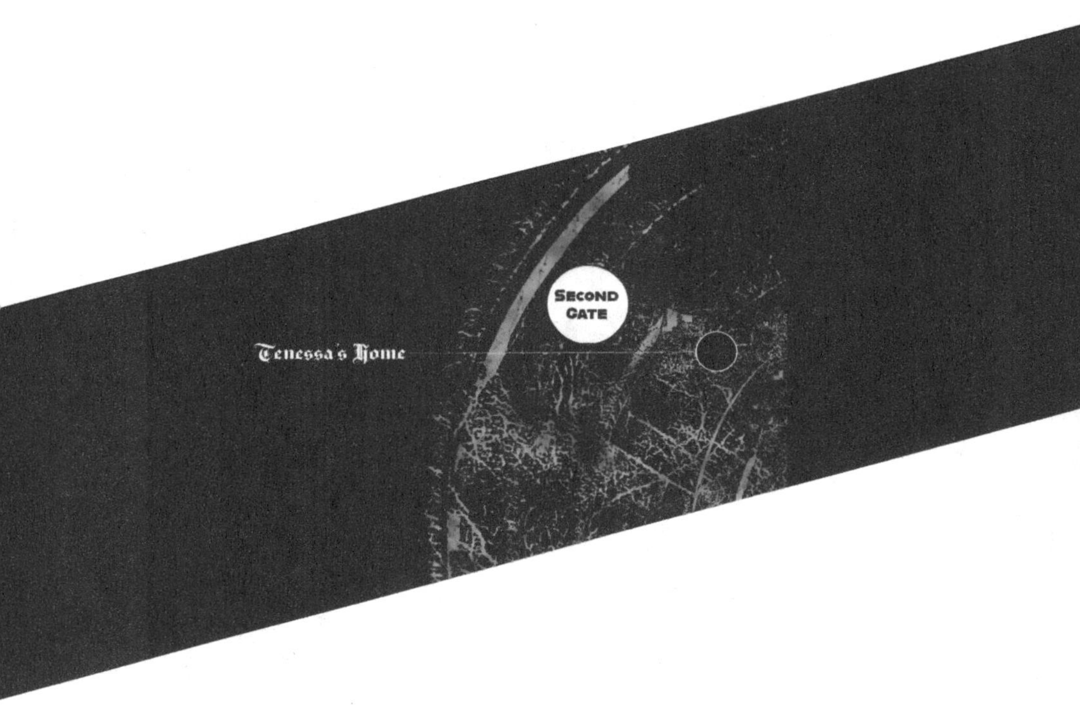

or as one day the Sphere will die, so too, those who remain in his world. Without me, they are condemned.

The words of Morlac as recorded by Adherent Laus

Simiad, Second Circle Magnate, sat at a wooden table pushed flat against a stone wall, leaving three of the four sides exposed. In front of him lay a meal consisting of three halved and roasted potatoes seasoned with lemon juice and cilantro, a mound of shredded green cabbage tossed with olive oil and a toasted flat bread; the bread appeared overly toasted. He sat in prayer above his meal: Fingers clasped together under brown beard, elbows on the wooden surface of the table with his head tilted upward as though a condemned man pleading for a final meal.

A dark painting hung on the wall beside him so that the bottom of the painting aligned evenly with Simiad's angular head. Framed with pistachio wood, the naturally stark contrast between light and dark grains negated the need for any stain or decorative design; a complimentary choice mimicking the shadow play of the painting which depicted a gangly boy peeping over a bush at a group of female bathers. A circle of torches provided enough light for the five bathers to set about their task despite the dark hour. Two of the women half-submerged in a lake, one actively scrubbing her left shoulder while the other floated on her back—breasts pointing to the heavens. The other three, depicted in various stages of disrobing, cast long shadows in several directions. At the corner of the painting stood the boy with a look more devious than curious, suggesting this as the latest in a series of previous encounters with the five nude bathers. The prickly forest surrounding the boy retreated into various shades of black and dark blues.

Simiad finished his silent prayer, grasped a silver knife, and cut into the potato nearest his cabbage. He turned his head, slightly, and considered the painting as he ate.

a taggle's painting

Delacroy

Certainty | Chastity | Fasting | Generosity | Joy | Orthodoxy | Peace | Honesty | Faithfulness

Troq dipped his feathered quill into a bottle of black ink. Then he blotted and scribbled and somehow managed to draw the shape of a sphere, his hands more familiar with a knife than quill. He set the writing device down onto a concave wooden block and folded the wordless note before sealing it with orange wax.

"Make sure Lyshmee receives this message," he handed the note to his apprentice, a taggle boy with red hair, disfigured ears, and a penchant for poor speech.

"'Tis a long journey to Second Circle. I'll be needing to buy food."

The cook handed Edran a leather pouch filled with five gold coins, "Buy a bag of apples from Nebon. Manage to bring some back with you and I may make some cobbler."

"And a sweet roll?"

Troq stood and shuffled his apprentice out through the door, "Yes, I gave you enough for a sweet roll."

"Yer a fine master," the boy stood in morning darkness, his red hair still visible.

"*You* are lingering. Go, and make sure you come back in one piece. The pots won't scrub themselves."

He watched the taggle boy as he snuck across the courtyard, disappearing behind a bush and then into the sewers below. Only taggles traveled the sewers. Any others, foolish enough to descend, soon went missing—their bodies left at the dark end of a dead end. Few in Delacroy knew about the sewers aside from the magnates and swads. Even informed residents thought them empty, for the taggles held their secrets well.

But he knew.

Troq shifted his attention to the softening sky. Darkness would soon turn red with dawn which meant he needed to begin preparations for the day. He closed the door to his room and traveled under the manor terrace toward another door leading to the kitchen.

"Boltmar is dead."

Phinx. Troq recognized the voice, though the taggle painter remained unseen under terrace shadow.

Troq turned slightly, speaking over his shoulder, "And the mark?"

"Carved into his chest. A gruesome task I'll not soon forget."

Troq closed his eyes, "And Remni?"

"Valun burned her inside the carriage."

He nodded, "A necessary sacrifice. I left a large amount of gold for you in my room."

"Pay a taggle, and you'll earn Morlac's favor," Phinx emerged from the shadows, raising a tattered scarf to his mouth, "May the Sphere protect us."

"And keep us in his light," Troq watched as the taggle returned to the sewers without accepting payment for his services, "And keep you out of Morlac's sight."

Moments later, he entered the kitchen to begin his morning routine. The fire pit still glowed. He added five quarter-split logs and stoked the fire until flames rose through the wire rack where the cook placed an iron skillet. Troq preferred the skillet nice and hot before he poured cake batter, allowing him to control the size of the breakfast cake; and he preferred them small and stacked, leaving room on the plate for eggs and sausage. This served as Troq's meal, one of two he ate everyday: the first meal before breakfast, and the last after everyone had their fill of supper.

Boltmar's manor required a staff of five cooks and eight apprentices, all of them answering to Troq. They arrived under a purplish red sky and just as Troq finished the last of his eggs. Everyone went about their respective tasks, and the kitchen quickly became a flowing current of bodies moving from table to fire pit, or from barrel to hearth. They entered and exited with intentional haste. Some scrubbed while others skewered or stuffed. One of the apprentices, Tilly, dropped an open bag of flour, sending white powder throughout the kitchen. Troq quickly relegated the yearling to peeling grapes. Soon after, the dejected apprentice left the kitchen entirely after Troq arranged a tray of grapes and goat's milk and then gave it to her to carry up to Boltmar's quarters. He watched her leave, pleased she gripped the tray hard enough for her knuckles to turn white, and by the way she carefully managed the swinging door.

Boltmar's final morning dish.

Troq did not pause long. He carried a full pot, filled with water and potatoes, and placed it atop the fire pit. Whether or not the magnate lay dead at the hand of his son meant little for him and his staff. The living would still need food. Even at that early hour, Troq knew the manor filled with visitors: Residents arriving to strike a deal, lobby on someone's behalf, or simply obtain useful information. And whenever the young apprentice arrived at her destination above, and upon finding Boltmar missing, she would return in alarm and inform the cook who would alert the swads, and soon after word would spread throughout the city. Such news meant more visitors would arrive—and visitors would expect a meal—so Troq resumed his morning routine.

Lomax sat watching the red morning sky from his customary position in front of his one-story home, his stiff back resting against a short stone pillar. He waited impatiently for Maldinado, as he did every morning.

"Morlac's boon upon thee, Lomax," Denam passed, already beginning his day.

"Favor and boon," he muttered irritably. The appearance of his jubilant rival in basket weaving meant Lomax had already lost out in securing a prime position within the marketplace. *Tasa Ro!*

Thousands more filled the street in front of Lomax as dawn brightened; turning red dirt into a cloud of dust which sat level with his increasingly disgusted face. He scratched at his gray-white beard, careful to avoid a large black mole along his left jaw line, and cursed Maldinado, again, for the growing delay. Then he wondered if the tailor, in fact, lay dead in his bed, leaving Lomax the victor in their long-standing wager. This happy thought brought him comfort for the next several minutes until he finally remembered his friend left the prior day to attend the Sorting, and likely wouldn't return to Fourth Circle for another couple of days. *Tasa Ro!*

It seemed the basket weaver grew more forgetful with each passing day, though he would never admit to such gaps in memory, especially to Maldinado. Instead, Lomax determined he would charge his friend the price of a new basket for making him wait so long that morning; and at least two gold pieces for allowing Denam to arrive first to the marketplace. *He owes me that much!*

"Morlac's boon upon thee, Lomax," Fanzir called.

"Favor and boon," Lomax stood with a twist to his back, and a subsequent crack, "Wait, we need to speak about your father. I spoke with him in the marketplace yesterday. He says he's worried about the condition of your home. In particular, he mentioned the baskets you purchased from Denam last week."

The beardless bookkeeper blinked anxiously, "But...I didn't purchase anything from Denam. You know I only buy your baskets. Why would my father say that?"

Lomax pressed his advantage over the young resident, "Are you calling your father a liar? Has he fallen so far out of Morlac's favor?"

"No, he's not a liar. I mean…but I *didn't* buy any denam-baskets."

Lomax patted Fanzir's shoulder, deftly pulling a gold piece from the man's pocket at the same time, "Age does funny things to the mind, Fanzir." *I should know.* "If your father isn't a liar… Perhaps his memory fades? You definitely don't want that information getting around."

Lomax considered his own mind. Though his fingers remained nimble, he struggled, at times, to recall even simple details like the name of Fanzir's father. *What is his name?*

"No, that would be bad," Fanzir agreed. The crowd stopped, forcing the two travelers to wait.

"Unfortunately, your father made his concerns known to the larger group gathered around my cart, yesterday——so that presents a problem," Lomax scratched under his chin. "Maybe you should purchase some of my baskets, so you can tell everyone you replaced your denam-baskets with lomax-baskets."

"But I don't have any denam-baskets," Fanzir protested.

"We both know that, but your father doesn't."

"You're right."

"Think of your father, Fanzir," Lomax patted the shorter bookkeeper's shoulder. "Morlac's favor upon him."

"Favor and boon."

"Why aren't we moving?" Lomax suddenly realized no one on the street was moving forward in either direction. Instead, they gathered closer together, speaking in whispers, "What is it? What's going on?" Lomax yelled.

"Boltmar's dead," someone in the crowd responded, "They found his body inside Fourth Gate."

Someone else added, "He worshiped the Sphere. They found him with *the mark*."

Phinx opened his blurry eyes to find Jennaween standing over him with a devilish look, holding a yellow glass oddly decorated with small, concave acorns and filled with goat's milk. Her grin made him pause, wondering if she had not, in fact, intended to douse him with the drink in order to awaken him; and felt suddenly grateful that he managed to stir from his slumber without her fiendish intervention.

"Late night?" Her husky voice lingered in his ears for a moment before settling softly into silence.

"I couldn't sleep," Phinx swiped the lukewarm glass from her, noting the playful disappointment which hung from her curved lips. He lay under sheet fully clothed; still wearing the same attire he wore the night before minus a silk scarf which lay in a careless heap upon the red stone floor. He threw sheet aside and spun his bird-like legs over the makeshift berth: two large wooden boxes and a wool-stuffed pad.

The sewers served as home to the taggles, offering secrecy and a faster way to travel, but they failed to offer the slightest hint of comfort. Despite the common perception of taggle wealth held by most Delcreans, any gold Phinx received did not, in fact, belong to him. The taggles pooled their earnings, mostly out of necessity, for while he may command several bags of gold in a single day—whether selling six or seven of his paintings or, after the gates closed, murdering an unsuspecting victim at the paid request of a politically motivated resident—a less skilled taggle may only earn a few coins over a week's period. Indeed, the sum of their collective effort barely paid for food, ale, and art supplies, so they lived together in the sewers, sharing every inch of habitable space whether hovel or corner. Ownership of these meager dwelling spots tended to change nightly according to whichever taggle arrived first. Thus, Phinx rarely slept in the same bed two nights in a row. One bed proved as uncomfortable as the next, so he found warmth in the arms of a woman—often a different woman each night—and on that morning, a particularly beautiful taggle from Fourth Gate.

Jennaween crossed her arms, causing multiple bracelets to jingle, "You couldn't sleep..." She wore her favorite blue shawl, and often crossed her arms to better wrap her hands and keep them warm, "And *still* you left me alone in my bed. I may as well be your sister as your lover."

He finished his milk and handed the empty glass back to her, "You were snoring. I didn't want to disturb you. Shook the walls you were so loud."

"We both know which one of us snores," she spit into the glass and wiped it clean using an orange cloth drawn from her pocket. "And you're a piss poor liar, Phinx. So, what's really bothering you?"

"Nothing," he reached for the discarded scarf, dyed red with sarlin root, and wrapped it around his neck; habitually hanging one end from his mouth. He chewed every scarf he owned to tatters, an oral fixation retained from his youth when he would chew on blankets until he fell asleep, a habit his mother, and several of his early lovers, tried unsuccessfully to break. The nibbling action helped him focus, usually while he painted or schemed, and the need for cynosure led to his excessive grinding that morning. He felt anxious, and with good reason.

"Just behind on a commission is all," he deflected her probing, deciding certain gruesome acts of revolution made for poor morning conversation let alone while in the company of such an attractive taggle.

"Does that mean you're in a hurry?" Jennaween bent over, shirt and shawl falling far enough forward to reveal an exotic and colorful winged tattoo between her nearly flat breasts. She placed the empty glass into a community box next to various other supplies including cookware, blankets, and tinder.

Phinx looked around and, gratefully, found the hovel empty of any other taggles, "Why, are you giving me a reason to stay?"

Jennaween repositioned shawl over breasts with a flirtatious smile, "If you wanted these you should have slept with me last night." She grabbed a leather pack from beside the wooden box, slid it over head and shoulder, and left with an air of satisfaction.

Phinx folded the linen sheet and laid it at the foot of the wool pad before following after his jilted lover, "Jennaween, wait," but she had already disappeared into another tunnel.

In her place, he discovered Beah. The shirtless taggle half-ran through the sewers, holding his head between hands and pulling fiercely at his long, black hair—disoriented to the point he nearly collided with Phinx.

"Beah? What's wrong?"

The taggle kept moving, however, muttering something unintelligible as he passed, "ninduin…"

"Beah!" But the crazed taggle continued to run. *Why aren't you in Second Gate?*

Phinx considered the odd encounter for only a moment. Other matters demanded his attention: Boltmar's body lay above in Fourth Circle, no doubt gathering a morning crowd. Though, judging from the lack of taggles traveling the sewers, aside from Beah and Jennaween, Phinx realized midday fast approached. News of any kind spread easily enough through Delacroy, carried by gold-tainted whispers, which meant news of the magnate's death would have already reached Fifth, if not Sixth, Circle—rumors of a nearly severed head, a burned carriage…and a mark of the Sphere upon Boltmar's chest.

Courtesy of Phinx.

And the Sons and Daughters of Oblation.

The taggle resumed his journey through a torch lit tunnel. Iron pipes above his head contained the city's sewage, leaving a dry, stone pathway for him to follow.

Valun chose the perfect spot to murder his father: unexpected and unseen. Though, as it turned out, neither entirely unexpected nor unseen. The impatient heir planned well enough, but he forgot about his father's cook, Troq, and, worse yet, the bastard neglected to pay a taggle to murder his father. *He would have made a poor magnate.* Fortunately for Phinx, the son would only assume his father's title, not his responsibilities.

And Valun doesn't suspect a thing.

The Sons and Daughters of Oblation needed a martyr, so Phinx did not try to prevent Boltmar's death. He simply watched and waited for Valun to leave. Then he carved into the magnate's chest. Troq, Father of Oblation, hoped to draw more worshipers of the Sphere out of the shadows. Thus, Valun inadvertently started a revolution, his selfish ambition serving as…*no, not Valun.*

Phinx started the revolution.

He shifted the scarf in his mouth. Despite his sexual prowess, Phinx had managed to remain childless…until that moment. He served as *father* of a revolution. He felt a sudden, strange desire for Jennaween just then. Not lust, more like desperation. He needed her—anyone, really—to stand beside him so he didn't feel so alone. And Jennaween offered him the closest option. His walk turned into a run.

Then he remembered Bella…and…Rayshin…Corralea…Kipla…

He stopped running. *Calm down. No reason to panic.* Yes, he served as father of the revolution, but no telling *who* might step forward as the mother.

Valun slept on his back—blockish head under a pillow. Left arm and leg lay pointed toward the baseboard, fully extended beneath linen sheet and a lightweight, red blanket. His right arm and leg rested in a bent position as though ready to run. The small man, much shorter than his reticent father, boasted thick shoulders and even larger thighs. And, though old enough to grow a beard, Valun kept his rigid face clean shaven to the point he shaved twice each day to counteract the almost freakish growth rate of his facial hair. With similar disdain for Delcrean tradition, he kept his black hair cut short, only slightly longer in length than his trimmed eyebrows. Thus, on that morning, his black whiskers and fuzzy head of hair scraped against a warm pillow as he breathed through an upward-slanted nose.

He awoke with a sly grin as sounds of panic filled the stone hallway outside his unsullied room. A spooked swad burst through a pair of wooden doors without knocking, then hesitated as she processed how best to proceed. Valun shouted through the pillow, "Get out!" He knew the swad, of course, for she had accompanied him the prior night—one of eleven hand-picked swads. This planned interaction provided Valun the opportunity to display an appropriate level of surprise and grief in order to divert suspicion.

"Forgive me, Valun. It's your father. The Magnate's body was discovered in Fourth Gate this morning." She closed the door, "He bears the mark of the Sphere."

Valun pulled the pillow from his face, "What?" The smile fell into doubt, his intended reaction replaced with genuine disbelief, "Are you certain?"

"Yes, left on his chest."

Valun considered the implications of the mark. All of the implications. He knew his father's secret, yes, but never would he renounce his father publicly. Delcreans beheaded worshipers of the Sphere, and their entire family. Someone must have witnessed his act of murder—or knew enough about his plans to plot against him. One of the swads. "You betrayed me!"

The swad shook her head, "No...no, forgive me, Valun." She opened the door and three more swads, none of whom served as part of his murder party, entered the room, "We arrest you for treason. Your father worshiped the Sphere. I hereby sentence you to death by beheading."

The room offered no escape. His sword lay sheathed on a small wooden table several feet away, but he would never make it in time. Valun swung the blankets away from his stout legs and barreled into his betrayer before she could reach for her own sword. Fool. They crashed to the ground and he gripped her head in his hands before she could recover. Her loose hair brushed against his bare forearms. Snap. Her body collapsed in death.

You dare betray me!

The other three swads swarmed him a second later. He almost wished they would run him through with one of their swords, but he knew they would never risk the beheading of a magnate's son. The execution of such a public figure would bring Delcreans from every circle. Beheadings brought gold. Valun's death would bring more gold.

The unshaven, devout disciple of Morlac struggled against his captors, but they held firm and bound him with ropes which cut deeply into his wrists and ankles. The tallest of the swads tossed Valun over his shoulder and carried him out of the room.

"Favor and boon!" He cried. "Favor and boon!"

The swads moved through stone corridors, their clanking steps ringing in unison with Valun's protests. At one point his shouts became violent screams, and screams turned into guttural growls. "I worship Morlac. You know I worship Morlac. I hate you, father. Grrraaah...I hate you!"

Servants gathered in the hallways, a few, though fully aware of the morning's developments gathered in disbelief, others emerged with puzzled expressions. Valun threw himself every which way, attempting to free himself of his captors. Then he saw Troq standing next to a young girl just inside the kitchen entrance, "Troq, tell them it isn't true. You've known me my entire life. Tell them I would never worship the Sphere. I worship Morlac." Valun stretched out his hands in a final plea, his face slick with sweat, eyes wide with terror.

"My master speaks the truth," Troq shouted. "He has never worshiped the Sphere. Favor and boon, Valun. Favor and boon."

"Troq!" But the swads removed Valun from his father's palace. His frantic shouting faded into the smell of bacon and simmering whispers.

Troq placed his bone-thin arm around the apprentice beside him. Tears coated her pale eyelashes; her round face splotchy. "Come, yearling. Our two masters have departed, but our task remains. We have many more mouths to feed."

Inindu

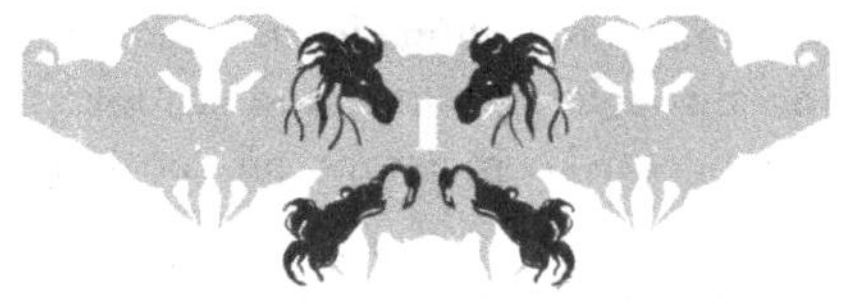

Sunrise brings separation and vile loneliness.

Inindu-horse:

I bide my time as a restless prisoner behind an unyielding, overly lacquered stall door. Tightly placed horizontal wooden slats form the lower section. Unpolished iron bars spaced wide enough in the middle for a horse to insert their head—my own private guillotine—rise upward from bottom portion to stout frame. I look beyond to the empty, middle corridor. A silver bay horse, two stalls down to my left, displays an annoying amount of curiosity. Any hint of movement snags his frenetic attention whether wandering rodent or slumbering horse. I see him every time I slide between these bars; him, and his flaxen mane. I retreat, once more, to my assigned dungeon. I stamp fiercely at the hard, uneven ground, moving sporadic piles of dry and splintered hay. My rider, my Inindu, departed early this morning. She filled an open barrel with tart, yellow apples prior to her departure, but they remain untouched. I'm not hungry.

I stick my head through the cold iron bars, again. Silver bay horse. Two stalls down. No other signs of life.

topi-Inindu:

I slept peacefully beside my horse, my Inindu, last night, as I always sleep, until Maldinado cruelly shook me awake. I left her savagely caged behind a stall door. She watched me leave with faithful resolve, her powerful head held high between iron bars, stoic eyes concealing her fear. Separation always brings fear.

When Adarian left, he never returned.

What if *we* never rejoin?

This dire thought stumbles recklessly into scattered emotions while

I follow a much more cautious Maldinado down a crowded, mostly sunlit street. He leads me through the elongated shadows of Second Circle toward an unseen dungeon keep, intent on speaking privately with a condemned woman.

"Why imprisoned?" I scribble hastily upon my slate board, and poke Maldinado's shoulder to get his attention. His shoulder once felt solid, firmer, but now it yields easily to the lightest touch as though nothing more than a dead fish.

"Lyshmee stands accused of copulation in a circle where such activities are strictly forbidden," Maldinado pauses for a concentrated sneeze, reacting to someone in the shifting crowd who never learned how to properly, and subtly, apply scented oils. "The swads found her with Penrem from Eighth Circle."

"Why does it matter?"

"Perhaps it doesn't. And I probably shouldn't give a damn, but something feels *off* about the whole story. Eighth Circle residents take a vow of honesty. Second Circle residents take a vow of chastity. Aside from Magnate Camen and his wife, I can't imagine a worse combination of residents in all of Delacroy. Think about it…Penrem gets executed if he lies about their affair, but if he tells the truth Lyshmee dies. And why would Lyshmee choose someone from Eighth Circle, anyway? And to what gain? Every other Delcrean Circle harbors known liars and, certainly, more capable and wealthy lovers. Choose any one of them and she likely avoids unwanted attention…unless she turned up with child, of course. So why Penrem?"

Why not Morlac? I again poke him in his quaggy shoulder with a chalk covered finger, perhaps a little impatiently, and point to my salted slate, "Why does it matter?"

Maldinado turns at my insistent peck—an ugly man, really, the curvature of his withered head fully visible under wisps of white hair. The furrows of his wrinkled face slink downward from indented forehead. Layers of dried and cracked skin culminate around the edge of his mouth like sliced, ripe fruit discarded and left to shrivel in the sun. In the Sphere's world he stood proud and tall. An enticing warrior. Here, in Morlac's world, he nearly topples with every hobbled step. He couldn't *carry* a sword much less wield one.

"I don't know that it does matter," Maldinado pauses to acknowledge a jovial passerby, "Favor and boon." He resumes speaking as though never interrupted, "But prior to the Sorting, I arranged a visit with Lyshmee, and Simiad would grow concerned if I failed to leverage such a rich opportunity. Whatever this grand illusion of Morlac's, and regardless what it may conceal, a thousand or more smaller deceptions occur in this city every day." Maldinado places a hand upon our shoulder and whispers, "Including our own schemes." Delcreans push pass us on either side, several pausing momentarily as they recognize the tailor, offering a quick greeting or a few lithe words.

Maldinado steps back and grabs at the worn lapels of his bright yellow robe as though gripping two ends of a frayed rope. He studies me with an odd twist of his mouth, "It's so strange seeing you here. Very strange… I'm not certain you really exist. Perhaps I fell asleep or passed beyond Ninth Circle and now lay at the bottom of the sea," he pulls nervously at his right ear, "Feels real enough." Then he quips, "*Return to your homes, the taggle said, Inindu enters the city.* Oh, but she's already here—and by special invitation of Maldinado. Yes, this will surely garner the Adherent's attention…and that of the guillotine, no doubt. I hope you're real. The real Inindu, I mean, or this will not end well. Probably die, anyway. Much to Lomax' delight."

He regresses with each word. The truth I revealed to him seemingly fades into madness. How can I fault him? Morlac's illusion feels complete. Everything about Maldinado's past likely seems a distant memory. And my past. How long ago did I hold Adarian in my arms? How many of the Adow…how many of my sisters did I witness take their first breath, and then their last? How many lives have passed before me?

Morlac's world. My father's world. None of it seems real.

I reach for Maldinado's hand, wrapping my fingers around his enlarged knuckles despite his cracked skin and the discolored dirt under his fingernails. *I've seen worse filth.* I place his callused palm against my cheek. Morlac wishes we both forget the world from whence we came, our true identities, but Maldinado's hand feels solid. He is…I am…real.

"Yes," Maldinado nods slowly. "Yes…" He pulls me into his weakened arms and lowers his grizzled chin to rest atop my head, "Yes, you are *the* Inindu."

Adarian embraced me often, and before him, and more frequently, the Daughters of the Adow. When Adarian died, however, I abruptly retreated from everyone until I forgot the warm touch of someone's embrace…the closeness and sense of comfort it provides. But this feels different. Adarian held me with passionate arms, and the Daughters of the Adow offered me the innocent love of a child. Maldinado's embrace strikes a chord of desperation and fear.

No doubt, he desires I wrap my arms around him, too, and assure him everything will turn out alright, but I refuse. I don't need him clinging to me, and I don't need his affirmation. I am Inindu. No, *we* are Inindu. Once, we were loved by Adarian. I push Maldinado away. I should never have left my horse, my Inindu. I head back to Second Circle stables, leaving the spurned tailor standing alone, free to chase local rumors and spread viscous gossip. Inindu requires my attention.

Not surprisingly, Maldinado does not follow.

The heavy stall door sits open as I arrive to find a familiar looking boy standing uncomfortably close to our horse; dust coats his red hair and disfigured ears. We knew him as Edran, a taggle boy from the Sphere's world. He runs a splayed brush over our satin mane and holds a fresh apple in his extended hand. We take it and eat ravenously.

"'Tis a rare thing to find this horse without her rider," Edran says.

"Rare to find an apprentice so far from his master," we write small so as to fit every word on our slate board.

"Troq sent me to deliver a message to Lyshmee."

Troq? We take the brush from the taggle's hand. *We will groom ourselves, boy.*

"But I be born in a stable, so 'tis thought I would visit the horses before I returned. And now I'm glad I did since I found you."

Aside from the intruding taggle, only nebbish horses populate the stable, thus we discard the slate board, allowing our rider to focus on grooming while our horse speaks, "Troq is here?"

"No," Edran sifts through the barrel for another apple, gathers hay into a stump-like pile with his foot, and plops down next to the open stall door. "Troq rarely be leaving his kitchen."

"Focus, boy. You're not listening. How are you here, in Delacroy? Where is Troq?"

"Fourth Circle," Edran takes a tiny bite from the top of the apple. "We be living in the magnate's manor. Well, 'tis mostly the kitchen where we live. Yer welcome to visit. We be getting all sorts of visitors every day. Sometimes late at night. I never see them, though. Troq makes me wash the pots and pans. I be washing the same ones four to five times a day. Eleven times, once. 'Tis my record. I be knowing every dent and scratch of every shape and size of every pot and pan. I don't mind the washing, really, 'tis the polishing I hate."

Our rider shifts to the other side of our horse, "Are you really here?"

Is this part of Morlac's illusion? Is this how Maldinado feels?

"I be asking you the same question," he leans forward, nibbled apple cradled between hands. "'Tis only a taggle boy you be seeing, a common enough sight. But I be hearing a talking horse. Of the two of us, which be real and whom the illusion?"

"This whole city is the illusion. Morlac's bland vision of the world. You've seen the dead?"

Edran wraps his teeth around the apple and nods.

"Can you see them now?"

"Nogwrh," Edran answers with a mouthful of mushed fruit.

No, I suppose not. If we cannot see them, how then the boy? *Perhaps our father remains free of the illusion?*

"What message did your master send Lyshmee?"

"'Tis a sealed message. I be a poor apprentice to betray my master's trust."

"Then you are also a fool. Any self- respecting apprentice knows how to open and reseal a message. How will you ever learn anything if you don't sneak around every now and then?"

"I'm not a fool."

"No, you're just a taggle. You do what you're told and think only as a last resort," we help ourselves to another apple and wipe at the juice as it runs down our chin.

"Yer not being very nice."

"Can I help it if I'm the reason yearlings cry at night? *Beware, Inindu!*" We stretch forth our hair, "Beware, Inindu." Our rider suddenly pounces forward, "Beware!"

But the boy doesn't stir.

Impressive...and insulting.

"Maldinado—or, rather, a feebler version of Maldinado—also went to visit Lyshmee." We would ask the boy about her, but we feel certain he doesn't know, "When he returns you will take us to our father."

"Fine. Yer horse be needing to stay here, though. There be no way to get a horse down into the sewers."

Stay? We don't wish to part again. We are Inindu. Once, we were loved by Adarian.

"Sewers?"

"'Tis faster to travel by sewer," Edran tosses his apple core aside. "For taggles, anyway. Maldinado be living in Fourth Circle, so he can take yer horse and we be meeting him there."

Our horse lowers her head. Our rider nods with resignation.

We are Inindu. But who are we when we part? Who are we without Adarian?

Maldinado

Certainty | Chastity | Fasting | Generosity | Joy | Orthodoxy | Peace | Honesty | Faithfulness

Maldinado used Mathay's shoulder to support himself as he walked along the shadowed corridors of the dank dungeon located deep beneath Second Circle. The hearty swad appeared indifferent, so the tailor accepted the aide with unspoken gratitude; his hip felt especially tight that morning after so much walking the previous few days. Mathay carried torch in-hand as he led him around a winding passageway and one oppressive door after another. Each iron barrier displayed a small sliding panel at the bottom, and a larger second panel at eye level, but offered no indication as to which of the cells held prisoners and which sat empty. Neither could he hear any of them. The swallowed clink of Mathay's silver ring which he tapped upon the hilt of his sword, and the absorbed groans from Maldinado whenever his hip locked up, served as the only audible sound along their dispiriting trek.

Typical of swads, and much to Maldinado's chagrin, Mathay did not wear a maldinado-robe. Instead, he wore a traditional royal blue kurta fashioned by Tymer, a small-fingered tailor from Seventh Circle. Few residents in Delacroy wore tymer-kurtas, but the swads single-handedly kept him in business. Worse, yet, Maldinado couldn't help but admire the tailor's work: Embroidered black silk sleeves and collar, and matching tight-fitting trousers, provided a nice contrast to the shimmering blue. A slit on either side of the kurta allowed the swads to hang their swords without bunching up the fabric around their waste. Maldinado found the design both practical and aesthetically pleasing.

From a tailor's perspective.

Maldinado the warrior, however, realized for the first time that the swads did not wear a single piece of armor. Compared to the warriors he once fought at the Battle of Quel, these swads presented little danger. *Did I ever fight such a battle?* Of course, Maldinado also lacked his customary Adarian armor and sword…and the energy of his youth.

Mathay stopped confidently in front of an indistinguishable cell door. He slid the top panel open with noticeable force, "Stand back, prisoner. Visitor."

The muscular swad lifted an iron shaft from its slot in the stone wall where it rested without any signs of rust. He swung open the well-oiled cell door, allowing Maldinado to enter. Inside sat a disheveled prisoner wearing gray, oversized trousers and matching sark. Her tangled, black hair hung over a dismal face, and her petite figure managed to hide behind an equally small presence—as though barely in the room. Maldinado struggled to recall ever meeting such a meek or demure Delcrean.

"Lyshmee?"

The woman lifted her eyes, though not her head.

Maldinado moved further into the room, but quickly stopped as a pungent smell sent him back to the doorway in a slow retreat, "Morlac's boon upon thee. My name is Maldinado, a tailor from Fourth Circle."

"I know of you."

"Then you also know of my generosity. Good. That saves us the burden of introductions," Maldinado took the torch from Mathay's hesitant hand. Then he moved forward and squatted down onto his heels for a better look at the prisoner's pallid face, "I heard all the horrible accusations against you, and those concerning Penrem. I'm willing to go in front of Magnate Simiad and plead for your release. He's a personal friend. He'll listen to me, but I need to know the truth. What really happened on the night you were arrested?"

Lyshmee lowered her gaze, "I slept with Penrem. Guilty as charged."

"I don't believe you," Maldinado glanced back at Mathay with an unspoken question.

"We caught them in the act—both of them still ass naked," Mathay responded.

The tailor stood with some difficulty, "Mathay, have you ever before barged into someone's home to find someone so convincingly engaged in such a lewd act? The only one strictly forbidden in Second Circle?"

"No," the swad admitted, "but I'm afraid your mission to liberate this whore is misguided, tailor. She is anything but innocent." The swad lingered on the last word as though relishing the idea. Maldinado held little doubt as to the abuse Lyshmee had already experienced inside these walls. Rumors suggested the swads, both the ones in Second Circle and those stationed throughout Delacroy, took full advantage of their intimate proximity to the condemned.

"Who was the informant?" Maldinado brought the swad's focus back to the inquisition, "How did you know Penrem was even there?"

"Actually, we didn't know anything about Penrem. We went to the house after someone accused this wench of worshiping the Sphere."

The Sphere?

"Who? Who accused her?"

"I...I don't recall."

Maldinado turned at the admission, "I find it interesting that bit about her worshiping the Sphere never emerged. Still...without an accuser... How fortunate, then, you found them in such a state. Copulation and broken vows make for better gossip, anyway. And with Penrem admitting to the affair it made any other charges mute." Maldinado handed the torch back to Mathay and moved to leave, "Well, Lyshmee, it seems I can do nothing to help your cause. I'm sorry. It seems you are destined to die one way or another. Morlac's boon upon your condemned soul."

"Favor and boon," Lyshmee whispered.

Maldinado slowly departed from the foul-smelling room, retreating back along the dungeon corridor without the aid of Mathay's shoulder. In that moment he felt certain as ever the arrests of Lyshmee and Penrem served only to cover up a much larger scheme; and one which somehow involved worshipers of the Sphere. If true, it meant he and Inindu would not have to stand alone against Morlac.

Maldinado limped noticeably, greatly favoring his right leg, as he entered Second Circle stables where he discovered Inindu openly conversing with a red-haired taggle boy. He instantly recognized the blacksmith's apprentice from Caduum, though both memory and boy seemed strangely out of place, "How did you get here?" He turned to Inindu, "Is he dead?"

"Maldinado?" Edran stood with an energetic bounce and dusted at the bits of hay loosely clinging to his legs.

"Disappointing, isn't he?" Inindu audibly replied. "Morlac turned him into a useless old man."

"I think I preferred the slate board," Maldinado reached for the matted lapels of his increasingly haggard looking robe. "A talking horse isn't good for my pride...or my sense of reality for that matter. Now I know for certain this is all in my head."

"You need to get past this belief you are losing your mind, Madar. Your memories of life in the Sphere's world are real. Delacroy is the lie."

"I am no longer a Madar; not sure I was *ever* a Madar." Maldinado snorted loudly and spit, "At any rate I made a poor Madar."

"Would you prefer I call you First Etabli?"

"You dishonor me."

"You dishonor yourself. Admit it. You want my sister to anoint you her First Etabli rather than Faunride; assuming Ayson ever dies. And she'll do it, too, the fool."

"Ayson be dead," Edran walked toward a warped barrel and grabbed a green apple with a thick yellow streak on one side.

Maldinado felt an instant panic, suddenly very aware of his former life; cursing himself for ever leaving the Sphere's world. "And the Adow? Did she survive? Nataline? Hintor?"

"Yer friends all survived," Edran replied between bites. "And Madic Baltin destroyed the Kul."

Maldinado leaned back against the stable wall. "May the Sphere be with them."

"And be keeping them in his light," Edran replied.

"Madic Baltin?" Inindu continued. "So, they found the five wolves?"

"'Tis our brothers they found," Edran lowered the apple. "Madic be giving his life to save us all."

"And where was our father?" Inindu asked.

"Hiate departed before the Kul be arriving."

"Typical. Why bother when he can send someone else to fight his battles?"

"The blacksmith is your father?" Maldinado asked.

"It's one of his chosen forms," Inindu responded.

"So, the Sphere is a blacksmith?" Maldinado turned to Edran with a confused look, "You're an apprentice to the Sphere?"

"Right now, he's an apprentice to a cook. And I need to speak to his master. Take me to our father, taggle."

"Wait," Maldinado suddenly remembered why he returned to the stables with such haste. "Lyshmee. She was accused of worshiping the Sphere. They were going to arrest her anyway."

"Lyshmee be saving a lot of lives, too," Edran dropped the apple core to his foot and kicked it up in the air a few times before it flew wildly to one side.

Inindu sifted through the hay to retrieve, and then consume, the discarded core.

"So, the rumors *are* true? About the worshipers of the Sphere?" Maldinado asked.

"Yes, the Sons and Daughters of Oblation meet in secret. My master be the Father of Oblation."

"Father of manipulation," Inindu sneered.

"How many are there?"

"'Tis hundreds spread throughout the city."

"That gives us an army," Maldinado considered the implications, "I may not carry a sword, but I can still lead a unit into battle. How do you communicate with them?"

"'Tis the taggles communicate with the Sons and Daughters of Oblation through the art they be creating."

"The taggles worship the Sphere?"

Edran shook his head, "No, only some of them. 'Tis enough, though. My master be conveying meeting locations and days using their artwork. The Sons and Daughters of Oblation pass through the Gates every morning and be searching for the out of place taggle. 'Tis that taggle be serving as messenger and tells them when and where the next meeting be occurring."

"Phinx!" Maldinado recalled the Eighth Gate taggle whom he encountered in Fourth Gate as he passed through on his way to the Sorting.

"'Tis a fine taggle."

"Tasa Ro! If I'm a tailor, I'm a blind tailor," Maldinado scratched at his scraggly beard.

"That explains the robe," topi-Inindu pushed past Maldinado and through the stall door.

He ignored the intended insult, "I should go with you."

Inindu-horse shook her head, "No! I need you to stay with me."

"Meet us at Fourth Gate," Edran followed the magenta-haired topi out of the stall. "You be finding us at Vitrec's stage."

"Does he worship the Sphere, too?"

"No."

Maldinado watched them leave for only a moment before the throbbing in his hip forced him to seek out a suitable place to sit.

Inindu-horse snagged another apple from the mostly filled barrel, "I need groomed."

The weary tailor looked at the discarded brush sitting beside a mound of hay, and then again at the talking horse, "This can't be real."

Delacroy

Certainty | Chastity | Fasting | Generosity | Joy | Orthodoxy | Peace | Honesty | Faithfulness

Prior to the hour when Mathay would make his most heralded arrest, indeed, before the sun started its descent on that same day, a red-haired taggle boy emerged unnoticed from the forgotten sewers beneath Second Circle. He walked casually toward the unadorned home of Lyshmee, a devoted scholar who spent her time translating ancient texts. He knew the scholar, but he dared not stop for a visit, for Edran carried a sealed letter which his master petitioned him deliver with haste to Fillop, Overseer of Second Circle.

Edran did not attempt to hide amidst the crowd; nevertheless, he traveled down the street as though invisible—benefiting, he chose to believe, from a prevailing perception of the adults around him that boys his age lived an altogether inconsequential life. Since he offered Delcreans nothing of value they quickly forgot his face, a useful trait which the boy's master often exploited. So, it happened that Edran delivered his note to a group of swads he encountered upon entering the dungeon keep in Second Circle. Later, when one of these same swads left to deliver the note to Fillop, none of the warriors could remember even the simplest detail about the boy. Perhaps most baffling to Overseer Fillop, however, when he asked from whom they received the note, the swads did not recall ever meeting the taggle boy. Edran, still standing in their presence, laughed with unheard boyish whimsy.

The overseer sent for Mathay and handed him the mysterious note.

Lyshmee: worships the god of another world.

"Take three swads and arrest her," Fillop ordered even as Edran completely vanished from room and memory.

As Mathay received his orders, Sons and Daughters of Oblation gathered together in the cellar of Lyshmee's home. They met believing the house empty, a harmless tale meant to protect Lyshmee's identity. But she did not, in truth, travel to Seventh Circle in order to visit with her parents; rather, she worshiped beside her brothers and sisters. And, like them, she wore a gold mask, and bowed low in prayer. Each worshiper of the Sphere also cradled a glowing candle in their hands. Their ritual consisted of lighting and extinguishing the candle at various intervals as dictated by a particular section of prayer. In periods of darkness Lyshmee mourned and wept, asking the Sphere to enter Delacroy. In periods of light, she praised the god of another world for blessing her with knowledge of his presence. The secret sect never met for more than one hour at a time, but still, whenever and wherever they met, they posted a lookout for they each faced certain death if ever discovered. Thus, Lyshmee and her fellow worshipers knew Mathay and his swads approached long before they reached Lyshmee's home.

"Forgive me Father," a Son of Oblation spoke to Troq from behind stair railing—the urgency of his message impeded a full descent into the cellar. "Several swads journey this way. We are revealed."

Lyshmee awaited Troq's response. Quietly, and without hesitation, he spoke, "Flee with haste. Go. Into the sewers until their suspicions are averted."

Thirty-three worshipers rose in unison alongside Lyshmee. They extinguished their candles and quickly filed out of her cellar without uttering sound or word, long accustomed to escaping detection. But as she approached the wooden stairs Troq pulled Lyshmee aside, "I must ask you to stay my daughter," he motioned to another, "And you my son. There is much at risk. I will need your help."

Moments later, Lyshmee hurriedly joined Penrem under the tattered blankets covering her yet unsullied bed; discarded robes and golden masks safely traveled the sewer tunnels below, along with the Sons and Daughters of Oblation—and Troq, Father of Oblation. Lyshmee maintained a sharp mind, so the tiny scholar fully understood the sacrifice she made in allowing the worshipers of the Sphere to escape. But if her death meant they remained undetected then she thought it a worthwhile offering. She did not fear death. Rather, she welcomed her demise, and longed to join the Sphere in another world.

"I'm Lyshmee," she lay motionless beside the cold and trembling Penrem.

"Penrem."

She touched his quivering leg, "Don't be frightened."

"I'm not…it's just…suddenly I'm in bed with a naked woman. I've never actually seen a naked woman. Somehow, I imagined it would be different. Not waiting here, about to die."

"They won't kill you as long as you tell them we're lovers."

"What about you?"

Mathay knocked loudly upon Lyshmee's front door.

She bravely threw herself atop Penrem, "It doesn't matter. Kiss me. They're here." She tossed the covers aside, thus removing all doubt as to the nature of their indiscretion.

Mathay kicked the door down and forcefully entered Lyshmee's home. She gasped and shrieked, and then she struggled to break free of Mathay's grip, but he did not let her flee.

Lomax pulled a straight black pipe from his smoke-filled mouth and exhaled. He sat cross-legged in front of a sparsely decorated merchant cart which he had pulled from storage; one of two badly damaged carts remaining when he finally arrived at the marketplace. His rival, Denam, sat closest to, and northwest of Fourth Gate, a position normally reserved for Lomax who, instead, found himself relegated to a spot furthest away from the gate—and from those travelers who emerged looking to purchase new goods. The basket weaver felt certain he wouldn't sell a single item so, as a result, he only retrieved three baskets from storage; each of varying sizes—large, larger, and handheld. The whole morning left him in a foul mood. But morning soon transitioned to midday, and smoke emerged from the compressed tobacco in his pipe to linger within the tarnished white whiskers under his battle-axe of a nose.

Lomax casually stared at the double-bellied woman who approached his cart, Tannessa, a swad heading home from her duty the prior evening. In appearance, she seemed quite unfit to defend the dungeon where he knew she stood guard each night. What she lacked in sword skills, however, she more than accounted for in devious schemes and powerful connections which meant the swads could not completely remove her from their ranks, so they relegated her to night duty. Fortunately for Lomax, Tannessa was his younger cousin. She also passed by the marketplace each day on her way home. This made her a valuable, and easily accessible, informant.

"Morlac's boon upon thee, Lomax," Tannessa's voice came from behind her tongue rather than her throat, as though each word disguised a gasp for air.

"Favor and boon. I suppose you know of the Magnate's death?" Lomax pointed the end of his pipe toward Fourth Gate, unseen in the distance to the southeast.

"Members of his family already reside in the dungeon."

"Naturally."

"We had to double them up—most of them, anyway. Valun demanded his own cell."

Lomax noted the number of people passing behind Tannessa, few of them gave his baskets a glance; at least three carried a denam-basket. "Not surprising given the fact he's betrayed most of his family at one point or another. No doubt they will eagerly march to their own death if it means Valun's head will roll that much sooner."

"It won't be as soon as hoped," Tannessa scratched beneath her tightly woven braid, raising her traditional blue tymer-kurta high enough that her brown skin was exposed beneath a slit at the side. "Valun asked for Morlac's judgment."

"He can do that?"

"He *is* Magnate now. It seems his father's death left an opening at the top."

"And Magnate's can only be condemned by Morlac," Lomax raised the pipe to his mouth. "That will draw quite the crowd."

"As large as any Nascence. Probably larger. Ninth Circle won't be able to hold everyone."

"Fourth Circle, then? Would Morlac really travel here?"

"I saw the Overseer writing the request before I left."

Lomax drew deeply on the pipe, suddenly struggling to remember his cousin's name...*Sa...no, something else...Reb...no, T-something—Tannessa! Yes, Tannessa*. His mind clung to her name as though fetching a fish from the sea, fearful of it slipping back into the water should he tempt fate and remove the hook, "Tannessa, it occurs to me that every severed head needs a basket."

"Naturally."

"And as you know, beheadings are a bloody mess. Of course, I've always felt denam-baskets were uniquely suited for the task. His baskets have so many holes in them, you know. The blood spills everywhere. It makes for a wonderful display, really, so I've left the head catching to him."

"Until now?"

Lomax pulled the pipe from his mouth, "Until now. Tannessa, I believe Valun deserves a basket *worthy* of catching his head; and certainly, now that Morlac will attend his beheading. Can you make it happen?"

"Yes, for a price."

"Naturally."

Three more travelers carrying denam-baskets passed in front of

Lomax's cart, but he paid them no attention.

Beah sat huddled in shadow against beam number 4–38–15. City sewage gurgled audibly through an iron pipe above, leaving a dry-stone pathway below. The chiseled markings remained consistent throughout the sewers: first number indicating the circle above, second associated with the tunnel, and a third mark as dictated by the total amount of supporting beams found within that same tunnel. The last number, therefore, descended or ascended according to the direction of travel. Thus, Beah need only glance momentarily at the pipes around him to realize he sat under Fourth Circle, but he remained no more aware of his surroundings than of the news about Magnate Boltmar's death.

Beah sat alone. Fluttering images of a much different world filled his shattered mind; one in which he slept uncomfortably amidst a circle of taggles in order to stay warm, his body snug against that of another, uncertain if he would live long enough to awaken the next morning. In this other world, Beah sought a blessing from his elderly uncle: A request to survive the Torment.

Beah did not survive. He died as he slept mere weeks into his journey.

In another world, he boasted how the Sphere would remember him because Beah served in the Adowian Army; a great honor even for a taggle. But the Sphere forgot him—left him to his fate within Morlac's world.

Beah gripped both ends of a green scarf, pulling downward until it strained his thick neck; black hair falling forward. The iron beam felt cold against his bare back, and the unforgiving stone floor beneath his checkered leggings offered him no comfort. He sat in shadow. His muscular body effectively hid the bone-thin body to which he clung while living in the Sphere's world. Beah closed his eyes.

Inindu.

Monster. Assassin.

How did she manage to enter Delacroy? And for what purpose? Did she seek to kill Beah?

No, she could have killed me in Second Gate. She must be after someone else. But as to whom she sought, he did not know.

"Beah?"

The terrified taggle jumped from his thoughts, momentarily struggling to locate any speaker until, finally, a taggle boy emerged from darkness, "Edran?"

"Beah, why are you down here? Shouldn't you be performing in Second Gate?"

Edran.

Beah's mind flooded with previously dormant memories of a blacksmith's apprentice from the Sphere's world. Edran. The boy from Caduum who joined them on the journey into Dragon's Torment.

"Beah, are you alright?"

Beah stumbled between memories of old and the new ones he thought he knew. None of it made sense. How could Edran exist in both Caduum and Delacroy? How?

Then Inindu appeared—half of Inindu—rider without horse, a beautiful woman who stepped lightly and without sound, yet her powerful presence fully consumed the air, leaving Beah both breathless and helpless. Fear seized every vein in his muscular frame even as her black hair stretched forth, reaching toward Beah with hypnotizing effect—lulling him into a trance with every slinking, shifting strand. As her silky locks brushed against his cheek, however, the taggle regained his fading wits with a desperate and sudden gasp.

Beah cowered from her touch. He scrambled to his feet. And he ran.

He ran. And he ran. 4–38–14…4–38–13…4–38–12… But when he checked to see how closely they followed, he found neither Inindu nor Edran. He slowed, and then stopped. Why did they not give chase?

He slipped deeper into the sewer shadows, reaching out to grip the solid pipe above his head, pulling himself upward to hide. He waited, his body wedged between wall and pipe, his mind fluctuating between two vastly different worlds. And a third…

The dead.

Did he only imagine the unmoving, lifeless forms crowding around him in Second Circle? Did Inindu use some trick of the mind, or somehow corrupt his vision? No answer emerged from the darkness, nor could he distinguish fact from fantasy with any level of confidence. Only the coolness of the pipe against his side, and the growing strain upon his arms, gave him any sense of reality.

Did Inindu manage to follow him into the sewers? No, Edran's surprise upon encountering Beah suggested otherwise. So, then, why did they travel this portion of the tunnel system? It only led to one location: The Magnate's manor.

Edran serves as an apprentice at the manor.

Beah suddenly knew who Inindu intended to assassinate: Boltmar.

Despite his perilous state of mind, he felt compelled to warn the

Magnate. Whatever Inindu's motivation, he knew she posed a threat to Beah's established life in Delacroy. He ran, though this time, he ran *toward* Inindu. 4–38–13...4–38–14...4–38–15... When he reached her, he continued forward without hesitation, pushing right past the surprised pair with unchecked strength. He shoved Inindu into the wall and sent Edran stumbling to the ground.

"Beah!" Edran called after, but Beah never looked back. Instead, he ran as fast as he could toward the ladder that would take him up into the courtyard of the Magnate's manor.

Troq walked calmly along the second floor, red stone corridor. His acknowledged seniority among the startled servants, coupled with the sudden lack of a Magnate on premises, left Troq in charge of the bustling manor. Accustomed to balancing his many tasks as a cook, Troq comfortably assumed the additional responsibility which, in that moment, included several pronouncements concerning the unexpected changes to the day's schedule and serving as apologetic host to the more than half dozen befuddled guests who remained asleep, drunk, or otherwise detained in their rooms—blissfully unaware of the morning's dreadful events. Troq found their ignorance slightly bemusing, if not surprising, for the manor often served as haven to those guests whom, having fallen victim to the many delights of the previous evening, needed time to recover. Indeed, a steady flow of regally attired visitors arrived each morning on official business, anxious to meet with Boltmar; and most of these aspiring visitants then found reason to dawdle the day away so as to garner an invitation to spend the evening celebrating with Valun; which included a room for the night—thus, a less refined, more ruffled group departed the next morning. With Boltmar dead and Valun imprisoned, however, several of the manor servants assumed the influx of visitors would subsequently dwindle substantially. Troq, somewhat roughly, informed them otherwise, for he believed the guests would continue to arrive, perhaps more than before, if only out of curiosity.

Yet even he found himself caught off-guard when Tilly arrived with news of a mad and raging taggle who had, only moments prior, stormed into the manor demanding to see Magnate Boltmar.

"The swads nabbed him," the young servant continued. "They're holding him in the small storage room."

The room in question held, among other items, several wooden containers of dried dates which Troq routinely stuffed with almonds, a favorite treat of Boltmar's. The cook arrived to find a pile of these dates spilling out of a hole in one of the many scattered barrels, all but burying a discarded green scarf. Six swads, several of whom displayed fresh wounds, held the shirtless taggle face down in the normally uncluttered room.

"What is this?" Troq barely contained his irritation over the chaos he discovered.

A vaguely familiar looking swad, grasping a large handful of the captive's hair, and bleeding freely from a bite mark on his hand, responded with a deeper voice than his boyish face suggested, "He insists someone is going to kill the Magnate." He raised the taggle's head with a fierce tug, "Tell him your tale, taggle."

"My name is Beah. I'm a taggle from Second Gate. Please, I must speak to Magnate Boltmar," Beah's swollen left cheek bore a nasty cut. A nosebleed filled his mouth, causing Beah to spit before continuing, "Inindu enters the city. Here to kill the Magnate. I came to warn him. Please, I must speak to him. Let me go!"

Troq knelt before the battered taggle, more than a little confused, "Boltmar is already dead."

"Dead? She's already killed him, then?" Beah stopped struggling against his captors, his taut body abruptly dormant.

"What do you know of his murder?"

"Inindu. *The* Inindu. She's down in the sewers. She came here from another world to kill...she killed the Magnate, though I don't know why."

"Should...should we investigate?"

No doubt the swad holding Beah's hair spoke out of duty, but the hesitation in his voice suggested to Troq he would sooner engage an armed thief than pursue Inindu in the shadows of the underworld—and, based upon his own strained encounters with her, Troq could forgive the man's apparent lack of passion. Unlike the swad, however, Troq did not hesitate to seize the moment, "Another world?" Troq had long anticipated Inindu's arrival. In fact, the morning unfolded much as he foresaw, but the babbling taggle before him proved an unexpected threat to his carefully cultivated schemes. Troq could not allow such disruption, "Tell me more about this *other* world, Beah."

Unable to turn his wilted head, the ground muffled his response, "The Sphere's world—I used to live in that world, but now I'm here, somehow. And she's here, too. Inindu. And I'm too late."

Troq stood and crossed his arms as though surveying a finished dish, certain the presented ingredients would provide a delectable course worthy of consumption, "You're from the Sphere's world? How did you get here? And how would Inindu enter the city if not by your hand? No, Morlac protects those who worship him. He would never allow Inindu to pass through the city gates. Nor do I believe there's an assassin in the sewers. Only a taggle may travel the sewers. But Boltmar did not die in the tunnels below, Beah. Someone murdered him in Fourth Gate where only taggles may wander after sunset, and now we've captured a taggle who claims to warn us about a death which has already occurred. You're mad, Beah. Mad enough to murder someone. And so, I think you are the assassin, Beah. You are Boltmar's killer." Troq stepped to the side of the door, allowing enough room for the six swads to exit, "Take him to the dungeons."

Beah twisted anew, "No! Wait. You're involved somehow. Edran. He's your apprentice, you must know something…you must know Inindu… let me go! He's part of her plan. You don't understand what's happening! We're all dead. I saw them. All of you are dead!"

For the second time that day, Troq watched as a group of swads led an innocent man out of the manor on their way to the dungeons. Well, innocent in a sense. Truly, Troq knew neither Valun nor Beah worshiped the Sphere. But Delcreans did not concern themselves with such matters as innocence or guilt. Rather, the causal accusation of a higher-ranking resident—or the mark of the Sphere carved into your lifeless chest— sealed the headless fate of scoundrel and blameless alike. Putting aside desperate interpretations of justice, therefore, Troq found political leverage and bags of gold proved more valuable within Delcrean circles; and as head of the magnate's manor, Troq gained possession of both in significant quantity. He reached for a handful of dates, popping two of them into his mouth, thoroughly chewing them, and using his tongue to pick at the portions of date wedged between his teeth.

"Back to work," he motioned to the servants who gathered to witness the unusual commotion for themselves. "You've seen what there is to see."

But he lied. They had yet to see, or understand, anything.

"Tilly," he caught the mystified girl's gaze and motioned toward the storage room, "Clean up this mess."

Inindu

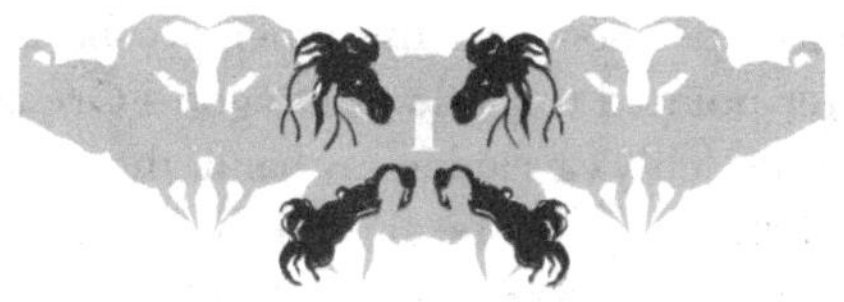

Edran strikes out again, but the grate at the top of the ladder does not budge. Locked. The third one from which we have attempted to exit. Still shaken from our encounter with Beah, Edran does his best to conceal his growing concern, but the taggle boy makes a poor liar. Shaken and newly scarred, for he skinned both hands and a knee when Beah pushed him down.

"'Tis another dead end," he whispers.

Though left unharmed by Beah, I cannot help but feel hindered, if not hobbled, by each locked barrier. I should have killed him when we found him huddled in the shadows. *Why didn't I kill him?* He will only get in my way. When I told Edran about meeting Beah in Second Circle, how I attempted to free him from Morlac's illusion…and how maybe that didn't work out so well, the red-haired taggle quickly changed our course of travel. Instead of heading straight for the Magnate's manor we now search along these abandoned tunnels for an unlocked entrance to the city above.

I reach the ground and wait for the boy to descend, "Lost?" I write.

"No, but there be a reason no one uses the sewers in this section of the city. 'Tis only a few open latches. I generally only be needing the one."

I retrieve a flickering torch from a secured ring in the stone wall next to the iron ladder, and then follow Edran further down the passageway. Our shadows merge, his only slightly shorter than mine in height. His gait stiff with age despite his apparent youth, and it hits me how little I know about him. He is my brother, yes, but we have never spent any significant time together.

He reaches into a burlap satchel which hangs over his shoulder, "Want an apple?" He withdraws one for himself and nibbles his way into a larger bite, tiny teeth marks barely breaking the yellow skin, prior to extending a second apple to me.

"What are your first memories?" I snatch the apple and tear into the juice-filled center.

"I remember the blacksmith forge, and how my master be driving his hammer into hot iron. He be fashioning hinges for a chest of drawers—

mine, in turns out—'tis the one I use when we be living in Caduum. 'Tis then my master pointed to a pile of Dragon's Ore and told me to be filling the bucket I suddenly carried in my hand, though I don't recall ever retrieving the bucket. My father be sick, so before he be dying, 'tis sent me away with only my goat to serve as the blacksmith's apprentice."

"No father," I write, "only Sphere." Erase. "Spoke you into being."

"Perhaps, so, but 'tis a better story, to be certain, if I be adding a sick father and a goat."

The taggle sounds annoyingly similar to our father. Whenever the Sphere assumes the form of Hiate he speaks as though he descended from a long line of blacksmiths. And when he assumes the form of Troq, my father speaks as though specifically chosen to protect the Daughter of the Adow—complete with an overzealous warrior's tale about his long, arduous history of rising through the ranks of the Adowian Army. None of it qualifies as reality, but for whatever reason, the Sphere insists upon the illusion. In fact, he alters the memories of his worshipers, so they never find reason to question the sudden appearance of Troq nor Hiate. And now this boy references a father who never existed despite his knowledge to the contrary.

I do not share their need for pretense, however. I witnessed our father speak the Adow into being, and the First Etabli after her. I imagine he did the same with our brother, though on the night Edran describes, it would seem laziness served as his impetus rather than any creative impulse my father may have felt at the time. Simply stated, he did not want to fetch his own Dragon's Ore, so he created an apprentice to haul it for him. Not surprising. My father always manipulates circumstances to better suit his purpose. Always.

Edran finishes his apple and veers left into another tunnel.

I spit an apple seed onto the stone floor, wondering why I follow this fanciful, foolish boy. After all, he seeks to lead me to Troq. When Hiate sent me into the Kul I thought I left the Sphere behind. My father, obviously, failed to mention he would see me on the other side, no doubt afraid I would then decide not to travel to Morlac's world. Another form of manipulation. *You were right to fear my response, father.* So, it seems I, too, eternally serve our father as nothing more than a sharpened, deadly tool in his unblemished hand. Thus, the reason I blindly follow a blind taggle, my brother.

Edran mounts another ladder and ascends toward an unseen grate. I leave the torch in a nearby ring, swallow the last of my apple, and follow. *Yes, father. I am here. How can I best serve your needs?*

This time the grate opens. We rise from the dark sewers into midday light. Several burlap bags, marked *beans* lay alternately stacked around the sewer exit, forming a waist high barricade. At least a dozen more stacks of various vegetables and fruits fill the small dirt courtyard. We emerge behind a solid stone structure, presumably several small living quarters attached to one another and extending out of sight to the right. A narrow opening to our left amplifies the noise from a mostly hidden road beyond.

Edran secures the grate and leads me out of the storage area into the streets of Delacroy, "'Tis not far to the Magnate's manor." Red dust hovers above the road, and Edran takes my hand to keep from getting separated. He points above the immense crowd toward three ruby towers, one much higher than the other two. All three towers peek over the inner wall of Fourth Circle, "Morlac's palace."

It puts the Fires of the Sphere to shame. Granted, I see only the one ruby palace compared to the hundreds of Fires of the Sphere which dot the landscape of our father's world. Still, I take certain pleasure in knowing Morlac, the god *I* created, outperforms my father in at least one area. The thought provides hope that, perhaps, some things extend beyond his manipulative reach even if I have yet to escape.

The boy's hand tightens and softens around mine as we walk. He silently glances back at me every few steps. The Daughters of the Adow once reacted in similar fashion. They watched for signs of my approval. I miss their gaze…their hands in mine, the warmth of their palm quickly turning to sweat. Ugh. I don't miss the sweat on their hands, and their faces, too. They would fall asleep in my arms and wake with soaked hair plastered to their gently sloping foreheads. They would awaken with such bright eyes…

The crowd surges forward and we follow at a comfortable pace. I recognize several faces, or rather, their souls; hazy reminders of another time and place—a land beyond this illusion. There, the woman with a mole on her chin. She managed a rundown inn. I killed her husband. There, the man with a speckled beard, once a traveling merchant. He sold leather goods and tightly woven blankets in his customary location along the road just north of Lor, long ago, during the Completion of the Yellow Moon. Did they both worship Morlac? I glance again at the ruby palace towers. *Is that how you bring them here? Did they worship you in my father's world?*

Inindu-horse:

I depart Second Circle stables, led away by Maldinado whom I've allowed to ride on my back if only to speed the journey along, for the sooner we reach Fourth Circle the sooner I will rejoin my rider, my Inindu. My current rider, Maldinado, clings to my soft mane with his mangled hands, using his left leg to steady himself while his right leg hangs useless against my sleek flank.

"Morlac's boon upon thee, Maldinado," the speaker boasts a fierce jaw line. "You acquired a new horse?"

I stop so he can admire.

"Favor and boon, Perinah. Yes, my hip makes it hard for me to walk these days."

"But your fingers remain nimble?"

Maldinado leans down to pat the man's shoulder, "Nimble as ever." The tailor runs his fingers under the collar of Perinah's robe, "I notice your robe is starting to fray. Visit me in the marketplace. I have a scarlet robe that will fit you well."

"I'm afraid the state of my gold is in worse shape than my robe," Perinah draws Maldinado's forehead to his own, two circles greeting four, "but I hope to change my fortune at Lyshmee's beheading. I'm wagering she is rescued."

"Everyone wagers the same, but the swads have new weapons," Maldinado pulls away, returning to a more comfortable position atop my back. "Best to save your money, Perinah. Spend it on a new robe."

Maldinado jams his left foot into my flank, attempting to urge me forward, but I am not an animal in need of goading, nor do I respond to such ridiculous behavior. I refuse to move.

"It seems you've purchased a stubborn mare," Perinah laughs. "No more stubborn than myself, though. You'll see. Someone will rescue Lyshmee and I'll make a fortune. Then I'll purchase three robes from you."

"And I will gladly sell them to you. Assuming I can ever get this horse to…"

I lower myself to the ground, causing Perinah to roar with laughter. Maldinado curses as travelers gather to watch their beloved tailor wrestle with his newly *acquired* horse. I am not his. He does not own me.

The Madar leans forward, "Please."

Perinah slaps my rump and I nearly run him through with my tail. But, instead of impaling his chest, I calmly sweep his legs out from under him.

He falls in a cloud of dust and amusement, oddly grateful for his sudden inclusion in the spirited proceedings. The crowd howls with delight, though I fail to see the humor, and again when Maldinado, admitting his thorough defeat, throws up his arms and finally dismounts.

I stand and continue my journey toward Third Gate.

The Madar takes a bow, predictably attempting to turn the moment to his advantage, and then hobbles after me with all the grace of a wounded warrior. Let him waddle. I'll not have him kick me ever again.

topi-Inindu:

The adorned hallway of the Magnate's manor is filled with hustling servants and ambling swads. Edran still holds my hand as one of the larger swads approaches with a gloved hand on his polished sword hilt, "State your purpose."

"Edran!" A young girl about equal to the taggle in height drops a stack of cream dishes, giving her pause before running forward—only to find her progress stopped by the swad, if not her mouth, "Edran, the Magnate's dead and Valun was arrested. They caught the murderer in our storage…"

"You know these two?" The swad interrupted.

Tilly nodded, "Don't you recognize Edran? He serves here with master Troq."

The swad looks more closely at my brother, "Oh, Edran, I didn't recognize you. Strange…I could swear you looked like someone else a moment ago. And who is this with you?"

Edran points to the slate hanging around my neck, "'Tis a new servant for my master. She's mute." He turns to the girl, "The magnate be murdered?"

The swad steps away, retracing his steps to a group of three peers with nothing better to do than stand in the hallway. He whispers something to them, shaking his head as all four of them look back toward Edran in puzzlement. Then my beauty captures their attention. I let them stare, but they soon turn away with disinterest. I am not Inindu without my horse. I am *less* than Inindu. Less than beautiful.

"I'm sorry, I need to clean up this mess, Edran. Troq is in the kitchen," the girl looks nervously at the pile of broken dishware, and then at two nearby older women each giving her a chastising look, "I'm sorry, Merrudi. I'm sorry, Myrtane. I don't know what comes over me that I'm always dropping things."

"Clean it up, girl. Then head upstairs to change the linens," Merrudi squints as she speaks.

Myrtane kneels down to assist, using one of the larger pieces and her calloused hands to shovel piles into the girl's apron, "Can't trust you to carry anything."

Edran's countenance alters with the harsh rebuke. His eyes follow after the girl, and he starts forward only to stop himself, but not before I notice. The girl notices, too, and assumes a position which enables her to keep an eye on Edran as he passes. Perhaps my brother sees clearly, after all. Well enough, at least, to notice the girl.

A moment later, Edran leads me down the large hallway, myriad servants and swads ignore our presence. The manor rooms extend outward from the squared hallway on both the first floor where we walk, and along the second floor above. The walls display giant works of art between each unadorned doorway; one of them depicts a magenta horse, a ward against Inindu. I find myself struck not by the presence of the rendering, but by that which I do not see, for while my image adorns every home, according to the taggle in Second Circle, I have yet to see a single image of Morlac.

Do they worship Morlac or Inindu?

The kitchen presents a blur of activity when we arrive. Servants busy themselves in every corner; most of them wearing crisp if slightly stained aprons. One of them washes pans in a large wooden basin while another slices several beets. Smoke rises from a skillet. Potato skins pile up. Discarded eggshells soar haphazardly through the air toward a metal slop bucket.

Not everyone in the room moves, however. Troq stands stoically beside an active fire pit. My father looks exactly the same as last I saw him in this form: White beard, deep wrinkles, and soft brown eyes. My sister always found comfort in his languid arms, and Troq always held *her*. Pampered her. Obliged her. Loved her.

Of the two incarnations my father assumes, Troq and Hiate, I definitely prefer the latter.

"You were much delayed, boy. Did you fetch the apples from Nebon?" My father noticeably engages my brother's gaze rather than look into my eyes.

Edran swings the sac from his shoulder, "'Tis a few less than when I first bought them. I be eating one or two on the journey back."

"Which is why I told you to purchase more than I needed," Troq takes the sac and turns away. "And who do you bring into my kitchen?"

"'Tis a mute I be finding in Third Circle. Yer a fine master and we be needing more servants, so I thought..."

"Take her to my room. I'll meet with her, shortly." Troq opens the sac and dumps the apples onto a table, "And come right back, boy. Selma has other things to do than wash your pots and pans all day."

Selma, a stout woman made more so by her hunched position on the floor beside the wash basin, nods in agreement. A dozen or more similar looking servants crowd the kitchen. His worshipers. Our father always surrounds himself with worshipers.

He hardly notices as we pass behind him on our way to the door, but I'm not so easily ignored. I write on my slate board, and then cozy up to him, right against his shoulder, "Apple?" I look up at him with innocence equal to that of any child asking their father for a favor. *Please, father, please feed me. Won't you look at me? You know how I depend on you for my survival.*

"Yes, of course, the boy probably kept them all to himself," Troq hands me an apple without looking, holding it a second longer than necessary as I snatch it from him.

Edran, less innocent but equally game, peeks around my back and extends a hopeful hand.

"Go on, boy. You can have another apple when I've turned them into cobbler."

Edran lowers his empty hand, "Master, is it true about the Magnate? Was he murdered?"

Troq leans hard on the table, lowering his head, "And Remni, too." I can feel a collective pause settle inside the kitchen. Only the simmering skillet indicates any ongoing activity as our father continues, "It's been a long morning. Go, boy. The magnate's death does not bring an end to our responsibilities. There are plenty of mouths to feed, and now two more with your return."

The servants resume their various duties.

I never met Remni, but I quickly decide I dislike her. Always the sentimental one, Troq reacts to the news of her death as he would to the Adow's passing. I wonder if my death would garner a similar response— no, not from this iteration of the Sphere. Hiate, on the other hand, would heartily toast my death with broth and beer. I miss the blacksmith.

Edran takes my hand and pulls me outside toward a grand courtyard and covered walkway which we follow for a short distance. He stops to open a wooden door, and motions me inside, "I best return, or Selma be skinning me alive. 'Tis my master's room. Wait here, he be joining you shortly." He lights a candle and closes the door upon exiting.

Yes, dear brother, run back to your master like a good little servant.

The small, sparsely decorated room contains a wooden bed frame with a thin mattress, folded wool blanket, and tucked linen sheet; a stout wooden table holding candle, parchment, quill, and ink bottle—grouped together beside a dark pipe and bulging tobacco pouch; a single dark-stained shelf mounted on the stone wall opposite the bed displays five stacks of leather bound books piled perfectly and vertically; and a black clothes chest, made of wood and reinforced with iron seams. I imagine Troq, used to far more extravagant surroundings, finds his living quarters more than inadequate. After all, he spends most of his time with my sister in her palace.

I take a single bite of my father's lone rationed apple and grab an unmarked book from the middle portion of the middle stack. Recipes. I throw it back on the shelf and proceed to adjust each stacked pile so that none of them have a straight edge. I unfold the blanket and toss it across the bed. Then, I fill the pipe. Troq always keeps a supply of good, fresh tobacco. The black and tan leaf strands, slightly tacky to the touch, smells unfamiliar but rich with spice. I place my re-gifted apple on Troq's writing desk, and light his pipe using the candle—wax drips onto the desk, cooling into a sizable glob before the tobacco finally begins to smoke. Each puff brings welcome warmth as my body slowly relaxes. Too much time has passed since I last shared a pipe with Troq…his one redeeming quality.

The door opens and my father quietly enters. He glances approvingly at my pipe, and curiously at the rumpled blanket, before closing the door. Then he starts to straighten his collection of unmarred books, turning his back on me, "I figured you could use a smoke. It is good to see you, daughter."

"Liar," I write.

"I trust you connected with Maldinado? He is known to visit the Sorting each year."

"Yes, revealed illusion. Beah, too," I erase and write, "Mistake."

Troq nods, "Beah arrived a few hours ago. He's no longer a concern, though. The swads think he's gone mad. They threw him in the dungeon." He finishes organizing one stack and moves to the next pile of books.

"Why are you here?" I shift the pipe to the other side of my mouth and inhale deeply.

"I've lived in Morlac's world ever since I left the Daughter of the Adow. Lived and waited for Hiate to send you here to Delacroy. I wasn't lying. It is good to finally see you, again, after such a long wait."

"Hiate? How?"

"How can we both exist at the same time, you mean?"

I shake my head.

"*Why* is the better question. I couldn't leave my world unattended. Your sister needed my help. Nor could I let you enter Morlac's world alone. You'll never admit it, but you also need my help." He moves to another stack of books, "I know you don't believe me, but I have always loved you."

"Touching. I despise you."

"Yes, and you don't like me as Troq, either. It doesn't matter. I still love you."

"You use me."

"I created you with a purpose, my daughter, as I do with all of my creations. We are here in Delacroy because you ignored that purpose."

I blow smoke at my father, then write, "Morlac?"

"He lives in a ruby palace at the center of the city. You'll never reach him there, but you won't have to because he will come to you. Valun provided a most convenient opportunity when he murdered his father. I didn't know if you would arrive in time, but I couldn't afford to waste the moment. And now here you are in Delacroy. Perfect timing, as always. But only half of my daughter, where is your horse?"

"With Maldinado," I twist the apple so Troq will notice the single bite. *I don't need your handouts, father.*

He continues to focus on his books, however, "Morlac will attend Valun's beheading which means he will come here to Fourth Circle, and you can kill him."

"Kill him yourself."

"You know I can't do that. Even if I was willing, he is your creation. Only you can destroy him."

"What harm is he?"

"Surely you've seen past this illusion. The dead? You recognize them? Morlac populates Delacroy with *my* people. He steals their light essence while they sleep. Given enough time he will steal everyone from me."

So that's how Morlac brings them here? Like a thief, he snatches them from you while they...while you sleep.

"The Adow?" I can't resist asking.

"Yes, he may even capture your sister. No one is safe," Troq moves to another stack of books.

So that's the real reason you sent me here. You need me to protect her.

"Hiate obviously convinced you to come. Now that you are here, will you hesitate to kill Morlac? His death is the only way you will return to my world—the only way any of us will return."

"You are trapped?" I find the thought amusing. My father...*my* father imprisoned. Of course, I share his misfortune as I sit in the same trap.

"When Hiate and I separated, we parted with the knowledge that I could never return without your aide."

I wonder...if killing Morlac opens a gateway back to my father's world, what happens to the souls who die in this world? "If someone dies here?" Erase and write, "Magnate? Remni?" *All the ones you've manipulated?*

Troq lowers his forehead against the bookshelf, again visibly overcome with emotion for Remni, "Necessary sacrifices. Too many sacrifices... They are forever lost."

The dead whose bodies I consumed?

Dead. Of course, they're dead. The dead are dead. Why do I care? I don't care. I devour the dead. Thus, the reason I don't like Troq: Too many damn emotions. They cloud the real issues, effectively disguising my father's schemes.

"Manipulating," I write.

Troq finishes straightening the final stack of unstained books, "If I didn't manipulate my daughters, they would never accomplish anything."

"I hate you."

"I can live with that as long as you kill Morlac," he grabs the blanket and begins folding, his gnarled fingers crisp with practiced movement. Still, he keeps his back turned, "Now, about this servant business, you and I both know you could never behave yourself. You would reveal us both within the week. I'll send you away on pretense you offended me."

"I *do* offend you." *Admit it, father, you can barely stand to look at me.*

"You *don't* offend me. I'm just not comfortable being in the same room as my assassin. It's nothing personal. I still love you," he replaces the blanket at the end of his bed and, avoiding my eyes, holds his hand out for the pipe. I'm finished with it, anyway, so I give it to him. He wipes my spit from the stem before placing it in his mouth, "Stick with Maldinado and wait for Valun's beheading. Morlac will attend. Strike him dead and we all go home."

Yes, father. Whatever you need, father. May I have another apple, father?

"And you?" I stand to leave.

"I must see to other matters which require my attention."

We all have our duties.

Inindu-horse:

We enter Third Gate as the sun nears the horizon, and with Maldinado, having apologized for treating me like a common beast, mounted on my back, once more. Though, I did make him walk another hundred yards even after he apologized.

"Well, the good news is we made Third Gate before sundown," Maldinado says. "The bad news is we will have to find lodging in Third Circle. They worship Morlac by starving themselves which means food is a bit scarce. Fortunately, I know a resident who tends to fast less often than others." I wonder if Maldinado's friend has any wia fruit. I haven't eaten anything since we left the stables this morning.

Third Gate appears sparse in comparison to the chaos we encountered at Second Gate. The pathway here lies straight rather than winding through every merchant booth and performance stage, both of which sit along either edge of the tunnel. And the crowd moves fluidly instead of shuffling en masse.

Maldinado leans down to my ear, "Can you spot Inindu in these paintings?"

The nearest painting, displayed on a feeble looking easel, appears unfinished. It mirrors the overall scarcity of the gate since much of the canvas remains unused. Similar to the works in Second Gate the artist relies on shapes, but the painting expands beyond the cube-like compositions we encountered previously to include three shapes: a yellow sphere, a red square, and a blue wedge. All three overlap near the top right of the canvas to form the rough outline of a horse. The rest of the painting is black and empty.

I nod my head in response to Maldinado's question. *Yes, I see a horse. No, I do not see Inindu.* These suggestive paintings hardly represent my beauty. How could anyone hope to ward against Inindu with such a poor depiction? Inindu is not a horse. Inindu is a horse and rider. *And I am without my rider, as I am without Adarian.*

topi-Inindu:

I sit at the back of a stall located in Fourth Circle stables, awaiting the arrival of my voice, my Inindu. I am alone. Edran returned to the manor for the night. He serves our father. And I serve our father…all must serve the Sphere. I lie down on a pile of hay and close my eyes to dream of Adarian. Tomorrow, Edran and I will travel to Fourth Gate and wait next to Vitrec's stage. I will wait there for my Inindu, not knowing how long I must wait.

Inindu (before)

Morlac was not the first to discover the god within. Others had previously sought after Inindu knowing if she, a creature more powerful than they could ever imagine, chose to worship them as a god it would serve as proof of their discovered deity. So, they traveled hundreds of miles, desperate to know the truth about themselves.

For this, they died.

Inindu killed them.

She killed them at the end of their journey when they asked her about gods and worship. Others, she hunted down long before their journey began, long before thoughts of personal ascension ever formed. In this manner, Inindu developed an intimacy with death. This, despite her own cursed immortality. Oh, how she longed for death when the Adow stole her beloved Adarian. And, again, as he lay dying in her arms at the Battle of Ire. The moment of his death haunted her, an image forever frozen in her mind. Alive, in a sense, for she could not escape the sound of his final breath. A hushed sigh. A diminishing exhale. She refused to let him die— refused to cast him from her mind. Indeed, Inindu clung to the memory of the slain Adarian. She wanted to embrace him, once more, in death as she had in life.

But Inindu didn't die.

She never aged despite witnessing a thousand births and a thousand deaths. Adarian had left her, and immortality left her feeling lonely, if not invincible. She knew pain and hunger and pain...and pain. So, she determined that if death would not occur naturally, she would find another means to die.

Inindu cast herself from the highest peak in the Nelic Mountains.

The Sphere sent a swift wind to catch her, gently returning her to firm footing.

She drove a sword through her body, but the Sphere turned the blade to water before it ever touched her skin. She drank poison, refused to eat...endured the coldest winter. But nothing Inindu attempted offered any hint of death. Finally, realizing the Sphere would never allow her to die as long as he lived, she decided to kill him, instead. And in order to kill her god, Inindu need only replace him with another god.

She found Morlac. Rather, he found her.

At any other period in her life, Inindu would have killed Morlac as quickly as the other aspiring gods who entered her cave deep within the Nelic Mountains. But on the day of Morlac's arrival, as it happened, she needed him as much as he needed her. No, something more. Morlac reminded Inindu of Adarian. He resembled her lover. His fierce green eyes...

"Yes, Morlac, you are a god," she knelt before him, thereby completing his transformation from inadequate man to powerful god.

Created to prevent just such an occurrence, Inindu performed the one act forbidden to her by her father. She no longer cared. Finally, free of her patriarchal protector, she turned her back on the Sphere even as he similarly refused to look upon her beauty. Once more, Inindu sought after death, longing to join her Adarian. Again, she flung herself from the highest cliff in the Nelic Mountains. Again, the Sphere called forth a swift wind and gently returned her to firm footing.

Still, she could not die. Still, the Sphere denied her Adarian's embrace. And she hated her father all the more.

Morlac

In the beginning...

Morlac towered above Inindu, rider and horse both genuflecting before him. And in that moment, the Sphere struck him with blindness, and a great pain arose from the depths of his bowels. He fell to his knees and grabbed at his torso with both arms, for the young god understood panic and fear like never before. He struggled to breath. All knowledge vanished. His name and former identity—former life—disappeared from his mind. He knew only pain and the darkness that overwhelmed him.

"So, *this* is what my father feared?" Inindu mocked him. Then she abandoned him.

Morlac sank to the dirt, alone and without conscious thought. Pain and agony ripped at his body. He tried to scream, but no sound emerged. Instead, a brown moth flew out of his throat. And another. But what he could not see, he could taste. Each moth crawled along his teeth; dust from their wings coated his lips. He lay in the cave retching hour after hour—unable to breath, unable to die, unable to escape the intense pain which seized him.

Relief arrived when moonlight flooded the cave, allowing Morlac to enter the dream world for the first time. He entered without the benefit of sleep. He entered as a stranger, powerless and unable to affect his environment. Thus, and despite temporarily regaining his vision, he wandered a desert land without understanding, encountering nothing except a graveyard of beasts—the final remains of a great pride whose bleached bones towered high above the sifting sand and sank deep enough to span two and sometimes three sizable drifts. Along with his restored sight, in this land he felt no pain, and no moth escaped his lips, yet he knew the body he left behind still suffered from the same afflictions. And so, he understood the benefits of illusion, and its ability to negate reality.

Back in the cave, the flow of moths exiting his body suddenly stopped. Morlac abruptly departed the dream world as the morning sun touched his face. In his blindness, he heard the fluttering of a thousand moths upon the cave walls. Thinking himself free of whatever curse befell him, free to breathe, Morlac quickly inhaled. Rather than inhaling the fresh morning air, however, a stream of moths filled his mouth. The creatures returned to his body with each breath, suffocating him and ravaging his throat without hope of mercy—the mercy death brings—or dreams, for he did not enter the dream world while the sun licked his wounds. Instead, he writhed and wriggled in anguish until, at last, the final moth touched his tongue and moonlight and dreams returned.

The cycle repeated. Over and over. Time held no meaning, and days passed without notice as Morlac remained alone in the cave, his life a ritual of daily consumption and nightly ejection. He lay on his back in the middle of the cave: Blind, terrified, and with his mouth fixed ajar.

And so, the young god remained until several months later when a taggle boy appeared at the mouth of the cave. The oddly well-clad taggle thought Morlac dead. He did not fear the dead, however, for taggles often awoke to find their face nestled between the living and those who passed in the night. Nevertheless, fear consumed the taggle when he discovered the majestic geyser of insects spilling upward from Morlac's motionless body and considered running until he noticed not one of the moths flew toward him. In fact, they completely ignored the boy, and the entire effect reminded him of the geyser in Yenul that mysteriously served as the bottom of a lake. Eventually, curiosity overcame fear, and the taggle watched with unrestrained wonder.

The well-traveled taggle had journeyed with his merchant master to Yenul, and then to Abre; and their thriving trade soon sent them from Adarian to Quel and even Caduum and Ire. Five days prior to discovering Morlac's body, however, the taggle's master fell dead. The overweight, gurgling merchant clutched at his left shoulder as he collapsed over the edge of the wagon, leaving the barely-clad and ill-treated taggle with a full supply of food and goods—and a road void of travelers. The boy stripped the fine clothes off his indifferent master, dug his teeth into a fresh melon, and turned the weather-worn wagon toward the Nelic Mountains. If anyone caught the runaway taggle, he reasoned, at least he would die with a full belly.

But nobody crossed his path until he happened upon Morlac.

His fear of moths kept him at bay for two days, but on the third day he ventured inside the cave. Under the circumstances, he assumed Morlac dead, but when the newly anointed god grabbed the boy's ankle, he immediately realized his mistake. Again, the taggle felt afraid. This wonder of nature had suddenly transformed into a creature of dangerous magic. He attempted to flee—kicking and twisting—but no matter how much he struggled to detach himself from the new god, Morlac's grip held firm. Finally, the boy prostrated himself and remained there, motionless, exhausted from his efforts to escape. The hours passed…and passed… and, reluctantly, the boy closed his eyes and fell asleep.

Morlac entered the dream world. After months of exploration, he no longer wandered aimlessly through the desert. Indeed, the graveyard of bones lay in the distance to the right of a winding path he traveled; and to his left grew a dense forest rich with speckled color amidst an array of tree leaves all displaying various shades of emerald. Morlac walked this path of white sand between life and death as he journeyed toward a crumbling tower and the rotting magenta doorway at its base which served as entrance to the Sphere's world. He turned the doorknob, upon reaching it, and walked through to the other side.

The dream world subsisted outside the plane of existence—a slight shift in reality that fully severed any connection to the Sphere. Morlac found he could see and walk and speak and interact with the world around him but, oddly, he could not taste or smell. And travel occurred instantly. He need only conjure an image of the destination in his mind. Thus, he envisioned a cave in the Nelic Mountains and, soon after, Morlac's ethereal presence hovered near the sleeping taggle…and his own detached body which still clung to the taggle's ankle.

"What is your name?"

The boy awoke from his slumber, "My master called me taggle."

"I am your god, taggle. I am Morlac."

The boy shook his head, "No, I worship the Sphere."

"The Sphere has forgotten your father, and he will never forgive your mother. He cursed you with a life of hardship—the life of a taggle. This is the god you worship." Morlac scanned the cave, "And where is this god? Have you ever seen him?"

The taggle shook his head.

"No," Morlac took hold of the taggle's ankle, ghost-like hand merging with a dormant hand of flesh. "Look, I am here before you. My hand clings to your leg. The Sphere has forsaken you, and I am now your god, taggle. See what power I possess?" Morlac motioned to the eclipse of moths, "Will you worship me?"

This time, the taggle nodded, "Yes."

"Then lead me away from this cave."

"Where?"

"To another world."

"Will I like this world?"

"Yes, you will find much peace, taggle."

The next morning, shortly after sunrise, Morlac released the taggle's ankle, and the boy assisted him to his feet, providing a shoulder for him to lean upon. The taggle led his newly adopted god, and the hovering cloud of moths, to the wagon he had stolen from his former master; re-stacking the supplies so Morlac could lie down comfortably. They waited until they could travel under cover of darkness and forest, always heading north toward Dragon's Torment. Morlac managed their supplies, mysteriously replacing every morsel the taggle ate; and he enhanced the food, so the youth would grow in strength and health.

Morlac, for his part, explored his new awareness. He discovered many more planes of existence, and he used this knowledge to subtly shift reality. So, it happened, upon reaching Dragon's Torment, the nameless taggle and his god completely vanished. Nearly three years later, beyond the far side of the Torment, and deeper than any map then stretched, they stepped through an invisible barrier to appear again at the edge of a great sea: The edge of the Sphere's world.

Morlac stood beside the dense, blue sea in physical form—outwardly unresponsive and without breath, for though he could shift reality, and assume ethereal form within the dream world, he could not escape his own body. Blindness remained, and also the eclipse of moths he consumed each day. And the pain. A parting gift from the Sphere meant to impair Morlac's ability to establish another world.

Similarly, he held no power over the land. Indeed, Morlac wrongly believed himself, as a god, capable of creating another world. But nothing he attempted allowed him to extend the land even an inch further out into the sea; and then he realized for all of his power to shift reality, each plane of existence, in fact, remained firmly rooted within the Sphere's reality. He could not create, only mold, and manipulate that which already existed. He must *build* a new world or destroy his old god. He decided to do both.

The taggle boy, ever faithful, stood beside him, for Morlac had promised him peace.

"Come, taggle," Morlac spoke to the boy when next he dreamt, "I must use your hands to build my world."

Thus, a nameless taggle fashioned Delacroy out of blood, sweat, and red stone. He erected a tower to encase Morlac's physical body, adding row upon row of irregular shaped rocks until, finally, the round chamber fully contained every moth which flew from Morlac's mouth. And the taggle aged. The taggle constructed a ruby palace around the tower, and the taggle aged. The taggle raised walls to encircle the palace. He built gates, manors, and sewers. And, at last, the taggle aged no more. With the city complete, Morlac blindly led the moribund taggle into the ruby palace where he lay him down to rest; and when the taggle closed his eyes, his light essence faded. He rejoined the Sphere, despite faithfully serving Morlac.

Lacking even one worshiper, therefore, Morlac suffered his fate alone within his tower chamber; in an empty city; in another world. Time passed, and the sea winds blew. Moths flew into and out of his mouth. Then Inindu caught his attention, for she traveled to Dragon's Torment. Beautiful Inindu. How familiar she seemed, but he held no firm memory of her. Yet, she remembered him. The Sphere's assassin sought to kill the god she had empowered. Morlac lit a fire and fashioned the Kul to serve as guardian of his distant world, and Inindu soon abandoned the hunt. Afterward, Morlac again shifted the planes of existence.

He returned to the dream world and the magenta door and he walked a thousand dreams until his journey led him to a dallic where several taggles struggled to survive. There he found a taggle boy who reminded him of the servant he had once encountered in a cave. He noticed a yellow glow surrounding the taggle's body, and Morlac inherently knew the taggle lay dying. Sympathy or sorrow or something much more desperate—self-preservation—led him to mimic the boy's breathing pattern. Then, when the glow seemed brightest, Morlac inhaled deeply—stealing the taggle's final breath. Indeed, he snatched his light essence. And when he exhaled streams of...not yellow, but red essence, Morlac suddenly understood how to kill the Sphere.

With clarity of thought and purpose, Morlac reached back to his tower in Delacroy and gathered wing dust from the eclipse of moths that tormented him endlessly. Near the taggle's dallic he pulled gusts of wind from a field of bloodgrass and added thickened white tears from his ivory-smooth eyes. Then, Morlac combined these ingredients to form a soulless vessel identical in appearance to the departed taggle. The dead body awaited the boy's light essence.

Morlac exhaled.

Red-colored breath. Light. Life.

Less than an hour later, Morlac snatched a second soul. And three more, again, before sunrise. So, unseen and unnoticed, Morlac opened the magenta door to the dream world night after night and liberated the dying from the Sphere's grasp. Each of the dead, or *nascient*, as Morlac soon named them, amassed near Delacroy. There they stood motionless and unadorned; their flesh weathered and rotting. The nascient. Worshipers of Morlac. He favored them, granting them the illusion of extended life. More importantly, he kept their light essence from joining the Sphere— kept them from sustaining the life of an old god.

Gan, Overseer of Adarian, slept with his rumpled head on Erisyte's exposed chest; his withered and wrinkled body contrasted starkly with the sculpted and bronzed chest of his young lover who slouched comatose against a padded headboard, his right arm wrapped around the ancient topi. Silk sheets and three tiger skins covered them both; mostly Gan, for the blankets barely covered anything of Erisyte. Gan, on the other hand, slept with an additional, tattered quilt over his gaunt frame, and laid one leg over the younger topi in an apparent attempt to stay warm. The bed sat awkwardly out of place in the center of a spacious room, beneath a large round window carved into the marble ceiling. Scrolls lay scattered throughout the rest of the room; piled across two desks, five chairs, and a marble crafted long-table all presumably intended to help organize the room.

Morlac sat at the cluttered table. He matched his breathing pattern to that of the young, beautiful topi: deep breaths and shortened exhales. Rarely, did Morlac encounter the opportunity to capture a soul so young and strong; robbing the Sphere of such vitality would surely hinder the old god and enhance his own presence.

Gan raised his head, "Have you come for me, at last?"

Morlac turned his attention to the Overseer, more than a little surprised by the question, "You can see me, ancient one?"

"Yes, I can see you, and I know your true name. I remember you from back when you still worshiped the Sphere. In case you're wondering, I *still* worship him, so torture me if you wish, I will not turn from my god."

"An ugly, if curious thought," Morlac leaned forward, "Why would I torture you? I have great respect for what you have accomplished in Adarian. Hmm, yes, more than you know, Overseer. You built a city, and for that I would sooner call you a god than torture you."

"There is only one god," Gan shifted onto his elbow while Erisyte slept beside him without stirring. "If not to torture me, then why are you here?"

"I come to collect the young one. He glows with the color of death, and if I do not save his soul he will be forever lost." Morlac, however, found his attention drawn toward the old man rather than the yellow light emanating from Erisyte, "How is it you can see me?"

"An old topi sees many things. Some real, some imagined. I find such matters difficult to discern, these days, so I no longer make the attempt. You may exist, and I may indeed see you, or perhaps I'm an old fool and you are merely a dream."

"A dream, yes," Morlac turned to the table and unfurled the nearest scroll, seeking to prove his presence, revealing a series of scribbled notes and several drawings depicting star positions and movement, "But not wholly a dream. I am real enough, and here in your world, if only for a moment."

"Then you have escaped the Torment?"

"Was I imprisoned? You think me somehow contained?" Morlac motions toward Erisyte, "Would I rescue his soul by capturing him, and deny him freedom? For what purpose? No, I am not your enemy, Overseer. The Sphere lied to you...he lied to us all."

"I find those with power are prone to lie," Gan scratched at his chest. "Schemes and deceptions and the like. I should know."

Morlac used one hand to pull at a cream-colored yiddick-shawl which he held loosely in his other hand, "So, you willingly follow a god who lies and manipulates?"

"I worship a god more powerful than me," Gan pulled the diamond patterned quilt up over his shoulders. "I learned a long time ago that politics boils down to position. Master the art of worshiping those with power and, eventually, you move up the ranks."

"Then you should worship me."

"That's called a conflict of interest, um... Your name. I almost called you by your real name, but you're no longer him, are you? No, they gave you a new name. Morlac. Well, Morlac, you see I can't worship you without offending the Sphere. And, like it or not, he's more powerful than you."

"Another name? Another lie. I *am* Morlac." Morlac pulled the shawl tight between his hands, "So many lies. Past names, and any suggestion that I am..." What? Weaker than the Sphere? Morlac could not escape that fact. But it did not matter, "Here is the truth, ancient one: The Sphere is dying, and any soul I fail to save will perish with him."

Gan sat up in his bed, "The Sphere is dying?"

"Yes, even a god can die. The Sphere is not the first god, nor the last. He is *one* god in a succession of many gods, just as the Adow is one in a succession of Adow; just as someone younger will one day take your place as Overseer of Adarian. The Sphere stole your soul from another world, before your previous god died, and I must do the same before this world ends."

"Then take my soul, too."

"How I wish I could take all of your souls!" Morlac struck down upon the table with an open palm, rustling the contents. Yes, how he wished to destroy his enemy with an all-encompassing strike. But, as the weaker god, Morlac could not risk such an assault, "But I do what I can, for now."

Again, Morlac mimicked Erisyte's breathing: long breaths and shortened exhales.

"Why can't you? Are you not a god?"

"Watch and know that I am now *your* god."

Morlac snatched Erisyte's light essence a moment before he ceased breathing. The kiss of Morlac: Yellow light turned red, and a body formed from dust and wind and tears.

"What is your name, pilgrim?" Morlac asked.

"I am Erisyte."

"I am your god, Erisyte," Morlac placed an arm around the dead man's shoulders, leading his newly fashioned body away from the vacated vessel upon the bed.

"Where will you take him?" Gan slid away from the cold and suddenly foreign shell beside him, turning a tearful gaze toward his lethargic lover standing in an odd daze next to Morlac.

"To another world."

Erisyte followed his new god to the other side of the cluttered room where Morlac opened an ornate double door to reveal, not the hallway beyond, but a red dirt road leading to the city of Delacroy. He stopped walking but indicated Erisyte should continue the journey.

"Will he be happy in your world?" Gan asked.

"Yes, he will find much peace," Morlac fluttered from existence, the effects of standing so close to his own illusion—the mind of the creator warping in on itself—a conundrum beyond the gods, it seemed.

"I will follow you Erisyte," Gan called out, "Even into Morlac's world."

Erisyte walked silently through the doorway, and Morlac quickly closed it behind him, sealing the passage to Delacroy. His presence solidified and he turned to Gan with a final word of compassion, "Rest, for now. I will return one day for your soul, and save you, as well."

Gan ran a hand over his wet cheek, "Then I will seek you in my dreams and in my prayers. Please, Morlac, keep Erisyte in your light."

Morlac opened the doors, their exterior painted magenta, and revealed an entirely different world. A desert graveyard. A lush forest. Morlac smiled, "I am the one who keeps him from the light, ancient one. For his sake, and yours, pray the Sphere never finds him."

Delacroy

Certainty | Chastity | Fasting | Generosity | Joy | Orthodoxy | Peace | Honesty | Faithfulness

Beah sunk to the damp floor of his dungeon cell. The wall, too, felt moist against his bare back, but darkness mercifully blinded him to the realities of his environment, and the presence of any other prisoners. Whether dead or sleeping, or simply not present, regardless, they remained silent. As for the sparse accommodations, he knew a small pile of hay and a discarded blanket lay to his left, for he caught a glimpse of them when his embittered swad opened the cell door to shove him inside; and he knew of a wooden bucket next to the door for defecation purposes. The only other decorations included a pair of long chains secured on one end to a bolt in the middle of the floor and shackled to Beah's wrists and ankles at the other.

The swads believed Beah a murderer and, admittedly, the taggle wondered how he would ever convince anyone in Delacroy of his innocence? How could he prove the existence of another world? Maybe he *was* mad. Yet, Inindu appeared real enough. He saw her…felt her hands wrap around his head. No, the Sphere's world definitely existed. Madness did not consume him. Neither did he kill Boltmar.

"Let me out of here!" He bellowed, "I didn't kill the Magnate. Please, I can lead you to his murderer. You have to listen to me."

"I'm listening."

The muffled voice sounded as though it spoke from behind the iron door. Maybe the swad? Slow to leave and willing to listen? "Please, open the door and release me."

"Over here, you fool. No one is going to release you."

"Who are you?" Beah searched to his left, eyes focusing on a small square-shaped hole where a stone wall met the dungeon floor, and a faint light emanating from an unknown source on the other side.

"Someone willing to listen. What is this you're claiming about the Magnate?"

Beah crawled across the cell floor with renewed hope, his battered face touching the wet ground as he spoke into the hole, "Inindu murdered him. I mean, the actual Inindu—the assassin from another world. She worships the Sphere. Please, you have to let me out of here. She is still in

Delacroy. There will be other victims."

"I am a prisoner like you. I cannot let you out."

"But...you have light?"

"I am Magnate Valun. Of course, I have light."

"Your father...wait, you're a magnate," Beah considered the implications. "Why are *you* a prisoner? Please, can you get me out?"

"It seems they found my father's body with the mark of the Sphere carved into his chest, and I can no more get you out of this ash heap than I can free myself."

"It was Inindu," something from above dripped onto Beah's nose. He wiped it away and continued, "Inindu must have carved the mark. She was with Maldinado. That has to mean something. Me and you are both innocent. Please, tell the swads. You're a Magnate. Tell them."

"Maldinado? Yes, that name means something," the voice sounded clearer as, Beah assumed, Valun moved closer to the opening between their cells. "Can you lead us to this Inindu? You are certain she was with the tailor? I don't know that it will matter, but if we are released can you find this murderer?"

"I am a taggle. We will find them."

"Pay a taggle, earn Morlac's favor..." The faint sound of clinking chains signaled an end to their conversation.

A moment later, Valun called out to the swads.

Phinx gracefully ascended the ladder, crossed an empty courtyard, and rapped five times upon a wooden door. A shirtless Troq opened the door slightly, and more fully when he saw the blond-haired taggle, allowing him entry; then closed it so they could speak in private. Phinx turned a stiff-backed desk chair around to face Troq who lit a pipe and took a seat on an unwrinkled bed.

The cook spoke first, pulling the dark pipe from his mouth, "We are close, Phinx. Morlac cannot ignore Boltmar's death. I can almost taste the revolution. Only one thing remains, though I fear you will not survive."

Phinx lifted a wet, silk scarf, dyed green with eodor sap, to his lips and started chewing, "The usual fee?"

Troq nodded, "Double." He scratched at his bearded throat with the stem of the pipe, "I need you to rescue Lyshmee. I sent word to her that she is not forgotten,"

"Edran?"

"Yes, he delivered the note, yesterday." Troq stood as though suddenly uncorked, "We cannot fail! Not now. Too much has gone into this moment. Boltmar. Lyshmee. Valun. Remni..." The last name sapped his energy. He sunk to the bed, once more, and pleaded with Phinx, "Rescue Lyshmee. Rescue her in the name of the Sphere—shout it from the guillotine when you pull her out from under that cursed blade. And let all of Delacroy know you and she and others throughout the city worship the god of another world."

Phinx tore into the scarf, sucking his own spit from the threads while he considered the idea, "No one has ever succeeded."

"A taggle never attempted the feat."

"Yes, well, we generally prefer less noticeably public displays of defiance," Phinx smiled at his own quip.

"Good because after you rescue her, I need you to run and hide. Flee to the sewers. Gather the Sons and Daughters of Oblation to you. Build an army. I will join you when I can."

Phinx stood and pulled the shredded green scarf from his teeth, "Make it five times my normal fee. May the Sphere be with me."

"And keep you in his light. You will have your gold."

Phinx watched Jennaween as she slept on a stuffed wool mattress inside the torch-lit hovel. The taggle spent several hours searching for her after departing Troq's room, but he didn't mind. Phinx preferred to sleep with Jennaween than in any of the available guest rooms at his mother's home where he typically stayed following any visit to Fourth Circle. His occasional lover slept alone in the hovel with her pierced nose pointed upward and her long arms inexplicably pinned behind her back. Her brown hair lay scattered in a wild mess, covering most of her face and shoulders. She looked funny and foolish—and she snored, but he didn't mind.

The taggle moved quietly to a wooden chest and opened it to find three bottles of ale. He pulled one out and removed the cork, leaning his back against the chest as he drank. He stretched his left leg out to the point where it touched the edge of Jennaween's mattress. Familiar, intense desire rekindled as he scanned every inch of her clunky, oddly-angled, slender, and altogether perfect frame; his feelings, no doubt, heightened by the enormity of the task set before him.

Rescue Lyshmee.

Troq's words lingered in his mind as he considered the time that remained: One day—two mornings—until the swads led Lyshmee to the guillotine. Every beheading promised a rescue attempt as a matter of tradition, to the point those who attended the execution placed wagers on the success of such an occurrence. But the attempt always failed, usually led by members of Seventh Circle who held an affinity for peace and maintained a general dislike for public executions.

Jennaween stopped snoring for a moment and Phinx watched her eyes to see if they would open, but it proved only a momentary pause. He raised a toast as she resumed, "Well spoken, my dear, whatever you said."

Second Circle would use anywhere from fifteen to twenty swads to guard Lyshmee, with another ten scattered throughout the crowd. Phinx would need to kill or capture all of them, or he would never reach the guillotine in time to rescue her. He set the bottle of ale on top of the closed chest, and then crawled on his stomach toward the mattress until his face hovered mere inches away from Jennaween. He ran his paint-splattered hand over her supple face, caressing her cheek and pushing hair strands back behind her ear. She felt warm…slightly damp with perspiration. He leaned down and kissed her forehead. Then her eyelid. Her neck.

She opened her eyes, smelled the ale on his breath and smiled, pulling him closer, "You found the ale?"

"I found you."

"It took you long enough," she kissed his lips.

"You're usually closer to the gate."

"I didn't want an audience."

Phinx pulled away, "You knew I would come?"

Jennaween sat up on her elbow, pulling at her tousled hair, "Men are as predictable as a loaf of bread. Add enough yeast and it will always rise."

Phinx pushed himself back until he sat against the chest, once more. He grabbed the abandoned bottle of ale and lifted it to his mouth, "I didn't…I mean…I woke you up so I could…I wanted to hear your voice."

"My voice? I'm your lover not your mother."

"Don't. Not tonight. I just want to talk."

Jennaween pushed herself out of bed, walked to the wooden chest, pulled a bottle of ale out, and sat next to the suddenly serious taggle, "Alright, what's on your mind?"

Phinx leaned his head back and stretched his left leg, "I'm going to rescue Lyshmee."

"Lyshmee, the condemned? Second Circle Lyshmee?" Her voice remained calm, if brazen, "So you want to die?"

"I'm starting a revolution. *We* are...the worshipers of the Sphere."

Jennaween set the bottle down a little harder than she likely intended, though Phinx could not say for certain, causing the glass to clink loudly against the stone floor, "It won't last five minutes. *You* won't last five minutes."

"I know."

She stood and walked over to the hovel opening, "So you came to say farewell?"

"I came to ask you to join me. If this succeeds, I'll need a place to hide."

"You know the taggles protect their own."

"I can't hide forever. Eventually, they'll come into the sewers."

Jennaween leaned down to retrieve her bottle and promptly took a swig of ale, "Then we'll stand beside you. Fight, if necessary."

"I'm asking you to die with me, not just fight."

"I know."

Phinx finished his ale and twirled the empty bottle in his hand.

"Why?" Jennaween suddenly asked, "What's wrong with the life we live?"

"Look around you. We're living in the sewers while Morlac lives in a palace. There's a better life out there. Somewhere. Maybe the Sphere offers us a better life. Maybe not, but if I die rescuing Lyshmee then at least I die striving for something better. I don't know..."

"Did you kill Boltmar?"

Phinx looked up to find her leaning somewhat tensely against the hovel wall, "No, Valun killed Boltmar. I simply unlocked the gate."

"Not surprising."

"And I carved the mark into his chest."

"Then you have *already* started a revolution. Everyone in Delacroy now knows about the worshipers of the Sphere. Whatever your plan was it worked. They already know. So why go kill yourself? Why rescue Lyshmee?"

Phinx dismissed the idea, "Someone has to come out of the shadows."

"So, they can see your face..." Jennaween choked on the remaining words.

Phinx lowered his gaze, and finished her thought,"...right before I die."

"Maybe you won't die."

He chuckled at the notion, "You mean, rescue Lyshmee and survive long enough to make it back to the sewers? Not likely."

"The taggles protect our own."

Phinx turned and fetched the remaining bottle of ale from the chest, "Will you join my revolution?"

"You knew I would."

"No, I *didn't* know," Phinx looked up at her intoxicating figure, "I wanted to ask."

Jennaween walked over, straddled his legs, and leaned forward to kiss him, "I'm glad you did."

Simiad slept on his back, his long beard spread out over a red and brown quilt, while one hand and both feet hung off the mattress. The Second Circle magnate stood taller and wider than former magnate Turnac, but Simiad did not receive a larger bed upon assuming the role from his master. He received an iron shelf. It hung on the stone wall beside his inadequate bed. Here, he kept a pair of spectacles; leather bound parchment sheets which he used to capture his thoughts or record the day's activities; and three candles which needed replaced every other day—or sometimes daily depending upon how far into the night he stayed awake; and two wine bottles. These particular bottles contained a red wine from Third Circle. Both bottles sat empty, and Simiad slept off the lingering effects of a late evening filled with spirited consumption.

"Forgive the intrusion, magnate," Fillop, Second Circle Overseer of the swads, who spoke as though unable to completely extend his lower jaw, his lips never fully articulating what he voiced in his head, waited for a response. Simiad snorted his way out of deep slumber, suddenly aware of the Overseer's presence without fully, or even slightly comprehending the reason for his appearance, "A message arrived direct from Overseer Narch. I am told it is a matter of some urgency."

Simiad rubbed at his bloated chest, and then moved upward to rub his eyes, still groggy with wine and sleep. Eventually, he sat up and held out his hand to the mumbling overseer, his senior in age by thirteen years, "Magnate Valun, again?"

Fillop handed him the note, "Your presence is requested."

Simiad cursed Boltmar for the seventeenth time that night. The magnate's death, and the subsequent arrest of his entire family, left a void within the ranks. As the least important magnate, therefore, Simiad assumed responsibility over Fourth Circle until such time as Morlac appointed a new magnate. Valun had sent Simiad several notes since his arrest, seventeen of them, each proclaiming his innocence. The newly appointed and recently condemned magnate had already proven himself an irritant. Since Valun outranked him, however, Simiad had no choice but to respond.

He broke the wax seal and read the scrawled, almost illegible note, a simple request imploring the magnate *come quickly*. Simiad, again, weighed his options, longing to return to his slumber. Finally, he sighed, "How long before dawn?"

"At least five hours."

If he left at that moment Simiad could reach Fourth Circle dungeon before the roads filled with travelers. A saddled horse would seem faster than the carriage, but he knew himself too drunk to stay in the saddle, "Give me a moment to dress. Prepare my carriage."

The overseer bowed and departed.

Simiad climbed out of bed and shuffled to an iron chest beside a dormant fireplace at which point he noticed a new bottle of wine sitting on the mantle. A gift from Fillop.

An escort of ten swads led Simiad's carriage through Fourth Circle. They moved with considerable speed, driving the horses in accordance with the magnate's orders, only pausing long enough to unlock the gates leading to Third and Fourth Circle. Simiad sat alone in the carriage, chasing wine with his tongue as it fell from his mouth—his beard soaked in several places, for the jostling of the carriage made it impossible to maintain a seal between his sluggish lips and the bottle. They reached their destination two hours before sunrise; horses breathing heavily as Simiad stepped out into the courtyard of the Fourth Circle swad barracks.

He handed the empty bottle to a nearby swad, "Find me more."

Narch, Fourth Circle Overseer, emerged from the barracks to lead the unsteady magnate to Valun's dungeon cell. The bald man held an impish gaze exasperated by both a retreating forehead and shoulder bones which sat even with the bottom of his unusually thin earlobes. He wore a ruby armband on his left wrist, identifying him as overseer, and Simiad couldn't help but notice the incessant adjustments Narch made to the armband as he walked beside him.

Tannessa, a rapacious woman, and the only swad on duty, carried the only torch amongst the party. Simiad knew her; rather, he knew her reputation and what she represented. Leverage. Power. This unwanted, porcine swad possessed more information related to Delcrean politics than Simiad could ever want or even afford to purchase. Indeed, though relegated to night duty, Tannessa held more sway than either of the two men who followed her through the dungeon corridors. His own dealings with her, solely restricted to that night's encounter, left him uncertain as to how she attained her information or why it granted her so much power. And, well, in that moment, he could not imagine caring any less about the state of her particular form of corruption.

Of greater concern, due to his unfamiliarity with the Fourth Circle dungeon, Simiad lost his way after only a few turns—neither could he, in his drunken state, remember from which direction they started. This mostly amused him, so he grinned stupidly while he walked, and passed the time by counting the number of wrinkles on the back of Narch's bald head: five. He marveled how the folds of skin spanned from ear-to-ear with four thinner wrinkles split evenly on either side of a thicker middle wrinkle. The magnate, filled with wine and curiosity, touched the back of his own head, but he discovered no wrinkles large enough to feel beneath his long, brown hair.

"Stand back, prisoner. Visitors," Tannessa opened an iron door, stepping aside to allow Narch and Simiad to enter the stone cell.

Several torches illuminated Valun who wore a loose-fitting smock over black leggings and rested comfortably upon an overstuffed mattress; unshaven but otherwise well kept. He rose, and sniffed the air with disgust, "Simiad...you're drunk."

"I am often drunk; and usually asleep at this time of night. But tonight, I am here at your insistence. Why?"

"I know who killed my father. Release me and we will take you to him."

"We?"

"The taggle in the next cell," Valun's chains jingled as he motioned to his right. "He says he witnessed Maldinado kill Boltmar."

"The tailor? I spoke with him during the Sorting. He sat atop my tower. He can barely walk; how could he have killed..." Simiad couldn't for the life of him remember the dead magnate's name. "Why is there a taggle in the dungeon?"

Narch spoke, "Beah, from Second Circle. He was arrested inside the magnate's manor. He killed Boltmar."

Boltmar. Yes, that was his name...the dead magnate. Simiad repeated the name several times in his head, unaware the others awaited his reply.

"Would you like to speak with him?" Tannessa finally asked.

Simiad nodded, "Yes, I need to speak to Boltmar."

Valun threw up his arms, chains clinking and shifting from where they pooled around his feet, "Tasa Ro! My fate rests in the hands of a drunkard?"

"Not Boltmar," Narch corrected the confused magnate, agitation emphasizing each word, "Would you like to speak with Beah, the taggle from Second Circle,"

Simiad knew the taggle, a gifted storyteller from Second Gate. Why did Narch lock him up in the Fourth Circle dungeons? "Yes, bring him here."

Tannessa waddled away to retrieve the prisoner.

"Beah didn't kill my father," Valun continued, "But he knows who did; and if not Maldinado, then the tailor is somehow connected to his murder."

Simiad shook his head, "You are not here because Boltmar was murdered." The magnate searched his thoughts, "You are accused... accused...of worshiping the Sphere. Finding your father's murderer will not change your fate."

"Magnate Simiad," Beah entered without bowing his unmarked head. "Please, you have to release me. The Sphere sent Inindu to kill Boltmar. None of us are safe until she is captured."

Tannessa pulled the taggle's chains, drawing him a safe distance away from the magnate, "He speaks madness."

"No, listen to the pure born," Valun urged. "Tell them about Maldinado."

"Maldinado is a warrior from another world—the Sphere's world. And Edran, too. Troq wouldn't listen to me, but I saw Edran in the sewers with Inindu."

"You speak as though you know this world," Narch accused.

"Yes, I lived there, but Morlac saved me, and brought me to Delacroy."

"You're not a pure born?" Valun stepped back with noticeable revulsion.

Simiad chuckled. *Pure born* only applied to magnates and taggles. The chaste residents of Second Circle, according to the unyielding laws of nature, need not concern themselves with such pettiness; neither could they improve their political leverage by simply birthing a taggle. Indeed, any established advantage required actual skill and hard work, for Morlac did not *give* anything to his worshipers in Second Circle; they earned every ounce of his favor and boon. Thus, Simiad found Valun's reaction, as the privileged son of a magnate, completely absurd. How fitting, therefore, as Simiad considered his role in that moment, both magnate and taggle relied upon his judgment…his inebriated and, in more ways than one, definitively *impure* judgment.

"I am a taggle," Beah responded haughtily. "In both worlds, as it happens."

"And I worship Morlac," Valun turned toward Simiad, effectively ending further engagement with the taggle. "Boltmar's murder and the mark they found upon his chest…someone plots against me."

Beah also turned to Simiad and pleaded his cause, "Please, Inindu is here for only one reason. She brings death to the city, and you may well be her next victim."

Simiad grinned with genuine bemusement, and of this he felt certain, for nothing he had tasted in the cheap wine that night qualified as genuine despite its ability to lift his spirits, "No one wants to kill me, taggle. I'm just an errand boy for the other magnates."

This time, Valun chuckled.

"Narch," Simiad said, "I am drunk, and none of this makes any sense. Find me a place to sleep and I will return later with a clear mind."

"You may sleep in my father's bed," Valun offered.

Simiad nodded, accepting the obvious bribe attempt, for it also presented the most practical solution.

Beah's chains rattled in protest, "No, Edran is there. It isn't safe."

"The cook's apprentice? He's just a boy," Valun said.

"He knows Inindu."

"He is not the only one," Simiad followed Narch out of the cell. "Inindu visits us all, and none more often than those who live in Second Circle."

Condemned

Maldinado

Maldinado left Inindu at Third Circle stables with a promise to return in the morning. Then he walked the short journey to Peeks' home—as with most of the tailor's friends, their relationship began after the Sorting when Maldinado offered him a room. Following a prolonged meal, therefore, filled with meandering conversation about those early days when last they shared the same roof, the tailor retired to his designated room and, for several more hours, lay uncomfortably upon his back, unable to sleep.

So, he allowed himself to believe another world existed, quieting his doubts if only for the moment. He lingered on hazy memories of Nataline and Hintor. *How much time has passed since I left?* Maldinado imagined them having lived a happy life in Adarian. *Are they still alive?* And Breline, his mother?

Will I ever see them, again?

Maldinado felt certain any action against Morlac would result in his own death.

He felt the loose skin on the back of his left hand. His hands, perhaps, served as the only similarity between warrior and tailor. Nimble. Confident. Adept. Whether sewing needle or sword, his hands never betrayed him, but...

How do I kill a god?

Delacroy

Troq awoke at the fifth knock. He opened the door to find Edran, "What is it, boy?"

"Magnate Simiad be here."

"No doubt, summoned by Valun."

"He be taking Magnate Boltmar's room, and asks his morning meal be delivered three hours after sunrise. He be more than a little drunk."

Troq nodded, "Simiad is always drunk. It's the curse of Second Circle magnates: All the privileges, but none of the power. I'll be sure to send him a glass of tomato juice in the morning."

Edran picked at a sliver of wood he found on the door frame, "He sent me to be fetching Maldinado."

"Maldinado? What does he want with *him?*"

"'Tis a secret to be certain."

Troq leaned heavily against the half-opened door, "There is more to Simiad's request than what he is revealing." He squatted down to the taggle boy's eye level, "Go, boy, and this time don't return. Find Maldinado and Inindu. Take them to the sewers. And find Phinx. I'll meet you as soon as I am able. Simiad will soon enough forget about Maldinado. He will be too busy with other matters."

"Lyshmee?"

"The revolution, boy!" Troq clasped both of Edran's shoulders, barely containing his excitement, "Morlac's destruction grows near."

"Master," the boy pulled back. "What be happening to Tilly?"

"May the Sphere keep her in his light."

Edran looked confused, "'Tis your light. Yer the Sphere, aren't you, master?"

"Yes, boy. I am the Sphere."

Edran suddenly embraced the cook, "Keep Tilly in your light. Don't let anything happen to her. She doesn't mean to be dropping things and breaking things all the time. 'Tis an accident."

"More likely, she is distracted by those around her," Troq smiled. "Yes, I will protect her, boy. Now go...quickly."

"I'll be needing gold."

Troq rose and retreated into the shadows of his room, emerging a moment later with a leather pouch, "Make it last."

Edran snatched the gold and walked quietly away, to the point of boyish exaggeration. Troq watched him as sadness filled his heart. Tilly he could protect, but the boy...

Another necessary sacrifice.

Edran discovered topi-Inindu asleep on a pile of fresh hay when he arrived at the dimly lit stables. The black gown she typically wore lay in a ring of fabric, discarded beside her slate board, leaving her naked body fully exposed. She slept as though stretching her back: Extended arms, with her right hand clasping her left forearm, rested above her tilted head and ever shifting black hair. The taggle boy stood staring at her full body, his eye level just high enough to peep over the stall door, his hand frozen upon the unturned latch.

He found her beautiful.

But mostly, he noticed her breasts.

"'Tis a strange thing to be sleeping without yer clothes," Edran spoke loud enough to awaken the horses contained within the surrounding stalls. "Time to dress. My master says we need to leave." The taggle boy stood tall, boldly taking another look at Inindu's bulb-like breasts before he turned and walked away. He didn't understand what he felt, but he liked what he saw.

Despite the early hour, several travelers already walked the streets of Fourth Circle on their way to either the marketplace, or Fourth Gate, or another Circle entirely. One of the travelers, a bone-thin woman—sweat dripping from the hair plastered around her ears—actually ran through the crowd. Edran and topi-Inindu joined the growing procession, eager to reach Fourth Gate and meet up with Maldinado and Inindu-horse.

Beneath the waking city, in the still quiet sewers below, Phinx held Jennaween against his bare chest. Though she lay asleep, he remained wide awake with a thousand thoughts of how to rescue Lyshmee racing through his mind. The most successful attempt to rescue a condemned prisoner occurred three years prior when Selpha sought to save B'tul, her much older husband. Her success proved particularly surprising considering the event took place in Sixth Circle, known for their large contingent of swads. The scheduled beheading, well-attended and heavily guarded, arrived with expectations that an attempt of significant proportions would occur due to its proximity to Seventh Circle. But the notoriously eager freedom fighters never appeared. Instead, a single woman made her way through the crowd, and though she lacked training or anything resembling a coordinated attack, Selpha actually managed to reach the guillotine platform. But as she tried to unbind her weakened husband, a swad ran her through with a well-placed sword. The doltish crowd cheered her death as loudly as they had rooted for her to succeed, grateful for the respite regardless of the outcome, for they traveled there to observe and enjoy—lacking the conviction to either liberate or impede. Thus, no one from the crowd stepped forward to assist Selpha. After her death, the swads beheaded her husband, his bare feet curiously touching his wife's crumpled corpse as the gleaming blade fell.

Hundreds of residents, but none of them offered any assistance. Hundreds attended every beheading, for the city announced each event weeks in advance to ensure maximum attendance. Hundreds of residents…against a handful of swads…

"Jennaween," he gently shook her listless body, "Are you awake?"

"Hmmm…"

"You were right. Taggles protect our own. What if we protected Lyshmee?"

Jennaween opened her eyes and lifted her head, "What are you talking about?"

"The crowd," Phinx moved out from under her and stood up to dress, pulling on leather trousers before reaching for his tunic. "Every beheading has a rescue attempt, but never more than a single person attacks, or at best, a small group. But never the entire crowd—most of them, anyway. So, what if the crowd was comprised of taggles? We could save Lyshmee. We could *actually* save her."

Phinx reached for his discarded green scarf, carelessly tossed the night before, and wrapped it loosely around his neck. Then he threw Jennaween's clothes at her, "Get dressed. I need your help." Her sudden scowl told him he should reconsider his request, so he knelt down close to her and gave her a kiss, "I meant, will you help me?"

"You know I will."

"We need every taggle in Second and Third and Fourth Gate, and we only have a day to spread the word." Phinx stood to leave, "Tell the taggles we meet in Third Gate, tonight. I'll meet you there." Phinx left…

only to return a moment later, "Sorry, you head to Second Gate. I'll take Fourth Gate and meet you in the middle."

Jennaween removed the wool blanket and began to dress. Phinx lingered long enough to enjoy her nakedness and myriad tattoos before departing.

Taggles emerged from the sewers into Fourth Gate carrying torches that cast shadows upon the walls, exaggerating their height and gestures. The line of taggles who ascended from below stretched the length of the ladder and several hundred feet back into the underground tunnel. The collection of performers, dancers, painters, storytellers and various other artists possessing skills in pottery, jewelry, wood and stone wore various vibrant colors which identified them as taggles: a dancer wore a yellow tunic with orange sleeves, slit and tied in the back to allow for greater freedom of motion; a musician had purple ribbons flowing from her untamed hair; a sculptor wore leggings with red and white vertical stripes; and a painter, chewing vigorously at the green scarf which both wrapped his neck and hung from his mouth.

Phinx actively moved from one taggle to another, speaking a quick word before moving on to the next, "Meeting, tonight. Third Gate."

Each taggle, upon hearing, nodded without speaking and continued with their morning routine. Aside from the painter's whispers, in fact, few of the taggles engaged in dialogue, choosing instead to embrace the customary silence of the morning for, soon enough, Fourth Gate would open to thousands of travelers and a corresponding wave of deafening sound caused by unchecked voices which echoed throughout the tunneled gate.

Vitrec, a storyteller, wearing his customary blue and orange scarf wrapped tightly around his neck, listened to the painter's message, nodded his acknowledgment, and then mounted the crowded ladder. He quietly muttered to himself while he climbed, a whispered story, one which he would unveil for the first time later that day:

Fourth Circle lies restless; every resident sits awake in their bed, staring out their window, fearful of what will happen to the old swad who walks alone in the street beyond their front door. The swad carries a long-barreled flintlock rifle and walks as old men walk—each step a barely salvaged stumble. They know he should not travel alone in the street, so they watch and listen.

The old swad shouts, "Why do you hide from me, Dsal Tiger? You cannot flee the hunter."

A fox appears from the shadows. The fox's white fur appears unblemished save for a black stripe which extends downward from her chin. The crafty beast does not run, for she does not fear the old swad, rather, she sits. She obeys Dsal Tiger.

"What message do you bring?" The old swad asks.

"Dsal Tiger does not flee the hunter. He does not hide."

The old swad fires his flintlock rifle, killing and silencing the fox. Then he pours gunpowder and a lead ball into the barrel and continues his march down the street as though drunk on wine...or love.

"Why do you hide from me, Dsal Tiger? You cannot flee the hunter."

A rabbit appears from the shadows. The rabbit's white fur appears unblemished save for a black stripe which extends downward from her chin. The tiny beast does not run, for she does not fear the old swad, rather, she sits. She obeys Dsal Tiger.

"What message do you bring?" The old swad asks.

"Dsal Tiger does not hide. What you seek you cannot see."

The old swad fires his flintlock rifle, killing and silencing the rabbit. Then he pours gunpowder and a lead ball into the barrel and continues his march down the street as though driven by lust...or greed.

"Why do you hide from me, Dsal Tiger? You cannot flee the hunter."

A swan appears from the shadows. The swan's white feathers appear unblemished save for a black stripe which extends downward from her chin. The graceful beast does not run, for she does not fear the old swad, rather, she sits. She obeys Dsal Tiger.

"What message do you bring?" The old swad asks.

"Dsal Tiger does not flee the hunter. He exists in shadow and light."

The old swad fires his flintlock rifle, killing and silencing the swan. Then he pours gunpowder and a lead ball into the barrel and continues his march down the street as though wandering...or blind.

In the street behind the old swad, Dsal Tiger follows. The tiger's white fur appears unblemished save for a black stripe which extends downward from his chin. He does not run. Rather, he sits as the old swad stops to speak with a wolf. The wolf's white fur appears unblemished save for a black stripe which extends downward from his chin. Dsal Tiger listens and waits. When the wolf lay dead, and after the old swad reloads his flintlock rifle, Dsal Tiger follows.

The residents of Fourth Circle huddle deeper under blankets as each shot rings out in the night. Throughout the night, Dsal Tiger follows. He does not fear the old swad, for he is Dsal Tiger.

Swads pulled open the large circular doors on either side of the tunnel, and Fourth Gate burst to life with a rush of sound and kinetic movement. Jugglers started tossing torches. Three performers mounted wooden stilts and began another day of pacing the delighted crowd. Choreographed swords flew through the air with practiced elegance. Flutes whistled above lutes. And within moments the tunnel filled with travelers who entered from both directions as though a herd of goats spilling into their pen.

On one side of Fourth Gate, entering from Fourth Circle, a diminutive pair of travelers seemed altogether swallowed by the crowd, for neither Edran nor topi-Inindu could see above the heads of those around them. And none of the passers-by wished them favor and boon or even gave them notice. The taggle boy led topi-Inindu toward the outer wall of the tunneled gate in order to better gain his bearings. Still, those who gathered around each of the elevated platforms and merchant booths made it difficult to pass beyond to the confined passageway which lay between the oddly angled taggle structures and the tunnel wall. Eventually, and after more than one inadvertent elbow to the face, the pair broke clear of the crowd, finally able to move freely. Several taggles standing along the back passageway gave them a sharp look, but quickly returned to their various tasks upon seeing Edran's familiar face.

When he and topi-Inindu finally reached Vitrec's platform they made their way back into the crowd, though they discovered no sign of Maldinado and Inindu-horse. They waited. Edran squatted and studied the feet of those around him, counting and losing track of how many people wiggled their soiled toes. Beside him, topi-Inindu attempted unsuccessfully to untangle her brother's mess of red hair.

Condemned

Maldinado

Morning brought a renewed spirit and clear purpose. Maldinado, riding atop Inindu-horse, determined he should reunite with Edran as quickly as possible. The taggle boy had mentioned worshipers of the Sphere: How many worshipers secretly existed within the walls of Delacroy? Could they wield a sword? Did they even own a weapon? Regardless of their skill level, Maldinado needed an army to defeat Morlac, so he would work with whatever Edran offered and sprinkle in a few of his own recruits with help from Lomax.

Lomax! Maldinado grinned at the image of his foul friend standing amidst the dead, clueless of the illusion known as Delacroy. *What wouldn't I give to find you out there so I could dance before your rotting corpse?* He leaned forward to better whisper into Inindu-horse's ear, "Any chance we can escape this world for just a moment? I need to find a friend."

Inindu-horse shook her head.

"Damn," Maldinado returned to his uncomfortable position atop her back, "Lomax will only think me mad if I tell him the truth." He thought about how best to approach and recruit the stubborn fool, "What if you showed him...like with Beah?"

She shook her head with noticeable irritation, suggesting he drop the subject and effectively crushing his vile hopes. Still, Maldinado lingered on the topic, formulating the framework of a scheme that would convince Lomax of the lies and deception around him. Then he laughed at the absurd notion, as though Lomax somehow thought otherwise, "He already knows Delacroy is a city of pretense." Maldinado muttered to himself as he stretched and straightened his back, "He's probably already figured out half the puzzle."

And the tailor felt immense joy knowing that he, not Lomax, held the missing piece.

Such knowledge would surely garner Maldinado much gold, leaving the basket weaver wholly humiliated, "The bastard will die if I torment him too long, though. He's always been the weaker one between us. He would, too. Tasa Ro! He would die and leave me here to fight alone if only to spite me."

Inindu-horse slowed to a trot and then a walk as they approached the outer tip of Delcrean residents seeking passage to, or through, the still distant Fourth Gate.

"Morlac's boon upon thee, Maldinado."

The speaker, Tania, a short and comfortably thin woman with a deep wrinkle on either side of her narrow mouth, walked alongside her son who appeared much older—and bearded—than the boy Maldinado sheltered several years prior, "Favor and boon. Is that Mendelsohn? Is the boy now a man?"

"And soon to be married," Mendelsohn replied.

"He'll need a new robe," Tania smiled. "We were hoping you might know a good tailor."

"When is the marriage? I will deliver the robe myself."

Will I? How much longer would Morlac's world even exist? How strange that a simple request for a new robe would cause Maldinado to pause. It seemed ages ago since he last held a needle and thread, as distant in that moment as the imagined feel of a longsword in his once scarred hands. Would he ever again sell his goods alongside Lomax in the marketplace? Would he ever again stand beside Hintor in battle? He struggled to merge the life he lived with the one he remembered, leaving him oddly detached from both worlds.

Mendelsohn and Tania looked at one another with a bliss only shared between mother and son; both grinning—the son as though asking permission to share more details; his mother resisting the urge to share the news herself. "In three weeks..." Mendelsohn finally confirmed.

"She's a lovely girl, Maldinado," Tania beamed. "I'll bring her by the marketplace, so you can meet her."

"I would like that."

"When did you get a horse?" Mendelsohn stroked Inindu's hindquarters, "She's beautiful."

"I told you that hip of his was getting worse," Tania looked at her son with a look of superiority.

He rolled his eyes in mock defeat and turned toward the tailor, "It's good that you purchased a few more legs."

Inindu-horse cocked her head, looking back at Maldinado. He shifted forward and patted her neck somewhat awkwardly, hoping to avoid another public episode, "Nobody ever truly owns a horse. Fortunately, she allows me to ride her on occasion."

"Oh, here," Tania reached into a canvas bag that hung from her shoulder. Eventually, she produced three gold coins and promptly handed them to Maldinado, "For the robe."

"This is enough for five robes."

Tania smiled at her son, "Then make a good robe."

"The best," Mendelsohn added.

Maldinado found warmth in Tania's eyes and, though certainly proud of her lovesick son, he understood the meaning of her discreet gift. The extra gold served as appreciation for what Maldinado did for them when he invited them into his home: He provided them with an opportunity to live a different life. Illusion or not, he decided to accept the moment as meaningful; and the gold it offered. "I will begin, immediately," he lied.

Could he possibly ask them to join his army? To sacrifice their happy life? He *must*. But he could not bring himself to squelch such charming ignorance.

"Morlac's boon upon thee," he offered in parting.

"Favor and boon," they both replied.

Maldinado and Inindu-horse entered Fourth Gate, though not without considerable difficulty. Aside from the usual congestion, residents constantly stopped them—recognizing Maldinado—to discuss matters of varying importance. The tailor hardly noticed similar interactions on his way to the Sorting, but on this day, as his two worlds coalesced into one mysterious reality, he found the frequent disruption simply added to the chaos already cluttering his mind. How many residents in Delacroy did he truly know, or did Morlac simply implant these memories? How much time had passed since Maldinado entered the Kul to awaken in Delacroy? Ten days? Seventy-eight years?

"Morlac's boon upon thee, Maldinado," the speaker wore a neatly-trimmed, black beard which augmented his angular face.

Maldinado recognized him immediately due to his recently gained and sincere admiration for the food merchant, "Favor and boon, Nebon." He dismounted, allowing Nebon to properly greet him: three circles touching four, "Come to retrieve your commission?"

"Um, yes, how did you know?"

Maldinado walked alongside the merchant, "I ran into Phinx on my way to the Sorting. Brilliant likeness of the Adherent. A gift?"

He nodded, "A decoration for my home."

Nebon, a stout man with thick arms, walked with a confident step. Maldinado imagined it would take several men to wrestle him to the ground, more with a sword in his hand. And it just so happened the tailor needed an army. He wrapped his arms around the merchant's neck and drew him close enough to whisper, "May the Sphere be with you."

The muscles in Nebon's neck grew tense under Maldinado's grip, but he did not pull away, "And keep you in his light."

"The time draws near when we must reveal ourselves. I will send word," Maldinado released the Son of Oblation.

"I am ready," Nebon turned his attention to a display of delicate objects fashioned from fragments of red and black glass.

Maldinado grinned as he turned back to Inindu-horse, "That's one. And Lomax will make two."

Inindu-horse whinnied and shook her head, her black mane billowing outward.

"This body may prove useless, but my mind remains sharp as ever before," he grabbed the lapels of his robe with a tug of marked satisfaction.

"Talking to horses now, Maldinado?"

The tailor recognized the voice, immediately. *Harian.* Maldinado's long-deceased spouse still tormented him daily by leaving her cousin behind to watch after him, "Morlac's boon upon thee, Harian."

"Favor and boon," Harian shouted at him, despite their proximity, as though she stood at the bottom of a well crying out to passers-by above ground. Then she embraced him in her customary hug and pulled his forehead to hers with hands more accustomed to milking a goat: four circles greeting four, "Does your hip bother you so bad you now need a horse? You dear poor soul; do you need me to help with anything? I could sell your robes for a few days, so you can stay home and rest. Just say the word and you know I'll take care of you."

"I'm fine. Thank you, Harian," Maldinado shuddered at the thought of sending Harian to the marketplace in his stead. Despite the opportunity to torment Lomax—and certainly his friend would suffer greatly having to listen to the overbearing woman for an entire day—Harian would chase away all of Maldinado's prospective customers. Indeed, he would never see another ounce of gold. The idea alone caused him to slip a hand into his pocket in search of tangible wealth, consciously counting each coin.

An image of the standing dead flashed through Maldinado's mind. *You mean the illusion of wealth.*

Still, the gold brought him comfort and the forbearance to listen to Harian speak.

"The marketplace hasn't been the same without you the last few days. And poor Lomax looks absolutely, horribly miserable. Everyone's buying denam-baskets it seems."

"The only thing denam-baskets are good for is catching severed heads."

Harian laughed with raucous delight and, awkwardly, for a moment too long, "That's what I keep telling everyone. I'm sure Lomax will sell more baskets, soon enough. These things go in cycles, you know."

"So, I'm told," Maldinado looked off into the distance, hoping to spot a familiar face in the crowd; or, really, anyone other than his dead wife's cousin, "Well, Harian, don't let me keep you. I'm sure you have a busy day ahead."

"Yes, yes, oh, I'm traveling to Second Circle to stay with my sister. There's a beheading tomorrow, you know. You should come. My sister has an extra room."

I can't imagine a worse idea. "I'm afraid I've already been gone from home too long. The Sorting is a worthwhile trip, but it takes me longer to recover each year."

Harian patted his right hip, her calloused fingers eagerly groping the edge of his ass, "Well, don't let it keep you down, too long. I want to see you in the marketplace when I return."

"I can't wait."

She bullied her way through the crowd and away from Maldinado.

The tailor turned his attention to Inindu-horse who raised her prehensile lips as though striking a grin, and snorted several times.

"You look foolish," Maldinado ran a stiff hand through his thinning hair. "And don't blame me. She's the cousin of my deceased wife. Assuming I ever *had* a wife. Either way, I'm stuck with her." His mind harvested a growing idea, "I don't suppose you could reveal a few things to *her*? Drive her mad like Beah?"

Inindu-horse started forward without responding.

"Shame…I wouldn't mind watching her runaway screaming."

"Morlac's boon upon thee, Phinx."

Maldinado found the taggle standing mesmerized beside a stage where three linen-clad dancers performed an intricate display of rising arms and delicate steps. The fluid weave of limbs and bodies encircled a single violinist who carefully caressed each string of the polished instrument—stretching haunting notes into an audible summons that pulled her dancing tormentors closer and closer until their choreographed movements broke against her like blanched waves upon the cliffs. Phinx placed a finger against his lips to quiet the tailor, but he need not bother for Maldinado felt himself entranced by the music and the visual display of long, white linen streams flowing about and around the barefooted dancers. They wore red gloves. And red paint covered their faces save around their eyes which they outlined in white.

One of the dancers slowed and fell with exaggerated, lethargic movement until at last she lay prostrate. The other two dancers pulled at her listless arms, red gloves serving as implied wounds. Then the violinist marched around the remaining dancers, attacking the strings with her bow, until each one fell victim to her chords. In this manner, the musician continued playing until, surprisingly, the first dancing victim stirred. Then another. And, finally, the last. No longer enchanted by the musical trickster, despite her ever more frantic notes, the dancers converged upon the violinist—surrounding her and forcing her to kneel within their midst until her music faded into the sounds of Fourth Gate. Their odd and sudden silence somehow squelched the otherwise overwhelming crowd noise with stunning impact.

The performance seemed ethereal, and Maldinado's thoughts temporarily transported him back home to Adarian where he felt a familiar desire to protect the Adow—to defeat any challenge which threatened her life if only for the honor of serving her...and in hopes of a kiss. He loved her. More than that, he *wanted* her. No, *more* than that. It seemed Inindu had correctly identified his true motives even if he remained blind to them until that moment in Fourth Gate.

Maldinado wanted to serve as First Etabli.

The tailor finally saw through the arrogant facade of the inner warrior who once shunned the title of Madar because he felt it beneath him. That warrior—he—desired a far more honorable position. Indeed, the warrior believed himself destined for greatness, a belief made stronger when at last he encountered Ayson, for the First Etabli appeared weak and the Adow so fervent. *How could she settle for such a fool?*

Like the dancers rising above a musical deception, however, the tailor realized the truth of the warrior's noble pursuit of honor. He did not love the Adow, rather, he loved what only *she* could offer him: First Etabli. With raw awareness, Maldinado acknowledged his former warrior-self sought the glory associated with serving as First Etabli. And the tailor felt the resulting shame of a life once lived. For the first time since Inindu revealed his past, Maldinado knew without a doubt he once lived as a mighty and proud, yet broken, warrior in the Sphere's world.

He *was* a warrior. He was *also* a tailor.

Two lives. Two worlds. But not, he knew, two separate men.

I am Maldinado.

"Favor and..." Phinx turned his attention from the performance. "Maldinado? Are you alright?"

"Forgive me," Maldinado replied, casting an eye at Inindu-horse who had buried her slightly whiskered nose into the tailor's back, a not-so-subtle nudge effectively stirring him from his daydream. "A beautiful performance, and one I don't recall having seen before now."

"You have witnessed the very first performance. Lilthian and her daughters have worked for several months on that piece," Phinx said. "Is this your horse, Maldinado?"

Maldinado ignored the question, patting the taggle on his shoulder, "Phinx, perhaps there is a quieter place for us to discuss a rather sensitive matter?" Then, leaning closer, "I worship the Sphere."

Phinx pulled away from the tailor with apparent mistrust, but Maldinado persisted, "Edran told me everything. It seems we fight a common enemy."

The taggle painter raised a green scarf to his mouth, took casual inventory of the crowd, and finally motioned for Maldinado and Inindu-horse to follow him to a spot directly behind Lilthian's elevated stage. They encountered a noticeably irritated violinist and two of her daughters. The mother sat and rose and sat again upon a wooden bench, discussing with some fervor the many mistakes which she and her daughters—the third standing nearby, doubled-over and touching her toes—made during the dance. And although Maldinado did not recall any such gaffs in their performance he did empathize with the mother, for despite his considerable skill as a tailor he had yet to produce, in his mind at least, a perfect robe. Whether seam or stain, cut or fold, every garment he produced contained a flaw however minor, hidden, or unnoticed by those who sought to praise or purchase his work. Unnoticed by everyone except Morlac, of course. Why else would his god wear a yiddick-shawl instead of a maldinado-robe?

No, not my god. I worship the Sphere.

Phinx led them away from Lilthian and her daughters, traveling further back toward the stone wall of Fourth Gate. Then he turned to the right and traveled a sizable distance before finally stopping. They stood in a cove of solitude behind a series of large, purple tents. Phinx dropped the scarf from his mouth, "May the Sphere be with us."

"And keep us in his light," Maldinado answered without hesitation.

"How soon can you gather the Sons and Daughters of Oblation? I need an army."

"An army?" Phinx pulled a silk fiber from his lips, "Then Edran has not told you everything. The Sons and Daughters of Oblation hide in shadows, neither willing to expose themselves to the light nor possessing the skill to defeat even the weakest of swads who would oppose them. I wish they really were an army, though. I could use such a force…but whatever your reasons I must leave such matters to you. The Father of Oblation has given me my own task."

"You *must* help me," Maldinado desperately needed an army. "Who else is there? The boy?"

Phinx pointed to the tailor's robe, "Is there anyone more qualified than the tailor of Fourth Circle? Yes, I suppose more than one person would take notice if a *taggle* declared himself a worshiper of the Sphere, but you, Maldinado, you are known throughout Delacroy. I swear, I see your robes everywhere. A proclamation from such a public figure would cause Delcreans from every circle to join…" He paused, apparently struck with an idea. Then he muttered, "*If Troq wants a revolution…*" Phinx patted the determined tailor on his shoulder, "If you want to raise an army, Maldinado, you will need to help me start a revolution."

The Madar stared at him without understanding, "The task you mentioned?"

Phinx nodded, "We are going to rescue Lyshmee. And if we survive long enough—if our revolution grows large enough—perhaps the Sphere will deliver us from Morlac."

Inindu-horse snorted an alarm and moved her head toward one of the tents.

Edran emerged, followed closely by topi-Inindu who quickly moved toward Inindu-horse, burying her face in the horse's mane.

Maldinado persisted despite the momentary interruption, "How are *we* going to rescue Lyshmee? And need I remind you no rescue attempt has ever succeeded."

"We use the crowd," Phinx said, "or rather, we populate the crowd with taggles."

Maldinado grinned at the notion, "It could work…against twenty or even thirty swads, and I've never seen more than thirty at a beheading. How many taggles?"

"Hundreds. We meet tonight."

"Yes…yes, we will certainly outnumber them, and only a fool would dare challenge an army of taggles." Maldinado envisioned the most likely swad positions around the guillotine platform, working through battle scenarios in his mind. If he could not lead the Adarian 45th through the streets of Delacroy he nevertheless savored the idea of leading an army of taggles who, though lacking experience with a sword, knew how to wield a knife. More importantly, the taggles worked in lies and shadows. They understood deception and subterfuge—highly skilled in the art of performance. And, according to rumors, they knew how to kill a man. *Can they kill a god?* Regardless, and though it pained him to admit as much, Maldinado could not imagine a more suitable army to lead in his battle against Morlac; not even the Adarian 45th which had never mastered or even bothered with the art of subtlety.

"And tomorrow," Phinx continued, "Maldinado, will reveal himself as a worshiper of the Sphere."

Maldinado found himself feeling jaded. He sought to raise—and lead—an army, yet Phinx gave the commands. Still, the tailor hesitated to openly question a taggle from Eight Gate whom he suspected...whom he *knew* dabbled in treachery and murder.

Phinx continued, "Once the city hears your declaration, others will question Morlac. They will all choose sides, and then the worshipers of the Sphere will have to emerge from the shadows. Troq will have his revolution...and you will have your army."

"More manipulations by my father?" Inindu could not hold her tongue any longer.

Maldinado watched bemused as Phinx stepped back in sudden fear, "Phinx, meet Inindu, the Sphere's assassin." He felt an admittedly juvenile surge of confidence, for he finally found himself one step *ahead* of the taggle.

"'Tis my sister," Edran grabbed Inindu's warm hand.

"The horse...the horse speaks?" Phinx stared in disbelief.

"I have many talents, taggle."

"Show him the dead," Maldinado suggested.

"I am not a jester performing courtyard tricks for your amusement, tailor. Besides, I cannot. Not since we entered Second Gate. It is enough that he worships the Sphere."

Once again, Maldinado ceded his authority—if not Phinx, then Inindu—leaving him to question his own role in the quest to kill Morlac. *Warrior or tailor, I'm a useless old man.*

"Manipulation, or not," Inindu moved closer to Phinx, pinning him up against the stone wall, placing her nostrils even with his terrified face. Then she slowly and visibly exhaled. Indeed, Maldinado saw strands of lightly tinted magenta breath flow forth from Inindu as though smoke from a pipe. And what she exhaled, Phinx inhaled, seemingly unaware of the gentle exchange of breath. Inindu continued her thought, "It seems I have no choice but to help you, taggle."

Phinx relaxed noticeably, and calmly reached out to stroke the black horse, caressing her forehead, "Such a beautiful creature." He spoke as though waking from a dream, "I'm sorry, what were you saying?"

Maldinado heard chalk scraping against slate. The mute resumed writing, her written message echoing the last words of the suddenly silent horse, "I will help you, taggle."

"And we welcome your assistance. It will take all of us...even this horse of yours, Maldinado."

The tailor stared at Phinx with renewed confusion. *What just happened?*

"What do you be needing from us?" Edran asked.

Phinx stepped away from Inindu, anxiously rubbing his thumbs over fingertips, "Travel toward the outer circles. Tell the taggles we will gather in Third Gate, tonight, after the gates close. I will spread the word here and in the inner circles."

"'Tis faster if we be taking the sewers. Maldinado can take the horse back through Third Circle," Edran pulled at Inindu's hand, but she resisted.

"No," she quickly added, "Take tailor." The topi embraced her horse.

"I think they've been separated long enough," Maldinado motioned, "Lead the way, Edran." Then he turned toward Inindu to offer a final word, "We will alert the taggles, and then meet you in Third Gate. Try and stay out of trouble."

Inindu flicked her tail, striking Maldinado full in the face as he passed.

"May the Sphere protect you," Phinx offered.

Maldinado brushed a strand of horsehair away from his tattooed forehead, "And keep you in his light."

Condemned

Inindu

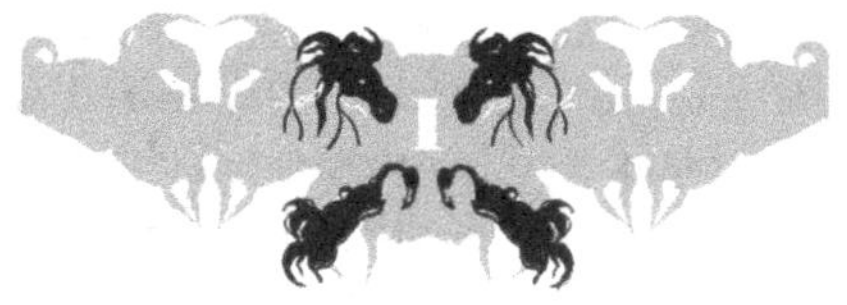

We watch Phinx disappear behind a tent, rejoining the vein of travelers coursing through Fourth Gate. We made a mistake in speaking to the taggle, though he will never recall the encounter for we erased the moment from his memory. He worships our father and, similarly, he fears our beauty. It seems that which Phinx embraces as truth simply blinds him to reality in a different manner, exchanging one illusion—that which Morlac created—for another—the manipulations of my father. First Beah. Now Phinx. Apparently, both prefer a life of ignorance. They will never survive the death of Morlac. The end of this world. Maldinado wants us to reveal Morlac's illusion, but they fear the truth. Phinx believes he exists only in Delacroy. Let him. Would he so eagerly start a revolution if he knew the fate which awaited him?

We leave the secluded area, squeezing between two tents. Men walk this path, not horses. No doubt, they never even considered making it wider. We find such an oversight disconcerting and loathe the rough feel of canvas upon our flawless flanks. We emerge as though a babe from the womb. We emerge as Inindu, made whole once more. Our legs clutch either side of our withers, back touching back, allowing our hair to merge with our tail. We *are* Inindu. Yet, we enter the crowd of travelers as nothing more than an illusion; that of our own doing, not Morlac's. A black horse and a black-haired mute. We hide our beauty. What Phinx and Beah deny, we willingly disguise; for if more taggles or Delcreans discovered the truth…if we revealed our magenta glory…if they heard our horse speak…or saw the dead. No, they *cannot* discover the truth, for they, too, would panic. They would flee from us rather than worship our beauty.

So, we will wear black.

That *they* may remain comfortably blind.

Our topi continues to ride with her back lying upon our horses' back. We watch these Delcreans approach with our horse's vision and watch them depart with our topi's eyes: A jovial man with a hesitant, mostly shuffling gait, whose beard matches the width of his gut, sidesteps us, and continues his dialogue with a sleepy-eyed companion who passes by on the opposite side. Neither one acknowledges our allure. *Not like Adarian. Once, he loved us. He found us beautiful.* A gray-haired woman, hugging a tightly folded, quilted blanket to her depressed chest, follows us, but she never raises her head. She simply walks where we walk, perhaps figuring we offer her some sort of protection from the boisterous crowd. And with good reason, for she can't weigh an ounce more than the blanket she carries. Despite her unspoken belief, however, we cannot save her from a predetermined fate. *We could not save Adarian.* Within moments, the crowd squeezes past our croup and swallows the woman whole.

The Delcreans pay us no more attention than they would an indiscernible rock in a riverbed. They do not concern themselves with our horse, for horses in this city provide their owners no perceptible travel advantage and, admittedly, we walk as slowly as those on foot. Neither do they find reason to engage with our mute, for they seemingly find the simple-minded and maimed unimportant in their quest to prove themselves faithful worshipers of Morlac; worshipers worthy of his favor and boon. *Once, Adarian proved himself. He served his Adow. We were no longer important.* Soon, they will know we are Inindu. They will no longer ignore our presence. But for now, we let them pass.

One such traveler carries a large oil painting, two hands tightly gripping either side of an ornate, golden frame. The painting depicts three persons, two of whom stand cloaked in shadow facing the third, a magenta-haired woman, who wields a bloodied knife. She holds the point downward, drops of red staining a green-linen tablecloth, her focus drawn toward the shadowed figures and an outstretched hand filled with gold and ruby gemstones. A hired assassin receiving her spoils. More than just the obvious reference to our magenta hair, the face of the woman also resembles that of our topi, leaving little doubt as to the identity of the woman. And, as we watch the traveler pass, we discover the painted outline of a horse—a blurred yet distinct magenta—reflected in the assassin's blood-streaked blade. Though clearly stagnant figures on canvas, we find the mirror-like quality slightly disorienting.

Our topi rises from where she lays, assuming a more typical rider-atop-horse position. The crowd remains oblivious, finding nothing unusual about the painting. Just another image of Inindu warding against Inindu. One of several thousand. But they do not see the truth. Beah. Phinx. All of Delacroy and their god.

Blind.

Yet, we wonder if these images truly serve their purpose. Quite literally, they failed to ward off Inindu. But why not depict us as dead, wounded, or suffering? Why not a magenta horse with a severed head? Morlac standing over our mutilated bodies in triumph? No, Delcreans do not brandish talismans meant to protect them from evil. Rather, these images glorify our image. Delcreans, it appears, worship us in their own, ignorant fashion: A reflection in the knife blade. Sculpted magenta horses. Our image decorates everything from baskets to vases and blankets. Reminders of a former life. Revelations of truth. Signs of beauty.

Your people do not worship you, Morlac.

They worship Inindu. Yes, in their blindness, and despite their fear, they worship us.

As they should.

Delacroy

Certainty | Chastity | Fasting | Generosity | Joy | Orthodoxy | Peace | Honesty | Faithfulness

Prior to Inindu's arrival in Delacroy, yes, while Maldinado still lay restless within the city, torchlight revealed the slick dungeon walls against which Lyshmee slunk deep into her knees, shielding her closed eyes. She braced herself for another assault by reciting a portion of *Etiolating Phlogiston*, an ancient text she once translated:

I see the fire that burns. It no longer blinds me, nor am I forced to look away. I can move my arm in and out of the flame as I would an ordinary prong. My arm lingers, but pain does not seize my senses...

Someone thrusted forth a torch, forcing light deeper into the dungeon cavity, illuminating Lyshmee's slight, shivering figure in a far corner. Light brought pain. But the expected attack never transpired. She opened her eyes to discover the lusty swad she awaited did not, in fact, stand at her dungeon door. Indeed, no swad stood anywhere in sight.

Instead, Waylon, a taggle sculptor she recognized from previous visits to Second Gate, stood just inside the doorway. He carried several sheets of parchment and an open leather pouch filled with various pieces of charcoal. She understood the implication. The taggle visited all the condemned prior to their beheading to better study their facial features which he then used to create numerous *Dissemination Poles,* a visual decree proudly displaying his work—a freshly sculpted wooden head—atop a long, ornately decorated pole; and carried like a trophy into the streets of Delacroy pronouncing a beheading—a traditional precursor to the guillotine. Indeed, the taggle's presence meant Lyshmee's death drew near.

Waylon did not bother to close the steel enforced door; did not even bother to remove key from lock. No doubt he realized, as did she, that Lyshmee possessed little ability to run...not this far into her imprisonment...not after so much abuse.

"Morlac's boon upon thee, Lyshmee." Waylon appeared a solid enough figure with thick forearms that resisted the age which had otherwise turned his hair white. He moved with noticeable courage, placing his torch into a brass ring beside the doorway before retreating to the dark corridor to retrieve a small wooden stool. He placed the stool directly in front of Lyshmee and took a seat, though not so close as to block the torchlight that tormented her unaccustomed eyes. She longed for darkness. Light seemingly aroused her senses. The room stank of filth and the sour odor of her unwashed body. Mold grew in the corners, along the edges of the walls, and under the pile of hay meant to serve as a bed.

"I am here to rescue you…in a sense," Waylon positioned the sheets of parchment on his lap and withdrew a stick of charcoal, oddly holding the short, black slab between thumb and pinkie. "That is to say a visit from Waylon often signals a marked improvement in the treatment of his subjects. Of course, you will soon lose your head, but they're not apt to place a wan neck under the guillotine. So, uncurl yourself," Waylon motioned. "You'll have no more clandestine visits from the swads. Unfortunate, really. If you had wound up in any other dungeon…"

Lyshmee slowly raised her head. Resist and he would likely call for the swads.

Waylon made several strokes, "The swads in Second Circle take certain liberties, of course. Not like other dungeons. I've seen them all. Carved more than a few Dissemination Poles in my time. None of the swads would ever damage your head, and I'm grateful for that bit of boon, but they do leave the rest of your body in dour shape. Figure it's on account they cover you up for the ceremony, so they think a few bruises won't matter. Second Circle is the worst, though. Not that I need to convince you," Waylon dug into the paper, pausing in his thoughts. "But all that's done and over with now. You may even come to enjoy your last days. Probably eat better than the magnates."

"I am a scholar," her voice sounded unfamiliar in her own head, more like a husky whisper.

"Your double misfortune, then," Waylon started on a new sheet. "Morlac favors taggles not scholars. Never have they beheaded a taggle. Lift your chin," Waylon pointed upward. "Used to be a time when one of these sketches would take me hours. I captured every detail as I typically would for a painted portrait. But I learned that a block of wood requires fewer details. Like corralling a wild beast. From what Waylon hears it's best to trap the animal unaware than go charging into the forest. A good painter can tame a canvas, yes, but wood remains untamed regardless of skill. For one thing," he pointed again, "Look to your left. For one thing, you must work with the grain. Never know what you'll encounter…not like a canvas where you can add a line wherever you want. Wood brings its own texture…its own detail. May find a pith fleck or something worse. I once ran into a gum pocket right in the middle of the forehead—made

Waylon look like a novice who couldn't handle his chisel."

He shuffled his stack of parchment, "Turn towards the wall. So, Waylon focuses on the lines of his subject's face. The position of his subject's nose and eyes…ears and lips. It's a much faster process, now. Studying for wood. Less time Waylon needs to sit sketching in filth and darkness."

"I am a scholar," Lyshmee spoke the words as though to reassure herself.

After several quick strokes, the taggle replaced his stick of charcoal in the leather pouch. He gathered himself and stood, "I will carve nine versions of your head. Soon enough, every Delcrean will know your face, yet the wood grain will mask your true identity. No one will care that you were once a scholar. They will witness your death, but your life will remain a mystery."

Waylon lifted the small stool and left the room. A moment later, he returned to retrieve his torch, "Morlac's boon upon thee."

"Morlac was a scholar," Lyshmee whispered these words of heresy even as the torchlight faded behind a closing dungeon door. She spoke them, but Waylon did not hear. Nor would anyone listen, she knew, taggle or otherwise, for Delcreans knew nothing of their god prior to the creation of his world. To them, he existed simply as *god*.

Lyshmee knew the truth, however. Morlac did not deserve her worship. He showed her no favor or boon.

"May the Sphere be with me," she cried out in the darkness, "and keep me in his light."

Weeks after visiting Lyshmee, Waylon entered Valun's dungeon chamber holding an open leather pouch filled with charcoal sticks, several sheets of parchment, and a torch. Valun scratched at his beard, ignoring the taggle. Reclined on an overstuffed mattress, he lay reading a thin leather volume: *Etiolating Phlogiston*—an ancient text, translated from original Delcrean by the scholars. Three sconces, ablaze and evenly spaced around the chamber, provided the light by which he read.

"I see the fire that burns," Waylon quoted a familiar passage. Valun turned his attention from the text. The taggle sculptor continued, "It no longer blinds me, nor am I forced to look away. I can move my arm in and out of the flame as I would an ordinary prong. My arm lingers, but pain does not seize my senses…" Waylon deposited his torch in a brass ring beside the open door, "Where would we be without *Etiolating Phlogiston?*"

"It brings comfort in times of trouble," Valun agreed. He spread the book upon his chest and reached for a silver tray at his side which contained cubed cheese and dried dates. Simiad sent along the book and food as an intended gift, though Valun considered them poor substitutes for a razor. His beard seemingly grew longer every minute. *How much longer, Simiad, must I stay in this wretched dungeon?*

Waylon exited the well-lit chamber. Returning with a small stool, placing it beside Valun's mattress, he sat with a sigh, "Some say it also brings trouble in times of comfort."

Valun took measure of the taggle: White hair and thick forearms. No doubt, Waylon, famed sculptor of the condemned. "Some have twisted the words of *Etiolating Phlogiston* for their own purposes," Valun agreed, watching Waylon pull a stick of charcoal out of his leather pouch.

This is happening? Tasa Ro! Simiad!

As the son of a magnate, Valun knew every Delcrean tradition including those typical of a beheading. Learned them to better enforce them. Still, he did not expect a visit from the sculptor, an occurrence of dire portent, for he assumed Simiad would delay the ill-fated carving of a Dissemination Pole. But it appeared Simiad had proven himself dafter than Valun ever imagined.

"I believe it written by one of the first taggles—fire performer, most likely. At any rate, it speaks of a transcendence achieved through art. Something I understand, that is to say, Waylon often experiences similar feelings when he carves the heads of his condemned. Morbid, I know." Waylon began to sketch.

Valun heard charcoal slash across the page. He watched the taggle's arm wiggle and stab with practiced rhythm. "What you achieve through art, I attain when I worship," he selected a date, having already finished most of the cheese, and pictured himself eating Simiad's head as his teeth tore into the shriveled fruit. "Even fire cannot burn me while I worship Morlac."

Waylon smiled, "Morlac? Rumors suggest you worship the Sphere."

Worship the Sphere... The accusation lingered in Valun's ears; the only reason he sat in a dungeon. The perfect execution of his father had somehow left him prisoner rather than magnate—forcing him to eat cheese and dried fruit instead of baked chicken and chopped carrots. Eating through a beard he detested; constantly scratching at his throat, pulling at each whisker—attempting to rid his face of an ever-growing disease.

Worship the Sphere? They dare carry his carved head on a stick? Proclaim his beheading throughout Delacroy? Send Waylon to carve his head? No! The taggle should carve a statue, instead—proclaiming Valun as magnate. Yet Valun wore no ring. His ascension ceremony never occurred. Somehow, even in death, his simpleton father remained magnate. His fool-hearted, dimwitted father still, inconceivably, held him captive.

Worship the Sphere! No! You will no longer mock me.

Valun abandoned his book, grabbed the silver tray—cheese and fruit scattering across mattress and stone floor—and leaped toward the taggle before another stroke of charcoal could sully the parchment. He swung the tray at Waylon's head, brutally connecting with cheekbone and right ear. The taggle fell sideways amid a flurry of flying parchment.

"I do not worship the Sphere!" Valun raised the tray and struck again. And again. He beat him repeatedly until the taggle bled and groaned and eventually passed beyond Ninth Circle. Then, with the silver tray still in his hands, twisted and badly mangled, Valun knelt beside the corpse and delivered a final, meaningless blow, "I am innocent!"

An unfinished sketch lay beside the taggle's outstretched legs. It displayed the face of the condemned: Rigid nose. Protruding forehead. Fierce jaw. And a cursed beard. Valun traced each infuriating line with his wide eyes even as three swads ran into the chamber. They drew their swords, pulling Valun away from the dead taggle.

"Simiad! Simiad!" Valun yelled, "I need a razor, Simiad!"

At the time of his death, Waylon's newest carving, the head of Lyshmee, sat atop a Dissemination Pole. Several red ribbons adorned the pole, flowing downward from the head. A herald carried the carving into Fourth Gate where Inindu glanced at it, briefly, though she traveled in the opposite direction.

The herald cried, "Second Circle!" He need not say anything more, for those who saw the Dissemination Pole understood the intended message.

Delacroy

Troq carried a silver tray through the halls of the manor toward the room where Magnate Simiad still slept, no doubt suffering from a hangover. The tray held Troq's prescribed cure for such a state in the form of a tomato breakfast: tomatoes, onions, cilantro, black pepper, and a touch of clear Delcrean rotgut prepared as an overly chunky soup. For a special treat, the cook had prepared a side of dried apricots coated with powdered sugar. Beside the fruit lay two notes, both written by Narch, Overseer of Fourth Circle, and delivered to the manor by a young swad only moments prior. As head of the household, Troq intercepted the eager swad, explaining the dour state of the magnate and suggesting a more suitably subtle approach which included a morning meal to accompany the news.

In fact, Troq personally delivered all important messages to the members and guests of the manor, as his duties dictated, and took full advantage of the opportunity to read each note—a custom he perfected while serving Magnate Boltmar prior to his death. He utilized a simple process involving a hot knife which he slid under the wax seal, allowing him to later reheat the underside and reseal the notes. Thus, Troq knew the contents of the first note which lay upon the silver tray: Valun requested a razor. And the second note: Narch's detailed report on the murder of Waylon at the hands of Valun.

The cook quietly opened the door to Simiad's darkened room. The magnate still slept, snoring loudly. After a moment, allowing his eyes time to adjust, Troq crossed to a small, empty table to deposit his tray with a louder than called for clink, and then he strode toward a window to fiercely throw open the curtains. Light streamed unmercifully into the room, causing Simiad to pull several blankets up over his cowering head.

"Breakfast sits on the table," Troq crossed the room to leave, "You'll find my food does wonders for that hangover. I will also ask a member of my staff to deliver a bowl of warm water and a fresh towel. Will you have need of anything else, this morning, magnate?"

A pillow muffled Simiad's foul response.

Troq bowed and exited the room, smiling as he went. It appeared the magnate did not remember his prior evening's request to fetch

Maldinado—the fortunate result of too much wine—neither did he recall sending Edran in search of the hobbled tailor. More importantly, news of Valun killing Waylon meant Simiad would likely ignore any further requests from the hot-headed young fool and return to Second Circle, leaving Troq alone to rule the manor.

Tilly crashed into him as he turned a corner. She carried an armful of carefully folded linens that reached above her head and skewed her vision. She fell to the ground even as they both struggled to salvage the suddenly airborne laundry, failing miserably in the effort. Troq stood dumbfounded above the shaken servant, remembering his promise to Edran. He failed to understand what attracted the boy to this clumsy little girl. Still, he acted with measured compassion, kneeling beside her to help gather the linens.

"Forgive me, Master Troq," Tilly scrambled to assist. "I didn't see you there."

"Likely, you couldn't see anything. You're carrying too tall a stack." He turned her chin with a gentle touch, ensuring he held her full attention, "You must see the path in front of you, or risk the destination. Come, we will each carry half."

He helped the flustered girl to her feet and led the way to a storage closet where they placed the recovered and refolded linens on a wooden shelf. Then he quickly sent her off to the kitchen to help with supper preparations. He followed after the girl, albeit at an intentional and much slower pace. Thus, he arrived at the kitchen several minutes later, only to discover Tilly cleaning up the remains of another mess, a broken egg this time, and under the watchful glares of both Merrudi and Myrtane. The two women cared for the yearling like two exasperated mothers: patient enough to coddle, yet desperate enough to strangle. Troq left them to their shared moment and retrieved what remained of the dried apricot dessert he had served Simiad, wrapping several of the delectable wedges in wax paper before continuing on through the kitchen to the courtyard beyond.

He followed a stone path to his room, retrieving and lighting his pipe upon arrival. Troq enjoyed smoking his pipe after serving the midday meal. Yes, *midday* meal, second of the day, though Simiad, no doubt, thought his day just begun. Troq did not approve of laggards. They irritated him. Even Valun, for all his faults, never slept so late as to miss first meal.

He bit down on the pipe with jagged teeth and sat at a wooden desk where he placed the wax enclosed apricot wedges. From his desk drawer he pulled a small lockbox made from polished red stone. Brass hinges matched the decorative lock. He placed the box next to the fruit; then stood to retrieve a book from the shelf above his bed: *Ingredients Discovered in San Riena*. A brass key tied to a thin red cord marked a passage which discussed the many culinary uses for birmly weed: thickener, being the most common. But the book also touched on the less widely known effects birmly weed produced when combined with other ingredients... such as apricots.

Troq set book on desktop and used the brass key to open the lockbox. Inside lay a collection of vials containing powders of various colors and quantity. Individually, the ingredients remained dormant, but mixed properly the powder would activate, turning as lethal as any poison. His calloused hands selected a vial of crushed birmly weed, white in color. He opened the vial and added two pinches to the apricot confection as though adding a sprinkling of powdered sugar. A fine disguise for a deadly treat.

Replacing the vial, Troq leaned back and pulled pipe from mouth. He licked the remaining, harmless powder from his fingers, savoring the piquant flavor of the finely ground birmly weed, and felt an undeniable sense of pride knowing it would enhance the tart dessert, providing his intended victim a sharp taste before death. Every cook in Delacroy embraced the finer aspects of murder. Not like Valun. Based on the rumors Troq had heard, the savage boy struck his father's body as though a butcher carving a pig. Worse. And without skill. No, murder required restraint—carefully selected ingredients and just the right amount of powder.

Troq returned key to book, book to shelf, and lockbox to desk drawer. He knocked the ashes from his pipe into a yellow glass jar he kept on the desk for such purposes and re-wrapped the suddenly malignant confection. Then he rose and left the room.

Lomax packed his straight, black pipe with a pinch of fresh sarlin root, tapping it down with a crooked thumb. Bits of the root slid under his overgrown thumbnail, joining several lodged bits from previous smoking sessions. Having no means of lighting the pipe, however, he surveyed the bustling marketplace until he spotted Darrol, a young boy whom he and the other merchants relied upon for various tasks. He caught his attention and curtly waved him closer.

The boy stood bare-chested underneath an orange maldinado-robe—a single black stripe encircling each arm served as the only design.

He kept his hair short, but it grew wildly along a series of scars which ran from his left eyebrow to just behind the ear. A clouded left eye, pupil white as a pearl, caused him to overturn his head whenever beckoned. Though obviously mauled by a beast at some point in his life, perhaps as an infant, Darrol had yet to confirm the rumor, or simply didn't recall. In truth, the yearling rarely spoke, certainly never enough to carry a conversation, nor did he speak well. Still, Morlac had shown the boy favor, sorting him into Fourth Circle where charity, in the form of gold paid by the generous though over-demanding merchants, kept him clothed and fed.

"Bring me Strade's candle, yearling," Lomax pointed toward the candle merchant who kept a vigilant candle. "I work better when I have a pipe between my teeth."

The yearling nodded and disappeared into the crowded marketplace.

Lomax, back in his customary position at the head of a row of several greedy merchants, and positioned closest to Fourth Gate, had already sold several dozen baskets that morning. But midday swayed most of the travelers toward food merchants, providing Lomax a much-anticipated lull. Reaching behind the merchant's cart, therefore, he retrieved a short stool along with bodkin, clippers, sheathed dagger, and a bushel of orange-tinted willow rods still damp from days of soaking. Denam wove *his* baskets with reed, but Lomax preferred willow, allowing him to produce much stronger baskets. He stared down the row of merchants along the north wall of Fourth Circle, searching for Denam, but the rival basket maker remained unseen behind the gathered throng of travelers. Nevertheless, Lomax smiled at the knowledge that anyone visiting Denam's cart that day would have already purchased their basket from Lomax.

Darrol returned with Strade's candle.

Lomax lit the sarlin root with a tilt of his pipe, "Favor and boon…" But he found himself unable to recall the boy's name.

Unaware, or unconcerned about the old man's fading memory, the boy had already run off to return the candle, or perhaps, to complete another task for a different merchant. They took turns paying the boy for his work, handing him two gold pieces at the end of each day, though Lomax rarely paid from his own pocket—relying instead upon the lifted generosity of his fellow Delcreans. His hands served him well even if his mind seemingly grew cloudier with each passing hour.

Darrol. Lomax suddenly remembered. *His name is Darrol.*

Oddly fatigued by the effort to recall such an inconsequential name, Lomax turned his attention, once more, to the willow rods, selecting six rods and his bodkin. This task, much to his relief, did not require thought.

His well-trained fingers wove themselves in and around the rods as he bored, pushed, and pulled the willow into the beginnings of a basket. Soon enough, a pattern emerged, and Lomax found himself transfixed by the mind-numbing process.

"Morlac's boon upon thee, Lomax," Tannessa's unmistakable voice broke his rhythm.

"Favor and boon," Lomax carefully moved his gaze from willow rod to the swad's swollen foot and back to willow rod. He found the sight of her foot—shoved into a burlap slip-shoe as though a furry mole attempting to scurry underground—quite amusing, but he did not smile at risk of insulting the woman, his younger cousin.

"No doubt you've heard of Waylon's murder?"

Lomax raised his gaze and withdrew his pipe, "The sculptor? I knew Valun murdered a taggle, but I didn't have a name. Why would he kill Waylon?"

"Unknown," she shrugged her broad shoulders. "He worships the Sphere. I imagine he would kill us all if given the chance."

Lomax returned to his weaving, "Does that alter the schedule?"

"No, we are still waiting for Morlac. Nothing will happen until then."

"Did you make the arrangements?" Lomax pulled a smaller rod through a bored slot in all six of the original rods.

"It seems the Overseer remains partial to denam-baskets," she replied.

He expected the response, for Lomax often engaged in treacherous dealings. He knew, in fact, it would take another three payments, at least, before Tannessa would *make the arrangements*. He could almost taste the sugar-sweetened sweat coating her all too eager fingers.

"I've tried to convince him, otherwise," she assured him.

Lomax paused in his weaving, reached back to rummage momentarily within the bushel of willow rods, finally emerging with a small leather pouch filled with…with… What? He realized it must contain gold coins, though he did not recall ever placing the pouch in the bushel; nor did he understand why he now held it in his hand. Whether or not she noticed his hesitation, however, Tannessa did not wait for his memory to return. Upon seeing the pouch, she promptly leaned forward on her swollen feet and slyly snatched the offered payment.

Lomax emerged from his momentary daze, recovering enough to continue the verbal exchange, a critical component of any bribe, "The head of a magnate is too heavy for a reed basket."

"That's what I keep telling him."

He struggled to recall how many payments he had already provided his young cousin, grasping unsuccessfully at fluttering thoughts. The entire exchange felt familiar, but the feeling failed to produce a tangible memory. He forced himself to focus. *Focus!* He could not afford such a worthless mind. The loss of gold, yes, but more than wealth he worried about losing his reputation. Delcreans devoured dimwitted fools, Tannessa more than any other. The woman cared little about family relations, and Lomax held few doubts she would sell him to an unwashed stranger if they offered her enough gold. What chance did Lomax have against such a force if he could not trust his own mind?

No! He tossed his fears aside, refusing to accept weakness in himself. Never again would he allow someone to take advantage of him the way… the way… *Jasper.* How he longed to forget *that* name. Many years ago, the older scoundrel betrayed a young Lomax. Jasper offered a simple scheme, and the promise of life in the Ninth Circle, but he also demanded more gold than Lomax had ever paid. The price forced him to steal from all his friends, including Maldinado—though the tailor never discovered the truth. In the end, only Jasper received an invitation to Ninth Circle, however, leaving Lomax poor and alone. In that moment, youthful hope turned to aged cynicism, and Lomax resolved to never again play the fool.

"I trust you will eventually convince the Overseer, otherwise?" Rumors suggested Tannessa often bested magnates, and even the Adherent. Only greed prevented her from persuading the Overseer, a simpleton by any measure.

"Naturally," Tannessa took her leave without the customary courtesies.

Lomax did not watch her leave, instead, his gaze turned toward Darrol who emerged from the crowd if only for a brief moment. The half-blind boy stared at the ground as though confused, unable to remember his errand—unable to act on his own behalf. Did Lomax rate any better? Would he find himself, one day, fetching candles to light the pipes of other merchants? Serving everyone and anyone willing to lend him a coin? The boy disappeared, no doubt recalling his task.

Lomax spat. He just needed to focus.

Tasa Ro! Focus, you old fool!

But the thought felt heavy and made him weary, so he turned his attention to the beginnings of a basket in his hands—one meant to catch Valun's head. One final, grand scheme. Surely, Morlac would take notice, and the Adherent would invite him to live in Ninth Circle.

Thankfully, his fingers wove the willow rods together without the need for thought. Only a single image filled his head: Jasper's dead body. Lomax had hired a taggle to kill the wretched man a few years after his betrayal, and the basket weaver had no intention of letting anyone get the best of him, again.

Troq sat waiting for Tannessa as she waddled up to her home. She often encountered a visitor upon her return from the dungeon; so frequent an occurrence, in fact, she placed a wooden chair against the wall just inside the doorway, allowing her usually apprehensive visitors a relatively comfortable place to wait. Shady dealings, she noticed, made most men squirm—sweat pooling in tiny forehead wrinkles, or cutting deep grooves around their quivering lips. Tannessa never understood their apparent distaste for disreputable affairs. She considered Delcrean schemes a practical matter and, certainly, a better option for amassing wealth than some misguided faith in Morlac's favor and boon. She knew too many of the powerful, and even the lowly decision makers to believe Delacroy rewarded the pious, nor did she cling to any aspirations of reaching Ninth Circle. Fourth Circle served her purposes much better, granting her easy access to most of the city's population as they traveled to and from the marketplace—those with gold, at least. Besides, over half the residents living in Ninth Circle routinely sent her gifts of the best wines and delectable foods available in all of Delacroy. Yes, she could garner an invitation to that most glorious of circles with but a single word, for she knew which secrets to flaunt when she wanted something specific. But, really, why bother? Tannessa lived a pleasant life and wanted for nothing.

Her visitors, on the other hand, always wanted something.

She recognized Troq, a kindly-faced cook, from her many visits to the magnate's manor. Magnate Boltmar had need of her services from time to time; and Valun, his devious son, more often. This served as the first time she had dealt with Troq directly, however.

He sat peacefully, as though lounging under the shade of a tree, and upon his lap he held a wax-paper package. Whatever this man wanted, Tannessa reasoned it a simple enough request, for he looked anything but skittish. Or, more probably, he had grown accustomed to dealing in secrets. For all her power, Tannessa suspected the cooks of Delacroy far more adept in tactics of manipulation.

"Morlac's boon upon thee," Troq began in greeting.

"Favor and boon."

Tannessa moved past him and through the door opening, and then proceeded toward a wide, open cupboard that stood against the outer wall of her front room not far from a thick, wooden table large enough to seat twelve good-sized swads. She pulled out a dark bottle and popped the cork, and then took a swig of the red wine contained within—never bothering to offer her visitor a taste. Her duties as hostess did not extend beyond the chair at her front door.

"How is my master, Valun?"

"Information is easy enough to obtain in Fourth Circle," she took another drink. "You must already know the answer to that question."

"Indeed," Troq dispensed with further pleasantries, no doubt eager to return to the responsibilities awaiting him back in his kitchen. "I would like for you to deliver this package to one of your prisoners. A taggle named Beah."

She eyed the package, "Food?"

"An apricot confection," Troq nodded.

"Poisoned?"

"Cream cheese and powdered sugar."

His response confirmed her suspicions about Delcrean cooks. Troq appeared far too comfortable standing there with both hands extending the well-wrapped and, most assuredly, deadly dessert. She set the bottle of wine on the table, suddenly realizing how easily the cook could have poisoned *her*. The lack of a front door meant he had access to her home, so nothing prevented him from rummaging through the wine cupboard prior to her arrival. Of course, he wanted something from her, so the notion made no sense. Still, she found herself wishing for a more anxious patron, realizing for the first time that a calm outward demeanor made her feel surprisingly unsettled. Even her cousin, Lomax, for all his experience in such matters, displayed an appropriate level of uncertainty when enlisting her services. This man, however, may well have held an unpeeled potato in his hands for all the concern he showed as he stood there holding the poisoned delight.

Nevertheless, she resisted his overture, "Delcreans don't like it when a prisoner dies before their scheduled beheading." Tannessa stiffened, she would not allow emotions to interfere with her machinations, "It will cost you three-hundred gold."

He withdrew, and then extended a small leather pouch, "As head of the magnate's manor, at least until my master returns, I have ample funding."

She took the package and accepted his payment, though judging by the weight, she knew the pouch did not contain more than 50 gold pieces.

"You will receive the rest in full when I hear word of Beah's death," Troq took his leave.

Tannessa thought better of voicing any protest. She typically worked under more favorable terms: half up front. At a minimum. But poison in the hands of a cook truly frightened her. Tannessa liked to eat...and drink, so she swallowed her outcry lest she find herself digesting a pinch of powdered death.

Delcrean Council

Certainty | Chastity | Fasting | Generosity | Joy | Orthodoxy | Peace | Honesty | Faithfulness

Shale, Adherent of Delacroy, finished reading the carelessly composed request—individual characters overtly curved, each point extending far beyond the standard length and written with an elegant flair which he found detestable. The circumstances called for a more formally crafted request which, in matters of politics, Shale preferred. But Valun possessed an uncouth hand, having only recently assumed the title of magnate. Still...

Did Boltmar teach you nothing?

The disapproving Adherent carefully refolded the letter and quite intentionally dropped it over the railing. It fluttered with all the grace of an injured moth, and he wiped at his fingers as if to remove lingering wing dust. Shale stood upon a small, wrap-around balcony overlooking the sun-drenched Delacroy. The protruding structure, composed of a crushed ruby floor and matching railing, a balcony of uncommon beauty and height, offered a rare full view of the orbicular city below.

Strange that you chose the shape of a sphere for your city, Morlac.

He often directed inner dialogue toward his god without expectation of response. Though, he wouldn't mind an explanation concerning the shape of Morlac's city, a thought he regularly repeated whenever he looked out from the balcony. A meditation, he knew, that arose from doubt. Indeed, Shale shared all his doubts with Morlac. No one outranked the habitual Adherent, so only his god could adequately address any misgivings. In return for his honesty, Morlac entrusted Shale with...

The adherent forced the thought from his mind before it fully formed. Instead, he stared out across the faithfully blind and unsuspecting city. Shadows that stretched out from each of the nine walls remained ever visible during the day, shifting with the sun and giving the city the look of a giant sundial. The ruby palace served as the gnomon—an unseen oddity unless one viewed Delacroy from such a height and from that particular balcony.

Shale watched as the sun approached the far horizon, immersing the city in shadow.

What would they do if they knew your secret, Morlac? If they knew our *secret?*

He considered delaying his duty until morning—a justifiable response to such a garish letter. But Valun stood accused of worshiping the Sphere and, according to Delcrean law, only Morlac could condemn the newly appointed magnate. Any delay on Shale's part equaled a passing of judgment and would inadvertently place him above Morlac, so he felt compelled to act quickly. Despite how mangled the request, therefore, it fell well within Valun's fleeting power to ask that Morlac attend his beheading ceremony and there decide the magnate's fate.

Shale left the balcony with somewhat forced urgency, two distinct lengths of white fabric trailing behind him like mist. Normally, he preferred the ethereal-like presence of the yiddick-shawl to the heavier, tighter-fitting maldinado-robe, though in this moment he casually questioned his garment choice even while he gathered the meandering material, wrapping it around his arm to better enable brisk movement through the palace.

The sun would soon set.

Once inside the palace, Shale traveled along well-crafted ruby corridors, passing hundreds of empty, adjoining rooms with unadorned walls. The interior resembled a glorified cave. Brightly lit, though. The cool air seemingly emanated natural light—Morlac's light—negating the need for torches during even the darkest hours. A useless light, for most of the rooms sat void of any furniture or decoration, and few people roamed the echo-ridden halls though Shale, per his custom, traveled to the highest balcony each day at sundown. Indeed, though he once thought the palace full of residents back when he viewed it from the city below, in truth, only three rooms displayed the scarcest signs of life. The first served as part-time living quarters for Shale containing bedroll, bucket, and a small wooden chest. The other two rooms...

Again, he forced the thought from his mind.

Shale paused in his journey, listening for an echo or any other sound along the hallway. Nothing save his own chest which heaved incessantly. He traveled alone and several floors above the palace staff. High above his god who suffered constant and great agony in the deepest portion of the inner tower. The adherent placed a stabilizing hand upon the crushed ruby wall, each red shard painstakingly fitted together and polished until even the tiniest of grooves disappeared to the touch—leaving an illusion of fractures. He slid his hand sideways along the wall, squeaking as he went...burning his palm. He could not feel a single crack. What the eye detected, his fingers failed to touch. He leaned his forehead against the perfect ruby wall and closed his eyes. How long had he served as

Adherent? How many nascient? How many times had Shale presented Morlac to Delacroy? *I am the keeper of your secrets.*

Shale's predecessor, T'thay, appointed him Adherent, and he initially embraced the opportunity, the highest appointment afforded Delcreans, with great enthusiasm and hope. T'thay did not live long enough to serve as mentor, but he did impart a few strands of wisdom; and when T'thay revealed those secrets, he shattered Shale's hopes as thoroughly as the facade of ruby along the palace walls. Hope then faded to memory, a memory that dwindled with each passing year. And in that moment, standing there with his moist breath forming a retracting film upon the wall, Shale knew for certain the cause of T'thay's death. His predecessor had finally lost all hope. Only doubt remained.

But then... Valun wants to see you, doesn't he? Morlac must be seen *by his people.*

He resumed his journey: One of duty which propelled Shale through the empty palace. He traveled hallways that wound downward at a modest grade. Then, he climbed a stairwell which took him deeper into the palace corridors, an unnecessary detour, really, but it allowed him to bypass the staff quarters. Soon after, he descended a long staircase. It encircled a stone tower located at the center of the palace...the very heart of Delacroy. Secrets. Lies.

The stairs led to a large, wooden door hung on four iron hinges, two on either side of the door, making it all but impossible to open from either side. Lacking both the traditional lock and a visible handle the door served neither as entrance nor exit. A small iron panel, concealing the only opening in the oppressive door, provided the only means of verbal communication between Shale and his impotent god. Still clinging to the gathered fabric of his yiddick-shawl, therefore, Shale used his free hand to slide the panel back. He looked through the hole, gazing skyward toward an opening in the tower within. Despite his hesitation in the hallway, he had managed to arrive moments before sunset.

Shale waited.

The iron felt cool against his palm. Iron panel. Wooden door. He stood on a squared landing where the stairs ended, forcing the traveler to turn left toward the door or return to the floors above. A staircase between two towers. The tower behind him formed from crushed and polished rubies. The one he faced, red stone. Only a sliver of space separated stone from ruby where they converged within an inch of the doorframe. That the first taggle chose to encase his god in stone rather than ruby served as another lingering meditation for Shale.

A tomb within a tomb?

Darkness brought a moth. It landed on the thin ledge of the opening from which Shale peered. It turned toward him and the emanating light beyond. Shale waited expectantly. A moment later the moth lifted in flight—beckoned by the wretched, unyielding presence of Morlac who stood at the center of the stone tower. The last moth…the one that would brush against Morlac's tongue before returning to the stone walls. Inhale. Moths. Exhale. Moths. A moment between when Morlac could hear with his own ears. All the time allotted to Shale.

Inhale.

"Magnate Boltmar is dead," he spoke quickly, clearly, and with confidence. "His son, Valun stands accused of worshiping the Sphere. He requests your presence at the beheading. Your counsel will determine Valun's fate."

Exhale.

The moth returned and crawled toward the opening. Shale slammed the iron panel back into place. A shiver ran up his arm. He hated the fluttering insects—imagined them swarming around his neck as he mounted the stairs. Still, he made the ascent slowly, for his next task offered no solace.

Simiad slept.

Several hours earlier, after drawing the curtains with belabored irritation, and consuming an admittedly delicious breakfast left behind by the otherwise insolent cook, the Second Circle magnate had promptly returned to the plush mattress where he fell back to sleep.

He awoke with a congested snort and lay there deciding whether he should return to his slumber, pruning the underside of his beard, dried and cracked fingers periodically emerging through thick tufts of hair like scar-riddled boar tusks. He stretched his toes, and then scooted himself several inches further down in the bed. It took him several more attempts before he finally touched the brass baseboard.

So, this is how other magnates live?

At his side lay a pair of spectacles, and under them two notes he had tossed upon the bed earlier without a trace of curiosity. He pulled the spectacles closer, lifting and dragging them across his face like an anchor that awkwardly hooked under chin, and then nose, before finally sliding into place. He felt around for the first note, using a line of light that streamed in from a slit in the curtains to read Valun's request for a razor blade. He sent it fluttering to the polished stone floor. Simiad turned his attention to the second note: News of Waylon's death. He also sent this note twirling to the floor. The magnate lifted the spectacles, allowing his listless hand to fall away.

He needed a drink.

Long before magnate titles and cheap wine, ambition fueled his every step. Indeed, a once chaste and sober worshiper of Morlac traveled to Delacroy the day after he turned thirteen, the age of passage for those seeking to enter their names into the Sorting. The young Simiad left his parents behind on the farm they tended in Rawlis, where he imagines they still live. After only one pilgrimage, he found himself sorted into Second Circle where he proceeded to learn and follow each of the male-specific tenants with meticulous care: Refrain from copulation. Avoid eye contact with a woman. Limit verbal engagement with women. Cover all limbs. Only eat food prepared by a man, and only consume the meat of a male beast. Limit personal study to the work of male scholars. Conduct business with male merchants. The list seemed endless, but the faithful Simiad thought it did not include *enough* tenants, so he added: Never sit in a chair where a woman last sat. And, for a time, he even went so far as to avoid brushing against women while he traveled the streets of Delacroy, but he abandoned this self-imposed stipulation when he fully realized the nearly impossible task of identifying a traveler's gender prior to an encounter. Too many traveled with their head down; or simply appeared out of nowhere as the crowd shielded their identity until they emerged beside him. Still, he did what he could, generally walking along the outside edges of the street to reduce the total number of times he inadvertently touched a woman.

His virtue soon turned into reputation, and then recognition replaced reputation. The thirteen-year-old pilgrim morphed into a thirty-one-year-old resident who caught the attention of Magnate Turnac. Simiad received an invitation to dine at the magnate's table, though they seated him at the far end and furthest from the magnate. Slowly, the ambitious newcomer displaced each of the residents seated ahead of him at the table until, at last, he sat at Turnac's right hand. So, it happened, when Turnac passed beyond Ninth Circle, Adherent Shale appointed Simiad the new magnate of Second Circle.

Soon afterward, the new leader received a request from Magnate Galeab asking that he hand-select and promptly deliver a virgin to his palace estate, for the magnate wished to "properly celebrate the occasion of Simiad's appointment." Simiad sent a note of strong protest directly to the Adherent, denouncing Galeab's request as repulsive and blasphemous, but Shale responded with an order that Simiad fulfill Galeab's request. In that moment, Simiad's faith turned to disillusionment. Several nights later, he sent a young virgin to Ninth Circle. She bubbled over with delight, of course, for Delcreans longed to one day receive an invitation to live in Ninth Circle. He watched her leave, forcing himself to gaze upon every inch of her fully covered body. Then he sent her off to *paradise*. Simiad imagined her screams when she discovered the horror that awaited her in Galeab's palace, and in that moment, he realized his new role did not grant him any real power.

He returned to his palace and poured a glass of wine.

Three years later, he simply pulled the cork and drank from a bulbous bottle. He sat on the edge of the mattress, his right foot resting upon one of two discarded notes. Brought up from Magnate Boltmar's cellar, Simiad took time to savor the swallow of tart, red wine. He detected a hint of spice in the aftertaste—the difference between a Fourth Circle wine and that of Second Circle.

He stood and walked across the mostly darkened room toward the curtains and lifted them with an effort, his other hand still clinging to the bottle. Sunset approached. Simiad let the heavy material fall back into place and blindly navigated his way across the room to the doors. Kome, Second Circle Post, stood just outside ready to attend his master.

"Magnate Simiad?" Kome's weathered voice aged his otherwise youthful features.

"Ready my carriage."

"At once," Kome bowed with a pause, awaiting further instruction. "And Valun?"

"No need to respond."

Simiad closed the door, knowing Kome would move hastily. He did not require additional information. Posts served as personal messengers of the magnates, selected for their *lack* of curiosity. He took another swig from Boltmar's wine. Then, abruptly, he threw the bottle across the room. It struck the small table, scattering his breakfast dishes, before falling with a loud clank onto the polished floor. It remained fully intact, failing to shatter. He could hear gurgles of wine spilling onto the floor—an altogether unsatisfying outcome.

Simiad turned and opened the door, once more, yelling down the hall toward the already departing Kome, "Wait! Send a note to Narch. No more razor blades for Valun. And let the guillotine fall upon his bearded head."

"Inverted?" Kome asked, unable to keep surprise from his voice.

"Yes, inverted! He worships the Sphere, and now I find out he murdered a taggle. The bastard doesn't deserve any of the customary dignities afforded the accused, nor certainly, those given to a magnate."

Kome bowed and departed.

I only pray he dies with his eyes open. Simiad closed the door. He licked his lips and turned, feeling his way through the darkness—crawling on the floor until his outstretched hand gratefully gripped the unharmed bottle of wine. He raised it to his mouth and drank what remained, celebrating his liberation from the petulant son of Boltmar.

Maldinado

Certainty | Chastity | Fasting | Generosity | Joy | Orthodoxy | Peace | Honesty | Faithfulness

Maldinado looked out upon the colorful gathering of scoundrels. Taggles. Thieves and murderers, and the most talented artisans in all Delacroy. An odd combination, but few residents ever witnessed the darker aspects of the true-born, and those who did wound up dead or otherwise found themselves the focus of a gruesome plot. The warrior within Maldinado noted how comfortably they moved—nimble and alert like deer grazing on a mountainside, yet deadly as a panther on the hunt. But the tailor side of him felt uneasy, for more than one of the taggles measured him, even those whom he recognized, an unwelcome though familiar face in their midst. He found mistrust in their eyes, if also a general lack of concern. They seemingly and universally determined that an old man and the diminutive mute beside him would offer little challenge should they have reason to act. Still, Maldinado felt certain that his life lay solely in the hands of the taggle boy, Edran, who sat between he and Inindu and just off the tailor's shoulder swinging his legs from a wooden stage as though completely unaware of any tension in the air. The boy's presence served to vouch for the only two intruders at the taggle gathering.

This spark of fear ignited Maldinado's spirits. Admittedly, he had doubted their ability to rescue Lyshmee. But taggle reputation combined with surprise would likely garner them an advantage and enough time to properly save the woman, for Maldinado suspected none of the swads would eagerly engage in battle with a taggle for fear of a blade to the gut—whether during the skirmish, or afterward while they slept. *Taggles protect their own.* Every resident in Delacroy knew the saying. Truly, only a fool would dare threaten let alone kill a taggle for risk of rousing the ire of the greater collective.

And I am a great fool. Maldinado touched his aching hip. *No chance I will survive this revolution.* Another taggle arrived, wearing a leather jerkin dyed blue with hessup leaf and oddly flexing thick fingers, and promptly gave him a calloused look as he passed. *I may not survive the night.* He laughed at the thought despite his discomfort. *You'd like that, wouldn't you, Lomax? You can tell Muriel how you outlasted me and grin all the wider when you tell her the part about how the "hobbled fool went charging into a den of assassins," then smugly add, "I knew he would find a way to lose the wager."* Maldinado sighed with the realization that his friend would doubtless win. Then he grinned at another thought. *Lomax will soon join the battle.* And, after all, someone must stand along the front line. *I may not survive, but I will not die before you, old man!*

"What I wouldn't give for five hundred more taggles," Maldinado muttered absently even as Phinx took the stage opposite and directly in front of where the tailor and his two friends stood. "Or five thousand..."

Edran shook his head, "It only be requiring the talents of a few taggles to entertain the masses..." The boy left the thought unfinished, distracted by a gouge in one of the planks comprising the stage.

The tailor nodded. *Only a few assassins to kill a god in his sleep.* Shadow warfare. Unfamiliar warfare. Maldinado understood power and strength in numbers. He knew how to seize a city with an army, their well-polished armor glinting between flames and smoke as they penetrated the walls. But given a hundred thousand of the finest trained warriors, such a force would never break through the nine circles of Delacroy to reach Morlac. They would never reach the ruby palace. This assault required stealth and schemes.

"Feeling like Madar?" Inindu wrote upon her slate board—rider sitting beside Edran on the otherwise empty stage; majestic horse within arm's reach.

"Thinking like one..." Maldinado replied. "Tomorrow, after we rescue Lyshmee, we will find ourselves in Second Circle while Morlac remains safe behind the walls of his ruby palace—we may as well try to assault the city from Dragon's Torment for all the threat we will pose from Second Circle. Dragon's Torment..." Maldinado recalled fighting alongside Hintor, "Not the worst of plans. At least then we would have an army."

"And you'd be much younger," Edran picked at a loose chunk of wood with his fingers.

"Young and useful," Maldinado nodded with unconscious agreement. Then, realizing what the taggle just said, he turned to glare at the boy. He well understood his physical limitations. He certainly did not need any more reminders.

As if the aged and broken body that served as his own private dungeon did not hinder him enough within Morlac's illusion, the city itself conspired against him—hunting him. Well, not really. True, Magnate Simiad sent Edran to fetch the tailor back to Fourth Circle for questioning, but Maldinado knew Simiad's penchant for drinking. No doubt, the lowly magnate had already forgotten his sending Edran anywhere to fetch anyone. Still, Maldinado felt uncomfortable, uneasy, and completely out of his element. Useless, and now a liability. Every aspect of the pending battle felt *off*.

"The point is," Maldinado continued, "we've chosen the wrong circle to start a revolution. Better to stage a rescue further into the city; rescue someone like Penrem. Yes! Penrem over Lyshmee. Suitable enough for our purposes and practically adjacent to Morlac's palace."

"Except Penrem 'tis not be losing his head," Edran countered.

"Lucky bastard," Maldinado casually slipped into the familiar Adarian 45th warrior's curse, spoken whenever they found the banner bearer still standing—and standing out—upon the battlefield.

"Not Penrem," Inindu erased the words and quickly scratched, "Morlac at Valun's death. Drawn to Fourth Circle."

Maldinado leaned heavily against the wooden stage, watching Phinx address the gathered taggles. The scarf enthusiast spoke ardently to the gathered taggles, though Maldinado barely heard a word above his own thoughts, "Yes, Morlac will attend Valun's beheading. But we may all wind-up dead before then..."

"'Tis the reason you be starting a revolution," Edran said. "The Sons and Daughters of Oblation be rising to stand with us against Morlac."

"That's something else I've been thinking about," Maldinado placed his hand on Edran's feet to stop the constant swinging motion. The restless boy only adding to his own anxiety, "Morlac won't leave his palace if we start a revolution. Which means we will *still* have to fight every swad in Delacroy if we have any hope of killing their god."

"He will come," Inindu wiped the slate with her sleeve, chalk flaking downward in a mist that frosted her simple black gown. "Pride will draw him out."

"Yes," Maldinado considered the idea. "A deadly thing, pride."

The three of them fell silent, turning their attention to the scene before them. Phinx, though a less than gifted orator, unlike some taggles, nevertheless commanded respect and spoke with a passion that elicited several head nods from the crowd, and his quick wits enabled him to divert raised objections. Maldinado found him altogether impressive, really. And the mood of the crowd seemed more favorable, in his estimation, than when they had first entered. At least, none of the taggles continued to cast the tailor a wary look. Instead, they turned their full attention toward the impassioned painter.

Pride...and taggles.

"Deadly," Maldinado continued his train of thought, "and not just for Morlac." He scratched at his scalp as though digging for ideas, "Saving Lyshmee does not alone qualify as an act of defiance. If we want a revolution, we have to capture the swads. And we must kill them. Preferably, a public execution. Delcreans must understand the choice we put before them: Morlac or the Sphere."

Edran nodded, "Only a god be defeating another god."

Inindu snorted, "I kill Morlac. Father can't." The creature seemed pleased with herself as she underlined the last word.

"The Sphere sent *us* to kill him," Maldinado agreed. "So, it is up to us to get Morlac's attention."

At that moment, Phinx pointed toward the back of the crowd and invited Maldinado to take the stage, prompting the tailor's...no, the Madar's portion of the evening. "May the Sphere be with us," Maldinado muttered as he started forward.

"And keep us in his light," Edran's eager voice trailed behind the Madar.

Maldinado glanced back at the boy. Not surprisingly, he had resumed swinging his feet, unable to contain his excitement. *What I wouldn't give for an ounce of that energy.* But nothing remained of the once young and proud warrior except Maldinado's mind...and his ability to command. He clung to both as he moved through the suddenly sneering crowd toward the stage that awaited.

Moments earlier, Phinx faced the crowd of taggles. His brothers and sisters. They stared at him. Indeed, he felt no better than Lyshmee, the condemned captive he hoped to convince them to rescue. Of course, the wooden stage from which *he* spoke did not possess a guillotine, nor did he have reason to fear death in that moment. Still, the thought brought little comfort to the painter-turned-revolutionary. Yes, travelers often watched him paint—a display of sorts—but whether they watched or not, Phinx need only focus on his canvas. He never saw the faces of those who gathered. But standing in front of the taggles that night, he held no brush in his hand and no canvas upon which to work. Phinx struggled to breathe. He loosened the already slack, red scarf from around his neck as though suffocating.

Everyone stared at him—stared...stared...waiting for him to speak.

Fool! Coward! Have you turned the craven?

He saw Jennaween standing off to the side, a short distance away from the gathering, but she held no sympathy. She danced, and as a dancer, she routinely performed in front of large crowds—always fearless. That's what Phinx loved about her. Unyielding fearlessness. Her presence caused him to smile and infused his voice with confidence.

"When Morlac created the world," Phinx paused, drawing the crowd's full attention as adeptly as any taggle performer. "He created a taggle. This taggle built Delacroy, and he built Morlac's ruby palace. This *nameless* taggle built every wall and every gate. He built *this* gate," he motioned to the cavern encasing them, "And we honor his memory through our own creations: every painting and every sculpture…our stories, our dancing."

Phinx turned, again, toward the beautiful Jennaween, "*Your* dancing."

He saw Diato, smoking a stubby pipe that protruded from an upturned lip, "Your acting."

He found Lilthian, a white ribbon woven into her braided red hair, "Your music."

Phinx pointed a finger at himself, "My painting."

Then he swept his hand over the crowd, "Everything we create honors the first taggle, or so I believed. But the truth is the first taggle was nothing more than a *slave* to Morlac. Our god whom we serve *used* him to build these walls. He drove him like a beast until he collapsed in death. And then Morlac found another taggle to enslave. And now *we* serve him. Why? Why do we serve a god who leaves us to live in the sewers? The *revered* artisans of Delacroy," Phinx sneered. "We are no better than sewer rats."

A voice bellowed from the crowd, "Better the sewers than the streets."

"Yes," Phinx agreed. "The sewers afford us moments of peace and quiet. We travel without restriction, and much faster than any Delcrean. But why is a taggle forced to live in the sewers? We should dine with Morlac! Taste his food and share his wine. We should sit at our rightful place of honor!"

Several heads nodded. Phinx stepped forward, squatting at the edge of the stage where he focused his attention on the closest taggle: Corralea—one of his many lovers and the one he visited whenever he passed near Second Gate. He hadn't noticed her in the crowd until that moment. Her soft cheeks. The way her eyes always sparkled. She wore one of his scarves, easily identified by the teeth marks and wear pattern he left on the edges of all his scarves. Not by coincidence did she wear that scarf to the gathering, nor did Phinx absently leave articles of clothing behind for just any taggle to wear.

Phinx spoke to Corralea as though caressing her esculent ear, "Is that not *your* rightful place?"

She nodded.

The painter stood to find Jennaween glaring at him. He ignored her and pushed onward, "We deserve a better life. Waylon," his mention of the murdered sculptor's name brought a collective shout of support, "deserved a better life! He deserved a better death!" Another shout arose, and this time Phinx allowed it to linger into silence. Then he pleaded, "If Morlac will not honor those who serve him—if he will not invite us to dwell in his palace—then we must turn to the god of another world. We must turn to the Sphere," Phinx watched the weight of his words settle upon their shoulders. "Some Delcreans already worship him. Yes, the Sons and Daughters of Oblation meet in secret, but we know their secret. We know why they gather, and where they gather. And we let them worship. More than worship, we let them live, for they could not move through our sewers unless shown the way by a taggle."

"They're cowards! Always wearing masks."

"They are cowards no longer," Phinx stepped forward, "I am one of them."

"You? You brought them into the sewers?" Several voices overlapped.

"No, I was not the first taggle to join their ranks. Someone else brought them into our home," Phinx cast a casual eye toward Edran, certain the boy, youngest of the taggles, granted the Sons and Daughters of Oblation access to the sewers. "Yet, we turned a blind eye to their presence then and now. Which is how I know that I am not alone. There must be others amongst us. But even if I do standalone..." He turned toward Jennaween, hoping she would finish the thought.

"We protect our own," Corralea half-shouted, drawing her lover's attention from the openly gaping Jennaween.

"Yes, we protect our own," Phinx nodded—he would have kissed the woman had the situation allowed. "So, what is to become of the Sons and Daughters of Oblation? I am one of them. And several of you have joined their ranks. Will we protect them?"

"Protect them? We don't even know who *they* are."

"Until now," Phinx pointed to the back of the crowd where Maldinado stood speaking with his two companions.

The tailor slowly approached, hobbling through the crowd. Jennaween joined him about halfway to the stage, offering Maldinado assistance as he climbed the stairs. Phinx flashed her a dashing smile as they mounted the final step, but Jennaween turned her back and, rather than return to the crowd, she continued to walk. He watched after her even as Maldinado began to address the taggles, oddly compelled to follow, but he could not leave the stage in that moment and, eventually, Jennaween disappeared around the curving tunnel. When Phinx turned his full attention back to the gathering, he noticed that Corralea, looking more than a little irate, also turned her back on him and departed—throwing his scarf in the dirt and, rather intentionally, and in his mind, unnecessarily stepping on it three times as she left. Two lovers spurned. The painter raised the scarf he still wore and started chewing, wondering what he had done to deserve such petty reactions even as he searched the crowd for another of his many lovers. He found Bella in a dazzling orange dress, thick black hair piled upon her ample and mostly exposed breasts. Kipla stood further away, several strands of colorful beads hanging from her ever-kissable neck. And Rayshin—one look at her green eyes and he forgot all about his other lovers.

Beside him, Maldinado spoke with a voice accustomed to commanding attention, "I am a Son of Oblation. I worship the Sphere."

Shaking himself from thoughts of love, Phinx surveyed his brothers and sisters as he would a finished painting. If they resembled a canvas, Maldinado served as the brush in the painter's hand. And in that moment, Phinx needed only to apply a final dab of paint with a confident stroke. He breathed calmly as he spoke, "Lyshmee also worships the Sphere, and we mean to rescue her."

Magnate Simiad closed his eyes and breathed deeply, allowing his body to move listlessly with the carriage. Sweat coated his brow and the edges of his beard. White-knuckled hands released their grip on a leather padded carriage bench, and he stretched his legs. Opposite the magnate, an unopened bottle of wine rolled back-and-forth atop another identical bench. The carriage moved through Third Circle on its way toward Third Gate, escorted by ten swads. The clip-clop sound of horse's hooves echoed softly. They moved without urgency through the dark, empty streets lit by torchlight which peeped into aphotic windows only to retreat at the sound of starving residents who moaned in their sleep, arms wrapped tightly around and subduing empty stomachs. Third Circle residents steadfastly denied themselves the pleasures and health benefits of food, seeking to prove themselves the most faithful of servants to Morlac—some to the point of death, too thin to see another sunrise. Though Simiad suspected those who did survive must often eat in shadows, succumbing to their weakness; and some, no doubt, ate and promptly disgorged.

The carriage hit a deep rut, causing the wine bottle to roll forward and over the bench onto his feet. Simiad cringed at the dull pain as the bottle struck the top of his right ankle, and then promptly retrieved the bottle from carriage floor. He felt the coolness of the dark purple glass, sliding a shaking hand over the curvature. Once, he lived a sober life, refusing to drink anything but goat's milk or boiled water. Once, he held to several such self-imposed maxims. Indeed, before assuming the role and responsibilities of magnate, Simiad lived as a devoted worshiper of Morlac denying himself any lusts of the flesh: love, wine, even food, at times.

Now, I drink until sunrise…and then again until sunset.

He had already finished two bottles that evening in addition to the one taken from Boltmar's manor. No, Valun's manor, now. *An abhorrent magnate.* But, perhaps, he spoke of himself. Simiad tossed the bottle away and back onto the opposite bench. It rolled with sultry rhythm—as tantalizing as a woman's jiggling breasts. Not that he would notice such things. He did not allow himself to notice any aspect of a woman lest he fall prey to his own desires. Lest he rank no better than Magnate Galeab and his vile requests for virgins from Second Circle. *An abhorrent magnate.* But, perhaps, he again spoke of himself, for he facilitated the exchange.

No, I am a better man than Galeab.

Simiad breathed deeply and closed his eyes as the carriage slowed to a stop. They had reached Third Gate. He listened as his swads opened the large circular door. He heard horses snorting. And he tasted the sweat coating his lips. The carriage rocked forward, slightly. Paused. And again, it rocked as the horses gathered the full weight of the carriage and the man inside, gaining momentum until finally settling into a steady tugging back-and-forth.

Simiad opened his eyes and found the bottle lolling with the lurching carriage. He switched seats, his hand fiercely embracing the alluring bottle. Within seconds, wine flowed down his parched throat, and his beard, drowning all thoughts of past maxims and personal aspirations.

Jennaween heard the horses enter Third Gate. She had traveled a fair distance from the gathered taggles, irritation with the man she loved hastening her steps. But the horses brought a sudden end to her temper-laden ruminations, for the sound could mean only one thing: Simiad had returned. *He is supposed to be in Fourth Circle.* But she knew that only a magnate would enter the gate after sundown, and only Simiad had reason to travel toward Second Circle.

She immediately turned to run back toward the gathered taggles, intent on raising the alarm. She ran with the grace of a dancer, quickly traversing the distance back to her sisters and brothers. But she did not run fast enough to avoid the swads. When they spotted her, the casual cantor of horses quickly turned into a curious sprint as the two foremost swads spurred their mounts forward, surprised to see anyone, even a taggle, walking the gate at that hour.

Jennaween started shouting, "Simiad! Simiad is coming!"

Taggles scattered as Jennaween arrived, two swads following closely behind. Her shouts of alarm merged with those of the swads who yelled, "What are you about? Why are there so many taggles here?"

She ducked under the outstretched hands of one of the swads who looked to capture, or otherwise trample her. The other swad had already dismounted and grabbed her by the shoulders. An unfortunate decision, and one that surprised her. *Why would you try to capture a taggle?* Jennaween smashed her assailant's nose with her elbow. He stumbled backward as she pulled two knives from her purple bodice. She closed the distance between them in an instant and slit his throat with a fierce crossing of her hands. Then she whirled gracefully, intent on tossing a blade at the other swad, only to find Phinx retrieving his own knife from the man's chest.

"Are you alright?" Phinx almost ran to her.

But she turned away, "Find Corralea. Simiad and his swads are coming."

"Then our revolution begins," Phinx kissed the side of her head. "Try not to die before the final battle."

His fool smile captured her breath, leaving her all the more annoyed with the dashing courtier.

"Seize them!" Maldinado commanded from atop the stage. "They must not escape."

"No chance of that," Jennaween scoffed.

The remaining eight swads, last of Simiad's escort, arrived to find two of their own lying dead. And while, apparently, their brothers in arms never paused to consider the situation into which they stumbled, Jennaween felt a pleasing sense of vindication upon seeing the look of unmistakable fear on the faces of all eight swads as she and Phinx and the rest of the taggles moved to surround them. Despite the advantage of sitting horseback, and the dominance their curved swords normally afforded them, none of the swads—shifting horrified eyes as fervently as their mounts raised anxious hooves—showed any semblance of confidence. Jennaween felt certain these men had never faced a willing combatant.

"Don't kill them," Maldinado called out.

"Would you have us perform feats of wonder for them, tailor?" Phinx, standing slightly behind Jennaween, echoed her own thoughts. This, too, infuriated her. *Stay out of my head!* She flipped the knife in her hand, switching from cool pommel to cold blade, and found her target: A young swad with rounded jaw and a tilted, long neck.

"No, I would have you execute them," Maldinado's words drew not only Jennaween's attention, but that of seemingly all the taggles; and even the swads turned. The feeble tailor continued with a surprisingly powerful voice, "The Sons and Daughters of Oblation worship in secret. They wear masks to conceal their true identity, so how can we know for certain whom among these swads follows the Sphere and who still seeks Morlac's favor? We must offer them a choice." Then, Maldinado spoke directly to the swads, "Publicly proclaim your allegiance to the god of light or face a public execution."

The force of Maldinado's words struck Jennaween, shattering her thoughts into a dozen different pieces. She willingly stood by Phinx, and if he felt the need to start a revolution then she would fight alongside him. Perhaps she followed him out of love, perhaps from a sense of duty. *Taggles protect our own.* Regardless the reason, she followed *him*…a taggle…a lethal assassin who garnered the respect of every true-born male, and the love of too many of her taggle sisters. She thought of Corralea just then. *Far too many!*

But what right did this nearly lame tailor, even one of Maldinado's famed repute, what right…indeed, how *dare* he stand above them on that stage and address the taggles as though he commanded an army. What weapon did he bring to the battle? Thread and needle? What use had she of a maldinado-robe when facing Delcrean steel—not to mention the wrath of the only god actually living in the city?

And what of my allegiance, tailor? She had never proclaimed any devotion to the Sphere, publicly or otherwise. She assumed the role of revolutionary for Phinx, alone. The gods be damned. And, she suspected, most of her fellow taggles felt a similar indifference toward the purported and ever-waging cosmic struggle. Yes, Phinx worshiped the Sphere, and yes, someone, if not Phinx, must have led the Sons and Daughters of Oblation into and through the sewers. But *she* did not. Jennaween trusted only what she could touch and feel. She believed in love, longing to share more than her bed with a lover, and she believed in creative expression. Nothing made her feel more alive than when she danced in front of a gathered crowd.

"Bring them to the stage," Maldinado's voice interrupted her thoughts. "We must know which god they serve."

Jennaween refused to move, at first. But when Phinx stepped passed her, intent on capturing the panic-stricken swads, she found herself following after him. *Who* she followed, however, whether one god or another god, whether taggle or lover, she had not yet determined. A taggle, certainly. No god, definitely. And as for a lover, well, she would leave Phinx to choose his own fate. Love her or die for another.

She again flipped the knife in her hand, gripping the pommel as though poised to strike Phinx from behind. *Corralea? Corralea!!! Really? Tasa Ro!*

Eight swads, bound and afraid, knelt before Maldinado. He meant to judge them. He meant to know who they worshiped. He meant to uncover their secret and unveil their chosen god. Then he would determine their fate.

And what of my allegiance?

A flood of emotions overwhelmed Maldinado. Visions of a former life in Adarian where his mother faithfully served as a Daughter of Oblation. Memories of times spent worshiping the Sphere. Times when his friend, Hintor, would mock him for displaying such unyielding devotion to the Sphere—a faithfulness born from his failure to protect the Adow at the Battle of Quel.

He suddenly found himself back in that moment…watching, again, as the Adow fell from the sky, Yenen's arrow piercing her chest. How helpless he felt. Unable to save her. And then, afterward, when he swore to protect the Daughter of the Adow as she assumed her mother's title.

And he did protect the new Adow: In the fields of bloodgrass, he killed her intended assassin. A worshiper of Morlac. A bastard who deserved to die.

But Maldinado also worshiped Morlac. Faithfully. Indeed, as a tailor living in Delacroy, Maldinado worshiped Morlac with never a thought given to the Sphere or the Adow. *What have I done?* He had failed both his god and his ruler. He wanted to peel his wan skin off, thinking such an act would somehow distance himself from the man within. *How often have I greeted travelers in Morlac's name?* Morlac. How often had he wished favor and boon on them from a god who wanted to kill—*kill*—his Adow.

Emotion turned to hatred as he looked upon the captured swads, perhaps seeing them clearly for the first time. Realizing who they represented: Morlac. He felt compelled to slit their throats without ceremony and without the opportunity to profess their allegiance to the Sphere. They deserved death for simply uttering Morlac's name. Then, oddly self-aware, his raging hatred flirted with compassion as the generous tailor—Maldinado, resident of Fourth Circle—temporarily overcame the protruding warrior of his past. Yes, they worshiped Morlac, but had he not also worshiped the god of *this* world. *Does their blindness to the truth somehow negate my own actions?* No. He could not accuse them without also condemning himself. They deserved the chance to choose their god.

"A test of their allegiance," Maldinado turned back to the anxious crowd. "Morlac or the Sphere. On this, we take our stand. May the Sphere be with us."

Only a handful of taggles responded, "And keep us in his light."

Not good enough. Maldinado spoke again, "May the Sphere be with us."

Phinx stepped forward and shouted his response, "And keep us in his light!"

Maldinado repeated the salutation. This time, a majority of the taggles responded.

Again. And again. Until all the taggles shouted a response. Not one of them, seemingly, held back. Excitement filled Maldinado's chest. He had found his army.

"What is going on here?"

Maldinado turned to find Simiad standing at the fringe of the gathered crowd. The all but forgotten magnate held a wine bottle in his hand and leaned heavily upon the shoulder of his young carriage driver, using the yearling for balance.

"Maldinado?" Simiad looked perplexed upon recognizing the tailor.

Maldinado found himself filled with regret bordering on grief, and his genuine fondness toward the oft-derided magnate—a friendship of necessity, certainly, but not without sympathy—caused him to hesitate in the moment.

Phinx, however, did not, "Seize them!"

Drunk and startled, the taggles captured Simiad and his carriage driver without a struggle, though moving the magnate from ground to stage proved a much more difficult task. He stumbled twice, taking several of his captors down with him. After a third such occurrence, several of the visibly ruffled and bruised taggles grabbed hold of his outstretched, swollen limbs and proceeded to carry him toward the stage. They deposited the tall, overweight magnate in a heap, leaving Phinx and Maldinado to help the clumsy oaf to his knees.

"We have captured ten worshipers of Morlac," Maldinado spoke to the crowd, avoiding Simiad's drunken and pleading gaze. "Who among you will stand against them? Phinx and I have confessed our allegiance to the Sphere. We need eight more. Who will admit to worshiping the god of another world? Who will stand against Morlac?"

Maldinado turned his gaze upon Inindu and Edran, still lingering at the back of the gathered taggles, but neither one stepped forward, apparently content to let him lead his army alone. Frustrated, he sought out others in the crowd. *One volunteer. I just need one, and more will follow.*

Men! Jennaween cursed the day she ever laid eyes on Phinx.

The painter stood on stage, chewing his teeth-beaten scarf like a goat chewing its cud. Folds of blonde hair fell downward toward a clean-shaven chin, framing his green eyes the way her hands did whenever she kissed him…whenever he cupped the small of her back with one hand, running the fingers of his other up and down her spine just ahead of the tingling sensation that followed.

Did he do the same with Corralea? *And where is your other lover now, Phinx?*

"Morlac never did anything for me," Jennaween shouted, stopping short of professing her allegiance to the Sphere even as she stepped forward and not so casually searched the crowd for her rival. *Taggles protect their own, even this fool of a man.*

"Nor for me!" Corralea announced.

Jennaween cringed upon hearing the woman's voice, yet displayed great enthusiasm, if forced, upon meeting Corralea's reticent gaze. She would not let the other woman see an ounce of jealousy. She did not understand, herself, why it bothered her so much that Phinx shared his bed with another—several women, actually. The great taggle lover. Jennaween knew his reputation long before their first kiss. He did not boast about his exploits in front of Jennaween, of course. He did not act the pig devouring slop. No, when Phinx held her in his arms he held her as though savoring the nuanced flavors of a handcrafted artisan cheese. The fact he washed the taste of her down with wine, and promptly reached for another curd of milk sliced from a larger, voluptuous wheel never even crossed her mind, in those moments of intimacy. And when he parted, for on those nights, she slept alone, Jennaween ignored any thought suggesting he may have chosen another woman over her.

But on that night, with so many taggles gathered together—with his attention given to multiple lovers—she found Phinx' reputation impossible to simply ignore. Even harder to avoid, and much to her astonishment, Jennaween noticed how Corralea's beauty seemed every bit opposite of her own features: Thick waves of cascading hair compared to Jennaween's too thin and impossibly straight mess of hair which she typically wore in a loose knot; or slightly tightened while she danced. And Corralea's perfectly formed hips. Her face, glowing with a permanent sense of joy that taunted Jennaween's gaunt cheeks and sallow eyes. Her unblemished skin. And the size of Corralea's bosom, vastly larger than her own near cutting board shaped torso. *Tasa Ro!* Just the sight of the woman made Jennaween feel inferior. Streams of familiar self-conscious doubts flooded her mind even as she and Corralea and six more taggles made their way toward the stage. Doubts that Phinx so often made her forget when he looked at her with unbridled desire. But she could not bring herself to look at Phinx just then. She did not want to find him staring at the other woman. She could not bear to know which of them he preferred.

The thought infuriated Jennaween. That Phinx would put her in such—put both women in such a position suddenly washed away all hints of jealousy. *How dare you judge me, Phinx! How dare you make me doubt myself!* She turned to find Corralea, wondering if the other woman experienced similar emotions. Surprisingly, she found an odd yet unmistakable sense of kinship in Corralea's eyes, an invitation of unity if not entirely one of friendship. Jennaween warmed to the unspoken offer and waited for the other woman to join her before ascending the stairs to the stage where ten captives awaited their fate. And one more who, if not given a choice between gods, would nevertheless choose one lover over all others. He did not yet know this, of course. But Jennaween felt certain that she and

Corralea had reached an accord of which they would confirm details, later.

Phinx would learn of their arrangement, soon enough.

When she finally stepped foot to familiar stage, followed by Corralea and the six additional taggle volunteers, Jennaween glowered at the once *mighty* taggle lover. She did not have to glance at Corralea to know the woman offered Phinx a similar look of disgust. The confusion and utter bewilderment that warped Phinx' typically self-assured countenance nearly made Jennaween smile, but she refused to allow such bemusement to reach her lips. Instead, she turned her attention to Maldinado.

"Strip them, we will need their clothes," Maldinado waited as his newly recruited taggles, nine assassins turned executioners, stripped the captives—eight swads, carriage driver, and magnate—and tossed their clothes into a pile at the back of the stage. Maldinado retrieved one of the swads' swords from the same pile, and then he aligned the taggles and captives—one taggle standing directly behind each captive save the still confused magnate. Simiad's death, should he choose Morlac, would fall upon Maldinado. He owed his friend that much, at least. If he must die...

The curved sword felt unusually heavy in Maldinado's hand, poorly made compared to the lighter Adarian steel he once wielded in another world. No, more likely, he lacked the strength of that warrior. Despite his ability to lead an army, slipping easily back into command, and regardless of his awareness of Morlac's illusion, Maldinado could not escape the bonds of an overly aged and beaten down body.

Still, he addressed the crowd and the captives with weapon raised, though it shook terribly in his feeble hand, "Now, let us choose our god. Let us see who will live and who must die."

Maldinado turned and attempted to point his sword at the young carriage driver kneeling below Phinx, thinking to threaten the yearling, youngest of the captives, into the first confession of fealty, but the tailor could not stop the weapon as he lowered it and so it fell ingloriously, traveling the full accelerated arch, until it rested at his side as though nothing more than a walking stick. He managed to keep his feet, however, if not his dignity.

The yearling sneered as he met Maldinado's gaze, seemingly daring the old man to face him—with or without a sword in hand. Maldinado did not shy from the unspoken challenge, "Let us see who will survive."

Phinx stood behind the young carriage driver, scarf firmly in mouth as he held a knife to the yearling's throat. The tailor could not help but marvel at the dichotomy of the childish habit occurring below the taciturn taggles' slightly squinting, deadly eyes. Few warriors, even those of the Adarian 45th, ever marched into battle with such calm confidence. Mostly, he witnessed wide-eyed terror and, as their leader, often sought to quiet unspoken anxieties. But the taggles needed no reassurances from *him*. Instead, Maldinado drew upon the strength of the assassin before him who held a knife to the throat of a yearling as though he performed nothing more unusual than a daily inspection of his blade. No, he did not draw upon his strength, rather, the taggles' tranquility in that moment compelled Maldinado to act—served as impetus, lest he fail to uphold his end of their deadly bargain. Clearly, if Maldinado sought to lead this band of taggles into a revolution, he must not falter in his responsibilities.

He approached the defiant yearling, "May the Sphere be with you."

The boy breathed deeply, and seemingly managed to extend his already long neck before shouting, "Morlac's boon upon me!"

Phinx slid his knife across the yearling's throat. Never shaven. Forever marred. Maldinado watched the yearling's body fall from life into death. He had hoped the boy would yield. Yet, war offered no mercy to the young. *The cost of a revolution.* If he held any doubts before, in that moment Maldinado stood once more as a warrior…faithful to his god.

Innocent blood dripped from the taggles' blade.

A curious silence turned to the much heavier hush of newly gained understanding, for the gathered taggles had all witnessed the stalwart yearling's death with a collective and unflinching gaze. Despite their noticeable indifference toward dastardly deeds, however, or perhaps as a result, the moment remained unobstructed. In a sense, hallowed. Maldinado suspected they shared a common level of respect that one so young would die so bravely. Regardless, private thoughts and concerns, if any, remained muffled by the inaudible crowd. The true-born understood more than most that Delacroy did not spare any neck, young or old. Most of them probably witnessed their first death, a casual glimpse of the guillotine, while suckling at their mother's breast. As such, they knew, as Maldinado knew, most condemned Delcrean yearlings, while they lay bound upon the bascule with their heads carefully positioned under mouton and blade, screamed for their parents, or anyone, to rescue them. Not this boy. This yearling had dared Maldinado to kill him, trusting that his god would save him in the end. But Morlac did not save him. He would not save any of them.

"And keep you in his light," Maldinado finished the otherwise prefatory greeting. In this case, marking the end. He moved to the next captive, older and visibly inspired by the boy who lay less than a foot from where he knelt before Jennaween. *And what of your allegiance?*

Maldinado offered him life, "May the Sphere be with you."

The smug swad shouted, "Morlac's boon upon me!"

Jennaween granted him death.

"And keep you in his light."

Corralea killed the next captive.

Simiad watched in puzzled horror as nine worshipers of Morlac died in succession, killed by Maldinado, a man whom he knew worshiped the god of Delacroy more faithfully than most—yet now claimed to worship the Sphere. Blood coated the stage, pooling in every cleft and depression along wooden planks that ran parallel with the line of bodies to the right of where Simiad knelt. His knees felt slick—the fabric of his leggings soaking up the blood to the point of saturation—moist as his chin under a beard that still clung to drops of sweat and red wine.

He needed a drink, but his hands grasped at air. Empty and bound behind his back. Yes, he remembered: One of the taggles had stolen the bottle he carried. He searched the crowd for the wine he craved. Surely, they enjoyed the spoils of their captured magnate. A bottle of wine. Simiad grinned at the absurdity of his position. He could offer them nothing more, for what more had Morlac ever given him?

Simiad struggled to maintain his wits. He faced an important decision. He knew that much. Maldinado wanted him to choose between Morlac and the Sphere. Important. Decision. *Lest I die...die if I don't choose correctly.* Maldinado worshiped Morlac. And Simiad worshiped Morlac. *No, Maldinado worships the Sphere...or Morlac...no, the Sphere.* He again searched the crowd, this time looking for an answer to Maldinado's question. Instead, as though taunting him, he found only wine. Several taggles raised cups and bottles in toast or boast, but none of them offered the magnate a drink. *Morlac or the Sphere?*

Suddenly, he felt the coolness of a dagger under his beard, barely registering the presence of Maldinado who stood facing the magnate. Simiad gazed at his friend with hazy eyes. The tailor's voice sounded displaced and garbled, as though speaking from behind a raised mug of ale, "May the Sphere be with you."

The blurred features of the tailor's face slowly solidified. Why did the most generous resident of Fourth Circle, or for that matter, the most generous resident in all of Delacroy, hold a knife to his throat? Simiad couldn't think. *Need to answer correctly...I need a drink.* Surely, Maldinado would grant him a bottle of wine if he answered correctly. *Morlac or the Sphere? Choose!* Simiad licked his chapped lips before finally responding, with slight hesitation after each word, "And...keep...me...in his... light?" *What has Morlac ever given me?*

Maldinado lowered the dagger.

Didn't he have a sword?

The tailor grinned widely as he and Simiad embraced, "And keep you in his light," he echoed.

One of the taggles brought forth several bottles of wine.

And Simiad consumed, faithfully.

Condemned

Inindu

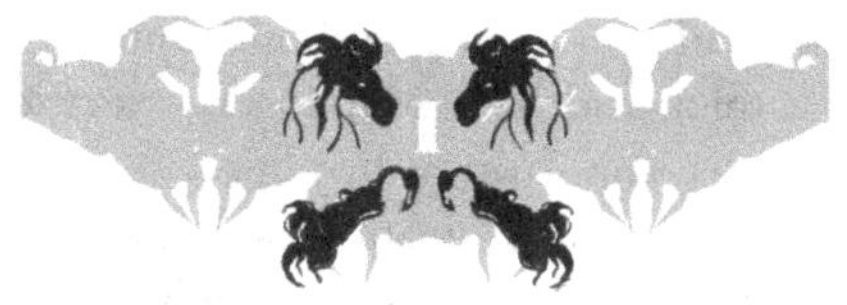

A bloody-ass affair, executions.

Edran looks away as Phinx slides his blade across the neck of the young carriage driver. Our brother sits at the edge of an empty stage. Though certainly accustomed to death, he refuses to watch the yearling die. We suppose it cruel to force the young to watch the young die—like feeding bacon to a pig. Still, the pig must eat. And the young must die. The first to die in every revolution we can recall, leaving the old to scrape their dried blood from doorposts, yet the battle never simply ends in the streets. It invades each home until even the old must act. And then the old die, too.

In Quel, when the worshipers of Morlac rose up in rebellion against the Sphere, they died. Will these taggles discover a similar fate? No. In Quel, both sides lost, for we refused to fight in that revolution, resulting in the inevitable outcome. But here in Delacroy we stand as part of the revolution. *Yes, father. We have finally chosen a side.*

The second captive falls. And the third.

Edran watches both swads die. As we suspected, our brother felt bothered by the boy's age, not his death. We want to provide him comfort as we once cared for the Daughters of the Adow. Once, when they would burrow into our embrace and ride upon our back. But intimacy and love and all such comfort vanished with Adarian's death, replaced with harsh realities and cold truths.

The young die, dear brother.

Edran's red hair sits flat upon his head, covering his forehead and ears, and gathers loosely at his shoulders. His cheeks look smooth as eggs, nose like a morning tulip. Green eyes, sharp as bramble, belie his age, but we cannot escape the truth of his youth. Our topi pulls him to our breast, and we can smell the dust in Edran's hair. All the same, we give his head a kiss.

Dear brother, even the young will die.

Across the way, Maldinado moves from one captive swad to the next, his robe covered in blood. He moves with confidence, if feebly. He kills without hesitation. A bloody mess.

Edran shifts his head into our lap and our topi runs her chalk-coated fingers through his thick red hair. Maldinado executes another overly zealous captive even as our drowsy brother closes his eyes. We, too, feel the fatigue of a long day—of death. And so, even as the last captive confesses his allegiance to the Sphere, and a celebration begins, the young one sleeps.

Maldinado raises a hearty toast, and the taggles drink.

While the young one sleeps.

The taggles exchange bloody robes for fresh clothing. They carry the dead into the sewers below and scrub the stage clean. All signs of the brutal execution erased from existence.

The young one still sleeps, and we dream of Adarian…

(before)

Prior to entering Morlac's world, yes, while we yet lived in a land created by our father, we climbed aboard the vessel, *Erin's Mast*, for its maiden voyage: Hemming trees for timber, sails woven together with flax fibers, and three towering cylen trees used for masts. The ship's merry captain stood below the mainmast greeting every invited guest. We nodded slightly as he thrust forward a stumpy hand in greeting, and then we quickly moved beyond the jolly sea ambassador to a position along the taffrail. We hated ceremonies.

We scanned the gangplank in search of our delayed sister, the Adow, and her First Etabli, Ig-Poy—both belabored with greeting rituals. We caught her attention and nodded coyly. She hated ceremonies, too, but lacked our knack for escaping the crowd. Behind our sister, various Madars and Overseers smiled and exchanged forced pleasantries; further out, Sons and Daughters of Oblation offered five supplications for every three steps they took; and amidst them all stood numerous warriors, effectively filling any remaining space upon the dock. The ceremonial voyage had seemingly gathered together each dignitary in the land, a detestable collection of frozen smiles and strategic encounters. They left us alone, thankfully, for we displayed no willingness to assist the political aspirations of the attendees, and, absent a formal title, they realized us incapable of turning their young ambitions into recognized achievements.

"You should know, I cannot swim." A low-ranking warrior of the Adowian Guard spoke as he approached: Black hair swirled about his face like smoke over fire. Tight beard. Green eyes. A square jaw that cast a shadow over his golden breastplate.

We looked away from him toward the choppy sea, "It makes little difference. I suspect we will all drown."

"The Adow will survive," he leaned against the taffrail.

Our sister, we noticed, found herself beset by a crowd which gathered around a smaller crowd which gathered around her, "Yes, those who can swim will no doubt save her." We stood close to him, close enough to see the variations of green in his fierce eyes—forest shadows merging with dandelion leaves. His eyes pleased us.

"When did you join the Guard?"

He smiled, obviously taking our question as an invitation. We did not mind. "Five weeks ago. I'm Adarian. What is your name?"

"You know my name."

"Yes, it seems everyone knows your name, but for all I know, everyone refers to you by the wrong name. Anyway, I thought it proper to let you introduce yourself."

We watched our sister as she encountered the elated captain, struggling to cling onto her fake and increasingly tense smile. Her desperate eyes sought ours, pleading for assistance—asking us to help her escape the bloated speech of the overly proper captain. But we did not save her. Instead, we turned our attention to Adarian, "My name is Inindu."

Adarian grinned, "Well then, I'm glad I asked. Rumor had it your name was *That Magenta Mongrel*."

He had our full attention, then. We drew back from the railing, certain Adarian sought to antagonize, but his casual demeanor suggested otherwise.

"Don't worry," Adarian waved his hands dismissively, "I won't share your secret. May the land forever know you as...um, well it's not a very nice name, actually. Why do they call you that?"

His sincerity disarmed us in that moment. Most men believed us beautiful, and incapable of the horrendous acts attributed to us in mostly whispered taggles' tales. They rarely displayed enough courage to ask us about the rumors outright, however. "It seems, that is what I am."

Adarian considered the idea for a moment before shaking his head, "No, I've known a few mongrels...a few bastards, too. You don't strike me as either." He turned back to the ocean, "I guess that settles the matter. I will have to call you Inindu."

We leaned closer, close enough to feel the warmth of his body beneath an otherwise chilly ocean gale. He provided a welcome distraction from the ceremony, "Call me whatever you like, but if you fall overboard, I won't save you."

Adarian grinned, leaning closer, "I may have lied about my ability to swim."

Behind him, our horse nuzzled her head between his legs, lifted, and promptly threw Adarian overboard, "Then there is hope for you, yet."

He flailed with surprise and gave a short bellow before striking the water below. Our topi mounted and turned toward the Adow. The captain's speech ended abruptly, halted by the sounds of Adarian's peril. We exchanged a glance with our sister as though to say, *you're welcome*; then we promptly charged the taffrail and lunged in after the cocksure warrior.

We landed lightly atop the rough water, however.

Adarian splashed to the surface; slick hair plastered across his wet face. He looked up toward the ship, but soon found us standing on the water, "What…you can walk on water?"

"Of course," we stretched forth our hair, ensnaring Adarian, and gently pulled him out of the water. We placed him atop our horse directly behind our topi, "I may have lied about my ability to save you."

Adarian wiped his eyes and pulled his hair back, "Now what?"

We looked up at the gathered crowd along the taffrail, shouts of concern merging with gasps of wonder, "I believe the ceremony is now over. The journey begins."

We walked across the water, taking a position at the front of the vessel. The befuddled captain gave orders to raise anchor. The Adow assumed her position at the ship's bow, seated upon a makeshift throne. She nodded toward us coyly before stating formally, "Let us proceed, captain."

Adarian wrapped his arms around our topi, and we led the ship out to sea.

Edran stirs slightly in our lap, turning over on his back and again on his side so that his nose is buried in our stomach. We run our fingers through his sweaty hair. He stinks and needs a bath. A sweaty nuisance. We pull our hand from Edran's head and use his clothes to wipe off the sweat.

Still, we hold him while he sleeps.

Condemned

Delacroy

Certainty | Chastity | Fasting | Generosity | Joy | Orthodoxy | Peace | Honesty | Faithfulness

Shale slid a polished, metal key into the iron lock; turned until he heard the familiar, oppressive click; and pushed the ornate, torpid door inward. The repugnant smell of formaldehyde and vinegar mixed with blood emerged immediately from the dark doorway, causing his right eye to quiver slightly and, despite his best efforts, his nose to crinkle. Returning the key to his empty pocket, he retrieved a burning torch from the ruby sconce beside the doorway. It served as the only torch in the otherwise illuminated palace.

No light in this room, only darkness. Here is where you hide your secrets.

Shale had sent his attendants away for the evening so, with several hours still remaining until dawn, the palace sat empty. Only he remained... and Morlac, of course, but his tortured god suffered in agony several hundred feet below where Shale stood at that moment. Yes, an empty palace except for Shale, Morlac, and those who slept within the darkness before him. *Sleep*. He did not allow himself to use any other word when describing the nascient.

A slight breeze blew outward from the room, causing both the torch flame to flutter and his yiddick-shawl to waver. Shale wanted to *throw* the torch into the room. He wanted to light a thousand torches and toss them in after the first until the fire set the wooden floor ablaze and chased every shadow away. Instead, he squelched his fear and entered the darkness.

He walked with knowledge of the room's deviant design: The uppermost, tiered corridor from whence he entered encircled a lower cavern, an observation deck made from wooden planks that cascaded down to a series of glass panels at its center. Each tier held a series of carved-out wooden benches complete with high backs. But if an audience ever gathered in this room, it occurred long before...well, the thought served as another of his lingering meditations. A discarded one, for he did not feel inclined to uncover the mystery of the observation deck. Indeed, he pushed down even the smallest of notions regarding its intended purpose as he navigated his way around the benches toward a locked iron gate that guarded a spiral staircase and the even more disturbing cavern below.

Shale cast the torchlight before him, willing the fire to descend fully into the lower level before him, but darkness kept the probing light from penetrating its depths. He nervously retrieved the key from his pocket and, overcoming his hesitations, opened the gate. Once more, he felt the urge to toss the torch inside, and again, he used his own fear as motivation to take another step forward.

He descended the spiraling staircase certain, though irrationally and without cause, he would encounter the nascient at every turn, but only darkness awaited his presence. At last, he reached the cavern floor and a heavy door fashioned with thick, wooden planks—perhaps the only room in all of Delacroy without an ounce of stone; certainly, the only room in the palace.

A thick, white fluid seeped out between planks, coating the entire door.

Here the nascient lay.

Though he could not see them beyond the torchlight, Shale knew he would find three wooden tables evenly spaced around the cavern. There lay the chosen ones. Selected during the Nascence festival when Delcreans gathered in Ninth Circle, cheering loudly as Morlac chose one of their own from the crowd—chosen to join Morlac and Shale in the ruby palace. But what the Delcreans celebrated, Shale hated. Dreaded. Feared.

Here the nascient lay, and the dead appear.

It felt like a doorway into another world whenever he stepped into the room beyond. A mirage. Aberration. If nothing more than a temporary vision. But he experienced it every time he crossed the threshold. He breathed deeply before unlocking the door. Then, he closed his eyes and entered the room.

He stood one step inside the room, he knew, but when he opened his eyes, the dead appeared in full light as though twenty torches had suddenly burst into flame. They surrounded him, looked down upon him from where they sat on the benches above; descended the spiral staircase behind him; standing in the room beside him as though waiting. For what he could not imagine. He shuddered under their collective and vacant stare. Decay dug into most of their faces until it reached bone, leaving deformed, circular holes in cheeks, chins, throats, and noses. Individual hair strands clung weakly to sporadically shattered skulls, stretching toward the ground as though longing to jump, to end the suffering, yet unable to release their tiny grip on life. Arms hung motionless. Feet remained planted. Nothing moved or breathed except Shale.

The dead appeared. They watched. And then they vanished.

Only a brief glimpse of the grotesque. Nothing more.

Seemingly alone, again, and grateful to have survived another viewing of the dead, Shale moved to the nearest table, careful to step around the slick white fluid that coated the split planked floor. He held his torch as though wielding a sword, however, for if the dead had truly vanished—and he still felt their vacant gaze—what remained in their wake left him no less unnerved. *Here lay the nascient.* Three tables. Three bodies. He inspected the closest of the creatures by thrusting forth his torch. The nascient still slept. *It* still slept. It had a name, once. Jowl. But only the body of the Delcrean remained, his shell barely recognizable: Pale skin stretched thin over twisted bones. Sunken face. Black hair and beard grown long and still growing. Closed eyes oozing the same thick, white fluid that covered the room—worm-like tears that pulsated downward over temples, filled its ears before spilling onto the table and then the floor where it pooled in every crack. The sight of it softly thrumming, threading its way over every surface, somehow climbing the walls like veins of mucus, caused Shale to brush at his neck, mistaking his yiddick-shawl for a strand of the substance as though it sought to devour him. The stench of the room made him want to vomit and never breathe again.

The nascient. Morlac's chosen vessels. Selected worshipers who unwittingly sacrificed themselves—their soulless bodies slowly altered; facial structures changed—all for the sake of appearances. The image of Morlac. Indeed, upon completion of the transformation, a process requiring several years, the chosen truly did resemble their god. They reflected his likeness in every way. But such a process, contorting the form of a man into that of a god, did not occur without consequences to the man. Indeed, and despite his disgust, Shale pitied the chosen. It seemed to him the white fluid they shed—*tears of the nascient*—spoke of the incomprehensible pain they endured. Particularly, during the early stages of their metamorphosis like the nascient who lay morphing on the table beside Shale. Painful, yes, but not without reward. Once fully formed, Delcreans would think the creature a god. Their god. Morlac.

Would they still worship you if they knew your secret?

Shale moved to the next table. Formerly known as Natiel. Dead. Living. *Does it really matter.* An altered existence, if nothing else, and a poor fate. Further along in the process, this nascient displayed the proper muscle structure, a shorter beard, and eyes that had shifted closer together. Its nose and mouth remained too high on his face, however, for Morlac had a stub for a chin; a sort of illusion resulting from Morlac's lower than normal mouth coupled with his elongated nose. Shale tracked the nascient's transformation by the position of the chin, always the last facial feature to come into alignment and complete the process. *His chin still needs work. Your chin?*

He navigated the darkness to a third table only to find it empty. Shale froze. The missing nascient stood somewhere in the darkness beyond. Silent. Awake, but unable to speak. Like the dead he had seen when he stepped through the doorway. Dead? Alive? Regardless, the nascient remained silent until Morlac inhabited their bodies, granting them a voice. Shale stepped forward until the light from his torch flickered upon a motionless, helpless figure. Once known as Sarke, nothing now remained of the man but his god.

A foul fate.

The nascient wore a white yiddick-shawl over bare chest and narrow shoulders, and a short linen wrap that hung from its waist; a tight, short beard that sharpened every angle of a square jaw line, and its long, dark hair—pulled back and braided—completed the disguise. Every inch of the creature resembled Morlac including its chin…and the eyes. Instead of pupils and irises, only two white orbs remained behind unblinking eyelids. They looked like two spheres of melted candle wax—cooled and smoothed over, yet unmistakably disfigured. Unmistakably blind like the god they once worshiped. *Once worshiped? Still worship?*

Another step. And another. The torchlight illuminated the far wall of the cavern, and Shale felt certain what he saw at the edge of that fluttering darkness would forever haunt him in the brightest of days; for directly behind the fully formed nascient lay the twisted remains of its predecessors. This terrible fate awaited them all, for the transmutation of the nascient did not end. Ever, he assumed. The most recent vessel of Morlac, along with several dozen of its peers, stood hunched over. Some slightly bent at the shoulders. Others with hands on knees. All of them sick-like, longing to vomit the last wisps of their existence, yet unable to exhale even the tiniest breath. Soon enough they would join the pile of deformed bodies that lay huddled together at their feet. A few of these creatures, the larger creatures, for Shale could see a noticeable difference in size, still held varying degrees of resemblance to Morlac; but the smaller ones did not. Shriveled and twisted inward beyond recognition, the skin from the faces of these smaller nascient connected head to knees like strands of melted cheese. Ankles joined hips. Fingers wrapped around toes. Indeed, these smaller nascient balled themselves up into blobs of ever-pooling flesh. But their suffering did not end there, for beyond these foul creatures Shale saw more nascient piled together in heaps that cascaded from the wall. These older, faceless, limbless creatures—spheres of mutilated life—appeared no larger than Shale's head; some smaller. Warped oval shapes. A few of them small enough to fit into Shale's hand, though the thought of touching the nascient, let alone holding one, made his stomach tighten. Worst of all, the same white ooze coated the spherical shapes. Not tears. No, Shale felt quite certain he looked upon what remained of their liquefied bones.

The chosen Delcreans. The honored vessels.

Their former selves had each entered Morlac's palace with great eagerness, blinded by promises of great treasure and a better life. And why should they fear? They achieved what every Delcrean desired. Chosen by the Adherent for their unyielding faithfulness, they followed Shale to the palace gates where Morlac awaited, or so they thought. Instead, they met the nascient, Morlac in transfigured flesh. They met their walking doom and happily followed the creature into Morlac's palace. But Shale did not select them based upon their level of displayed faithfulness, rather, he chose them according to a predetermined height and weight, those who already resembled Morlac in body structure, for it hastened the change process.

Of course, they did receive a small reward. For all of one day, Shale facilitated the illusion of honor and celebration. Each of the chosen received new clothes. The seldom-used kitchen staff prepared a feast. And, in a sense, they truly did converse with their *god*, for Morlac indwelt in the nascient during these times, granting the soulless creature life and voice. So, the chosen asked their lifetime's worth of questions and listened intently to each response until, inevitably, they fell asleep, convinced they would live forever in this paradise. *But they never awaken, do they?* At least, not as themselves. Only the nascient awoke, and then, only in blindness.

Their transformation took two years, and then they resembled Morlac for about a year before they noticeably hunched their shoulders, leaning into the decay that would eventually suck them inward into nothingness. Aside from Morlac making an appearance at the annual Nascence, however, Shale rarely had need of them. One of the benefits of worshiping a reclusive god. Thus, he kept the nascient locked inside their cavern and did his best to forget they ever existed. But Valun's beheading necessitated his interaction with the creatures. Yet another reason, Shale decided, to dislike the condemned magnate.

"Follow me," Shale wondered if the creature truly understood the command, or if something else compelled it to walk. He once tried to fetch one of the nascient without speaking. It stood motionless until, finally, he spoke. But whether his voice triggered something within the creature or Morlac simply tested Shale's faithfulness, he could not say for certain. Regardless, he performed his duty and turned to leave. The nascient, covered in the same white slime that coated everything in that room, needed a bath. And, lest he leave the palace half-naked, clothes befitting a god.

Upon exiting the cavern, somewhat unexpectedly, for his thoughts remained for a time upon the nascient, Shale once again entered the world of the dead. Light surrounded him and perhaps a hundred forms, maybe more, suddenly appeared to fill the cavern above him. Not dead like the nascient. Not soulless. No, these creatures possessed a knowledge of life. They clung to it. Not in any visible sense, for their freakish and wretched forms reflected the monstrous illusions normally found in the lost dreams of the damned, rather, Shale felt an unmistakable stirring within his being as though the fingers of the dead fondled his spirit with a perverted envy that sickened him. Left him quivering with fear. They wanted to breathe, once more, but in their haste to taste the air—in their desire to possess Shale's body, possess the only living thing in their midst—their unseen ghosts careened off one another. Shale could feel them colliding against his chest. But just as surely, he knew, that whatever remained of the dead scattered into the dark existence of oblivion. Their last, desperate, gasp before succumbing to an unfortunate fate. The dead vanished.

Shale stepped through the cavern door, and the nascient followed. Not for the first time, he wondered whether he had seen an illusion, or momentarily escaped one. The dead wanted him. Their touch lingered for longer periods each time he encountered them. There, in the doorway. Yes, always there. But in other places, too. Unexpected places, and more and more frequently as though they hunted after him.

How much longer can I escape their grasp?

But in these matters, at least, he kept his thoughts to himself. He did not discuss the dead with Morlac, for Shale feared what he might hear in response—bad enough, he knew about the nascient.

(before)

Sarke lay sleeping, his mostly empty wine glass spilling into a crimson pool upon the crushed ruby floor. Shale sat with his arms around knees not far from Morlac, god of Delacroy, who lounged expectantly upon several cushions. Morlac listened. The blind and ever-tortured god indwelt in—consumed, rather—a physically altered and freely offered gift of a body: nascient. Shale called for two nearby attendants to clear the absurdly large feast that had long since cooled. Most of it uneaten; untouched. Unseen. Morlac longed to sample the many culinary delights—to taste anything but the moth dust that coated his tongue. But try as he might, the illusion he created did not transcend the Sphere's curse. He could not taste or feel or see. Only the dream world, it seemed, offered him any escape from his afflictions including the eclipse of moths, escape from his rotting body.

Shale, too, had restrained himself from eating anything more than a few grapes, though Morlac had shifted the illusion several times during the meal as a means of tempting the adherent—buttered and seasoned mushrooms; steamed asparagus with flakes of sea salt; and boiled lobster—but Shale had remained stalwart throughout, refusing to eat in front of Morlac if his god could not also partake. An outward lie, for Morlac knew the doubts of his most faithful servant. The nascient greatly bothered Shale, and he often devoted the majority of his daily meditations upon the mysteries of the transmuted creatures. Morlac listened and dismissed them. In truth, the nascient troubled every adherent. All of them. Everyone who served before Shale. And Morlac accepted their misgivings without offering any explanation, for he knew himself to be a god and, he reasoned, a god does not need to explain everything to his followers. What he did, he did for his own reasons, and for the benefit of the souls he rescued from the Sphere's world.

In the nascient, Morlac had found a means by which to enter his own illusion. A disfiguring, of sorts—a twisting of light essence—but necessary. If he never appeared in Delacroy, his worshipers would soon follow the god of another world, and Morlac would die without worship. All gods die if nobody worships them. So, Morlac sacrificed the life of one nascient each year. Well, he sacrificed their light essence. He caused each of these chosen ones to believe themselves Morlac, the creator of the illusion. As such, their existence warped in on itself. Their light essence dwindled into oblivion. But, for a time, Morlac could indwell them.

He watched Sarke breathing from inside the nascient. The creature he possessed called himself Morlac and believed himself a god. It had a different name, once, but it could no longer recall such matters. So, it happened, Morlac, or perhaps Morlac, or a different Morlac snatched the light essence from Sarke and began working on the alterations required to create another Morlac. He left enough essence to sustain Sarke's body—enough to transform its physical features—until he returned the greater portion.

Morlac motioned to Shale, "You may take him, now."

Condemned

Delacroy

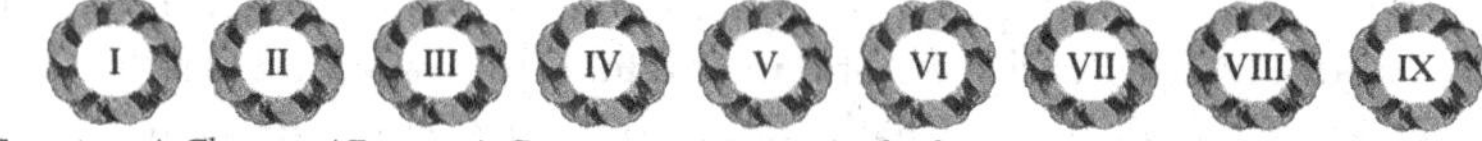

Tannessa led Beah down the winding dungeon corridor away from his repugnant cell. She noticed the sour scent of piss still lingered on her befuddled prisoner, though she could do nothing about the odor short of bathing him. She didn't typically notice the various smells of the dungeon. They blended together under years of memories and the passage of time, until her senses grew numb to even the strongest odors like the scent of death. But she seemed more alert than usual on this particular night. She found herself studying every flickering shadow along the wall; could feel the dips and elevations in the stone floor beneath her swollen feet. And she could smell the piss.

"Where are you taking me?" Beah's iron chains, binding his feet and hands, clamored as he walked. His tri-colored leggings—saturated, heavily soiled, and torn in several places—looked in better condition than the rest of him. His bare chest, slick with grime and sweat, appeared sickly in skin tone, and displayed several grisly sores. A bruised and swollen face seemed all the larger under his matted black hair.

"You have a sponsor," Tannessa lied.

Though not a common practice in other parts of the city, residents in Fourth Circle often paid Tannessa the gold required to provide a prisoner with a warm meal and, despite her usual tendencies to the contrary, she rarely kept the gold for herself in matters that involved food. After all, a warm meal for her prisoners usually meant a warm meal for her. It also brought conversation—however good or poor.

For although Tannessa portrayed a powerful figure within Delacroy, with connections to every important resident throughout the city, she mostly lived her life alone. Indeed, she spent her nights as the lone guardian of the dungeon and slept by herself during the day. Only a handful of men had ever warmed her bed, and none for at least the past seventeen years. In fact, and aside from her many bribes and secret dealings, Tannessa lived her life in relative silence. Not that she ever complained. The gold she swindled served her purposes, well enough. It paid for her food, certainly, and she enjoyed a diverse menu. But conversation, rather than gold, served as the main reason she accepted bribes even if they never strayed from business-related topics, for, of course, no one ever ventured into personal discussions with her. She maintained leverage, not friendships. Nevertheless, her dealings usually included some form of dialogue.

"But who would sponsor *me*?" Beah asked.

"Pay a taggle, earn Morlac's favor," Tannessa shrugged. "You're a taggle, so it could be anyone who felt a need to make amends. Or, perhaps, they felt sorry for the murdered taggle."

"Murdered taggle? Who?"

"Waylon," Tannessa responded flatly. "We found him in the cell next to yours."

"*Valun* killed him?"

They descended a set of stairs, Tannessa pushing Beah in front of her rather than risk strangulation or a desperate attack from behind.

"What of Inindu?" Beah inquired. "Did they capture her? Please, you must listen to me. She came here to destroy our world."

"Inindu comes to us all at one point or another, but Morlac will protect us, taggle."

They turned and followed a corridor which gradually widened, eventually leading to an open cavern. At the far end of the room, a mantled fireplace emitted heat and the scent of seasoned meat. A large and pitted wooden table awaited them, complete with two sets of dinner plates, bowls, goblets, and eating utensils carefully laid out nearest the skewered meat; worn benches on either side of the table. A silver tray, placed between place settings, held an apricot confection topped with cream cheese and powdered sugar.

"You haven't seen what she can do…her power…" Beah continued to ramble.

"Her power does not compare to Morlac's," Tannessa positioned Beah at the table and fetched a wine bottle from the mantle. "Where is your faith, taggle? Would you have me believe she exists beyond Morlac's reach?"

"There is much beyond Morlac's reach," Beah attempted to seize a piece of the apricot dessert, no doubt propelled by a dormant hunger newly aroused with the scent of warm food, but to Tannessa's delight, his restraints prevented him from grasping anything beyond his tin plate and the empty goblet.

Tannessa poured the wine with a steady hand, "My mother used to say dessert is a blanket that covers a good meal, and wine is the bed frame. Disrupt the order of any meal, and the meal will surely disrupt your sleep."

"I haven't slept since I met her," Beah buried his throbbing head in both hands. "Since I saw the dead. They're all around us. Here, even. Listen! I used to live in another world. The Sphere's world. Everyone there worships the Sphere instead of Morlac. We hunted them—I hunted them—we killed worshipers of Morlac," he accepted the filled goblet and consumed most of the bitter wine with a loud gurgle and a final gulp. "Morlac fled the Sphere's world, but not far enough. She found us. Inindu has entered Delacroy. Somehow...I don't know how. I won't go back. I can't return to the life of a taggle. Please," he lunged for Tannessa's arm, but she calmly withdrew beyond his reach. "We must stop her."

"What do you mean return to the life of a taggle? You *are* a taggle," Tannessa pointed out.

"No, you don't understand. In the Sphere's world, I was nothing more than someone's property; like a goat, grateful to fill my stomach with whatever scraps fell from the table of my master. Here, we are tru-born. We serve only ourselves and our art. Here, I am revered. There, I was taken at birth and disfigured."

Tannessa sliced into the blackened pork, shaving several long strips, and shoved one of them over her lower jowls. The warm juice rolled off her tongue like butter sizzling across a hot skillet and spread its pleasing smoked flavors throughout her mouth. She had learned the recipe, which included a mixture of paprika and dried mustard, from a mumbling swad who had long since passed beyond Ninth Circle.

"*Here*, you reside in a dungeon, and you're about to lose your head," Tannessa reminded her prisoner, "and you eat whatever scraps I allow you to eat."

She scraped several marbled strips from her wooden serving tray until they fell off the edge and landed on Beah's smaller plate, but he sat unmoving; shoulders slouched under the weight of her words. She found his demeanor oddly comforting.

"Eat," Tannessa gave him one more of the loose strips before moving to the other side of the otherwise empty table where she proceeded to eat straight from the serving tray and drank directly from the wine bottle. Beah had his portion, after all. And her manners only went so far.

"I lived with my uncle," Beah began. "In the Sphere's world, I lived with him. I helped him build a hut using only grass and mud. He grew older than everyone else in the dallic, so we considered him blessed by the Sphere, and many taggles came to him asking for blessings. Most taggles there die young and forgotten. But my uncle found favor with the Sphere, and the other taggles in the dallic reasoned that if the Sphere bestowed blessings upon my uncle, he, in turn, could provide them a blessing. Taggles there are desperate creatures…though, the taggles here…we are naïve in this world.'

'Anyway, I resisted asking him for a blessing, at first. Maybe I expected him to simply gift me a blessing for no other reason than our kinship. But eventually, I too asked for his blessing: I wanted to survive. I wanted to live a long life like my uncle. He informed me I had to earn his blessing by smuggling a yearling into Adarian," Beah stabbed at his meal. "I refused."

"Morlac offers his favor freely," Tannessa sprayed droplets of wine as she spoke.

"Yes," Beah agreed. "Morlac provides favor and boon. Even now… this meat…the wine. What did I do to earn anything I possess? I survived the Sphere's world. Morlac saved me. He brought me here and gave me more than I ever dreamed, but I remained ungrateful. I responded in the same manner with Morlac as I once did with my uncle. I *expected* his blessing."

Beah rose with a jangle of chains, "But now I realize my error."

Tannessa sunk her chipped back teeth into a strand of fat and motioned for Beah to resume his meal. The gristle slid between her molars and became lodged there.

"Inindu did not come here to destroy Delacroy," Beah took his seat. "No, Morlac must have brought her here so I could earn his favor. Finally, I will earn my blessing."

Tannessa worked the fat loose with her tongue, moving it to her front teeth so as to chew it more effectively. All the while, she considered the impassioned prisoner across from her: his carved muscles and broad frame. Strength surrounded him like a stone wall, yet she knew the strong died as easily as the weak when poison entered their body, regardless of whom they worshiped.

"If nothing else," she pushed the silver tray toward him, "you've earned dessert."

"Favor and boon," Beah smiled as he bit into the apricot confection.

Tannessa rose and waddled over to the fireplace to carve out a second helping of pork. Chains clamored loudly behind her; the bench screeched slightly backward; and Beah fell with an indiscriminate thud. She paused at the sound, observing how closely death resembled the sound of a pouch filled with gold. How the regretful silence that followed a bribe exchange mirrored the last, quiet sigh of the dead. And then, she found herself alone once more…alone with simmering pork.

Tannessa filled her plate to overflowing and returned to the table.

Condemned

Maldinado

Certainty | Chastity | Fasting | Generosity | Joy | Orthodoxy | Peace | Honesty | Faithfulness

Maldinado rode in the magnate's carriage opposite Simiad who slept with his head against the padded leather wall. Edran sat atop the carriage, guiding it through the dark streets of Second Circle. Phinx escorted them, serving as one of nine taggles masquerading as swads. Inindu served as the tenth swad, though Maldinado couldn't help but think her diminutive frame offered cause for concern.

He shifted uncomfortably. The jostling of the carriage bothered his hip. Despite his growing mental awareness, and acceptance of the warrior within, his body remained unchanged. It ached. He felt old. Muscles that once surrounded and supported freely moving joints relinquished their grip, seemingly the moment he had entered Delacroy, giving way to calcium deposits and arthritis. It took every ounce of his strength to wield the sword to which he clung as fiercely as Simiad held the wine bottle on the bench beside him.

Maldinado reached across his own body and peeled aching fingers away from the leather corded hilt. His entire hand had grown stiff with the prolonged effort required to lift and move the weapon. It fell with a clamor to the floor. *Let the young carry these burdens of war.* He needed a long and much lighter knife. *Assuming this works.*

Fillop, Second Circle Overseer, represented the greatest risk to Maldinado's small band of masqueraders. He would most definitely greet Simiad upon his arrival, and if he looked too closely at any of the swads, Fillop would surely discover their ruse and force Maldinado to take alternative action. Routine often dulls the senses, however—Maldinado told himself for the fifth time—and darkness would provide them with a greater disguise than even the tymer-kurtas they wore; add a few hastily crafted tales and the whole venture may actually work.

It seemed worth the risk, at any rate. If Simiad failed to arrive at his destination, it would raise alarm and most likely delay Lyshmee's scheduled execution. Alternatively, Maldinado debated letting Simiad walk into the dungeon and issue commands until they simply released her, but an unseen rescue, however successful, would do little to spawn the public revolution they needed.

The Madar rubbed the palm of his stiff hand. Subterfuge stretched the limits of his strategic training. He felt far more comfortable on an open battlefield, positioning larger forces. And he missed Hintor. It felt strange heading into a battle without his friend alongside…without his calming banter.

Simiad snorted and shifted in his seat. Maldinado questioned his own reasoning in placing so much responsibility upon the shoulders of a drunkard. But what choice did he have other than to trust him? Before the Sorting, Maldinado felt fortunate to know the magnate, fortunate to gain the ear of a magnate despite Simiad's lack of status among his peers. The relationship elevated Maldinado to a position of influence. Few Delcreans could make a similar boast.

Depending upon the magnate as a prime ally during a time of war fell into a completely different category, however. Maldinado wondered how much Simiad would even recall of the night's events. For that reason alone, Maldinado decided to accompany the magnate back to his manor. For that *same* reason, Fillop had always kept close watch over Simiad. Most Overseers had little to do with their respective magnates aside from the occasional briefing or public appearance. No doubt, Fillop longed for such meaningless interactions. Instead, Maldinado knew the Overseer slept at the manor, and took it upon himself to escort his master to and from the carriage, allowing him to better ascertain and curtail any inebriated decisions or potential situations that demanded his immediate attention; or that of his swads. The carriage slowed. Maldinado breathed deeply.

When it stopped, Simiad awoke with a groan, but slit eyes suggested he hoped to return to his slumber, "Maldinado, you're still here?" He closed his eyes, again.

The Madar leaned forward and grabbed the magnate's knee, "You know I am. Wake up!"

Simiad rubbed his eyes.

"Remember, I'm here for a visit."

"Yes, of course, tailor. You can stay with me in my manor. It will be good…" He closed his eyes.

Maldinado sat back, "All the better. You sleep. I'll explain."

Edran knocked once upon the carriage door prior to opening. Outside, Phinx quickly hurried the masquerading swads to a position on the opposite side of the carriage where Fillop promptly appeared. The overseer approached the carriage without expression, flanked on either side by a swad. He looked well-rested despite the late hour; no doubt, Maldinado realized, Fillop slept when his magnate slept. Late nights, late mornings.

"Good evening, overseer," Maldinado emerged from the carriage, determined to maintain Fillop's attention upon himself and Simiad. "I'm afraid our good magnate raised one too many toasts, and I...and I..." He purposely skipped the last step down from the carriage, feigning a drunken stupor, and promptly stumbled forward without completely losing his footing. Then his hip locked up, unexpectedly, causing the tailor to fall hard on his elbows. Maldinado gritted his teeth against the pain, again longing for his more youthful warrior's body. Then he rolled onto his back, grinning stupidly as he stared up at the overseer, "And I may have drunk a little too much wine, myself."

Fillop pointed to the fallen tailor and mumbled orders to the swad at his right hand, "Take him to the guest quarters." And to the swad on his left, he mumbled, "Help me with the magnate." Fillop never even glanced at Phinx or any of the other mounted swads; and Edran, smartly, remained behind the carriage door to better hide his face.

The overseer, with assistance from one of the manor's swads, pulled Simiad's lethargic body forward and out of the carriage. Together, with practiced effort, they all but carried the magnate inside and alongside Maldinado who only required help from one of the swads.

"Slow down, there, yearling," Maldinado spoke partly for show, partly due to his unexpected fall which left him hobbling more than usual. "You're making my...you're making...my head hurts. I like your chin."

Maldinado grinned with outlandish delight. So far, so good. The ruse had worked.

May the Sphere be with us and keep us in his light.

Phinx waited until Fillop and Maldinado entered the manor before dismounting, signaling the other taggles to do the same, and then he began removing the loose-fitting tymer-kurta. Underneath, he wore his more colorful taggle clothing and a fresh, white scarf designed with jagged patterns dyed blue with hessup leaf. The pattern slipped its alignment by several threads on one end, so his mother gifted it to her son. He placed the disfigured end in his mouth and shoved the discarded tymer-kurta into a saddlebag.

He looked about, waiting for the other taggles to finish dressing. All of them present, he noticed, except Inindu. For that matter, Phinx couldn't recall when he last saw her. Whereas he rode at the head of the magnate's procession, Inindu rode at the rear. Phinx questioned her inclusion in their masquerade, but Maldinado insisted. Or, rather, Inindu insisted, striking her slate board with a piece of chalk that crumbled into bits of powder with each stabbing motion. The mute seemed to hold an unusual influence over Maldinado.

Phinx caught Edran's attention and motioned him closer, "Where's Inindu?"

"She be meeting us again in the morning."

"Where did she go?"

"'Tis a mystery to be certain."

Phinx waited for the boy to provide more information, but Edran quietly climbed back atop the carriage without concern. Dumbfounded, chewing his scarf with vigor, Phinx looked back down the road they traveled only to find an empty street.

Tasa Ro!

With Simiad and Maldinado inside the manor, the taggles need only return the horses to the magnate's stables and disappear back into the sewers. A simple enough plan to execute despite their slightly inebriated state. The celebration in Third Gate had extended deep into the early morning hours before one of them, likely Maldinado, had realized they needed to return Simiad to his manor lest someone discover the magnate missing. Those chosen for the task—those only slightly less drunk than the majority of the taggles or, like the boy, actually sober—had performed remarkably well considering the challenges they faced, not the least of which required them to stay mounted. Far from skilled riders, anyone watching the procession of riders approach the manor would have immediately known them for impostors. And only the darkness allowed them to don the blood-stained tymer-kurtas; in some cases, still damp.

Phinx, for his part, had drunk enough ale to feel lightheaded even as he stood outside the magnate's manor, staring down the dark street, but he retained enough of his wits to remember the plan.

"As long as she stays hidden," Phinx shrugged and grabbed the reins of the black stallion, rubbing its nose and noticing, for the first time, the white glaze that covered its left eye. "A cataract-stricken horse? It's a wonder you didn't throw me off..." Phinx clutched his gut, suddenly remembering Jennaween. She brought him the horse; saddled it for him. He thought her anger over Corralea diminished. Did she still withhold her forgiveness? But, "She had to know there were other lovers." Again, he looked at the horse's eye, "Surely, she wouldn't..."

He led the gathered taggles away from the quiet manor; one hand gripping leather reigns, the other hand pulling at the scarf he held between his teeth. They stabled the horses and stored the carriage, and then quickly disappeared into the sewers below. As he descended the steel ladder, Phinx considered his available sleeping companions.

"She had to know..."

The disgruntled swad half-carried Maldinado all the way to a disarrayed guest chamber, crossed the cluttered room, and ungraciously discarded the tailor face down on a dusty mattress. He left without lighting a single candle and shut the wooden door with more force than Maldinado felt necessary. The tailor stopped grinning when he rolled over and waited for his eyes to adapt to the darkness.

Familiarity with the room informed Maldinado's path as he rose from the bed and navigated his way to a large window which led out to a small balcony. Wooden crates littered the rug-covered floor, some broken, some still containing wine bottles. Even without the benefit of a light, he knew the room smelled of must because of all the straw, tossed aside whenever the manor servants retrieved another wine bottle for their magnate. Tangled strands of straw stuck to everything in the room: fabric backed chairs, floor-to-ceiling curtains, and piles of folded blankets.

Few Delcreans claimed a magnate as friend. Fewer still ever slept at a magnate's manor, or knew of the mostly impoverished, and certainly childless, life of the Second Circle magnate. Maldinado knew the truth. Simiad lived in loneliness. No lover. No family. No one to mourn him on the day he passed beyond Ninth Circle. Maldinado knew the truth because he lived with that same sense of loneliness. The reason for their friendship. Loneliness bonded them.

He opened the window and walked out onto the balcony. It overlooked Second Circle and First Circle, but Maldinado looked beyond Delacroy to the extended land that lay beneath an all-consuming, darkened sky. *The land of the Sphere.* There, fires lit the night, rising high above the walls of Adarian and every other city; altars constructed for worship of the Sphere. Here, unlit and too far to see. The Adow—and his feelings for her—only a fading memory. Did she still live? How much time had passed since he entered Delacroy?

A familiar loneliness settled upon his shoulders.

So, I've started a revolution. For what purpose? To kill Morlac, yes, but then what? Would the Adow greet him upon his return? Or would he die in Morlac's world?

At that moment, he noticed a figure on the horizon—atop the outer wall of Delacroy. *The Adow of his memories!* She rode atop a horse and galloped along the length of the unguarded wall as though she ran over nothing more than a field of bloodgrass. He could only see her shadow, a faint impression against the darkness, but in her shadow, he detected a golden glow. And then, just as quickly, the glow and the Adow disappeared.

He rubbed the illusion from his tired eyes, turned back to the guest chamber, and again navigated the scattering of wine crates. A moment later he returned to the balcony with an open bottle in hand. He raised a toast to old friends and past lovers.

"A useless toast if ever there was one," Inindu said from the shadows of the balcony.

Maldinado nearly dropped the bottle, "How did you…when did you…"

"I don't feel like sleeping in the stables, tonight," Inindu said as the slender topi slunk further into the able-bodied horse.

Maldinado looked out over the balcony and into the distance below, "How…"

"For someone who hasn't sipped a drink all night, you're muttering like a fool," Inindu closed her eyes. "I'm tired, Madar."

He shook his head in wonder, "Then I drink to your honor and beauty, and leave you to your slumber."

"Now *that* is a worthwhile toast."

Morning arrived as sharply as the knife held threateningly to Simiad's bearded throat. Maldinado's knife. The magnate struggled to absorb his surroundings, struggled to identify his attacker. Sunlight blinded him. *Why did Fillop open the drapes?* All remaining thoughts lay buried under the weight of his latest hangover.

"May the Sphere be with you," Maldinado seemed to shout.

Simiad stared at his attacker, his vision finally coming into focus. He saw an older man: white whiskers grown into a short beard, a mound of white hair that drooped over a wrinkled forehead, and sporadic age spots dotting his gaunt face. Simiad thought for certain he recognized the thin, old man. *Maldinado? Why is Maldinado here?* Clipped memories surfaced from the previous evening: An attack in Third Gate, his swads— all slaughtered, and the words that saved his life…

"And keep you in his light," he whispered. Then, a little louder, "Are we to begin each morning in this fashion, old friend?"

Maldinado withdrew the blade, "Only today, old friend. You tend to forget more than you remember."

Simiad retrieved an unopened wine bottle from the mounted iron shelf beside his bed and began searching for a corkscrew, "If I could forget, I wouldn't drink so much."

Maldinado slid off the bed to retrieve the discarded corkscrew from the floor, and then reached for the bottle in Simiad's hand as though offering to assist. Instead of removing the cork, however, Simiad watched in horror as the tailor slid the corkscrew into his pocket and, more alarming, walked across the room to place the wine bottle atop the fireplace mantle,

"I need you sober."

Disappointed, Simiad scooted himself to a seated position, his legs still under the covers, "Is this to be my penance, then?"

"Drink all you want, tomorrow," Maldinado returned to Simiad's bedside with a noticeable limp and a knife which he held as though nothing more than needle and thread. "Today, we rescue Lyshmee."

The beheading. Simiad *had* forgotten.

A knock on the door interrupted their discussion. Fillop entered, "Forgive the intrusion, Mag..." He halted at the sight of the knife wielding Maldinado. The Overseer drew his sword, "Your orders, magnate?"

Simiad, struck by the force of the moment, suddenly realized Fillop could easily overpower the older and physically impaired Maldinado. He needed to only utter a command and Maldinado's revolution would end as quickly as it started. Simiad could return to his drinking...return... *Return to what?* To his insignificant life as Second Circle magnate? Yes, with a simple command the revolution would fizzle without ever catching Morlac's attention.

Or Simiad could allow Maldinado to live.

"Fetch me that bottle of wine from the mantle," Simiad pointed, much to the surprise of both men. "Your knife, Maldinado, you were describing its finer details," he held out his large hand and swiped the blade from the dumbfounded tailor. "It seems Fillop thinks you mean me harm, the result, no doubt, of his rather bad habit of entering my room without invitation."

Fillop sheathed his sword and bowed his head, "Forgive me, magnate." He half-ran to the mantle where he retrieved the blue tinted wine bottle and hastily uncorked it with a corkscrew he likely always carried in his pocket.

"I wish to bathe," Simiad swiped the bottle and took a prolonged drink, allowing the tart white wine to rekindle his senses. "We have a beheading, today."

"But you never...I mean, of course. At once," Fillop gave Maldinado a cautious glance before continuing, "If I may, you are most *energetic* this morning."

Simiad spun the knife in his hand and again raised the wine bottle to his lips. *I do feel good.* For the first time in his life, he wielded power—real power: Maldinado's life. The fate of the tailor's revolution. The fate of every Delcrean. Perhaps, even, the fate of Morlac.

The fate of a god...in my hands.

He could force the other magnates to grovel at his feet. Yes, he felt quite energetic.

"It's the sun, Fillop," Simiad lied, "You've denied me the morning sun all these years, but Maldinado has opened the drapes and I find the light most agreeable."

Fillop departed with a bow and a mumbled apology, closing the door behind him.

"I was wrong to doubt you," Maldinado gently disarmed the magnate, returning the knife to its sheath at his waist.

Simiad tightened his grip upon the wine bottle.

The tailor smiled, "And right to *mis*trust you."

Simiad laughed at his friend's double-speak, "You have started a revolution, Maldinado. Trust is forfeit." *Leverage takes precedence.* He rose from the undersized mattress, "Let's eat. I'm starving."

Sunlight gleamed off the Second Circle guillotine. Left surprisingly dormant, if not forgotten, for far too long. Phinx stood several feet away from the usually gruesome apparatus marveling at its pristine condition: Sharpened blade; visibly oiled grooves, allowing the mouton and blade to fall unimpeded; no trace of blood on the bascule and lunette—nothing left of previous executions. *How do they remove the blood?* The taggle considered the streaks of dried blood that had pooled within the creases and ridges of his fingers, discoloring his nails. No, just flecks of paint, oil stains, nothing more. Yet... He ran both hands down his hessup-dyed, wool tunic. He had washed the blood from them using water, salt, and lemon juice, but no matter how much he scrubbed...he felt the blood.

How many lives had he taken without any reflection the day after? Enough to match that guillotine? At least. Yet, he had awakened that morning convinced the yearling's blood still flowed between his fingers. Foolish thoughts. Phinx tucked his hair behind ears and focused anew upon the guillotine, forcing himself to look with a painter's eye—to absorb and record every detail. It struck him, then, as too perfect. In all his previously painted depictions, Phinx presented the guillotine as something more rugged and abused, as though never cleaned. *No guillotine should look that polished.* Without the gore and splattered blood and rust… *a sterilized death.*

"Contemplating your own demise?" Jennaween asked as she passed him. She must have followed him.

Phinx tugged at the red scarf around his neck. His favorite article of clothing felt tighter that morning for more than one reason—really, ever since Jennaween encountered Corralea, "Are you still angry?"

"No," she snapped her orange shawl crisply behind her, shifted it under loose brown hair, and wrapped it over bare shoulders.

Earlier, awake and alone, Phinx had emerged from the quiet sewers below where most of the taggles still slumbered. He wanted to scout the area and plot his path of escape. Their rescue plan called for several groups of taggles to surround and disarm, capture, or otherwise restrain each swad. If all went well, Lyshmee's rescue would occur in a matter of moments. If something went wrong…

Well, as his mother often stated when handing him another scarf, "Find a way to make use of what's left."

But what *did* remain? What remained of his relationship with Jennaween? His collection of lovers? He had wondered if she would ever speak to him again after all her fit throwing over Corralea. But there she stood, returned to him. Unable to escape his particular set of charms. The part of him no woman could resist.

"You had to know you weren't…I mean, love needs…*I* need variety," Phinx stammered despite his improved level of confidence. *I was right.* He wanted to say. *And you were wrong for expecting me to act any different than I've always acted.* Instead, he settled for a less accusatory approach, "Corralea is one of my many lovers, you know that. You had to have known that. But I don't love her any more than I love you. I love all of you equally, if for different reasons."

A few early travelers moved along the street, some already staking out a spot near the stage to better view the pending execution of the condemned, but Phinx and Jennaween retained enough privacy to continue their discussion without embarrassment. Foolishly, he later concluded, Phinx counted this as his good fortune.

"You need variety?" Jennaween looked back over her shoulder at him, and in that moment any perceived advantage Phinx had gained and dared to flaunt quickly vanished under her brazen, though disturbingly gentile gaze, "Yes, Corralea and I discussed your need for *variety*. We discussed many things last night. Bella was there, too. And Rayshin. And Kipla."

"What?" Phinx tugged at his seemingly suffocating scarf, "All of you...together?"

Jennaween turned to fully face him, flashing a wicked smile, "Like you said, last night, 'Taggles protect their own.'" She looked past him, then, "Isn't that right, girls?"

Phinx slowly followed her gaze, shifting his head and his feet, until he could see the four women standing behind him: Corralea...her soft cheeks; Bella with her long, slender nose; Rayshin's voluptuous lips; Kipla...oh, he could linger upon her neck for days.

"Taggles protect their own," they stated in unison.

"You've had all of us at your pleasure, sharing our beds whenever you desire," Jennaween continued. "Well, we're sick of sharing, so now you'll have none of us. How's that for variety?"

Phinx watched in horror as each of his jilted lovers turned an overly dramatic shoulder and briskly walked away without a second glance.

Only Jennaween remained.

He faced her with upturned, paint-splattered, pleading hands, "You had to know..."

"Yes, I knew. We all *know* what you are, Phinx: The great taggle lover. And we accepted our various roles in your life...until last night. A revolution changes everything, and when I saw you looking at Corralea... well, things are different, now. I'll help you start a revolution, and I'll die for your cause because I'm a taggle, but I won't share you with another woman. I won't die knowing you loved someone else." Jennaween looked around cautiously before continuing, "We're in the middle of a war between gods. One of them will most likely kill us in the end. So, choose your lover—choose whose arms will hold you as you take your final breath—and do it quickly lest you die alone. And then I will die alone. Don't you dare make me die..." She paused unexpectedly, stabbing at her tear-filled eyes. He had never seen her cry before, "Don't you dare!"

Phinx reached for her, but she pulled away, "No, you don't get to hold me. I told you I won't share!"

Thus, Jennaween passed by him and followed after his other lovers.

Phinx waited for her to steal another glance at him, but she never turned.

Suddenly everything about his life had changed. Father of the revolution. Lover of none. Nothing felt right. Nothing felt real. He wanted to chip away at the dried paint of the canvas before him until he scraped it clean and could begin anew. But it seemed he no longer held the brush.

"Wait, they want me to *choose*?"

SEVERING

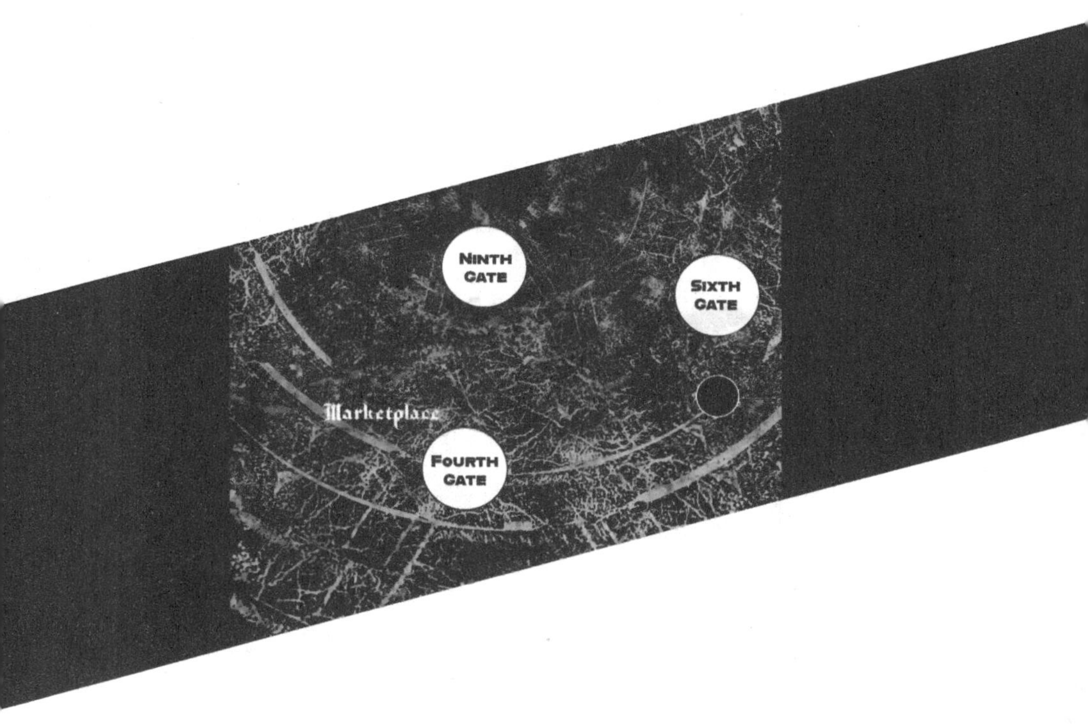

Those who do not worship Morlac faithfully, in word or deed, and any resident known to worship the god of another world, will die on the guillotine—upon the severing of their head from body.

By Order of Magnate Orpheum, Ninth Circle

hale, Adherent of Delacroy, prepared a simple meal of boiled rice, chopped carrots, and a spattering of peas. He poured oil over the mound he had piled on a wooden plate and added a buttermilk biscuit which he grabbed from under a burlap cloth that covered a ceramic bowl. He ate near an enormous fire pit, leaning against a center counter section made from butcher block. The kitchen sat empty and cold most evenings, for Shale more often found himself settling for a dry supper than not—but on this night he welcomed the warmth of the food in his belly and the heat against his skin.

He stared at the lone decoration adorning the walls: a painting that hung above the doorway, striking in both its placement upon the wall—well above common sight lines—and in its blue-toned color pallet which represented the only blue in the otherwise red palace. In fact, the painter had used several variations of blue to depict a fierce ocean, a cloud-riddled sky, and a distant mountain range. In the foreground, upon dark cliffs that jutted outward over the sea, stood the figure of a lone traveler, his back to the viewer. A shock of red hair offered the only contrasting color tone. The painter constructed the scene using a triangular composition, merging the cliffs with the traveler so that his head served as the uppermost point. On either side of the figure, in the distance, angled shadows represented the horizon, and served to direct the viewer's eye while also emphasizing an unseen object in the distance upon which the traveler so intently focused.

As he studied the painting, Shale did not concern himself with made up stories about the traveler's past, nor did he ever linger upon the visible peaks. Instead, he too, dwelt on what the painter had somehow hidden beyond the painting. The severed portion.

a taggle's painting

Delacroy

Certainty | Chastity | Fasting | Generosity | Joy | Orthodoxy | Peace | Honesty | Faithfulness

Lyshmee stood quietly inside her dungeon chamber, arms extended to the side whilst three other women busied themselves with dressing her, having already bathed her, and pampering her according to the traditions reserved for beheadings. One of the women clothed her in a formal, white murat-gown complete with gold interlay and a long, red train. Murat, a Second Circle seamstress, preferred gowns with a high waist. This particular gown, too heavy for Lyshmee's slender frame, paired the high waist with a low-cut neckline elegantly accented by sleeves designed to sit lightly about the shoulder. Unfortunately, the slightest movement by Lyshmee caused the sleeves to fall toward her elbows.

The oldest of the three women shook her head for at least the third time and readjusted the sleeves, "Your arms grow straight out of your neck, same as my youngest."

Another of the women, taller than Lyshmee, pulled at her thick black hair, tugging upward with great effort—intent on exposing every inch of Lyshmee's neck. Pins scratched and dug into Lyshmee's scalp until, finally, the woman had inserted enough of them to keep her hair in place; or simply could find no more room to add any more of the tiny daggers. In the end, carefully fashioned curls sat atop Lyshmee's head and cascaded over both her forehead and the tips of her ears. Though, *regrettably* and *disturbingly*, according to the hairdresser, the curls failed to conceal Lyshmee's earlobes which remained quite attached to her neck as though day lilies waiting to bloom. The woman also commented on her overgrown, *weedy* eyebrows, and Lyshmee's sunken cheeks that resembled *rotten squash*. With a final, resigned sigh, the woman added a white lace coiffure. Lyshmee would symbolically remove the thin shawl as she approached the guillotine.

The last of the women dug under Lyshmee's fingernails with unpleasant force, and then under her toenails. She aggressively filed the nails and vigorously rubbed oil into the surrounding skin, mumbling inaudible curses all the while. No doubt, Lyshmee assumed, chastising her for a dozen or more appalling blemishes discovered during the process.

At last, all three women backed far enough away to view their collective work. And when Lyshmee lowered her arms, both sleeves fell.

Mathay entered the cell, broad shoulders easily supporting a royal blue tymer-kurta. His eyes traveled down Lyshmee's body and back to the areas with exposed skin, tapping a silver ring upon his sword hilt. Then he slowly circled around her and placed a menacing hand on her bare shoulder. His sinister touch made her cringe, a distressing reminder of those first few weeks in the dungeon when the swads took turns raping her; Mathay more often than the others. She tried to pull out from under his terrifying grip, but he held tight and led her out of the filthy cell and away from the three women who visibly, if silently, displayed their disapproval of Mathay without offering an ounce of sympathy for her.

Seven swads, standing guard in the corridor, fell in line behind Lyshmee and Mathay. And cheerfully skipping in front of her, as though part of a wedding ceremony rather than escorting the condemned, several yearlings littered her path with so many white lily pedals that, per tradition, they forced Lyshmee to trample the flowers with her every step. Lyshmee recalled her own days as a flower girl, gaily broadcasting pedals without concern for either the symbolism or the accused. She had thought it all a grand festival back then, unaware of the ugly truth, for her mother whisked her away long before the guillotine blade fell.

Lyshmee smiled at one of the yearlings walking before her, a girl with straight red hair and a missing front tooth, who stopped skipping to sneak a peek at Lyshmee's dress, "You have beautiful hair," she spoke with a delicate, if somewhat fractured, voice.

"I wish it was black like yours." Suddenly embarrassed, the girl ran to catch up with the other yearlings, but continued looking back at Lyshmee, forgetting to broadcast her pedals until one of the boys reminded her.

The procession moved out of the dungeon and up a multi-level staircase, stopping at an open archway that led into the crowded street. Lyshmee breathed deeply, enjoying the fresh air away from her musty cell, and closed her eyes if only to escape the moment. She opened them again when Mathay forcefully prodded her forward.

Then the red-haired girl, along with her fellow skipping yearlings, disappeared into the crowd.

Lyshmee suddenly gasped for air, her tiny frame struggling to expand wide enough to breath. And then she wept. She had thought herself ready for that moment, convinced she fully understood the sacrifice she had made to protect the Sons and Daughters of Oblation. She had survived every violation of her body, withstanding the physical abuse and the lack of food. None of it broke her. None of it made her cry. But she never envisioned the red-haired girl, and she hated her captors all the more for including the innocent yearling in such an ugly affair as death.

May the Sphere be with you, she prayed, *and keep you in his light.*

"What's your wager?" The tone of inquiry seemed particularly jolly, emphasized by the man's extended jaw and plump skin surrounding fingertip dimples. He wore a leather biggins hat, dyed yellow with birmly weed; loose hanging ties elongated his otherwise fatty features. The hat designated him as Gold Keeper at the beheading, collector of wagers. Three yearlings assisted the keeper, one pushed whilst the other two pulled a wooden dray filled with bags of gold coins. It proved easy enough for Simiad to track their path through the gathered crowd, an exaggerated wave of movement that, if not for tradition and greed, would otherwise have created an unfriendly commotion.

Despite several hands raising gold around his head, Simiad managed to pass the Gold Keeper a small pouch, "Magnate Simiad. Second Circle. Seventeen coins. Failed rescue." Tradition dictated the magnate place a wager. Decorum suggested a magnate should never wager against his own ability, and that of his swads, to prevent a rescue attempt. And general disregard of his role as Second Circle Magnate left him traversing the streets like everyone else in order to place the expected wager.

The collector of wagers unceremoniously added Simiad's gold to his overfilled dray and recorded the wager with a charcoal stick on the outside of a scroll, his fingers covered in black dust. Previously written names appeared smeared to the point of being unreadable. The keeper smiled and moved to the next attendee, "What's your wager?"

"Maldinado. Fourth Circle. Twenty-six coins. Successful rescue."

Ignoring his own established tenant to never brush past a woman while traveling the streets of Delacroy, Simiad pushed his way toward Maldinado, "A wager?"

Maldinado smiled shrewdly, "I have reason to believe my wager represents an opportunity. Though I fear yours will only serve as a donation."

"It's tradition," Simiad shrugged. "But not without merit since I've never lost."

"Until today."

"Then consider it my gift to the cause."

The two moved through the gathered crowd toward a small, elevated stage a short distance from the guillotine. Though Simiad dwarfed Maldinado in both girth and height, the older, frailer tailor drew most of the attention. One Delcrean after another, every few feet, offered the tailor the traditional greeting.

"Morlac's boon upon thee, Maldinado."

A large woman approached the tailor. She wore two red-beaded necklaces. One of the strands hung low to her sizable waist, while the other rested tight against her bloated neck.

Maldinado froze mid-step, apparently recognizing the annoyingly boisterous voice, "Favor and boon, Harian."

"I didn't think you were coming? I guess that new horse of yours does help you get around, though."

It seemed every word Harian spoke required a corresponding hand gesture, or a tilt of the head, or a shift of the hips that made Simiad wonder how anyone could possess so much fervor. Her abundance of passion and energy struck out against his chest like relentless gusts of wind until he felt certain he would forever depend upon her to provide every ounce of air he wished to breathe. He found her utterly exhausting.

"Oh, you have to meet my newest friend. You two will love each other. I was just telling her about you and how you couldn't attend the beheading on account of your bad hip. But here you are. Morlac's boon, can you believe our good fortune? Maldinado right here in Second Circle. Now, I wonder. Where did she wander off to?"

With a polite shrug of his shoulders, Maldinado left Harian to her own mis-wanderings.

Simiad followed closely behind, eager to distance himself from the talkative woman, "Deftly done."

Maldinado shuddered, "My dead wife's sister. I swear no matter how far I travel from Fourth Circle, or during what time of day, I always encounter that woman. Lomax thinks I should marry her, so she'll stop paying me so much attention, but I'm secretly hoping this crowd will swallow her whole and finally end her annoyingly happy existence. She's enough to make any man want to move to Second Circle."

"An unexpected benefit, but yes, celibacy done properly certainly fails to...um, attract all potential suitors."

"Morlac's boon upon thee, Maldinado," thus began another exchange.

Simiad started counting the number of greetings they each received, and when they finally reached their destination, Maldinado's total greetings outnumbered Simiad's by fifty-three. Fifty-four greetings if he included their second encounter with Harian. For a moment, Simiad considered arresting the tailor—he could expose Maldinado as a worshiper of the Sphere. Well-acquainted with feelings of jealousy, however, Simiad kept silent and instead focused on the opportunity at-hand; that, and visions of the other magnates prostrating themselves before him.

Upon arriving at a poorly constructed staircase, one which led to a much sturdier wooden platform, Simiad parted ways with Maldinado and climbed the stairs. A few moments later, Simiad sat on a wooden box that someone had placed in roughly the middle of the platform. There, he awaited the accused. Other magnates sat on padded chairs whenever they presided over beheadings. But he tried not to think about such matters. Galeab, Ninth Circle Magnate, pronounced judgment from the comfort of a golden throne. This, too, he dismissed even as he attempted to ignore the sharp discomfort already emerging in his lower back due to the hunched-over posture he assumed upon first taking a seat on the small, wooden box.

But he did not dwell on these pesky little differences.

Things will change, soon enough.

Maldinado positioned himself at the base of the platform staircase. Responsibility for Simiad rested upon his shoulders. If the magnate gave them away, if he said anything aside from pronouncing judgment, Maldinado would kill him. Admittedly, the stairs presented a challenge for the hobbled tailor. He could climb them, but not well. Then again, he wondered about his ability to catch and kill a younger man as big as Simiad. Holding a knife to the throat of a drunkard, or to one who slept, required little skill. Assaulting a sober man presented an entirely different challenge.

Simiad had proven his allegiance earlier that morning. Still, he represented the greatest threat to Maldinado's rescue plan which relied upon isolation and surprise. Any warning given to the swads by the magnate would result in a foiled rescue attempt. If Simiad played his role, however, if he simply pronounced judgment and nothing else, Maldinado felt confident the taggles dispersed throughout the crowd could quickly overpower the swads.

And what of his friends? *Friends.* The word sounded foreign. Friends of the tailor, yes, but his inner warrior saw them only as potential threats. Simiad. He had almost killed his friend—twice, within the span of only a few hours. Harian, Perinah, Peeks…Maldinado had encountered each of them on his way through the crowd. Would they choose to join his revolution? If not, he knew the warrior inside would not hesitate to kill them. *Lomax?* Would he kill his closest friend if Lomax chose to worship Morlac? *That's one way to outlive him...* No! Maldinado buried the thought.

A cheer arose, signaling Lyshmee's appearance. The revolution drew near.

Fillop, Second Circle Overseer, rarely left Simiad's side, but the execution of a prisoner shifted his attention elsewhere. Thus, at the time of Lyshmee's arrival, he stood stationed in a nearby home, beside an upstairs window overlooking the guillotine. He held a flintlock rifle in his hands. Two swads, one standing beside Fillop, the other kneeling between them, also held rifles at the ready. They scanned the crowd for anyone attempting to rescue Lyshmee.

"Morlac's boon upon thee," Fillop raised his rifle, slightly.

"Favor and boon," his swads responded.

The overseer glanced to his left and across the street at a similar home where three more flints stood watch at a second-story window, their weapons barely visible within the shadows. He shifted his focus to a rooftop directly opposite his position. Three more flints; armed and ready. And another two stations to his right. Five stations. Fifteen flints. It seemed overly cautious for the routine beheading of a prisoner without repute, but Fillop's experience in handling Simiad's various drunken blunders taught him that a cautious approach frequently prevented larger issues. Appropriately satisfied with his established defenses, Fillop returned his attention to the prisoner in the street below.

Phinx gnawed at a purple scarf as Lyshmee passed. He stood less than twenty feet from the guillotine. Five swads, each wearing traditional blue tymer-kurtas, escorted the condemned prisoner through the impeding crowd. Several feet ahead of them, another three swads, wearing red tymer-kurtas, forged a pathway with swords drawn, hoping to dissuade resistance. Phinx studied the facial expression of each swad, searching for any sign of concern, but they seemed not to notice the increased number of taggles attending the beheading or, if they did notice the brightly-dyed clothing of the easily identified tru-born, they proceeded without distress.

So far, so good.

When the swads reached the staircase leading up to the guillotine, they shifted responsibility of the prisoner from those wearing blue tymer-kurtas to those in red. No longer required to forge a path, therefore, the three lead swads assumed escort duty. When the largest of the blue-clad swads released his grip on the condemned, however, Lyshmee lifted her coiffure and straightaway spat upon him. Phinx and those around him roared with laughter, and gamely cheered the act of defiance, if only briefly. The swad wiped his face and, fully embracing the moment, licked the spittle from his hand with a nasty grin. The crowd around Phinx erupted, and immediately a murmur began circulating in the distance as to the reason for the commotion.

"Brilliant!" Phinx lauded the brief skirmish as though applauding a performance. All intentions aside, he appreciated a good show.

But the scuffle ended when the afflicted swad moved to join his blue brothers-in-arms. They spread themselves out through the crowd, effectively establishing a perimeter around the base of the platform. Phinx turned his attention to Lyshmee. She climbed the stairs, following her red-clad escort, and took a position at the edge of the platform—clearly visible from where Phinx stood. Lyshmee looked out over the crowd to where Simiad sat all alone on a stage opposite the guillotine. The five blue swads below, having successfully transported their prisoner to her execution, turned to face the magnate. So, too, did the crowd.

Phinx stopped chewing on his scarf. He scanned the area immediately surrounding the stage, hoping to find Jennaween standing nearby; or one of his other lovers. He found none of them. Instead, he estimated thirty or more taggles stood within fifty paces of the platform, all anxiously awaiting the pronounced judgment from Simiad, for Maldinado had emphasized the need for them to rescue Lyshmee *after* Simiad confirmed her execution—not prior. Thus, Phinx and the other taggles waited.

And waited.

"Lyshmee, of Second Circle," the crowd fell silent as the foremost red swad bellowed forth the accusations against the prisoner.

Based on where they stood in relation to the prisoner, Phinx knew the designated role of the three swads who addressed Simiad: Standing directly in front of Lyshmee, Orator. To her left, Executioner. And the swad on her right, Body Removal. Should the Executioner die during a rescue attempt, one of the other two swads would assume his duties. As such, the taggles needed to capture all three swads before the blade fell.

The stout orator continued, "Accused of worshiping the Sphere.

Found copulating in her Second Circle home with Penrem of Eighth Circle. During an account of his relationship with Lyshmee, as recorded by Somering, Appointed Recorder of Delacroy, the honest and forthcoming Penrem confirmed what our own, honorable Mathay, arresting swad, witnessed with his own eyes." The orator motioned toward the largest of the blue swads. The one upon whom Lyshmee had spat. Then he continued, "The accused offers no account of her actions. Therefore, by order of Fillop, Overseer of Second Circle, the prisoner is presented for execution by beheading. We will act according to your order, Magnate Simiad."

All three swads bowed even as Simiad stood to pronounce judgment.

Maldinado gripped the knife at his waist, awaiting any hint of warning from Simiad to his swads. *Remove her head.* The tailor wished only to hear those words. Any other word from Simiad, and Maldinado would storm the stairs; or stumble up them. *Crawl?* The whimsical thought made him long for Hintor. *My friend.* Hintor had a way of making Maldinado laugh prior to every battle.

He looked up and out over the crowd, half expecting to find Brink carrying the banner of the Adarian 45th. But Brink lay dead. He fell in the battle at Dragon's Torment, far away from where Maldinado stood in Second Circle. He smiled at the thought and softly muttered, "Lucky bastard!"

Phinx tore into his scarf, pulling on it as much with his hand as with his teeth. He scanned the crowd, once more, suddenly desperate to find Jennaween. Nothing. The moment of revolution arrived, and Phinx faced it alone.

"Remove her head," Simiad stated.

The taggles sprang forward all at once; seemingly, from everywhere a blue swad stood guard. Phinx let the scarf fall from his mouth and dove toward Mathay. Someone else wrapped their arms around Mathay's legs, causing him, and Phinx, to topple over.

On the platform above, the executioner, unaffected by the unified attack, led Lyshmee to the guillotine. The other two swads took positions at the top of the stairs, swords drawn. Lyshmee dutifully removed her coiffure, and the executioner proceeded to strap her onto the bascule.

Cheers erupted in response to the coordinated uprising.

Phinx rammed his elbow into the back of Mathay's neck as they hit the ground together. The added force effectively planted the swad's face into the dirt and, as a result, he stopped struggling against his assailants. Realizing the blow must have knocked his opponent unconscious, Phinx grabbed the swad's fallen sword even as three more taggles converged on Mathay's limp body.

"Stay with him," Phinx instructed. "The rest of us will take the platform."

He ran to the staircase, but several taggles had already beaten him to the steps including Corralea. Simultaneously elated and mortified, for his lover specialized in corruption not murder, Phinx cried out, "No! Corralea, wait!" But Corralea continued her assault and, upon reaching the top of the stairs, inexplicably attacked the two awaiting red swads without waiting for help. *Fool woman!*

Phinx watched in horror as she flung herself at both swads, the first of several taggles who rushed forward. The orator almost casually deflected her initial knife thrust and just as easily ran her through with his curved sword. Then, he used her body as a shield against the onslaught of taggles, but the attempt only hindered his ability to defend himself. Within seconds, five taggles, including Lilthian and her three daughters, dancers from Fourth Gate, threw the mutilated body of Corralea's killer from the stage. The other swad stood strong, wounding several taggles before a knife in the back, thrown from somewhere in the crowd, finally knocked him off his feet.

Phinx reached Corralea, but already she lay dead. He cradled her body, momentarily oblivious to the chaos surrounding him. *Choose whose arms will hold you as you take your final breath.* Jennaween's words echoed harshly in his mind.

The executioner slid Lyshmee's head into place under the guillotine blade and lowered the lunette.

Seven more taggles rushed the platform, daggers in hand, focused on the last of the remaining swads. But as they did, flintlock rifles shattered the air. Lead bullets ripped through the taggle force—killing or maiming several of those already on the platform, halting those along the staircase.

Blood splattered Phinx' face as Diato, a taggle actor from Fifth Gate, collapsed to one knee in front of the painter, having taken two bullets in the chest—wounds otherwise intended for Phinx. The actor pulled at the purple scarf around Phinx' neck, "Leave her. She's dead." Diato looked out at the crowd, eyes widening with sudden horror, "They're all dead."

Three more shots, all fired in succession. One of the bullets whisked by them, but the other two bullets struck Diato in the back. His body went limp. His bloodied hand slid down Phinx' scarf until, at last, he released his grip and fell into death. No one else moved. On the platform, or upon the stairs. In a moment, the executioner would release the blade and sever Lyshmee's head.

But then the executioner fell to his knees, moribund. The third bullet had lodged itself into the base of his skull and, with a final, garbled breath, the executioner died. Only Phinx and Lyshmee remained alive amongst those who littered the platform.

topi-Inindu:

Strands of my hair extend throughout the room where Fillop and his flints tried so gallantly to hold their positions, but they never stood a chance. I stand silently at the window, one arm on Edran's shoulder. My brother kneels at the same window, flintlock rifle still smoking in his hands. My brother, assassin. Lyshmee's savior. Behind him, three cocoons hover within my black hair which flows freely and wildly, consuming the room as though a thousand vipers converging upon their prey. I savor the taste of their flesh in my hair, and I hunger for more.

Lyshmee opened her eyes. She still lay horizontally upon the bascule, hands tied behind her back with her head placed under the lunette, but the blade remained locked in place. She waited for a rescue, but nobody released her.

She couldn't see much. To her left, at the base of the guillotine, the body of her executioner. The wooden planks of the platform, and between them the red dirt of the street below. The anxious crowd. No one spoke a word. No one moved, as though suspended in time. She spotted a familiar face: A girl with straight red hair and a missing front tooth. The yearling, her flower girl, stood in front of the crowd, not far removed from the platform. She stood calmly watching Lyshmee, waiting.

"I hope they rescue you," she whispered.

Lyshmee embraced the yearling's innocence, "Me, too."

Me, too.

"Tasa Ro!"

Maldinado stepped onto Simiad's platform with a stilted hop. He could finally see clearly: The pile of taggles mixed with swads, their bodies lay in awkward heaps upon the opposite platform. Lyshmee still locked into the guillotine. And not a soul willing to move.

"Flints?" Maldinado asked Simiad. The magnate stood behind him.

"Several of them," Simiad replied. "High…over there, and there," he pointed. "It appears Fillop has us surrounded."

"Your Overseer is the worst kind of irritant."

Simiad shrugged, "I've always thought him a faithful commander. Depends on your point of view, I suppose; or which god you serve."

Maldinado ignored Simiad's last remark, racing through his available options. *Wait!* He turned toward the magnate, "Faithful, you say? Let's find out just how faithful…" The Madar drew his knife, "On your knees, old friend."

"Again, with the knife?" Simiad obediently knelt. "This is becoming a habit. And not one I enjoy."

"Fillop!" Maldinado wrapped one arm around Simiad's head and held the knife to his neck. "The rescue is complete. You are defeated."

A scream served as the only response. An endless, breathless, relentless scream. Maldinado searched the edges of the crowd but couldn't determine the source. Then a weave of swirling blackness shot out of a second story window some distance down the street. *Inindu!* He recognized her hair, immediately. It seemed to fill the sky, rising higher and higher until it far exceeded the heights of the nearby homes. Those who had gathered for the beheading stood mesmerized by the spectacle.

Someone shouted, "Inindu!"

Several more echoed the sentiment, convinced Inindu had entered the city.

She's here, alright. Though, Maldinado could not imagine what she had planned aside from showing off. But when Fillop's head appeared within the black weave of her hair, only his head—eyes alert, mouth screaming—Maldinado suddenly recalled the stories from the tailor's youth that described Inindu as a monster. A demon. Eater of the dead. And in that moment, he believed every story. Did he choose the wrong god? What cursed creature did he invite into the city? *Favor and boon!*

The severed head floated upward against the blackness, rising violently like a feather in a gale. Fillop's screams filled Maldinado's ears, seized his chest, and coursed through his veins. He felt every ounce of terror as though it emerged from his own mouth. Indeed, staring up at Inindu's captive, still holding a knife to Simiad's bearded throat, Maldinado understood why Fillop screamed. This was a battle of the gods, and the battle they waged pitted friend against friend, brother against sister, husbands and wives. Maldinado lowered his gaze from Fillop's head to the taggle dead. Artisans. Their future works of beauty forever lost. A revolution, no matter how just the cause or which god he followed, would destroy the city. Yes, he understood why Fillop screamed.

He, too, screamed. He howled with guttural exuberance. He raged against all the chaos of his mind, the pain of two lives lived. His lungs cleared themselves of the putrid air he breathed. His voice blared over Fillop's, forcefully drawing the crowd's attention. Others joined him. Howling and yelling and shouting. Then the screams stopped. Fillop fell silent. Maldinado breathed, once more. The crowd waited.

Fillop's head vanished behind the blackness of Inindu's hair which slowly parted in the center, and an unmistakable spherical shape appeared—a hole in the darkness, a view of the sky. Light.

"The moment is yours, Madar," said a familiar voice.

Maldinado turned to find Inindu-horse standing on the platform behind him. He couldn't recall seeing her come onto the platform. Though, admittedly, he had found the head and the hair more than a little distracting. But there she stood. A terrifying creature. No, oddly, her fierce presence brought him comfort, for she had traveled through Morlac's illusion with him. She served as his source of truth, however deadly or fierce, for what was real apart from Inindu? They alone lived in this world of the dead. He waited for Inindu-horse to speak further, but she offered nothing more.

Maldinado gathered himself before turning to address the stunned gathering, "Lyshmee shall not die, today, for she is a Daughter of Oblation. She worships the Sphere." Maldinado pointed to the follicle sphere in the sky, "All of you serve as witnesses that the Sphere has not forgotten his daughter. Release her. And may the Sphere be with you."

"And keep you in his light," the taggles responded, though somewhat hesitantly.

"And keep you in his light," Simiad whispered.

Corralea's body lay at Phinx' feet. Diato's, too. Several more taggles lay scattered across the platform, or on the stairs where those still living huddled together, leery of...everything and anything. Rifle shots and screams and signs from the gods and severed heads—Fillop's head, surrounded by a wildly wavering shadow, had inexplicably floated in the sky above the crowd. A severed head. In the sky. And it screamed as though still alive, and then Maldinado screamed as though possessed, and others, too, and Phinx had bellowed along with them.

He didn't know why.

Corralea's death? Diato's sacrifice? No, death did not bother him. He specialized in assassination methods, frequently sharing a room with a warm corpse. Poison. Strangulation. Blood dripping from his dagger. He never flinched, and he never failed. His services fetched more gold than any other taggle, and for good reason. Those who hired Phinx often gained political or financial leverage as a result. Competition in the marketplace? An older sibling blocking your path to the magnate's seat? A witness to your misdeeds? *Pay a taggle, earn Morlac's favor.*

His brush with death did not cause him to scream, either, for his dark affairs placed him at the edge of life—his own, and that of his targets— each time he entered into an assassination scheme. No, he knew all too well how quickly life faded into death. A blade to the gut while walking along a crowded street. A sip of wine amongst friends. A soft pillow after a long day. The end. Death arrived without warning. Phinx never felt his life at risk, and he never felt safe. He found such terms meaningless even in the midst of rifle fire while attempting to rescue a condemned prisoner.

But he did scream. He yelled at the god who wanted him to lead a revolution. A god who then proceeded to take love from him. The first to die. Corralea. Yet, Phinx felt...nothing. He thought himself in love with her, but he barely knew her. He could have painted her every curve from memory but, aside from the taggles, *who* exactly would mourn her death? He did not know her parents. Did she have siblings? Whom should he notify? Instead of feeling broken, as though someone squeezed the blood from his heart, Phinx felt shame and guilt. He should mourn her. *He,* if anyone. Yet, nothing. The roar he released sprung from a lack of feeling. Emptiness.

In the silence that followed, Phinx realized he did not blame his god for Corralea's death.

He hated himself.

Still, the Sphere needed him to lead a revolution. *Tasa Ro!* The god had all but appeared, and if that did not qualify as enough of a sign, only Phinx remained alive on the platform. The Sphere needed him, and so did Lyshmee. Gently shifting out from under the bodies of Corralea and Diato, Phinx rose and walked over to the guillotine. He wondered how many flints remained, half expecting to feel the impact of a discharged lead ball at any moment. But the flints held their fire, and Phinx reached Lyshmee without further opposition. He raised the lunette, slid her out from beneath the blade, and untied her hands.

"The Father of Oblation sent me to rescue you," Phinx told her.

Lyshmee embraced him, unable to hold back her tears, "Thank you." Uncertain what else to do, Phinx wrapped his arms around her, his own emotions still equally overwhelming.

Jennaween...

He searched for her amid the crowd, longing to hold her once more, but she remained hidden. He could only hope she survived. No doubt, she survived. He couldn't imagine the swad who could win a fight with Jennaween, neither did Phinx wish to fight with her any longer. He wanted her to know she could die in his arms, and he in hers; and when she died, he wanted her to know it would mean something to him. Not like Corralea. Never again.

The taggles celebrated around him, but the gathered residents of Second Circle did not share in the excitement. Phinx could see it in their eyes. Horrifying signs in the sky followed by talk of the Sphere sent several of them, those near the edges of the crowd, scattering for their homes. The ones who stayed stared at Phinx or Maldinado or the dark curtain still wavering in the sky and attempted to absorb the implications of what they had witnessed.

Phinx looked toward Maldinado, knowing what came next. The rescue of Lyshmee provided a public stage, but it lacked the impetus required to birth a revolution: Bloodshed. Not taggle blood. Delcrean blood. Personal choices and deadly consequences.

"Gather the swads," Maldinado shouted. Then he addressed the unseen flints in the windows above the street, "If you fire upon us, I will kill your magnate."

Pockets of movement emerged throughout the crowd as taggles pushed their captured swads toward the guillotine. Those taggles closest to the homes from which the flints had fired, boldly rushed their positions, and moments later emerged holding confiscated rifles high above their heads as they escorted the flints to the platform.

Phinx pulled back from Lyshmee, reassuring her, "You have nothing to fear. The Sons and Daughters of Oblation will soon be revealed."

He left her standing there and began gathering the bodies of the fallen taggles beginning with Corralea. Several more taggles assisted, and together they laid the dead along the back of the platform. Eight taggles had died during the rescue attempt. Phinx knew them all: Corralea, Lilthian and her three daughters, Diato, Brendt, and Hethor. Several more had suffered wounds. The swads showed similar signs of battle. Four dead, the three red swads who stood guard on the platform, and a blue swad with so many slashes it proved difficult to tell which of the wounds had actually killed him. Phinx had four of the taggles pile what remained of the swad dead on the street beside the platform. Then he turned his attention to the living.

In total, the taggles captured thirty-one swads, shoving them below into a line that ended near the top of the staircase. Jennaween brought the last of them, and the biggest. She emerged from the crowd, carrying a sword, and dragging a bound Mathay behind her. He had obviously escaped from where Phinx had left him lying unconscious. When Phinx caught a glimpse of her, he immediately walked to the edge of the platform, "Jennaween." But she did not look up. Either she did not hear him, or she purposely ignored him. It didn't matter. The sight of her lifted his spirits. The presence of Jennaween—covered in red dirt; her orange shawl tied around her waist rather than over her shoulders; strands of brown hair hanging out in several directions—her presence filled the emptiness.

"They saved me," Lyshmee knelt and called down to the red-haired flower girl.

"I knew they would."

"Where are your parents?"

"They never made it through the Sorting."

Lyshmee lay on her stomach and motioned the girl closer to the stage. "Lift her up," she shouted to several taggles below. A moment later, she held the orphan in her arms, "My name is Lyshmee."

"I know," the girl ran her fingers through Lyshmee's black hair.

"What is your name?"

"Alanna."

"Well, Alanna, would you like to stay with me?"

"Yes," she hugged Lyshmee's neck. "You smell pretty."

Lyshmee squeezed the girl tightly.

"Let it be known," Phinx heard a murmur move through the crowd as Maldinado spoke. Curiosity. Fear. Mothers pulled yearlings closer. Some in the crowd sought to escape. Others stood confidently. The tailor continued, "The Sons and Daughters of Oblation worship the Sphere. We stand in opposition to Morlac. We will destroy him and any who worship him. You know me as Maldinado, tailor of Fourth Circle. Now you will know me as a worshiper of the Sphere. And I will know which god you follow. I will know who stands with us, and who opposes us." He pointed to the spherical shape in the sky, "Can you deny the existence of the Sphere? Where is Morlac, now? Who will save you from my blade? Make your choice and reveal yourself."

Then Maldinado pulled Simiad to his feet and dragged him to the edge of the platform——fully capturing everyone's attention. Phinx marveled at Simiad's performance. The terrified look on the magnate's bearded face conveyed the perfect amount of intensity when, in reality, falling off the platform presented a greater threat to his well-being than did Maldinado's knife since Simiad had already professed his allegiance.

"May the Sphere be with you," Maldinado shouted.

"And keep you in his light," Phinx and the taggles replied.

Maldinado turned to Simiad, "May the Sphere be with you."

"And keep me in his light," Simiad replied with a touch of trepidation in his voice.

"Strong performance," Phinx muttered softly. "Really, well done."

He observed dozens of surprised looks in the crowd. Lyshmee, too, let out a small gasp of wonder, no doubt wondering why a worshiper of the Sphere had condemned her to death only moments prior. The taggles, meanwhile, cheered as Maldinado released Simiad. *All part of the show.* Then, right on cue, Maldinado's horse knelt slightly, allowing the tailor to mount. Phinx had suggested this portion of the plan for, as a painter, he understood focal point and visual balance. Though Maldinado spoke loudly enough, his withered frame diminished his presence and detracted from his message. Atop the horse, though...

A remarkable horse. Phinx found himself oddly compelled to paint the beast.

Maldinado waited for silence, "Bring forth the accused."

Phinx grabbed the first swad in line and pushed him to the same spot from which Lyshmee had previously stood to face Simiad's judgment.

"May the Sphere be with you," Maldinado said.

Still holding the swad's arm, Phinx felt the man's muscles stiffen as he spat his reply, "Favor and boon!"

"Magnate Simiad," Maldinado transitioned, "This swad is a known worshiper of Morlac. We will act according to your order."

"Remove his head," Simiad returned to his wooden box and took a seat. Despite his sizable girth, the magnate seemed pathetically small beside the horse and the mounted tailor. Mostly due to the horse, Phinx realized, before pulling the worshiper of Morlac over to the guillotine where he secured the newly condemned prisoner to the bascule; slid him into place; and lowered the lunette around his neck.

"What's your wager?" The Gold Keeper, clinging to his yellow biggins hat, hung out of a nearby window. The crowd erupted in cheer and applause, "Will anyone rescue this worshiper of Morlac?"

"Gold Keeper," Maldinado called. "You owe me a fair amount of gold. I wagered twenty-six coins on the successful rescue of Lyshmee, and there she stands."

"As my title suggests, I keep the gold," he shrugged with zany enthusiasm. "But I worship the Sphere, so consider your wager a donation to the cause. May the Sphere be with you."

"And keep you in his light," Phinx joined the jolly and collective response.

"Keep your gold then," Maldinado tugged at his robe. "And your head."

"Most generous, Maldinado," the Gold Keeper swung his hat in a half-circle and bowed his head with grand flair. "The tailor of Fourth Circle is rightly known for his generosity."

Then the blade fell.

Phinx turned back to the guillotine, stunned to find Jennaween with her hand on the release handle. The swad's head rolled awkwardly, his body twitched.

"May the Sphere be with us," Jennaween spoke quietly, her eyes filled with a thousand emotions as she met Phinx' gaze.

Another cheer.

Phinx embraced her with a desperation that matched her own grip, "And keep us in his light."

topi-Inindu:

I listen to the guillotine fall. Over and again the swads declare their allegiance to Morlac. Then, the sleek whine of sliding metal. A sickening thud. The resulting cheer. Edran sits against a wall just inside the doorway of the room I otherwise consume with my hair. He listens. I listen. The guillotine falls thirty-one times. Then it stops.

I pull my hair back into the room. It swirls all around me searching for more bodies to consume. But one cocoon remains of the three I captured in this room. I long to devour him, but Fillop must serve another purpose. His vessel emerges from the black strands of my hair. I unwrap him. First his head, and then all of him. I slowly, painstakingly withdraw my hair from his succulent warm body. His eyes burst open. In an instant, he springs into consciousness ready to battle his unknown assailant, but he only sees a taggle boy and a diminutive mute. He sees what I want him to see. He freezes, confused and terrified.

I write a message on my slate board, "Run. Tell Morlac. Tell everyone."

My hair begins to swirl, once more. Lest he find reason to stay.

Fillop runs. He bolts through the doorway, down the stairs, and into the city beyond.

Edran nods, "Yes, he be telling everyone."

I am coming for you, Morlac.

Lyshmee stiffened at the sight of the thirty-second swad to take the platform: Mathay.

Phinx and Jennaween dragged him forward to face Maldinado and Simiad. He stood about ten feet away from Lyshmee. Rope bound his hands, but she could not avoid shivering at the memory of his touch. She pulled Alanna closer to her chest. The orphan girl slept, fading shortly after the ninth beheading.

Best you sleep for this.

Blood dripped from the raised guillotine blade. Severed heads lay strewn across the platform like apples spilled from a basket, some falling to the crowded street below. Headless bodies, like a pile of festering manure, cascaded outward from the guillotine. The stench of death rivaled the pungent smell of Lyshmee's dungeon cell. But nothing on that stage repulsed her as greatly as Mathay.

The accused swad stood confidently, his chest jutting outward. He cocked his head to the left, finding Lyshmee where she sat, and the girl in her lap. He sneered, "A child? I knew you was a whore."

Thankfully, Phinx punched him in the back, silencing the bastard. Jennaween took a grip of his hair, bringing Mathay's attention back around to Maldinado and Simiad. The man could not die soon enough for Lyshmee's liking.

"May the Sphere be with you," Maldinado said.

Mathay smiled like a rat and boldly proclaimed, "And keep you in his light!"

His words echoed in Lyshmee's ears. *What?* Surely, Mathay worshiped Morlac. No Son of Oblation would rape her…would treat her with such disdain.

Simiad's voice dripped with excitement, "Release the honorable Mathay. He worships the Sphere."

"No!" Lyshmee cried, but no one heard her plea.

A celebration erupted. Jumping. Shouting. Drinking.

Lyshmee watched in horror as Phinx removed Mathay's bonds. The swad rubbed his wrists, and then raised them in celebration, garnering another round of cheers from the gathered taggles. Even Maldinado and Simiad applauded him. But when he glanced down at Lyshmee, Mathay grinned in a cold-hearted manner that sent shivers down her spine.

She hated him. She hated every inch of his snide grin. Yet, he lived.

After everything she had sacrificed. How could the Sphere allow this man to live?

Maldinado couldn't believe his good fortune. *Their first swad.* He had begun to think none of them would ever turn against Morlac. But, finally, success. The same shoulders he leaned upon when he visited Lyshmee in the dungeon would now support the revolution. *The Sphere is with us.* Yes, the taggles managed to rescue Lyshmee, and they presented a formidable force, but Maldinado needed a thousand more Delcreans to join their ranks if they had any hope of overthrowing Morlac. Preferably, well-trained warriors like Mathay.

Despite the impromptu celebration, however, Maldinado could not yet conclude the proceedings. There remained the matter of his friends—new ones and old ones. Everyone in the crowd. The moment of truth had arrived. *Will they follow?* He held up his hand and motioned for silence. The celebration fell to a hush. Maldinado, still mounted atop Inindu-horse, searched the masses for the one person who agitated him more than any other: Harian. He found her easily enough. She waved at him, her hand fluttering above her head like a hummingbird. He felt certain this would come back to haunt him, but in that moment, he welcomed—needed—her boisterous manner.

He stared at her for a lengthy period, stared right at her chubby face, "Now *you* must choose." Harian stopped waving and started smiling with anticipation. Maldinado continued, "Will you stand with me, Harian?" She nodded with great fervor.

Maldinado had to wait for subtle laughter in the crowd to subside, "May the Sphere be with you."

Harian responded with a yell, "And keep me in his light!"

Cheers followed. And then, with several of those gathered soaking in the euphoria of the moment, a chant emerged under the cheering. It rolled back and forth, and grew to full volume, "May the Sphere be with you…and keep you in his light."

Maldinado nodded with the knowledge of victory. Simiad, Mathay, and Harian stood revealed as Sons and Daughters of Oblation. The taggles. And a tailor from Fourth Circle. The revolution ignited in front of his eyes. Yes, and it burned wildly. Maldinado wondered how many battles it would take before Morlac noticed this fire. Once again, he thought of Hintor and their constant berating of Brink, the banner bearer of the Adarian 45th.

We need a banner.

He scanned the crowd, settling on the Gold Keeper still hanging out the window, rocking and shouting.

He will do. Maldinado smiled. *Lucky bastard!*

Severing

Inindu

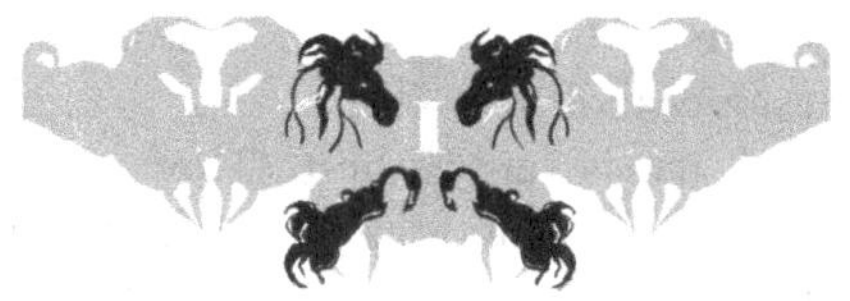

They gather, as men will, to discuss matters of war. Maldinado moves with newfound authority. Phinx grants him cursory nods, if not his full attention. Understandably, he measures every word the Madar mutters against his own devised schemes. A skilled assassin. Like us, but not like us. He could never kill a god. Our topi sits atop our horse, forcing those gathered to look upward when they speak to us, if only to remind them of their proper place. Men need such reminders; even our Adarian needed the occasional intimation. It seems men don't understand anything beyond the sword in their hand. These men, more than some. They stare stupidly at us, wondering why we stand amongst them, wondering who invited us to this gathering of selected heroes. They think we are *only* a mute and a horse. They do not know we are Inindu. *We* held Fillop's head above them. *We* sent the Overseer into the city to spread fear—announcing our presence to Morlac. No, these ignorant men do not know. They do not understand. We remain hidden from them lest fear destroy them, ending their revolution before it begins. We let them believe they witnessed an act of the Sphere. We let them believe they are the chosen ones… invincible. Men like to feel invincible. And these men need hope, so we allow them to rally around their own perceived brilliance. Still, we will not allow them to look down upon us. We are Inindu. They will give us their respect—offered or otherwise.

"Third Circle will not resist," Simiad swallows another drink of wine from a dark, rotund bottle. "Honcherub and his swads are too weakened from fasting," he points toward the broad-shouldered swad to our left. "Why, Mathay could take them single-handedly."

"Agreed," Maldinado forcibly takes the bottle from Simiad and passes it around to the rest of those gathered but, we notice, it quickly finds its way back to Simiad's hand. "Third Circle will join us if we offer them an ounce of food, or they will simply ignore us. Either way, the threat we truly face awaits us in Fourth Circle."

Phinx interjects, "Which is where we hold the advantage."

"The sewers," Maldinado continues with a nod. "That and I have a few connections. We will make appearances in the city, secret visits in hopes of recruiting others. They think our resources limited, but we will build an army right under their feet."

Mathay folds thick arms over his chest, "How many do you think?"

"Hard to say," Maldinado motions to Phinx. "How many Sons and Daughters of Oblation do you think are hiding in the city?"

Phinx looks up at Edran who is sitting on the stage, swinging his feet, as is our brother's habit, "What do you think…maybe two or three hundred in each circle?"

Edran nods, "At least that many."

We see Mathay attempting to total the figures in his head. A fisherman would more easily pry a turtle from its shell. Amused, we write a number on our slate and wait. The sound attracts his attention. He turns expectantly. Our topi blinks several times in succession, innocence disguising guile, and we continue to wait. Finally, realizing we have no intention of assisting in his endeavor, and then determining the task too great, Mathay quietly states, "Several thousand."

We turn our slate around, so he can see what we wrote, "20,000."

"At least twenty thousand," he says with a lingering eye. He tastes our beauty with a slight lick of his upper lip; barely perceptible. He is not the first to crave our body, nor is he the most repulsive. Indeed, we find his warrior physique most appealing. Powerful, honed shoulders—a groove for every one of our fingers.

Despite their typical arrogance, we savor the men we encounter under these conditions. War serves them well, and they are never more attractive than prior to battle. And, of course, they are drawn to us. We serve as their inspiration. Our men. Our warriors. We ride with them, and they ride *for* us—never losing sight of our beauty. In moments of desperation, we give them strength. In strength, purpose. They live and fight and die for us. And we loved the greatest of them: Adarian.

These men do not compare to our lover, but they are not without individual merit. Together, they remind us of Adarian: Maldinado, though far removed from the warrior whom I snatched from my sister, still retains his wits. Simiad, despite his drunken state, brings political influence. Mathay will help recruit more swads. Even Edran. Our brother represents the loyal servitude of Adarian. And Phinx…well, Phinx is the lover. How we savored Adarian, the lover. Love motivated him as much as anything, and it motivates Phinx. Yes, we imagine Phinx is often *motivated*.

"Twenty thousand against two hundred thousand," Maldinado continues.

"More will follow," Phinx says.

"Maybe," Maldinado concedes, "but right now we can only concern ourselves with known allies."

"The revolution represents only one of numerous challenges currently facing Fourth Circle," Simiad wipes his lips with the back of his hand, his beard slick with sweat and wine, "Boltmar's death and Valun's imprisonment leaves Narch and his swads in the precarious position of relying upon Shale for their orders."

"The Father of Oblation acted wisely," Phinx says.

We consider the idea, momentarily, wondering if our father has *ever* acted wisely or, rather, if he simply serves his own needs. He is a man, after all.

"Regardless, they will certainly defend themselves," Mathay crosses his arms, one over top of the other.

Maldinado nods, "Yes, when Fillop reaches Fourth Circle and tells them what occurred here, they will take up arms and defend themselves; but aside from closing Fourth Gate, they will not act without first consulting Shale. That gives us the time we need."

"Time for what?" Mathay asks. "Forgive me. Having just joined this lovely revolution, I'm still fuzzy on the details. Aside from taking on every swad in Delacroy, what are we hoping to accomplish?"

Maldinado grabs the lapels of his robe with a confidence reminiscent of his prior life, "We are going to kill Morlac."

Mathay laughs, "You want to kill a god? Is that all? Tasa Ro! We only have to get through seven circles worth of armed swads in order to reach him."

Edran pulls his knees up to chin, "'Tis a difficult task, to be certain."

Simiad shrugs, "We won't have to go any further than Fourth Circle. Morlac will come to us. As magnate, Valun cannot be condemned to death by anyone other than Morlac. If we reach Fourth Circle, we reach Morlac."

Phinx drops the scarf from his mouth, "Now I understand...the Father of Oblation...Boltmar's death. It all makes sense." We suddenly wonder if Phinx also chews on the hair of his many lovers; the scarf serving as temporary appeasement. We want him to taste our hair. It extends toward him, ever so slightly.

"You ramble, taggle," Mathay turns to Maldinado, but Phinx interrupts him before he can speak another word.

"A careless insult," the taggle produces a knife with impressive speed and, just as quickly, it disappears, "often leads to a hasty death."

Mathay starts forward, but Simiad and Maldinado hold him back,

"I've paid all I care to pay the taggles in my lifetime, and I no longer seek Morlac's blessing."

"So, you say," Phinx smiles with deadly aim.

Mathay settles down, speaking to Maldinado without backing away from Phinx' cool glare, "How do you kill a god?"

Kill a god? Wrap those sculpted arms of yours around him and squeeze, Mathay. Our hair shifts toward the warrior. Hmm...how we relish men of war.

"I imagine you kill him the same way you kill anyone," Maldinado responds. "A sword. An arrow."

Mathay's eyes widen, "Flintlock rifle?"

Maldinado takes an enthusiastic step forward, "I was wondering about them. How do they work?"

Mathay shrugs, "Mostly, it means we won't have to get close to Morlac in order to kill him."

"Or them, to kill us," we write, drawing the attention of every man. Yes, gathered heroes, look upon our beauty. Honor Inindu. Let us serve as the reason you fight this revolution as we once inspired Adarian.

"True," Maldinado agrees. "They can kill us just as easily, but we have the advantage of surprise. Mathay, how many flintlocks do we have?"

"No more than ten, but Third Circle will have at least that many, too."

"Probably double..." Simiad mutters bitterly.

Maldinado nods, "Simiad..." The tailor pauses before continuing, "I'm entrusting you, old friend. I need you to deliver Third Circle. Take Mathay with you, and dress a few more taggles in tymer-kurtas. Make them think every swad in Second Circle has joined the revolution."

"More important that the swads, take food," Phinx reminds him, drawing a fierce look from Mathay.

A careless insult followed by a carefully placed one. No doubt, an attentive lover, as well.

Phinx casts a bemused smirk in response to Mathay's unspoken challenge but, for now, their silent quarrel is allowed to simmer without further infraction. We find these riffs are not uncommon between men. They often suffer from jealous bouts when we join their midst. We are a worthwhile pursuit, after all, so we allow them to fight. Mathay would quite easily dispatch Phinx in a duel of strength, and Phinx would best the swad in a duel of skill, but we are only interested in the duel that leads one of them to take us into their arms. In this regard, Phinx and Mathay are equally matched. Either one will serve our purposes.

"Yes, food," Maldinado agrees. "Take a cart full of food. Let them know all followers of the Sphere will feast. We have no reason to fast."

"Find Nebon," Phinx takes another jab at Mathay. "He is a food merchant and a Son of Oblation. You will need his help if you hope to deliver Third Circle."

"Phinx and Edran," Maldinado continues onward, as men are apt to do, oblivious to the undertones of the gathering. "The three of us will slip into Fourth Circle and meet with the Sons and Daughters of Oblation. Inindu, you have command of Second Circle until I return."

"A woman?" Mathay and Simiad simultaneously interject.

Maldinado smirks, wrinkles gathering under his gray eyes, "Yes, but you have nothing to fear. This woman doesn't speak."

The tailor wisely avoids our piercing eyes. *For now, Maldinado. We do not speak, for now.*

"Who is this mute that you would include her in our council?" Mathay crosses his considerably thick forearms.

Simiad tosses away the now empty bottle, "I've been wondering the same thing, tailor. She makes for a strange traveling companion."

"But a perfect companion in bed, I wager," Mathay laughs.

Of course, we are the perfect companion in bed, as Adarian can attest. He dares laugh at the thought? For the briefest of moments, we consider revealing *exactly* who we are—wrapping Mathay in strands of hair, bringing a swift end to his impertinence. Wrapping his body...his every muscle...wrapping our hair around his every muscle...

"She's the devil 'tis come for Morlac's soul," Edran hops down from the stage and stands beside our horse, stroking our nose. "And *yer* souls too, be they still in yer possession."

Mathay and Simiad, even Phinx, are taken aback, uncertain how to respond.

We restrain our planned assault on Mathay's torso, lowering our head to more fully embrace our brother's touch. A soft caress. Prolonged strokes. Every pass sends ripples through our collective body. We can feel his touch in the deepest reaches of our throat—both of them. This is what we desire. These men do not understand. Only Edran understands our needs. Men. All of them bested by a boy. We were wrong. These men are nothing like our Adarian.

"And that is all you need know," Maldinado concludes without a trace of humor.

They gather, as women will, to determine positions of power. Our topi sits atop our horse, forcing those gathered within Simiad's manor, to look upward when they speak to us, if only to remind them of their proper place. Women need such reminders; even our sister, the Adow. Each of them, all of the Adow throughout time, needed the occasional intimation. Women don't embrace anything beyond their own opinions. Roles are forced upon them rather than accepted. These women judge every other woman in the room, seeking leverage and opportunities to exploit weaknesses. They refuse to believe *we* are truly in command. Civility notwithstanding, they would pull our topi from atop our horse with only a moment's notice, if we allowed them to get close enough. They think we are *only* a mute and a horse. More than think, they act. The attacks are subtle, yet precise. Indeed, these women disguise every devious forward assault with polite laughter, and retreat with disingenuous self-admonishment. We loathe such feints of battle. A woman at war serves only one woman.

Still, we have gathered, so we must win this war. From atop our horse.

"How could a mother leave her own child?" Lyshmee reclines with the ease of newfound freedom. Her adopted daughter, Alanna, lies asleep in her lap. We quickly decide neither of them pose a threat. One is a child, though, admittedly, we have faced many formidable Daughters of the Adow in the past, but this girl is not one of them. The other is already a victim of the revolution. Their collective if unseen wounds run deep. Neither is properly nor emotionally equipped for this battle. They have each other. That is enough for them.

"They left her because they never wanted to be a mother in the first place," Harian eats the remains of a dozen frosted pastries from a tray. She is Maldinado's closest relative in this world, so we must entertain her, *apparently*. Food moves her into the category of follower, however. Keep her mouth full and she will struggle to say anything beyond the kind of murmur that is coupled with a boisterous nod. We can manage her, if we must.

Jennaween looks out a large eight-section window and raises a bottle of warm ale, "Sign me up for the childless life."

"You know Phinx wants ten children?" The comment comes from one of seven women all of whom sit on cushions and huddle together around a raging brazier embedded into the floor. We are certain they each have a name, but they all look and act the same. We don't remember which of them is whom. Let Phinx worry about such matters. They're his lovers. A collection of scarlets. Yes, that will serve our purpose. We will call them all by the same name: Scarlet. The seven Scarlets of Delacroy. Eight if we count Jennaween...

"Phinx wants ten lovers, not ten children," Jennaween retorts, easily sidestepping their attack. So, she refuses to be counted as a Scarlet? We shall see.

"Can you imagine *me* with ten suckling babes?" A Scarlet asks no one in particular.

"At least *you* have the equipment, honey," another Scarlet points to her flat breasts with a sigh.

Lyshmee kisses her daughter, "Sometimes, I wish none of us were equipped."

"How bad was it?"

"Prison is no place for a woman," Harian answers. A dab of frosting hangs from her double-chin. "I can't imagine what you endured."

"I don't want to talk about it except to say I hope some of our newest warriors don't survive the revolution."

Jennaween leans against the window, "I fear none of us will survive."

You may not survive *this* battle, Jennaween. Yes, we determine she presents our only challenger within the gathered group of women. Her displayed indifference to the game afoot is an effective, yet obvious strategy. She will yield to us, in time.

"Women always survive," Harian says. "The men go out to battle and leave the women behind."

Jennaween lifts the bottle to her mouth, "Tell that to Corralea."

"Lilthian and her daughters, too," one of the Scarlets adds.

Harian withdraws a half-eaten pastry from her lips, "I saw one of the girls die."

"They were dancers."

"They had these ribbons that never stopped wavering...it was beautiful to see."

Truly, Jennaween is a skilled combatant. Already, the women rally behind her. If we strike now, we will lose the battle. We must wait patiently and strike at the proper moment.

Jennaween turns back to the window, "Now their bodies lay forgotten upon the guillotine platform."

"The Father of Oblation says the dead should be burned," Lyshmee runs her fingers through Alanna's red hair. "That way they are joined with the Sphere."

"You mean, not cast them into the sea?" Harian asks.

"I can't imagine being burned. It feels disrespectful."

The idea of a sea creature devouring a rotting body seems more awful than fire; or something swimming around our horse's legs. Sick...slick... disgusting creatures of the sea. Though, they do taste delightful when properly cooked. We especially enjoy broiled brown crab with a hint of curry.

"They're dead. They don't care."

"I care," Jennaween counters, masterfully. "We enjoy the magnate's food while our friends lie rotting in the sun. Taggles protect our own, even our dead. If we follow the Sphere, then let them be burned. Why do we delay?"

"I suppose we simply forgot they were there..." Harian admits.

"Then let them forget about us, too, if we would dare allow their sacrifice to go unheralded," Lyshmee says.

"And what of your sacrifice?" Jennaween probes. "You don't have to speak of the horrors you experienced for us to know the truth. We rescued your body, but you've already given your soul to this revolution, Lyshmee. That, too, should be honored."

"With fire?" Scarlet gasps.

"Yes," Jennaween has complete control of the room, now. She walks over to where Lyshmee and Alanna recline. She kneels and takes Lyshmee's arm, "A symbol on the skin. A tattoo. Will you let me brand you with a flame? Let me honor you in this manner, please."

"I would like that very much, Jennaween."

"All of us, then," Jennaween stands to address the room. "For Lyshmee, a flame on all of our arms—a symbol of her living sacrifice. And the names of the fallen. We will wear their names, and we will remember them."

We admit this taggle is a worthy opponent but then, of course, we have previously defeated the Adow—all of them. Jennaween will fall in similar fashion. The moment of our attack draws near.

"Oh," Harian bursts into laughter, "I could never do such a thing. I have too many folds on this old body. A tattoo would just get lost."

"That only means your body can hold the most names," Jennaween places her hand upon Harian's leg and kneels beside her, "You have the ability to honor the fallen more than all of us. Please do this. For me... for them."

"Oh my, it seems I have no choice."

"As you said, women will survive, and so must the memories of those who pass into the flames," Jennaween turns to the Scarlets. They all nod eagerly.

She turns to us, expecting us to agree. She actually stares at us with wide eyes—not even bothering to ask the required question. We suppose, from her vantage point, she thinks we pose no threat to her newly established kingdom of women. Poor girl. She mistakes us as nothing more than a mute and her horse. We are tempted to play the role. We are tempted to allow Jennaween to sit upon her throne of power, however temporarily. She *did* work hard for the privilege, we admit. Still, this is war. These are women. And a woman at battle only serves one woman. Unfortunately for her, we are Inindu, so Jennaween must learn her place. Yes, they shall all bow before our throne.

Our horse speaks, "Curse the dead. Remember the living, and pray they are willing to sacrifice more than death." We turn to Lyshmee, "Pray they sacrifice everything. Their bodies *and* their souls."

It seems we have now managed to capture their attention, so we leave the room, pausing long enough to enjoy the look of complete surprise upon Jennaween's face. Upon all their faces. Except the sleeping child, of course. Poor girl, she never stood a chance. Jennaween, not the child. This is a woman's game, and women don't keep secrets from one another. Now they know our secret. It's our gift to them.

Hereafter these women will control any room they enter, for unlike men, all of whom fear secrets—men always assume the worst and lose their heads with even the smallest uttered word from our horse—yes, unlike men, women savor secrets. They use secrets like currency, buying and trading for other secrets. Oh, these women will send whispers throughout the city. News will spread faster than even the terrified Fillop can shout. These women will share what they now know to be true: We are Inindu, and we have entered this city.

Morlac

Morlac walked along a winding path of white sand. He moved through the dream world at a brisk pace, familiarity dulling his senses to the surrounding environment. A lush landscape grew out of the darkness to his left, filled with clumps of red and blue flowers growing out like bushes; open areas of green grass; and small, unassuming trees that offered light shade to passersby. To his right: a graveyard rose out of dust that swirled in low, slithering circles; severed bones of various sizes and shapes stretched upward or outward at odd angles. The road split directly in front of Morlac near the foot of a stone tower. The noticeably longer path to his left continued deeper into the colorful garden, but the shorter path to his right ended at a magenta doorway at the base of the tower. The tower mirrored the two contrasting sides of Morlac's path: strands of ivy covered nearly every stone on one side, while multiple stones on the other side slowly crumbled away with each passing breeze.

He focused on the doorway, an entrance to the Sphere's world, and came to a halt just as his hand touched the metal latch. Something felt out of place. His senses re-engaged, and he looked back toward the graveyard. The scattered bones no longer resembled their past life forms. The relics of larger beasts mixed carelessly with smaller remains, as though hastily discarded. Yet, he knew the pattern. Daily visits to the dream world burned an image of the bones into Morlac's mind, creating order from chaos. One tusk gave him pause as he scanned the graveyard. It jutted out of the ground, rising well over nine feet into the sky. Beside the tusk stood a boyish figure clothed in white, barely perceptible, yet unmistakable.

Dream Walker.

Morlac knew the yearling: Adelic Hon, a taggle created by the Sphere and given life with a touch from the Adow. When Morlac first encountered Adelic Hon, the taggle wandered the dream world aimlessly; struggling to navigate his way through the desert land to the path of white sand, temporarily trapped beyond the tower and blind to Morlac's presence. But their encounters steadily increased in frequency leading up to this moment. At long last, Morlac felt certain the boy could see him. And though the distance between them only spanned a few hundred linear feet, Morlac stood without fear of attack, for the dream world offered no direct path from graveyard to the tower. That which Adelic Hon saw, he could not, as yet touch.

Nevertheless, Morlac knew the moment marked a shift in their relationship.

He pulled at his beard, wondering what kind of battle the taggle boy waged against him. Admittedly, the dream world still concealed much from Morlac, but he decided this puzzle must wait for another day. Alas, he gave a slight bow in the direction of the young hunter, then spun on his heels and entered the tower.

It served as a doorway into the Sphere's world, and on this night, it brought Morlac to a small room in Lor. The walls glowed with the flickering flame of a mostly extinguished candle that slouched over an unattended candlestick. A merchant, bald and wrinkled, slept on a thin mattress supported by four wooden posts. Several wool blankets lay draped over the merchant's frame, pulled up to his chin; three fingers peeping out from under and firmly clinging to them. Strands of hair grew wildly out of the visible top portion of his right ear, and his eyebrows stretched toward one another without touching. His face resembled a weathered and pitted tree stump, folds of skin shifting with every intake of breath.

Morlac matched the merchant's breathing pattern and snatched his light essence. At least, he tried. Something or someone prevented him from saving the merchant. Indeed, his body relaxed in death.

Morlac knelt beside the body, placing a hand on the merchant's face, "I am your god, pilgrim. What new power keeps you from me?"

Moments later, Morlac re-entered the dream world to stand once more upon the path of white sand. He slowly closed the magenta door behind him and looked out across the graveyard toward the enormous tusk, but Adelic Hon had vanished. The taggle had not thwarted him. No, something else had changed.

He opened the door and entered the tower, once more, but he did not travel to Lor. Instead, he entered his own world—the world of the dead—and stood on the road to Delacroy. He saw the dead all about him for miles in every direction. He had saved them from the Sphere's world. Transported them to Delacroy and the outer lands using the dream world. There, they slowly migrated into the city. Morlac kept them alive, but only barely. Their bodies rotted, seemingly with each step. But within the illusion he created for them he offered them full and rich lives. It proved the best he could manage until he could somehow sever their connection to the Sphere. Until he could kill the god of another world. Until then, his worshipers had to live between two worlds. One filled with life, the other populated by the dead.

Into this world of the dead Morlac traveled. If something had changed, he would find it there. If he could no longer rescue the dying from the Sphere's world, he would visit the dead one by one, night after night. He approached the closest of his chosen. Erisyte. He knew all of them by name, cared for them; watched over them like a shepherd. Erisyte's face still held a touch of the smoothness it had in life, but decay had slightly altered his flesh tone and thinned the skin around his eyes.

"What is your name, pilgrim?" Morlac asked.

Erisyte's pupils widened, "Erisyte." His voice sounded like the echo of rust-laden chains turned into a whip and used to strike at an iron door.

"I am your god, Erisyte. Do you know my name?"

"Morlac."

"Yes," Morlac nodded with relief. "I am Morlac. I have not forgotten you."

He left Erisyte and moved to the next motionless form. He asked the same questions to each of the dead he encountered in the outer lands, seeking to know whom they worshiped, for he knew at least one of them no longer followed him. Perhaps more. He could think of no other reason for the loss of power he had experienced. So, he searched the outer lands, and if he did not find the unfaithful there, Morlac would move into the city. Though, certainly, he doubted any of those who had made it through the Sorting would turn their back on the god to whom they swore allegiance. The god who offered them favor and boon in exchange for their outward displays of devotion.

Yet, something *had* changed. Doubt. Disbelief. Something drained his power. When Inindu chose to worship Morlac, he received his power. Thus, he inherently knew that if no one worshiped him as a god, he would no longer exist. He knew because he employed the same strategy against the Sphere. Steal the followers and kill the god of another world. Morlac needed to find the unfaithful, wherever they stood. And when he found them, Morlac would...

What? Consume their light essence?

Death in this world—still the Sphere's world, no matter how close to the edge of his world Morlac had traveled—meant their light essence returned to the Sphere. It would *always* return to the Sphere until the day when the old god lay dead. A day when Morlac would take his rightful place and, at last, absorb all light essence into his own being. Until then, however, death meant Morlac would lose both a worshiper and their essence. The Sphere would grow stronger and Morlac weaker.

Not that Morlac avoided death. In fact, he encouraged it so long as it occurred *within* the illusion. There, he fostered and glorified death. If someone died in the illusion, they appeared again on the road to Delacroy, and their journey began anew. An endless cycle that provided a sense of completeness for his followers. A start. An end. And a constant, passionate pursuit of Morlac's favor and boon. Oh yes, death within the illusion provided Morlac so much than simply allowing the Delcreans to grow old and apathetic. A torrent of adoration compared to the barely audible whispered prayers from an indifferent pilgrim. But he could not kill them in the Sphere's world. So, he would find those who lacked faith, and he would thrust them far beyond the illusion of Delacroy out into the untrampled lands at the edge of reality.

There, in solace, they would forget their own name and the name of the Sphere.

There, they would learn to rely on Morlac, once more; seek his favor and boon.

There, kept far from the illusion, they would beg him to let them die, but he would keep them alive.

Always alive. Always. The dead never died.

Severing

Delacroy

Where did the taggles go?" Lomax stared in disbelief at the empty stages, tents, and booths that populated Fourth Gate. At first, he thought it another trick of his mind, but the hundreds of travelers in the vicinity convinced him otherwise. Equally dumbfounded, they all attempted to comprehend the sudden disappearance of every taggle in Fourth Gate.

"I didn't even know taggles could leave the gates," Denam, his rival in basket weaving and unlikely companion, blessed with a sound mind and ageless complexion, shook his head in disbelief.

Both basket weavers, along with their fellow merchants from Fourth Circle, had abandoned the marketplace moments earlier to see the mystery of Fourth Gate with their own eyes. What began that morning as simple annoyance—complaints by various travelers lamenting the absence of their favorite taggle performer or artist or storyteller—quickly turned to early afternoon shock and then fear; bringing more travelers into Fourth Gate until, finally, even the merchants felt compelled to investigate.

"Fourth Gate is cursed," several onlookers agreed.

Lomax nodded and quietly added, "Morlac's judgment." He wrapped his arm around Denam's bony shoulder and pointed farther down Fourth Gate, "That's where they found Boltmar's body. He had the symbol of the Sphere carved into his chest. This must be Morlac's judgment upon Fourth Gate…for displaying the symbol of the Sphere."

Darrol, adopted servant boy of the merchants, standing close enough to Lomax and Denam to overhear their conversation, suddenly grabbed Lomax around the legs, "Don't let them take me."

Lomax reached down and held the boy's head, "We have nothing to fear, boy. Morlac only condemns worshipers of the Sphere." He pulled the yearling's chin upward until he could see into his eyes, "Do you worship the Sphere?"

"No," he shook his head.

"See. Nothing to fear."

Denam walked a few steps forward before turning to face his marketplace rival, "Are you saying the taggles worship the Sphere? This is their judgment?"

Strade, a skilled candle merchant, stood near enough to casually eavesdrop; right up to the point when he turned his large, hourglass ears much too quickly to escape detection. Lomax relished the moment, fully aware of his surrounding audience. He considered his answer as though inhaling through the tight stem of a lit pipe, allowing the moment to draw more attention…attract more eavesdroppers. Finally, he exhaled as though releasing a stream of lingering smoke, "Morlac's judgment upon them. Yes, it appears the taggles worshiped the Sphere and met their doom."

Denam, Darrol, and at least nineteen others from what Lomax could tell—a mix of merchants and travelers standing around him— responded in chorus, "Morlac's judgment upon them."

Lomax listened intently as whispers raced through the gathered crowd, echoing his accusation and, most gratifyingly, dozens of heads soon nodded their agreement.

"If the taggles worshiped the Sphere," Lomax spoke loud enough to again draw the attention of those around him, "Then the artwork they created is also cursed. Morlac's judgment upon anyone possessing any item made by a taggle. Burn it all!"

"Morlac's judgment upon them," the crowd responded.

Lomax took great satisfaction in watching various signs of fear surface upon the faces and in the eyes of those nearby; and, as the gathered residents considered all the taggle art they possessed, some politely took their leave only to struggle mightily as they attempted to move through the crowd—desperate to escape Fourth Gate and, no doubt, return to their homes so they could destroy anything linking them to the taggles.

Yes, surely this would bring Lomax favor and boon.

Others close by turned their attention to the more easily accessible items: All the abandoned taggle art displayed throughout Fourth Gate. Paintings, pottery, jewelry, and carvings. They shattered clay pots and ripped apart jeweled necklaces and bracelets. Someone grabbed a torch, lifted a painting above their head, and set it ablaze. The oil painting, a portrait of a scarcely clothed old man, seated as though in deep thought, ignited into a blanket of fire that wholly covered the wilting canvas. More paintings followed, and within moments a bonfire of artwork burned in the middle of Fourth Gate. Then, Lomax watched as several crowd members snatched embers from the fire and lit nearby wooden stages, tents, display shelves, and easels. Smoke billowed upward to fill the tunnel.

Lomax and his band of rioters gasped for air—coughing and wheezing.

Panic replaced fear. The fire spread. Those closest to the flames realized their mistake too late. They ran toward Lomax, pushing against the crowd, attempting to flee, but the flames consumed their screams. All around them, travelers trampled one another in their attempts to escape the flames. Black smoke rolled toward Lomax, engulfing him and his fellow merchants before exiting through the circular gate behind him.

Nearly blinded by the smoke, Lomax lifted Darrol into his arms and pushed his way toward the back wall of Fourth Gate. More than once, he planted an elbow into the rib cage of passerby or stepped on someone's foot. Despite his age, he retained the strength of his youth—enough of it, at least, to move away from the main flow. Moments later, however, faced with no other option, he reentered the mass of bodies cascading toward the exit and forcibly shoved without discretion. Darrol buried his scarred face into Lomax's shoulder, clinging to the basket-weaver's neck with arms that threatened to choke him. The smoke thickened around them; screams gave way to coughing.

Lomax felt a sudden push against his right knee and a stranger's fingers grasped at his lower leg, causing him to lose his footing. Instinctively, he reached out to grab the shoulder of the person ahead of him...a bony shoulder. Denam. His rival didn't bother to turn, desperation driving him forward. But Lomax recognized him all the same, and he kept his grip, using Denam as he would a walking stick; still holding Darrol with his other arm.

Finally, Lomax and Denam and Darrol emerged from Fourth Gate. Behind them, dozens of Delcreans scattered out of the opening in stumbling waves of arms and legs. Some continued to run. Others gathered at a safe distance and stood to watch.

Lomax patted Denam on the shoulder as they stared at the rising smoke, and the few visible flames that suggested just how quickly the fire had spread, "Morlac's judgment, upon them."

"Morlac's judgment," Denam and...and some boy agreed.

Lomax stared at the boy as he would a stranger, struggling to recall his name. *Darrol*. The boy's name was Darrol. Still, it took several more minutes for Lomax to remember how he knew the boy.

Shale, standing on his balcony, saw the surging mass of black smoke rise from Fourth Gate. The nascient stood beside him, disturbingly lifeless despite its ability to walk and move. Bathed and groomed, the creature wore a red tymer-kurta inlaid with gold and swirling embroidery, cream trousers, and a matching yiddick-shawl. The nascient faced the same direction as Shale, gazing at the smoke without visible concern. Blind. Lifeless. A creature without a resonating presence. Almost...dead.

The lack of curiosity about the smoke, indeed, the complete absence of emotion from the nascient served as an irritant, yes, but it paled in comparison to Shale's discomfort regarding the creature's dormant chest. It stood without inhaling, without exhaling. Not a single breath. Stillborn.

When his predecessor, T'thay, revealed the nascient, Shale did not, at first, notice this particular oddity. Admittedly, his own feelings of horror disguised several truths, for truth, Shale later discovered, acts as the appointed keeper of secrets. Equal to that of any skilled scoundrel or thief, truth properly revealed serves to divert attention from that which remains concealed. Morlac in the flesh. The chosen no more. A life revealed. A death concealed.

Of course, Shale rarely paused long enough to notice the stillness of the creature during their awakening, or during his preparations for the nascient when his duties forced him to touch its slime-laden torso. No, during these times Shale had to focus all his attention to the endless squelching of his own revulsion lest he vomit. But there upon the balcony, as he stood beside the creature—and despite the rising black smoke— Shale remained ever cognizant of the fact the nascient did not, would or could not, breathe.

The height of the balcony provided Shale with grand perspective but left him in noticeable silence, for although he could see the evidence of a tragic event occurring, he remained too far removed to hear the terrible cries of the residents below. Tragedy witnessed without the wailing. He often contemplated the general quietness of his existence: The solitude of his favorite balcony. The empty rooms. His lack of companionship within the ruby palace. A god in the palace dungeon; one who screamed without ever uttering a sound. Shale lived an undeniably muted life. Oh, attendants interrupted his solitude, on occasion, but even they spoke sparingly—or quietly delivered a written and, therefore, soundless correspondence.

He turned away from the sky, focusing instead upon the nascient's freshly oiled hand and trimmed fingernails. The arm hung at the creature's side like a limb suddenly snapped torpid. Shale exhaled. *And how long must I hang at your side? When will I pass this burden to another?*

"I smell smoke," Morlac spoke with a hollow, lingering voice, effectively disrupting the silence.

Shale did not bow before his god. Not before this creature. No, he would not allow the ends of his white yiddick-shawl to gather about his own feet. Besides, serving a blind god meant Shale did not have to bow. "The city burns," he started to point then halted mid-motion. *No, I guess you wouldn't see no matter where I pointed would you?* "Fourth Gate, I believe, or near Fourth Gate. It is difficult to tell for certain."

"Fire. A symbol of the Sphere," the nascient spoke with perfect animation of mouth and chin. It crossed its arms, liken to any man pondering such thoughts. But its shoulders did not rise. Its chest never extended outward. It did not breathe.

"Much has occurred during your absence," Shale forced himself to gaze upon the creature's ivory-coated eyes in preparation for the coming journey through Delacroy. Their subsequent interactions with the residents meant he would need to publicly participate in Morlac's deception. "The fire, for one, though, that is a recent development. More pressing is the matter concerning Boltmar and his son. He is the reason I awakened the nascient. Valun is accused of worshiping the Sphere and awaits your judgment."

"Interesting. Yes, this may prove useful," the nascient moved with fluid legs and a firm step, and it groped the air until its hand found Shale's shoulder. Despite the exertion, Shale couldn't help but notice the nascient did not take a single breath, "I cannot stay long, though. I must return to the dream world with haste. Here *and* there, it seems I must judge the unfaithful."

Shale turned his back to the smoke rising from the city, guiding the creature toward the palace interior, "Then we shall leave at once." He had no wish to prolong his interaction with the nascient.

"I remember you being taller. About here," the creature momentarily raised its hand to a position slightly above Shale's shoulder, but quickly returned with a firm grasp, "Perhaps you shrink with age?"

Shale straightened his back, but soon enough he wilted again beneath Morlac's grip.

Whether or not he had shrunk, he certainly felt old. And he carried an even older burden.

Later that morning, having left the nascient in an austere waiting room just inside the palace entrance, grateful for the respite, Shale walked down a winding pathway leading to a small, white stone hut. His predecessor had called it the *white box*. It stood near the corner of the palace, detached and unadorned, large enough for a single attendant. The attendant stood ready to arouse a full legion of servants should Shale have need of them. But he rarely had any need, so the servants mostly stayed in their quarters conveniently built just off the palace gates. Each attendant, working a standard three-hour shift, would stand with their arms folded behind them and keep their feet together like a statue, lest Shale find them slouching or, only slightly worse, sleeping. The attendants lived in Ninth Circle, chosen by magnate Galeab to serve their god, allowing them to reside closer to Morlac than any other resident in Delacroy aside from Shale and those honored residents chosen by Morlac to live in his palace.

If only they knew your secret…

But they didn't know. Only Shale knew. Only he lived in the empty palace. Shale ordered the white box attendant to prepare Morlac's carriage, and then send a message to Magnate Galeab alerting him of Morlac's pending emergence from the ruby palace; and he gave another order to fetch Overseer Ristan, asking her to present herself, and the entirety of her swad unit, as escort for her god.

"At once," the stout attendant bowed with practiced form.

Shale watched him leave, measuring his gait. He walked with obvious haste but stopped short of running. Each controlled step sustained his momentum without overextending his center of balance. Shale most certainly approved, and he determined to make mention of the attendant in his next letter to Galeab.

The adherent breathed deeply, savoring a familiar silence.

Eighteen. Eighteen nascient. One more than the total number of awakenings his predecessor had performed. One more creature presented to Delacroy, professing it as their god in the flesh. *More accurately, an abomination.* The journey ahead proved equally concerning to the adherent for the city brought crowds and endless shouting. Noise. The thought alone made his ears ache. Thousands of people would soon scream sentiments of worship. They would stretch out, hoping to touch the hand, or any portion, of Morlac. They would want to touch Shale's hand, too. Every hair on both his arms recoiled at the thought of their touch and, already, he longed to return to the solitude of his balcony.

Instead, he returned to the waiting room and the nascient therein.

The attendant returned to Shale even as the sun moved behind black smoke, resulting in a premature dusk. More than just return, he brought news from Fillop, Overseer of Second Circle: Revolution!

Revolution *and* a creature of magic and horror. Inindu.

Shale nodded and dismissed the animated attendant, barely disguising his relief. "It seems our journey has ended before it ever began," he addressed the nascient without turning to face the creature. "I will send word to Narch and have Valun brought here, instead."

The creature tightened its grip upon Shale's shoulder, "Inindu. She has come for me, at last. Nothing changes. I will go to Valun. I do not fear Inindu. She worshiped me, before. She will worship me, again."

You? You never go anywhere. You're a captive in a stone tower. No, you do not fear Inindu because you will never have to face her. You send me and this creature to face her.

"Very well," Shale pushed the words from the edge of his mouth as though heaving a large boulder off a cliff. He led the nascient out of the waiting room, "We will go to Fourth Circle, as expected. We will go, and we will take every swad from the inner circles with us. We will squelch this revolution."

The palace gates opened and Morlac's monstrous carriage emerged, pulled by nine powerful horses. Despite the darkness brought on by the smoke, the ruby encrusted exterior of the carriage glimmered. Overseer Ristan, mounted atop a black gelding and flanked on either side by four hundred swads from Ninth Circle, all of whom carried a torch, led the grand procession into the palace courtyard. A crowd of Delcreans, including Magnate Galeab, standing atop a hastily assembled stage, cheered wildly, and lobbied for position in hopes of glimpsing their reclusive god, but the nascient did not reveal himself to them.

"My god," Shale mouthed the cumbersome words, keeping his voice well below a whisper, as he practiced the traditional salutation by which he must address the nascient upon their exit from the jeweled carriage.

My god…my god…

Delacroy

Certainty | Chastity | Fasting | Generosity | Joy | Orthodoxy | Peace | Honesty | Faithfulness

Go, Tilly. Go on."

Troq watched the girl walk down the crowded street. She still appeared distracted after having dropped a half-dozen eggs on the kitchen floor earlier that morning. Every day brought a new accident. Some days, Tilly dropped or broke something seemingly every hour. In fact, Troq felt certain the girl ranked as the worst servant in all Delacroy. If not for his promise made to Edran to look after the girl, Troq would have dismissed her days earlier after she swung a broom handle into a collection of wine bottles—each one crashing to the stone floor in a burst of vibrant color and dreadful sound. He only hoped she could manage to find her way to the marketplace and back again without incident. She carried a pouch of gold, enough to buy everything on the list he had provided her.

"And don't forget the basket. One from Lomax," Maldinado added. The denam-basket he had used to store potatoes unexpectedly burst near the base several days prior; damaged because of poor craftsmanship rather than, surprisingly, anything the girl may have done.

The shuffling crowd slowly absorbed the absent-minded girl. Troq waited several moments, creating greater distance between him and the girl, and then he, too, entered the mass of travelers. The morning sun shined brightly above and fully revealed by the time he reached his destination. He took a seat in the familiar wooden chair just inside Tannessa's doorway and waited patiently. Time slipped away. Finally, after nearly two hours had passed, and as a murmur rose from the crowd outside, drawing his attention, Troq left Tannessa's home with gold still in hand. He would return to pay the debt he owed her another day.

When he saw the sky outside, a pillar of black smoke rising from somewhere on the other side of the city, drawing the attention of travelers—several stopping to point as if those around them could not readily identify the cause for concern—Troq understood the reason for Tannessa's delayed return. The swads had more pressing matters to attend.

"The revolution," Troq uttered to himself.

He could not fathom the reason for the smoke, or what portion of the city now burned, though, for a moment, he wondered if Tilly somehow managed to set the marketplace ablaze. He wouldn't put it past the girl. But, no, he knew what the fire truly signaled. Troq shifted his gaze slightly to the left where he could see the uppermost portion of Morlac's ruby palace, "No doubt, he will require something to eat upon his arrival."

The cook reentered the street and made his way to the magnate's manor. Morlac would come to Fourth Circle for Valun's beheading. The revolution would necessitate he stay for an extended time, and during his stay, Morlac would sleep at the manor—the only place in Fourth Circle worthy of his presence.

Lomax stood leaning against the front of his merchant cart, resigned to his misfortune for while the fire still burned, only curiosity would pass between visitors and the merchants in the marketplace on this day. They arrived in droves, more travelers than Lomax had seen in weeks, but their gold coins remained pocketed. Some of the merchants had already given up the effort, or never returned from their excursion into Fourth Gate— dead, most likely. But Denam, the only other basket merchant in Fourth Circle, remained in the marketplace, and Lomax refused to leave all the gold, or even the potential for gold, to his rival. If Denam stayed, Lomax stayed. Besides, he knew other ways to gather gold.

"Morlac's boon upon thee, Fanzir," Lomax wrapped an arm around his unwitting victim while simultaneously lifting a gold piece from Fanzir's pocket, deftly concealing the coin in his own pocket.

"Favor and boon. What happened here?" Fanzir spoke without turning his attention from the smoke.

"Morlac's judgment," Lomax spoke loud enough to attract attention. "The taggles worshiped the Sphere, and now they burn inside Fourth Gate." Lomax climbed the back wheel of his merchant cart, elevating himself above the crowd to further draw the attention of those gathered nearby, "First Boltmar. Now the taggles. Worship the Sphere at your own peril." Then he looked directly at Fanzir, "And what remains of the taggles?"

Fanzir feebly sought an answer in the faces of those who stared back at him. Finally, he shrugged, "Their artwork?"

Lomax smiled with wicked satisfaction, "Yes, their artwork. Morlac's judgment upon anyone who possesses the art of the taggles! Make your penance here. Renounce the Sphere and the hellion taggles who worship him. Pay your tribute to Morlac." Lomax jumped from the wheel and grabbed one of his baskets; one of his larger baskets. Then he pulled the coin he had snatched from Fanzir and held it up for all to see, "Pay your tribute to Morlac, here. Then return to your homes and cast aside the work of taggles." Lomax dropped the gold piece into the basket and turned to Fanzir, "Pay your tribute to Morlac, Fanzir. Or Morlac's judgment be upon you."

Fanzir fumbled with his pocket of gold, eventually pulling forth three pieces and hastily tossing them into the basket, "Please, no judgment."

"Morlac's boon upon thee, Fanzir," Lomax said with a slight bow of his head.

Fanzir sighed in relief, "Favor and boon."

"Return home and cast aside..." Lomax changed his mind. He had a better scheme. *Tasa Ro! What was it?* His mind seemingly grew cloudier every day. Then, "No! Bring your taggle art to Fourth Gate. Cast it in the fire. Let Fourth Gate burn until every work of art is turned to ash. Let it burn until smoke fills the sky, and the sun remains unseen from dawn to dusk. Let it burn until we are rid of every artifact of the Sphere. Only then will the darkness lift. Only then will we be free of Morlac's judgment!"

A chant began, "Morlac's judgment! Morlac's judgment!"

As Lomax had hoped, his message ravaged the crowd. Useless feelings of curiosity and apprehension turned into a profitable fear of judgment and resulting conviction. The chant he started quickly spread, and those in the crowd who may not have heard Lomax speak initially, nevertheless, found themselves caught up in a flow of people that deposited them at Lomax and his pile of baskets. They had no choice but to drop a gold coin into the lomax-basket. The first one overflowed, so he added another lomax-basket, and then another. He ran out of baskets, and the gold simply piled up until only the top of the first and tallest basket remained visible. To everyone who dropped a coin, Lomax wished them favor and boon—all of them until his tongue swelled and his lips chapped and still, he blessed them. He wished them favor and boon until his voice grew hoarse. Until he lost it completely. Still, he blessed them in whispers.

All the while, less than two-hundred yards away, Fourth Gate burned. Lomax watched as the residents who lived closest to the marketplace brought forth their canvas paintings, leather-bound books, wooden carvings, and any other piece of taggle artwork they possessed and tossed it all into the fire. This pleased Lomax and it pleased the gathered mass. They started jumping, still chanting. Fourth Gate turned into a roaring furnace. The red stone encircling the entrance turned white from the heat. Those who ventured too close to the fire—some struggling to heave a heavy object into the flames, some simply too adventurous—burned to death. This, too, pleased the crowd. Jumping. Chanting.

"Morlac's judgment! Morlac's judgment!"

"Morlac's judgment," Lomax agreed when they looked to him for confirmation. *If only Maldinado could see me now. It's just like him to miss this moment. Foul friend.* Still, Maldinado would get to watch him parade through Fourth Circle on his way to Ninth Circle. *Surely, the adherent will send notice when he hears about my faithfulness.*

Folds of smoke billowed upward from the circular mouth of Fourth Gate. Ash floated on the stagnant air and fell in flittering waves. A dark haze replaced sunlight. Darker strands of smoke sifted through the black haze like serpents navigating moonlit fields.

And into these fields stepped Tilly.

Chaos encircled her. She found herself pushed one way and just as quickly shoved in another direction. She clung to the brown maldinado-robe of the stranger in front of her. She clawed at the slick arm of the woman beside her. The crowd started jumping and chanting. Tilly took an elbow to the nose. She tried to jump with them. Someone stepped on her ankle, shattering it with their weight. Tilly fell in agony. She screamed, but no one heard her above the chanting crowd. She writhed upon the ground, attempting to avoid the jumping Delcreans. Someone stepped on the side of her face, her ear. A shoe scraped her back. The jumping continued. Three people tried to fill the space where Tilly fell. Two of them tumbled on top of her, the weight of one snapped her arm. They both scrambled to their feet lest they, too, get trampled like Tilly. Neither offered the girl assistance. The jumping continued.

Closer to the fire, Tannessa, along with every available swad in Fourth Circle, struggled to clear the street of potential kindling. Wooden carts, hay bales, banners, stools, poles, and numerous other hazards littered the marketplace. Fourth Gate itself presented little danger to the city, Tannessa knew, for once the fire began, its stone walls morphed the gate into nothing more than a large kiln. But this kiln had an open door. The heat kept anyone from getting close enough to close it off, and if the fire managed to spread into the city... Fourth Circle offered no means of escape. Thousands would burn as they attempted to flee toward Fifth Circle, or Sixth Circle after that, or Seventh Circle—each circle smaller than the last. Eventually, they would simply run out of room. Leaving only two options: Die in the fire or get trampled to death.

"Put too much wine in the barrel, you burst the barrel," Tannessa struggled to push one such wine barrel away from the flames. "And these fools are *feeding* the fire!"

She felt sick to her stomach, for she rarely exerted so much effort; and standing this close to the fire, she found the heat unbearable. Sweat gathered at her throat, pooled between her breasts, and ran down the inside of her thighs. It lubricated the folds in her belly, dripped from her hair, and stung her eyes. Worst of all, the falling ash absorbed her sweat, forming a black paste which coated every inch of exposed skin. She finally succumbed to her exhaustion and took a seat on the upturned barrel. Her fellow swads continued in their various efforts, pulling flammable objects away from the flames until the pile resembled the foundation of a yet unlit bonfire. Fortunately, the swads had ample room to maneuver, for the crowd arched away from the furious heat emanating from Fourth Gate. All except the mouth of the fire where they continued to toss artwork into the flames.

Never had she witnessed such an event.

Then, the mass of gathered fools started jumping with an absurd amount of untethered energy and, sitting there motionless in that moment, Tannessa could feel the resulting tremors beneath her feet. She saw artifacts of the rarest kind carelessly passed overhead and tossed into the fire. Smoke filled her nose, tainting every breath. Her tongue tasted like sweat and ash. And only the constant ringing in her ears rose above the pulsating chant of the crowd.

For perhaps the first time in her life, Tannessa felt powerless. No amount of gold would bring an end to this madness. Despite her endless connections, she could not enlist anyone to assist...

Flints.

She stood at the thought, feeling every harsh ounce of bodyweight settle back over her creaking knees. Absent the presence of Overseer Narch, who had left for Fifth Circle earlier that morning, along with Overseer Fillop from Second Circle, the swads of Fourth Circle had turned to Tannessa for leadership. She did not qualify as the best of them, but she knew the worst about them—all of them. Thus, no one had opposed her command, or at least, they did not verbally oppose her.

Tannessa grabbed hold of the closest swad, nearly tearing the tymer-kurta from his chest. She pulled his oversized ear down to her sweat-laden lips. Even so, she had to shout above the crowd, "Bring me the flints, and any extra rifles you can find. Go!"

At least sixty able-bodied flints accompanied the swad upon his return several minutes later. He carried an additional three flintlock rifles in his arms, handing one to Tannessa. She lined the flints up in three rows: twenty lying on their stomach, twenty kneeling, and twenty standing. They loaded their rifles and, at her command, took aim at the portion of Delcreans gathered closest to Fourth Gate. Closest to the emerging flames. Tannessa raised her arm.

For the briefest of moments, her awareness of colors appeared magnified. It seemed everyone in the crowd wore the muted colors typical of maldinado-robes: Yellow with white lapels. Orange with cream lapels. Brown with beige trim. Tan with designs made from bronze thread.

She lowered her arm, "Fire!"

Three rifles misfired, but a volley of seventeen lead balls ripped into the front lines of the jumping and chanting Delcreans. It hit them like the stroke of a scythe sheering rows of wheat. The wounded fell backward with the force of impact.

Inexplicably, the jumping and chanting continued, "Morlac's judgment! Morlac's judgment!"

"Fire!"

Another eighteen lead balls. Half of them piercing gut, shoulder, or thigh; the other half went awry, striking dirt, stone, and cloud. Puffs of white smoke blew out the side of the rifles, quickly subdued by the dark haze of the blaze. After two volleys, eleven Delcreans in total lay wounded or dead. The jumping horde slowed with sudden apprehension, their chanting fading with confusion.

"Fire!"

Sixteen lead balls fired. Thirteen struck their target. All movement and chanting ceased, abruptly. The wounded groaned. Several wailed. The fire cracked and roared within the gate turned furnace. But Tannessa, for the moment, had seized control of the crowd.

"Enough!" Her shout sounded more like a returning echo, for she struggled to project her typically muffled voice. Fortunately, those Delcreans who could hear Tannessa passed her words through the line in low murmurs.

"Would you burn the entire city?"

Someone yelled, "We would burn the artwork of the taggles and rid ourselves of the Sphere's artifacts! Or face Morlac's judgment!"

A cheer erupted, quickly subdued by those wanting to hear from the newly appointed leader of the swads.

Tannessa recognized the voice, though she could not see him, "Lomax?"

"Tannessa?" Like a mole burrowing underground, upheaving dirt on both sides, Lomax moved through the crowd.

Ash continued to fall, a few flecks landing on Tannessa's eyelashes. The swads she commanded busied themselves by reloading their flintlock rifles with black powder. Those whose rifles misfired, checked the angle of their flints or ran their thumb along the frizzen to gauge the hardness. Fifteen bodies littered the street less than twenty yards from where she stood. Blood stained their maldinado-robes and formed brown pools in the red dirt. The crowd withdrew from the wounded, fearful of Tannessa's particular style of judgment. Five of the wounded no longer writhed, no longer displayed any signs of life.

Lomax glanced briefly at the fallen Delcreans before turning to Tannessa, "Worshipers of the Sphere hide within our midst. First Boltmar and Valun. Now the taggles. Morlac's judgment upon them. Let them burn."

Tannessa considered Lomax a generally ugly man: Elevated shoulders that seemed always on the verge of sliding down into a more proper position on his torso; large hands that hung from too-thin arms; three moles which marred his weathered face; a white beard that stretched well above his cheekbones; and wrinkles which fell from his forehead like the coils of a snake from a tree. Despite his awkward appearance, however, Tannessa felt a certain affection for her older cousin. Like her, Lomax was an opportunist, and a skilled manipulator. More importantly, he recognized the power she wielded, and made it a point to speak with her every morning as she passed through the marketplace.

"There is another way," Tannessa formulated her scheme even as she spoke, trusting Lomax to adjust accordingly. "Fire is a symbol of the Sphere. Those who worship the god of another world believe fire will unite them with their god. Do we dare assist them in their quest?"

Much to her delight, Lomax responded perfectly and without hesitation, "Morlac's judgment upon those who would honor such a request."

"Let us, instead," Tannessa pointed in the distance behind her, "make use of Valun's guillotine. Is that not more agreeable than burning the entire city?"

Lomax stepped forward and turned to the crowd, "The guillotine!

Denam-baskets for worshipers of the Sphere. Lomax-baskets for those who follow Morlac."

The suggestion confused her. Based on previous conversations, Tannessa knew Lomax had long wanted his baskets positioned beneath the guillotine for all to see. After a moment's reflection, however, she marveled at the skill of her merchant cousin. Who among them would dare purchase a denam-basket, again?

Adding to his leverage, Lomax started a new chant, "Denam for their heads!" Which soon morphed into, "Denam for heads!" And eventually, "Denam heads! Denam heads!"

Tannessa ordered her swads to gather up the wounded and the dead. Then she led them, along with Lomax and the rest of those gathered, toward the guillotine originally intended for Valun. Dead or wounded, Tannessa's swads slid the condemned into position under the blade and their heads fell into a denam-basket.

After every few executions, Lomax raised the head-filled denam-basket, blood seeping through the woven reeds until it dripped onto his white hair and ran the length of his arms, "Denam for their heads!" He passed the denam-basket to the awaiting crowd and then held up a lomax-basket, "Lomax for their penance!" This too, he passed out into the crowd. Obediently, those gathered tossed gold coins into the lomax-basket until the weight of the gold forced them to lower the basket to the ground. Only the denam-baskets circulated overhead, serving as warning to any who would worship the Sphere.

Again, Tannessa marveled at her cousin's cunning.

The final body placed into position beneath the guillotine already lay near lifeless. Though broken and bloodied, the girl's body did not display any bullet wounds. Simply trampled. The blade fell, and Tilly's head landed in a denam-basket. The gold Troq gave her, now taken from her body. The list of goods she carried, long forgotten. As Lomax leaned forward to pass the denam-basket to the crowd, the basket unexpectedly slipped out of his blood-coated hands. Tilly's head rolled into the dirt, blood slowly flowing from her neck like the yolk of a fractured egg.

Troq pulled another potato from the ruptured denam-basket, placing it on his cutting board. Though he sliced it evenly, each resulting sphere retained the uneven flaws of its beaten, original whole. He gathered the pieces with the edge of his knife and tossed them into a sizzling skillet. Added salt and stirred.

"Selma," he spoke to the stout woman standing on the top step of a wooden ladder. "Have you seen Tilly? I sent her to the marketplace this morning. She should have returned hours ago."

Selma placed a freshly cleaned large pewter platter on the bottom of an overly crowded shelf. The task had already forced her to traverse the ladder several times with stacks of dishes in order to clear space for more dishes on the shelf. Typical of her, she did not take shortcuts when it came to cleaning, or when storing various dishes, pots, pans, and utensils around the kitchen. Troq served as cook. Selma served as caretaker—a task made easier without the presence of children, of course, but Edran, Tilly, and any number of other children often appeared over her shoulder, sent by Troq to assist with the washing of dishes. As such, whenever a child went missing, every servant in the manor, along with the cook, assumed Selma knew their whereabouts.

"No, Master Troq."

"See if you can find her. That basket won't hold any longer."

Dishwasher. Child herder. Troq thought she would happily abdicate the latter, but Selma acquiesced and climbed down, "Yes, Master Troq." She folded the ladder and moved it out of the pathway, but she left the remaining dishes piled on the countertop as if to remind him of the task he had *actually* hired her to perform.

He took a step forward, allowing Selma passage. Then he reached for the wrapped block of aged cheddar and the hand-sized shredder he kept above the cold box. A minute later, he moved the cheese over sharp circular grooves with long, graceful strokes. The cheese curled away from the harsh grater, falling like molting skin onto the rustic brown potato slices he had sizzling. He allowed the shredded cheese to melt over and around the flawed edges of the sliced spud before he removed the skillet from the fire. Using an oversized spatula, he transferred the resulting pile of dairy and starch into a serving bowl.

Myrtane entered with news, "Master Troq, Overseer Narch sends word. Morlac will attend Valun's beheading. Our god, and Adherent Shale, will arrive this evening. We are ordered to make the proper preparations."

Troq smiled warmly, "Thank you, Myrtane." He pointed to the potato dish, "As you can see, I anticipated their arrival. Have the magnate's quarters dusted and light the candles; and Valun's room for Shale, I believe.

The adherent is used to more luxurious accommodations, no doubt, but it is the best we can offer under the circumstances."

"At once, Master Troq," Myrtane turned to leave.

"And send Merrudi here to the kitchen. It seems all my help has abandoned me."

Severing

Delacroy

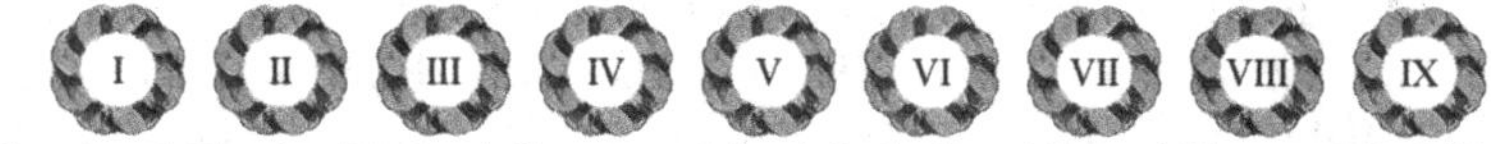

Maldinado, Phinx, and Edran climbed out of dark sewers into the darkness of the smoke-filled air, silently replacing the grate behind them. The smoke burned their eyes, but they could see their surroundings well enough, having already adjusted to the darkness of the sewers. They stood in an alleyway behind the stone wall of a series of double-stacked homes, the taller stone wall that encircled Fourth Circle at their back, creating the illusion of a canyon. Wooden doors leading into lower-level homes, all of them closed from what Maldinado could see through the haze, offered the only breaks in the pattern. Beside each of these doors sat two large, open barrels. Twice a month, horses pulled a water cart through the alleyway and attendants filled the barrels. As such, the residents diligently kept the pathway clear of debris. The water barrels also indicated the poverty level of the residents. Wealthier residents, such as Maldinado, preferred wine. Indeed, every Delcrean *preferred* wine. Water carried disease and tasted like dirt. Maldinado cringed at the thought.

Fortunately, Fourth Circle residents worshiped Morlac through acts of generosity. Quite often, therefore, the poverty stricken would open their door to find a bottle of wine tucked discreetly behind the water barrel. Maldinado searched behind several different barrels before finally finding one such bottle. The fact it remained unopened meant the person residing behind the door likely visited relatives or friends in another circle. Ignoring the bottle, Maldinado opened the corresponding door and entered the home. The alley stretched in either direction for miles, offering no outlet to the street, so the abandoned home provided the three of them quick passage.

"What is burning?" Phinx asked.

Maldinado closed the door, "I don't know."

Light flooded in from the open entryway where a torch hung on the exterior side of the door post. Mostly barren interior walls and a lone wooden chair greeted them. A side wall extended outward in a failed attempt to provide privacy from passersby. Seen during the day, and from the correct angle, however, Maldinado knew from experience the residents within found themselves completely exposed. Seen during the night? Maldinado trusted the shadows of the open room concealed them.

If not for the small painting hanging above the chair, barely visible in the dim light, Maldinado would have thought the home more permanently abandoned. The painting style matched the style of Fourth Gate, depicting the mostly shadowed profile of a man. The only source of light in the painting, smartly positioned to align perfectly with the real torchlight streaming in from outside, fell upon the figure's right ear, a portion of the surrounding cheek and throat area, and the gray wall behind the figure. Maldinado felt certain the painting's alignment did not occur by chance.

Phinx paused to study the brush strokes, "Shardell. Strange to find one here. She died before I was born."

"Probably a gift," Maldinado rubbed at his hip, "or inherited."

"Valuable. Whoever lives here should sell it."

"Perhaps they are unwilling to part ways with it."

"'Tis likely an inheritance, then," Edran decided. "A reminder of someone."

"Do you know who lives here?" Phinx asked.

Maldinado nodded, "Yes, I know everyone in Fourth Circle, but I couldn't tell you which one of them lives in this particular home. They all blend together."

"Then you have never been in this room. You would have remembered *this* Shardell painting if you had seen it before. If I survive the revolution, I will remember this moment." Phinx wrapped his checkered, yellow scarf around three fingers, "I have only ever seen five other Shardell paintings in all of Delacroy."

"Why so few?" Edran asked.

"She died young. Beaten to death by a jealous lover when she was not much older than you are now, Edran."

"Edran's older than he looks," Maldinado moved toward the entrance. "We can't linger. We have too much to accomplish."

They entered the darkness outside, and parted ways upon reaching the street. Phinx and Edran sought out the Sons and Daughters of Oblation, and Maldinado sought those residents who he thought would join the revolution, starting with the foulest of his friends.

Lomax slept beside his wife, Muriel. For a moment, Maldinado just watched. His friend struggled to breathe, the effects of age and tobacco. Not for the first time did the tailor invade the basket weaver's home. In their younger days, Maldinado often awakened Lomax from sleep. The two of them would sneak away from Muriel, though never far, typically spending half the night in the empty street just outside Lomax's home drinking wine and telling stories about the travelers they met in the marketplace the prior day. As they grew older, late nights transitioned to early mornings. Maldinado would arouse Lomax and they traveled to the Sorting together. As they grew even older, however, Lomax stopped attending the Sorting, so Maldinado stopped waking him.

So much had changed since the tailor last saw his friend.

The sound of Lomax snoring remained the same, however.

"Lomax," Maldinado spoke without concern for Muriel. If she could sleep next to that fool of an ox, Maldinado had no fear of disturbing her; nor had he during any of his previous visits, "Lomax, wake up."

His friend shifted upward into his pillow, fighting to maintain his dreams. Maldinado licked his finger and stuck it into Lomax's ear, "Wake up."

The old man lifted his head and stared silently at the bastard who dared to interrupt his slumber.

That bastard proudly smiled like a dolt, "Get dressed. I'll grab the wine."

Maldinado walked into Muriel's kitchen. For as long as he could remember, Muriel kept a curtain hung in such a manner as to conceal the shelves where she stored the wine bottles. Her sense of hospitality meant she did not display any signs of wealth. Lomax thought it a silly gesture, but Muriel exhibited many peculiarities, most attributed to the insecurity she felt about her black teeth, so the curtain remained. Lomax said it made her happy, but that greatly shortened the tale. At some point in their marriage, Lomax had wanted something. Maldinado could no longer remember the details. Perhaps, he wanted to smoke his pipe indoors. Regardless, Muriel seized her opportunity and made a deal in exchange for the curtain.

Maldinado stared at the plain brown curtain. His life as a tailor felt strangely more distant than his prior life as Madar of the Adarian 45th. He felt closer to Hintor in that moment than he did to Lomax, longing to raise a pint of ale from inside Three Horns Tavern rather than toast with wine at the edge of an empty street in Delacroy. But he shook the thought from his head. He needed Lomax. Hintor lived in another world. Lomax lived in Delacroy. Thus, Maldinado lifted the curtain and selected a bottle from the highest shelf.

Lomax emerged from the bedroom, shirtless and with an unlit pipe in his mouth. He pulled a candle from the wall and lit the tobacco leaf. Hot wax pooled on the rim and ran down the concave bowl of the pipe. He replaced the candle after a few successful puffs of smoke, "Where've you been?"

"Building orphanages."

Maldinado followed his friend out of the home. They took a seat in the street. Lomax, per his custom, sat balanced on his heels, placing his back against his favorite stone pillar; same as he did every morning while he waited for Maldinado to pass along the way. Maldinado sat with his back against the opposite pillar and stretched his legs, adjusting the angle every few minutes to keep his hip from growing too stiff. They passed the wine bottle between them.

"You're getting as bad as Muriel with all your ailments," Lomax picked at the dried candle wax that had gathered on his pipe. "Did you just get back?"

Maldinado nodded, "I couldn't sleep, so I figured I would drink, instead. And get news from the marketplace. You can start by telling me why there is so much smoke in the air."

"Fourth Gate," Lomax leaned forward onto his wide, calloused toes. "We found it empty, this morning. All the taggles suddenly vanished. I saw it with my own eyes, and you know how much I hate to leave the marketplace." He took a swallow of wine and held the bottle out for his friend to take. Then he continued, "I may have said something about it being Morlac's judgment. I mean, Boltmar died in Fourth Gate. Now this? And I may have suggested we burn everything the taggles touched."

"*You* started this fire?"

"No, not specifically. Someone else lit the fire. I merely started the inquisition."

Maldinado set the bottle on his leg, "An inquisition?"

"To find worshipers of the Sphere and abolish every last piece of taggle artwork," Lomax stood and paced between the two stone pillars. "They worship him. Why else would they vanish? Morlac judged them. It's the only explanation. And Morlac's judgment be on any who worship the Sphere." Lomax stopped suddenly, "Destroy anything you have purchased from the taggles, Maldinado. I wouldn't want you to lose your head over a set of colored beads. Oh, and I'll need you to help me gather the gold. You wouldn't believe how much gold," he pulled five coins from the pocket of his linen trousers. "Baskets filled with coins! I had to leave most of it in the marketplace, but no one will dare take it from us. Except Tannessa. We will have to share with Tannessa. She's the one who suggested the guillotine. Much safer than fire..."

Maldinado struggled to his feet, leaning warily with his hand atop the stone pillar, a stark contrast to the joy that emanated from Lomax. He thought about not telling him the truth. He could remain silent and simply disappear back into the sewers. His friend would never know. But images of the dead filled his head. Lomax deserved to know the truth. Also, Maldinado needed allies he could trust, and he trusted no one more so than this man. He decided to take the risk.

"While you were busy with your inquisition, I started a revolution."

This time, Lomax appeared taken aback. He pulled the pipe from his mouth and scratched his beard, staring down his nose when he finally spoke, "A revolution?"

"I was not always a tailor..."

Maldinado proceeded to tell Lomax the tale of his life as a warrior in the Adarian 45th. How he followed the Adow into Dragon's Torment. About Inindu and how the two of them rode into the Kul, and how they discovered the dead.

Lomax reached for the bottle of wine and took a long draw. Then he sat down.

Maldinado joined him and continued his story, "I met up with Inindu at the Sorting. She opened my mind to the truth, somehow, and she can do the same for you: She can show you what lies beyond this illusion, show you who you really are, and you'll remember the life you once lived in the Sphere's world."

Finally, he told Lomax about the rescue of Lyshmee and their quest to kill Morlac, though he did not mention the taggles, specifically, or their plan to use the sewers, "It will all happen here in Fourth Circle. When Morlac arrives for Valun's beheading, we will march. Join us, Lomax. Fight beside me."

Lomax sat in silence for several minutes before finally replying, "You've gone mad, old friend. Did you sleep with some infected scarlet? Drink a slow poison? Who, exactly, did you encounter at the Sorting?"

Maldinado leaned his head back against the stone pillar, "I am not mad, and I am not the only worshiper of the Sphere."

"Who else?"

"Simiad."

"First Boltmar and Valun. Now Simiad? Are all the magnates corrupt?"

"The Delcrean Council has long been corrupted," Maldinado motioned for Lomax to pass the wine bottle. "But not all of them worship the Sphere."

Again, Lomax sat in silence for a long moment, "What of Muriel?"

"We can keep her safe. I'll take her to Second Circle. She can stay with the other women."

"How?" Lomax stood, but he did not pace, "How will you take her there? Fourth Gate burns. How are *you* even here?"

Maldinado did not respond. He remained seated, allowing Lomax to judge him and choose for himself.

The basket weaver crossed his arms and drew on his pipe, staring at Maldinado. Memories of younger days passed silently between them. A lifetime unspoken. Each bearing the weight of the moment, both faltering.

"No," he finally decided. "I worship Morlac. I cannot fight with you."

Maldinado stood then, grasping for Lomax's shoulder rather than the stone pillar. He reached up and wrapped his hand around the back of his friend's neck, drawing him closer to his face until their foreheads touched. Lomax did not resist.

"Then I fear we must part ways. I leave you to your inquisition."

"And I leave *you* to your revolution."

Maldinado closed his eyes and savored the smoky smell of his old friend one last time. How many times had they embraced over the years? He released his grip, "My father used to quote a proverb: *Young men march out to war, but the old man knows there is no reason for haste. The battle will come to him, soon enough.*"

"Which father?"

Maldinado chuckled, "Both of them."

Lomax placed the pipe between his teeth, "Do you remember Jasper?"

"The one the adherent invited to live in Ninth Circle?"

Lomax nodded, "He came to me with a story about how I could live a different life in a different circle. I gave him every last coin I possessed, and some that I stole. Some of that gold came from your pockets."

"He died, if I remember correctly."

"He betrayed me, so I had him killed."

"Why tell me now?"

"It seems my mind is fading. To the point I may not remember Jasper tomorrow, so it feels right I should finally tell you," Lomax tapped the charred tobacco from his pipe. "Besides, it appears I will, in fact, outlive you, as I've always said. Farewell, old friend."

"I've yet to lose that wager," the tailor countered wistfully. Then he nodded, "Farewell, old friend."

"Probably forget all about you by morning. Couldn't even remember you went to the Sorting."

"You're the worst kind of friend," Maldinado turned with a tear coated smile, and slowly disappeared into the haze and darkness of the night.

Shale leaned forward on the plush, red velvet cushion, grabbing the edge of it, and stiffening his arms against the constant jostling of the carriage. The nascient sat stiffly across from him, same as the previous seventeen. Each time prior they had traveled in silence, for while he frequently spoke *at* his god, sharing his every doubt, Shale had refused to speak with the dead; beyond what duty required. But age had tempered his feelings of horror and layered his doubts. Doubts he could not share with anyone else aside from Morlac. Despite the creature's presence, therefore, Shale focused on the god it held within, pushing past his revulsion until his lingering meditations finally rose to the surface.

"Why choose me?" It proved easier to look at the carriage floor while he spoke, "Why entrust me with your secret?"

"I have no secrets."

"No secrets?" Shale motioned toward the nascient, "What about this creature you force me to parade through the city? That body was once a faithful worshiper. He trusted you...and you betrayed him."

"There are things you don't understand," the lips moved but the face failed to wrap them with any visible expression; one of the many reasons Shale shielded the nascient from prolonged public view.

"So, help me understand," Shale forced himself to look into the nascient's ivory eyes. "You are my god. If not you, then who will lift my doubts?"

The nascient reached for Shale's shoulder with a cold hand, "I betrayed no one. The worshiper who fills this body willingly shares it with his god. He is helping me in my battle against the Sphere. I only wish I could remain in the city longer, but my focus is required elsewhere."

Shale pulled away from the cold touch of comfort, "When will it end? This curse? When will you be free of your torment?"

"My torment is only in physical form. It means nothing. I spend my time in the dream world stealing souls out from under the Sphere's nose. He is powerless to stop me. In time, his world will come to an end. No one will remain there to worship him."

"Yet, he grows stronger in our world," Shale folded his arms and looked at the wavering red velvet curtains that hid them from onlookers. More than onlookers. The dead, too. Standing motionless along the street, reaching for him, seeking to pull him from the carriage. Flickering images that left him frightened. Curious. A loose thread at the corner of the curtain caught his attention. He reached over and attempted to pull it off, but the stitching held firm. He tugged slightly, opening a crack to the city beyond. Only the street. Real people. Nothing of the dead remained visible, but he knew they would return.

"You're the adherent," the nascient continued. "Deal with the problem. I built the city to survive without my presence. But it won't survive if you never intercede."

"You constructed nine spheres. You built a city in the image of the Sphere."

The nascient lifted the curtain, obtusely sticking its hand out to wave. The crowd cheered.

A brief glimpse of the dead. Then gone.

"I give Delacroy what they desire. The shape is familiar to the souls I bring into this world. It helps them transition peacefully. I use the image of the sphere to bring Delcreans closer to me. Each circle grows smaller in physical size, but what I require of my worshipers greatly increases as they move through the city. I entrust them with more knowledge, as you well know."

Shale yanked more forcefully on the loose thread. Still, it held. Through the resulting crack he again saw the dead, "There was a time I fully embraced you. I held no doubts. Then you chose me as Adherent."

"Your doubts prove your faithfulness to me, Shale. You cannot worship me if you don't question me."

He turned his attention away from the dead and the loose thread. He folded his arms and again looked at the nascient, strangely growing unaware of the morphed body, "Why is Inindu in Delacroy? How did she enter our world?"

"I admit, I do not know." Morlac's words brought him no comfort. Visions of the dead brought him no comfort. The carriage sped through the streets of Delacroy. Smoke wafted through the closed curtains.

Phinx had hurriedly pulled a yellow-checkered scarf from the pile of silk scarves he kept. As a result, and with a desire to return quickly to the two travel companions he had left behind him in the sewers, neither of whom understood his desire to fetch a new scarf, he absently forsook his habit of searching for the one blemish which had otherwise caused his mother to gift the scarf to her son. As he moved through Fourth Circle, therefore, unable to properly examine the silk fibers due to darkness, he found the lack of knowledge greatly bothered him. In truth, Kinu did not *gift* the scarf to her son, she gave him a puzzle to solve. Whenever she discovered a flaw in the design, something only she could typically see, Kinu threw it into a pile for Phinx to wear. In a sense, she gave all of Delacroy the best of what she had to offer, but she gave her worst scarves to Phinx. Only he bore witness to her flaws, and that transformed each scarf into something unique and special.

He loved his mother and, in her own way, though she denied they represented tokens of affection, Kinu kept her arms wrapped around her son's neck every moment of every day. Absent a flaw in the scarf, however, or the knowledge thereof, Phinx felt awkward, as though he suddenly wore another man's boots. He found it so uncomfortable, in fact, he had yet to put the new scarf in his mouth. Instead, he twisted it around his fingers and settled for chewing strands of his hair.

When, at last, he reached the home where his parents lived, and as he approached the torchlight flooding their main entrance, Phinx paused to inspect the length of the scarf: White backing with yellow squares; each side of the square about half the size of his forefinger. He marveled, as he often did, at his mother's skill with a loom—fibers pressed so tightly together they appeared smooth as a sheet made of silk; as though she snatched her designs from nature, rather than crafted them. Phinx measured every square against his finger, but not one line exceeded or proved inferior to the others. After several more minutes of inspection, searching for sheering, minor tears, or variance in the dye, he relented and altered his tactics.

"Mother," Phinx found Kinu working in a side room, sitting at her loom like she often did until deep into the night, at times greeting the sunrise. "You've given me an unblemished scarf."

"You came all this way to question my eyesight?" Kinu, cursed by age and strain, looked at her son over a pair of rounded glass spectacles.

Phinx fell against the door frame with familiarity, "No, I came to tell you to leave Fourth Circle. It seems I've started a revolution."

"You start many things," Kinu finished interlacing the weft, swung the batten, adjusted the healds, and began anew with the weft.

"This is serious, mother."

"Oh, very well," she paused her weaving to look at him over the spectacles, eyeing his scarf. "Third row, fifth square. The birmly weed dyed that section of the fiber darker than the rest. Looks more orange than yellow."

"No, that's not..." Phinx grabbed his scarf and quickly found the blemish. Suddenly, he felt as though her arms had wrapped warmly around his neck. "Thank you, but that isn't what I meant. The revolution is a serious matter. You need to leave Fourth Circle. Go visit that friend of yours in Seventh Circle." Phinx put one end of the scarf in his mouth.

"Your father is bedridden. You know I can't leave," she spoke as though holding a conversation with the loom, never shifting her focus away from her weaving.

Phinx turned toward the bedroom where his father had slept, mostly uninterrupted, for the past three years. He had fallen asleep, one night, and must have lost his head in the dream world. When his father awoke the next morning, he mumbled every word and lost function in half his body.

Phinx knew the reason Kinu worked so long into the night: She feared sleep would take her the same way it had taken her husband, "How is he doing?"

"I asked him if he planned on dying today, but he insisted on breathing. I'm holding out hope he will give up and die tomorrow, though."

Phinx nodded at the familiar exchange.

Despite her harsh words, Kinu provided his father with the best of care. Whether looking after him, or weaving, she rarely left the home. Fortunately, Delcreans considered it improper to purchase silk goods in a marketplace. Instead, patrons traveled to a weaver's home where they conducted business in a more intimate setting, allowing them the privacy required to properly trial the various outer and *under* garments. Of course, some homes provided more intimacy than others. As a yearling, Phinx often spied on his mother's female patrons, and quickly discovered a fondness for the many varying shapes of a woman's body. Rather than punish her son upon discovery, however, Kinu invited him into the room and asked for his honest critique of the garments. At first, the women found him charming and giggled at his innocence. But when he grew into his features, and closed the gap in age, charming turned to delightful; then fetching. Eventually, they found him most pleasing.

Kinu never spoke harshly of her son's actions.

"I killed someone, mother. Several, actually. I killed a yearling," Phinx offered the confession without conviction or need for forgiveness. Per his custom, he told Kinu about all his shady dealings.

Kinu widened the stretch of warp threads, "The young are the first to die in any battle. If they weren't prepared to die, then they shouldn't have opposed your revolution."

Phinx pulled gently on the scarf hanging from his clenched teeth, slowly sliding it out of his mouth, "I may die tomorrow."

Her fingers stopped moving. A moment later, they resumed pinching and pulling the fibers, "May the Sphere be with you."

"And keep us in his light."

"We both understood the risk when we joined the Sons and Daughters of Oblation. This is not our world. We belong with the Sphere."

"The Father of Oblation wants his Sons and Daughters to reveal themselves. No more masks," Phinx pushed himself away from the door frame. "Will you stand with me, mother?"

Kinu looked over the glass frames at her son, "We both know I've never worn a mask." She returned to her work, "I've never left your father long enough to attend one of their fatuous gatherings. I worship the Sphere right where I sit, every day. But if you're asking me to stand with you and fight a revolution? No, I won't do that. I cannot. I will stay here and die with your father. But you knew what I would say before you asked."

"Yes."

"Don't doddle, son. This is no place for a leader of the revolution."

Phinx watched the familiar rhythm of her hands. They grew more deformed with every visit he made, but Kinu refused to yield.

"You'll find a bottle of ale on the counter. I thought your father may want a drink, but he doesn't seem to be in the mood."

As Phinx left his mother's home, he raised a toast. Then he wept.

Edran picked at his nose, removing a crusted flake with his finger. He wiped it apathetically on the rough, stone wall of Denam's bedchamber. The wealthy basket weaver slept separately from his wife. She lay resting in a room further down the hallway. The home, while much smaller than a manor, included nine bedchambers, large enough to house a brood of children, but Denam's wife had never conceived. To fill their home, therefore, Denam and his wife often hosted guests for several months at a time, and always kept an empty room for those in need.

Though Edran rarely saw the basket-weaver without a pleasant smile during the day, Denam displayed a distinctly serious expression while he slept. Deep, darkened grooves dug into his cheeks, stretching down past his mouth from where they attached to either side of a solid nose. Edran had seen those grooves ripple like ribbons whenever Denam laughed; his deep-set eyes turning bright, gently held in place by the massive cushion of his raised cheeks. His pleasant demeanor compensated for a lack of craftsmanship and served as the foundation of a fruitful business. Indeed, he had attracted many of the thousands of patrons who visited the marketplace each day until it seemed everyone in Delacroy owned a denam-basket.

Edran knelt beside the merchant's bed, inches from Denam's face. He stared at the middle-aged man for a moment, feeling his soft breath upon his chin. Then, he blew quietly into his face, and nearly burst into laughter when Denam twitched his nose. Finally, the boy spoke, "Denam... Denam. 'Tis time to be waking up."

Denam's eyes opened, and immediately his face lit up with recognition and a grin, "Edran, my boy. Your breath stinks."

"Celery sticks."

"Do you bring word from the Father of Oblation? I suspected someone might visit me tonight, considering the uprising in the marketplace."

Edran sat back in confusion, "What uprising?"

Denam motioned the boy further from the bed so he could move his legs out from under the blankets. Then he provided Edran with details about how the fire in Fourth Gate started, and about the burning of taggle artwork, and then he told him of the massive number of beheadings.

"Who?" Edran asked.

Denam wrapped his arm around the boy and brought him closer, "Rab and Elsane. Lewhit. Several I didn't know, probably from the inner circles. A girl, too, the poor thing. Put their heads in my baskets and passed them overhead and all around the crowd. 'Denam heads' they call them, now. May the Sphere be with me."

"And keep you in his light."

Denam stood, "Enough about the inquisition. You bring news of the revolution, yes? I heard tidbits, but I found it hard to steer anyone away from discussions about missing taggles and the fire."

Edran nodded, "The revolution 'tis begun. We be marching on Fourth Circle with Inindu leading us."

"Inindu? Here, in Delacroy?" Denam half-bounced, managing to contain his excitement only after crossing his arms and biting his upper lip.

Edran climbed atop the feather bed, walked along the edge, and jumped to the ground, "The end be near. 'Tis time to remove the masks. Be ready to fight when Inindu marches."

Excitement turned to sternness. Denam pointed to a dark-stained wardrobe in the corner of the room and motioned for Edran to follow. The merchant pulled at the bottom drawer, lifting away several maldinado-robes and a selection of yiddick-shawls to reveal a long, curved sword lying underneath, "I am ready."

Commotion from the street brought swift concealment of the blade. It sounded like thunder to Edran's ears, but louder and longer and, instead of fading, the sound grew closer and even louder. The taggle boy followed Denam to the entrance of his home, and then further still, until both stood outside near the street. Torchlight lit the night, piercing through the lingering, smoky haze. The entire horizon glowed, and Fourth Circle watched, brought forth from their homes by the light and accompanying deep thrumming. Residents and onlookers lined the street as far as Edran could see.

Hundreds of horses with mounted riders, each of them carrying a torch, rounded the street. They rode ten abreast and wore the royal blue tymer-kurtas that signified them as swads. The riders passed with singular purpose, few of them glancing to either side. Behind them marched thousands more, filling the street as thoroughly as the travelers who visited Fourth Circle most days. These swads, too, carried torches. A smaller unit of riders followed. Though still in the distance, Edran recognized several of the higher ranking Delcrean council as they approached: Overseers Fillop, Narch, and Tristan. Fillop rode fully erect, displaying no signs of the fear that had chased him from Second Circle earlier that morning, though Edran wondered how he would act if he saw Inindu, again. Behind this procession, a team of nine black horses pulled Morlac's carriage into view. It gleamed in the torchlight. Every inch sparkled with crushed rubies, stealing Edran's attention away from the overseers. The carriage stretched at least three horses in length and, the boy guessed, sat five broad-shouldered men across. A dozen swads surrounded the carriage, preventing anyone from getting close to their god. And behind Morlac's carriage, Edran saw a nearly endless procession of marching swads.

"This is what we must fight?" Denam wondered.

"'Tis a massive army, to be certain," Edran agreed.

No doubt, the army emerged from Fifth Gate which lay far beyond Edran's vision and several hundred yards in the distance to his left, and they marched toward the magnate's manor which lay far beyond Edran's vision to his right. The only portion of the street Edran could see, the space between gate and manor, contained swad following swad following swad following swad...

Overseer Narch pulled away from the procession, unexpectedly, trotting forward along the edge of the street. He reared to a stop in front of Denam and Edran, "Morlac's boon upon thee, Denam."

"Favor and boon, Overseer."

"I trust you have room for the council, this evening?" The bald man spoke without concern of refusal, for Denam never refused a guest. Then he nodded slightly upon seeing a woman standing in the doorway of Denam's home, "Tell your wife we will need food and wine. I can provide both, if you wish?"

Denam stretched his arms wide in a sign of welcome, "No, that won't be necessary. I am a poor host, indeed, if I fail to offer the full extent of my hospitality. My home, my food, and my wine are yours, Overseer."

Narch tapped his ruby armband, "You, boy, haven't I seen you before at the magnate's manor?"

"To be certain," Edran bowed. "I serve as apprentice to the cook, Troq."

"A fine cook."

"Yes, Overseer."

"Yes, good...good. Assist with the meal preparations, boy. Let us see how much you have learned from your master."

"Yes, Overseer. At once."

Severing

Inindu

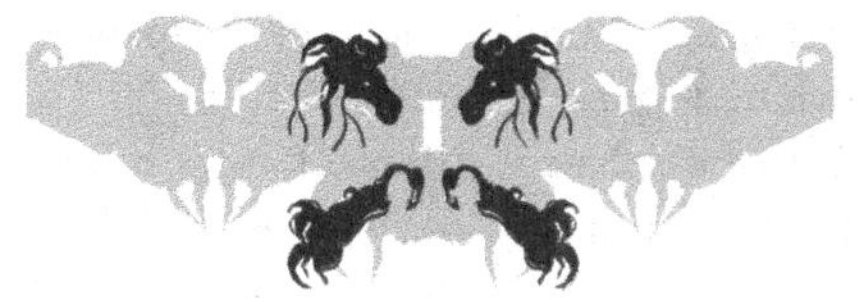

Simiad and Mathay lead our revolution into Third Circle. We are a collection of taggles and misfits. A few swads. Barely more than several hundred mostly untrained rebels, the majority of whom carry torches instead of swords, but no one in Third Circle stands in opposition. No champion from Third Circle rises. No shadowy figure awaits us on the horizon, seeking to bring a halt to our passage. Magnate Honcherub yielded, as predicted. Now, Simiad and Mathay ride in front of us with an air of victory and, in the case of the shirtless Mathay, an intentional display of muscle. A pointless display. Most of the residents we've encountered in Second Circle, and now Third Circle, hide in fear, unwilling to choose one god over another. Thousands of them sit in their homes, while only hundreds choose to fight. It is enough to make us miss our sister. The Adow would never allow such indifference.

The Gold Keeper—newly elected banner barer, though he still wears his yellow biggins hat—carries our symbol of the revolution: A black sphere, outlined in red, against a white field. Even here, in another world, Maldinado chooses to follow the banner of the Adarian 45th. It hangs limply from the top of a Dissemination Pole—the same pole which, less than a day earlier, carried the sculpted likeness of Lyshmee's head, heralding her pending execution.

We look over to where Lyshmee, Jennaween, and Harian walk beside a gaggle of women. Jennaween leads them. These women watch us as they walk, not with eyes of spite or malice, rather, they watch with reverence. Then we notice they each display a new tattoo upon their forearm. There is something familiar about the marking. They do not reflect the names of the dead, as they had discussed. No, this is a single shape, outlined in magenta.

A horse.

They tattooed the image of our magenta horse upon their arm. A ward against Inindu.

Jennaween raises her arm in the air, forming a fist. Then all the women raise their fists in succession, displaying their tattoos. Even the girl at Lyshmee's hip shows her marking. We stop walking. They stop walking.

No, not a ward *against* Inindu. A sign of allegiance to Inindu.

The men continue to pass without concern.

It occurs to us that our hair is still black. Our horse is black. But these women honor the magenta horse of legends told. The one we only half revealed. They honor Inindu. They follow Inindu—not some listless flag from a lost world. Not the shirtless Mathay. Not the drunk magnate. No, they follow Inindu. They raise their fists to Inindu.

And the men continue to pass without concern.

We hide our identity from these people, but perhaps we underestimate them. The men withdrew in fear when we revealed the truth. These women…worship us. Our father can barely stomach our presence, yet these women tattooed our image upon their arms.

We consider Morlac's world anew, the drab architecture and subdued colors. We see a resident of Third Circle who sits in her entryway, not far from where we stand in the street. She wears a black gown that stretches up over her head, so that only her gaunt face remains visible. Her cheek bones jut outward, far exceeding the natural frame of her face, eyes disappearing over the edge of the resulting chasm. Her skin gathers in wrinkles around haggard lips and stretches over chin and nose. So much power at his disposal, and *this* is the world Morlac chose to create? We turn back to Jennaween. *What fate awaits you?* If she knew the truth, would a tru-born so willingly worship the Sphere? But she doesn't worship the Sphere. She follows Inindu.

We are Inindu.

Our topi mounts our horse.

Men continue to pass without concern. In the distance ahead, the Gold Keeper carries the bouncing banner of the Adarian 45th above our heads. Simiad and Mathay lead the procession. These men follow a drunkard and the scum of all swads. They willingly follow two scoundrels.

We turn back to the women. Do they not treat us like a god? Are we not worthy of worship?

Yes, father, we are worthy. What you ignore, they adore.

Our topi smiles even as we reveal our full magenta color. Magenta horse. Our magenta hair soars wildly in the stagnant air. Our horse speaks well and loudly, "I am Inindu."

I am your god.

The women cheer.

The men finally stop marching. They turn at the commotion taking place at their rear and find our revealed beauty. We move forward, leading our army of women.

"Inindu does not ride behind a man," we announce. *And we will no longer bow to them.*

The gathering of misfit warriors dutifully, if hesitantly, parts to either side of us until we reach Simiad and Mathay. They sit atop their horses, eyes wide with wonder. Horror. It's difficult to tell which, what with their mouths agape in such a manner, "Jennaween. Lyshmee."

Both respond, "Yes, honored Inindu?"

"Perhaps these men will offer you the use of their horses? I find horses prefer a woman rider. Men tend to squeeze their legs, too tightly, when mounted."

"What magic is this?" Mathay's chiseled torso distracts us from his otherwise ignorant and brutish nature; or, perhaps, we simply prefer to look elsewhere whenever the dolt speaks.

"Inindu." Simiad slides off the grey gelding with all the grace of a potato falling from a basket, but hands the reigns to Jennaween with a much more polished bow, "Did Fillop tell you nothing of the legends from the old world, Mathay? She was the first to worship Morlac, and the reason he now hides behind nine walls of stone." The magnate lowers his head, "Forgive my blindness, honored Inindu."

"You are incapable of seeing anything. You are always drunk."

"I have never found reason to stay sober," he rubs finger and thumb over the whiskers surrounding his mouth.

"You knew of my existence. That is reason enough."

Did Morlac ever possess any greater knowledge? We exist. That is enough for anyone.

"I was a fool. I see that, now. I will never drink again, honored Inindu."

"Only a greater fool than you would make such a promise. Trust me, I know. My sister, the Adow, has chosen a few of them as First Etabli. No, Simiad, you will surely drink, again. And when you drink, raise a toast in my honor, but I warn you: Never speak of my beauty when you are drunk. You cannot possibly convey, nor adequately describe my beauty in a state of drunkenness."

Simiad lowers his head, once more, "I fear sobriety will not aide in my attempts to describe your beauty, honored Inindu. Even the greatest of taggle painters would struggle to capture the treasure of your presence."

We nod in agreement, "Well, certainly, all who tried have failed in the attempt. Even Beaug."

"Who?"

"An artist from another world," we turn our attention back to the city and Third Circle. The girl who once sat in her entryway now stands. Hundreds more have emerged from hiding. It appears, we managed to draw them out, "Join our revolution. I am here to kill Morlac. I am here to lead you to another world. A better one. One where no one will starve."

The girl is the first to join our ranks, but she is not the last. Others follow in her path.

Mathay, however, still sits atop his chestnut mare, glaring at us with utter disdain, "I will not bow to a woman." Then he points to Lyshmee who stands a few feet away, hand extended and ready to receive the reigns, seemingly doing her best not to vomit, "And I will not give my horse to a whore."

Fair enough. In an instant, we stretch forth our hair and pull the proud warrior up off his horse, wrapping his every muscle with our unbreakable bounds. He starts to speak, again, so we help him close his mouth. We hold him in the air above Lyshmee, high enough for our gathered army to see clearly. *This* they must witness.

"Mathay, of Second Circle," we announce. "Accused of raping a resident of Second Circle. Known to physically harm and ravage all females under his care." He struggles mightily against our grip and, pathetically, emits several muffled groans. We continue, "Since no one wants to hear how the accused might try to account for his actions, in this matter, and by my order, the order of your god, Inindu, the prisoner is presented for execution by beheading. I will act according to your wishes, Lyshmee."

The redness in the woman's eyes tells us just how much she hates him. The tears that well up in her eyes tells us the sacrifice our father asked of her had nothing to do with death. And when Lyshmee turns her head away in shame, her image, in that moment, is forever burned into our memory. Mathay should have died under the guillotine.

"Remove his head," Alanna speaks for Lyshmee, her adopted mother.

We consent. We sever Mathay's head by consuming his body.

The swad's head lands with a thud at Lyshmee's feet. She stares at the dirt-laden head of the man who tore into her body, but she takes no pleasure in his death.

Alanna suddenly kicks the head away from Lyshmee's view, sending it into the shadows of an alleyway twenty feet beyond. She hugs the legs of her adopted mother, and Lyshmee wraps her arm around the girl.

We turn to other matters of concern, "Gold Keeper, toss that banner aside. Jennaween will mark those who follow Inindu. That is all we need see."

Simiad quickly raises his arm, turning his attention from where

Mathay's head disappeared into the shadows, "Allow me to be the first."

"No, that honor was Jennaween's."

Lyshmee mounts her horse, placing Alanna in front of her, and waits beside Jennaween. They raise their fists as we pass, and we are unexpectedly grateful for their worship. We lead the new revolution, *our* revolution, toward Fourth Gate. We are a collection of taggles and misfits. Nothing more than several hundred mostly untrained rebels, the majority of whom carry torches instead of swords. We lead women. We lead men. We bow to no god, and no one stands in opposition. We are Inindu.

REVOLUTION

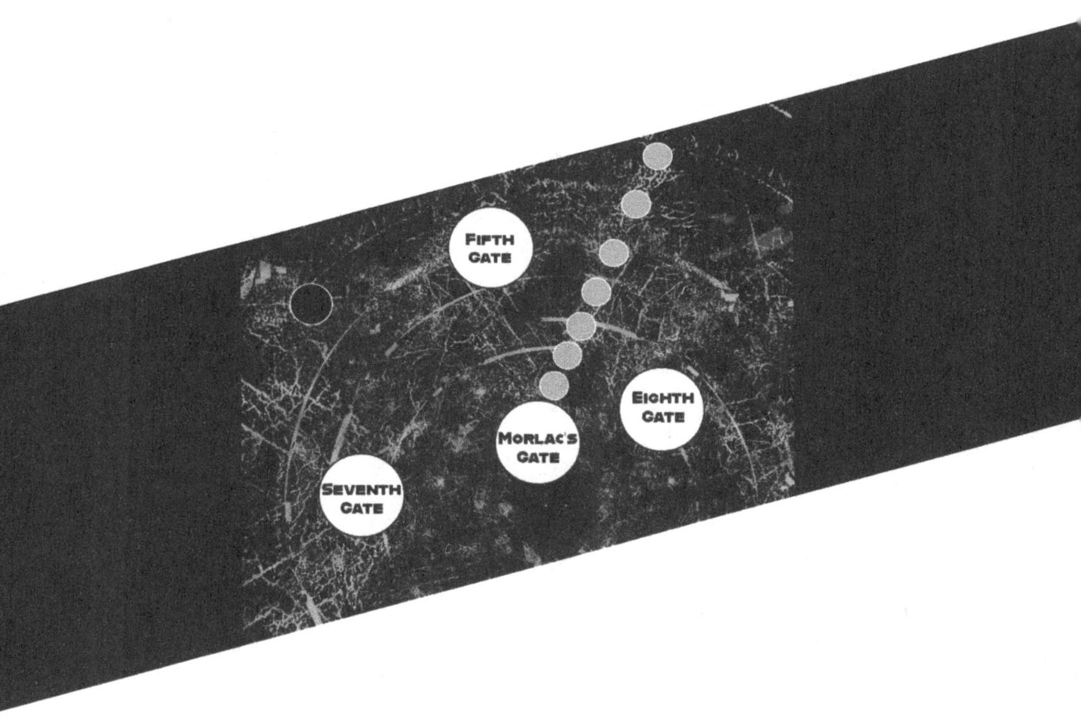

erhaps such battles occur in the outer-lands, certainly
I hear rumors, but Delacroy will never face a revolution while Morlac
lives within the city.

Early Ruminations from Overseer Ristan

(*Before*)

Boltmar awoke in the middle of the night, habitually unable to sleep. Remni slept beside him, her dark, coarse braids scattered across Boltmar's gray-white beard and bare, depressed chest. Only the touch of her breath upon his ethereal skin offered any sign of life, for he could not detect any movement corresponding with her breathing. Though wilted and heavily drooping on one side, a candle still burned on the nightstand beside the bed he shared with his lover. Wax flowed and gathered and dried in bark-like grooves along the gold candelabrum. The waning flame glowed about the magnate's room, casting light upon the only painting in the room.

The restless magnate stared at the painting as he did most nights, moving from one reproduced battle scene to the next; and from warrior to warrior. A great conflict occurred behind two central figures. One seated...collapsed, really. In her arms she held a fallen champion in the moment before his death. She gazed upon him, and he at her, as tortured lovers often do. A love once captured, suddenly lost. Boltmar felt a kinship to the lovers, finding himself and Remni in their eyes, for he, too, would soon succumb to death and leave her behind. Their time cut short.

What wouldn't he give to have met Remni as a younger man? What wouldn't the woman in the painting have given to save her champion? Magenta hues and ever-darkening shades of gray cast the moment into the space between life and death, seemingly lifting the lovers off the canvas and away from the battle that raged behind them.

Boltmar slowly slid his arm out from under Remni and shifted himself to a seated position, placing two barely stuffed pillows behind his back and against the dark-stained headboard. He reached for the remains of a cherry pie, his second slice of the evening. Troq had topped the desert with an almond crumble using slivered almonds, rolled oats, and a healthy amount of brown sugar. The magnate slid a bite into his zestless mouth and turned back to the painting.

A magenta figure, almost imperceptible, stood behind the lovers and the battle. All but hidden within the shadows of the ruins that outlined the horizon. Inindu. Death. If not a participant, certainly the cause of the depicted revolution. She stared out from the shadows toward the lovers. No, beyond them. Boltmar often felt as though Inindu looked directly at him, and he wondered if she saw in the magnate what he saw in her: Death.

a taggle's painting

Delacroy

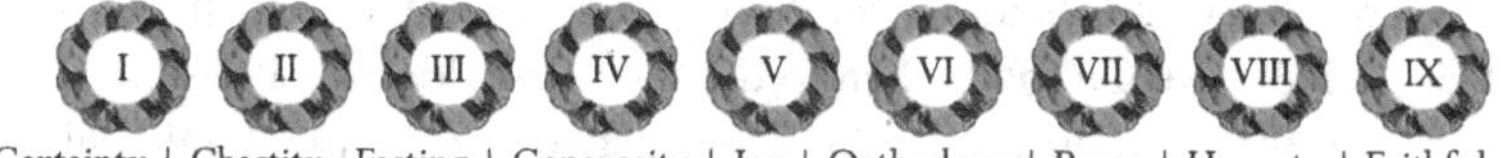

Troq bowed as Morlac entered the manor, guided by Adherent Shale and a small escort of stoic-faced attendants, "My god, we are here to serve your needs." He resisted the urge to vomit the words, managing to deliver them eloquently and, he thought, quite skillfully. After all the trouble Morlac had caused, Troq finally stood mere feet away from his enemy. But the time for action had not yet arrived. The recipe for killing a god required the proper ingredients and time to simmer. With so much still at risk, he would not dare exchange years of planning and manipulation for a single moment of unsavory behavior.

The row of servants lining the manor entryway also bowed, demonstrating varying levels of grace and poise. More importantly, given the relatively short notice, they had managed to prepare the manor and still arrive at the grand entryway for the formal greeting without a moment to spare. Troq took great pride in their hasty accomplishment.

"Would you have me show you to your quarters, or first to the dining hall?" Aside from cheesy potatoes, Troq had also prepared blackened chicken breast, toasted rice, and yellow squash.

Shale responded, "You may deliver all meals and visitors to my quarters. No one is to disturb our god. I, alone, will attend to his needs. Kindly lead the way."

Morlac, with a hand on Shale's shoulder, followed behind Troq.

When Troq returned to the hallway, he found that none of Morlac's attendants had moved from their positions. They still stood guard on either side of the main entryway. The manor servants, much to Troq's satisfaction, had also remained in place. Seeing to his duties as master of the manor, therefore, he gave instructions to several of the servants. They promptly departed. He dismissed all those who remained, and then turned to Morlac's attendants, "Follow me to the dining hall."

The attendants looked uncertainly at one another, but no one took a step.

Troq lowered his head in deference, "I prepared a feast. If you will not eat, I shall have the food taken to the swads outside. But I should warn you, it is not wise to offend a cook." He turned toward the dining hall.

All twelve attendants followed him.

They ate well, but not enough to please Troq. He sent a servant, along with several helpings of leftovers, to feed the swads in the street. The servant returned to inform the cook that the army covered every inch of the street. They lay in rows or gathered in limb-awkward clumps in a vain attempt to gain a few hours of sleep before sunrise, making it impossible, the servant claimed, for him to traverse any further than the edge of the manor steps. He recounted how those swads closest to the servant had lunged at him, snatching the pewter plates away with a hunger that sent the servant skittering back to the manor, abandoning hope of ever retrieving the dishes. Troq thought it a poor excuse for losing expensive dinnerware, however, and sent the servant to scrub the cellar floor as penance.

Selma, having finally returned from her search for Tilly, had followed the servant into the manor. She received more than one suspicious look from Morlac's attendants who had resumed their posts at the entryway. Troq noticed she gave them a few looks in return. He motioned for her to follow him into the kitchen.

"Did you find her?"

"No," Selma snatched up a horsehair brush from where it hung on a hook by the door. "I walked all the way to the marketplace. There is no sign of the girl. Maybe she left the city and returned home to her mother." She squatted near the wash basin and started scrubbing, "I've never understood parents who put their yearlings into the Sorting. *Intentional Orphans* is what I call them. No mother should ever intentionally abandon her child. Some of us have dishes to scrub. We don't have time to waste looking for foolish girls." She pointed back toward the door, "Every swad in Delacroy is out there. It wasn't an easy task getting back here, you know. Tilly probably got lost. Maybe she took a wrong turn on the only street in Fourth Circle. You know she could manage to do it. Clumsiest girl I've ever seen. If any of my yearlings could, she..."

Troq noticed the tear flowing down Selma's fat cheek, "Selma, I have served as father to many of these intentional orphans. The kitchen seems to naturally draw them to us." He leaned against the counter and folded his arms, rubbing at the slight ache in his elbows, "Something about yearlings always needing to eat, I suppose." He chuckled at a memory of Edran stealing apples.

And memories of Inindu eating apples. He stopped smiling.

"Selma, listen to me," Troq lowered his voice and slid into a squat beside her, lest any passersby overhear.

Troq had entered Delacroy as an orphan, a fact not overlooked during his sorting into the city. Delcreans did not *own* one another, but the wealthier residents often employed servants, and most of the servants in Delacroy arrived as orphans—intentional orphans. Short of bribing the magnates, the only sure way to make it through the city gates meant telling the swads you never knew your parents; or describe how they died miserably. So, when magnate Boltmar, three years after taking the ring from his father, needed a new cook to replace the nearly dead one he employed, Troq heard his name called during the Sorting.

The orphan served as apprentice to the austere cook, and when his teacher eventually passed beyond Ninth Circle, Troq assumed his kitchen responsibilities. He expanded the menu and added more spices to the shelf. The new recipes pleased Boltmar and, soon after, the magnate steadily increased Troq's responsibilities until, at last, he gave him oversight of the entire manor.

The changes Troq made, thereafter, went mostly unnoticed. He operated on the fringes, slowly shifting tasks away from the servants he knew worshiped Morlac; or replacing them entirely. He added less than faithful servants to the staff and proceeded to encourage their many doubts. He spoke of secret meetings where Sons and Daughters of Oblation gathered to worship the Sphere. But although Troq openly served as the Father of Oblation, he kept his worshipers hidden from one another. Thus, they worshiped the Sphere without ever knowing the identity of the person who worshiped by their side.

So, it happened, when the swads escorted Valun away from the manor, arresting him after having murdered his father, they removed the manor's last remaining worshiper of Morlac.

Selma wiped the tear from her cheek.

"Tilly worships the Sphere," Troq continued. "Edran, too. Merrudi. Myrtane. All of them. All the servants. They are all Sons and Daughters of Oblation."

"May the Sphere be with us."

"And keep us in his light," Troq stopped short of revealing his own identity, though. If she knew...if *they* knew his identity, they would have pitted him against Morlac. But only Inindu could defeat the god who slept in the bedchamber above. But then, Troq himself had no intentions of killing Morlac, rather, he planned to expose him. The worshipers of Morlac deserved to know the truth about their god.

"Selma," Troq helped her up from where she knelt by the wash basin. "Listen to me. I'm telling you *everyone* in the manor worships the Sphere. There is an entire army outside, yes, but Morlac sleeps in our midst. We have the enemy in our hands, we only need to act." He took the scrubbing brush from her hand, tossing it back into the water, and then he took both of her hands into his own, "I am speaking to you now as the Father of Oblation. I am asking you to make a great sacrifice, my daughter. Will you help me?"

"Yes, father."

He pulled her into an embrace, burying his bushy white eyebrows into her musky hair, "Sunrise is only a few hours away. That gives us enough time to prepare breakfast. Head to the storage room and fetch a bag of apricots. I will gather the others. We must work together. No more masks."

Troq left the kitchen using the back door and quietly walked the stone path to his room. He retrieved the vial of white powdered birmly weed from the polished stone lockbox he kept in his desk drawer. Then, compelled to stay longer and relish the moment, he packed his pipe and lit the tobacco. He stood at the doorway for a time, breathing deeply, sending puffs of smoke into the night. The smoke drifted and faded away.

Necessary sacrifices. Admittedly, he asked for much from his children.

He pulled the pipe from his teeth and set it on the desk, "Necessary sacrifices..."

Troq left the room and systematically hunted down every servant in the manor. He asked each of them to make a necessary sacrifice, and they all agreed. They gathered with him in the kitchen: Thirty-three Sons and Daughters, and one Father of Oblation. Men. Women. Two children. All of them orphans. They lit a candle and said a prayer. For the first time, without masks.

When sunrise came, only Troq and Selma remained in the kitchen. She laid out fourteen china plates. He arranged apricot confections. She gathered two of the plates and placed them on two wooden serving trays. He added a drop of cream cheese and sprinkled generous amounts of powdered sugar. She poured buttermilk into a red-stained, glass pitcher. He poisoned the fruit with birmly weed. She carried plates to the attendants, dutifully seated in the dining hall. He carried the serving trays upstairs to Shale's bedchamber.

Morlac's attendants fell without a clink or groan, for behind them stood twelve servants—each of whom held a linen cloth with which they caught the heads of the collapsed dead. Myrtane latched the manor entrance. Merrudi walked to the adherent's bedchamber and listened for sounds within. Hearing nothing, she opened the door and found Shale's body collapsed on the floor, an apricot confection fallen from his grasp. She went to the railing and motioned to the remaining servants below.

The Sons and Daughters of Oblation turned to Troq. He stood in the kitchen entrance holding a large butcher knife. He walked unhurriedly down the length of the hall and led his servants up the stairs. Together, they entered Morlac's room.

Prior to entering Morlac's room, yes, while Troq stood smoking his pipe in the darkness outside his room, his apprentice, Edran, pulled Overseer Narch's bald head out of the suddenly misshapen pewter bowl which still contained remnants of a milky mixture of vermicelli, sliced dried dates, and poisoned saffron. Seven more Overseers lay with their slacken heads atop the marred, wooden table in varying positions. Ristan had plummeted chin first, her disheveled hair covering her entire face. Fillop had fallen to the side of his bowl, tipping it in such a way that, in death, he appeared to lap at the dish with his languid and strangely extended tongue.

Edran let Narch's head fall back into the bowl, "'Tis a recipe I learned from my master. Though he be none to pleased if he discovers I forgot to add the almonds."

Denam and his wife returned from the shadowed depths of their home. They each carried the unseen burdens of a private conversation, but their eyes signaled they had reached an accord about whatever they had discussed. Edran did not pry and, really, the dead sitting at their table offered the couple no real alternatives.

"Yer certain, then?" Edran asked.

Denam nodded, his smile ever-present if heavier in his despair, "The swads will not accept any reason we give for our departure. We must stay, if only to fulfill our role as hosts in this ruse."

"Denam is too well known for his hospitality," his wife agreed softly.

The merchant chuckled wryly, "Well, our recently departed guests would likely argue, otherwise. I'm afraid there's no way to salvage my reputation, now, once the city hears about this mess." He knelt to face the boy, "I envisioned myself joining a grand and epic battle in the marketplace, but the Sphere deems it best that our journey end here."

Edran stepped forward to embrace the couple, "'Tis no one be making a greater sacrifice. May the Sphere be with you."

"He is always with us, Edran. And we will soon be with him," Denam stood with visible resolve. "And that is what I will remember when I lie on the guillotine, staring down into my own denam-basket. Now, go, before we are discovered."

Obediently, Edran stepped to the entrance. Only a spattering of torches remained ablaze. Horses snorted and stamped their hooves. Swads shifted against the packed dirt of the street where they lay, most of them mumbling curses and recalling nights of greater comfort. Edran paused to steady his breathing. Then he slipped onto the pathway and the street beyond. Several swads looked in his direction, showing only faint interest. Edran felt waves of blood coursing through his neck and arms. He knew the swads had no reason to suspect any savagery—they viewed him as nothing more than a boy—but he couldn't escape the tension that came with every peripheral movement. It filled him with excitement same as he felt when he fired the flintlock rifle, and when he served poisoned saffron to the gathering of Overseers. Too often, the adults around him relegated Edran to performing menial tasks. He fetched dragon's ore for Hiate, or he carried messages for Troq. He stayed with the horses or they had him wash the dishes. Worse than chores, however, in battle, they kept him at the rear for fear of harm. *No longer.* He had saved Lyshmee. He killed the overseers. Edran had now stepped forward to fight in Delacroy, twice. He also, in that moment, stepped between legs, arms, and travel packs. Although he traveled along the street's edge, swads and gear and limbs of swads cluttered the winding pathway, considerably slowing Edran's progress. He still hoped to conscribe several Sons and Daughters of Oblation prior to sunrise, but his sluggish rate of travel diminished his prior aspirations.

He wondered, briefly, if Tilly liked him. It seemed an odd thought in that moment, but it lingered, nevertheless. More than lingered, he wanted to tell Tilly how he killed the Overseers, and about Denam and his wife staying behind so he could escape. But Tilly, he knew, lay asleep in the manor, leaving Edran to journey alone.

Revolution

Delacroy

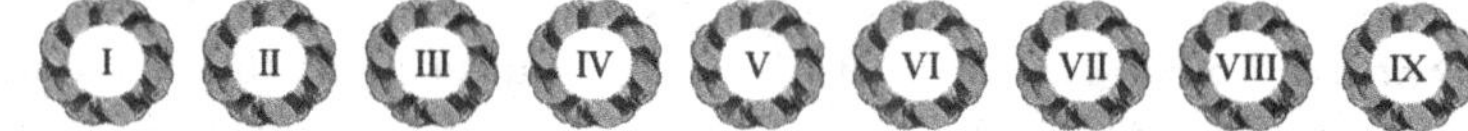

Certainty | Chastity | Fasting | Generosity | Joy | Orthodoxy | Peace | Honesty | Faithfulness

While the army fully populated the street near Fifth Gate, and around the magnate's Manor, they had not yet filtered into the marketplace. Thus, Lomax moved through this area of Fourth Circle quickly and without opposition, pausing only long enough to investigate the condition of his newfound wealth. The baskets of gold he *shared* with Tannessa, a fact he remembered more clearly when he discovered she had taken the precaution of posting a rather menacing looking swad to guard their gold. Rather than fill his pockets with any of the coins, therefore, and at the risk of encountering the swad's ire, Lomax decided to continue with his journey.

A handful of travelers, strewn around the marketplace, slept in makeshift bedrolls or lay atop hay bales. Residents of Third or Second Circle, Lomax assumed, unable to find better accommodations while they awaited passage through Fourth Gate. Even at that hour, as Lomax passed the open gate, the bowels of the tunneled structure still glowed, and a shadow-like column of smoke continued to rise. On any other night, Lomax may have stopped and offered the stranded travelers a more suitable shelter, but not on this night.

He nodded to Yeri, the Torch Keeper. The able-bodied man ran the length of Fourth Circle every night, lighting torches; and, again before dawn to douse the flames. His presence in the marketplace signaled the approach of a new day. Yeri smiled at Lomax and pointed to the bow-legged man running with him, "My new apprentice." The much older Yeri looked far more spirited compared to his weary apprentice.

Lomax nodded an acknowledgment, "Morlac's boon upon thee."

"Favor and boon."

Torchlight faded to the background, as Lomax moved in the opposite direction of the Torch Keeper, but his eyes adjusted to the pre-dawn darkness easily enough. He passed a pile of clutter to his left, remnants of Tannessa's effort to prevent fire from consuming the city. He made his way around the elevated guillotine. Beside the platform lay a collection of denam-baskets and the severed heads of the condemned which they contained. The swads had tossed the bodies into Fourth Gate to burn, but they left the heads as warning to any resident found worshiping the Sphere. Lomax scratched at his beard, shuttering at the smell still permeating the smoke. Moments later, he opened a squealing door and entered the swad barracks. Retrieving a torch from the entryway, Lomax headed to the dungeons below.

He stopped, suddenly.

How did I get here? Where am I?

Lomax looked around, trying to decipher his location. It looked familiar. *The barracks.* But he could not recall traveling there. He wandered for a time. Lost. Certain Maldinado had played a cruel trick. Eventually, Lomax followed the murmurs of conversation that echoed along stone walls. He found a heavy-set woman sitting on a tiny wooden stool in the corridor just outside an open dungeon door. Though he could not see into the shadowed crypt, Lomax heard a man's voice.

It sounded familiar. *Valun?* Yes, Valun's voice.

"Lomax?" Tannessa stood up from the stool upon seeing the merchant, and clumsily closed the iron door.

She knows me. I must know her... Tannessa.

"Tannessa? Why are you here?" Lomax couldn't think clearly. Why couldn't he think?

"I'm here every night," she replied. "Why are *you* here?"

"Tannessa?" Lomax glanced behind him, unable to recall traveling down the hallway. *That's odd.* He turned back to his cousin, "I'm glad I found you. I come with news about the revolution. Gather your swads. The worshipers of the Sphere plan to attack Morlac at Valun's beheading."

Tannessa stared at him as though gauging his well-being, "How do you know?" She brushed hair from her reddened face.

How do I know?

"Maldinado," Lomax lowered the torch, slightly. "He leads the revolution. He made a visit to my home, tonight. He shared their plans with me in hopes of enlisting me. I came straight here."

"And where is Maldinado now?"

"I'm not certain. Still, in Fourth Circle, I presume."

Tannessa grabbed the tiny stool by a leg and slid past her older cousin, "So, you just let him go? The leader of the revolution is wandering freely around Fourth Circle?"

Lomax followed her, "Tannessa, he is like a brother to me. I will not fight him."

The blow caught him by surprise. The short woman spun on her stubby legs and swung the edge of the stool at Lomax, splitting his left earlobe and sending him careening into the stone wall. Darkness mixed with light as the torch he carried fell from his hand. He followed it to the ground when Tannessa struck another blow. The torch burned his leg, but Lomax could only defend against the assault above.

"Stop…Tannessa, stop…"

"Did you come here to kill me, Lomax? Kill me and take all the gold for yourself?"

"No! No! I came here to warn you."

"Lies!"

She struck again. His arm went numb. Her next blow sent Lomax into darkness.

Tannessa dragged Lomax's body from the corridor into an empty dungeon chamber. She had thought her cousin above the role of a fool but, "In death all things are revealed. Morlac's judgment upon you."

She stepped out of the chamber and considered her next move. Morlac. Maldinado. Everything seemingly centered on the beheading. She returned to Valun's cell, avoiding the streaks of blood along her path, and opened it to find the freshly shaven magnate pacing irritably. On the stone floor before him sat a bowl of clouded water and a wad of cloth, but the razor she provided him remained noticeably missing.

"Who was that?"

"You took the razor?"

"It's mine. You gave it to me."

"Magnate Honcherub only paid for one shave."

"I'll send him more food. You'll get your gold."

"That may prove a difficult task with Fourth Gate currently in flames and, from what I hear, Honcherub is otherwise occupied," Tannessa replied. "It seems your claims about Maldinado were true. The tailor leads a revolution."

"I knew it!" Valun extended his chains. "Release me."

She knelt beside the bowl, carefully moving it out of his reach, and dipped her hands into the water. Blood immediately tainting the surface. She rubbed at her fingers, "Morlac travels to Fourth Circle, no doubt hastened by Overseer Fillop who brought news of the revolution. Now, I hear the revolution marches on Fourth Circle. It seems they all want to attend your beheading, and it occurs to me if we stop that particular event from happening, then the revolution will falter and Morlac will return to his palace."

"Yes, yes. Release me."

"But then, beheadings bring gold," Tannessa tossed the cloth into the bowl, watching it absorb the red liquid. "And the death of a magnate brings even more gold," Tannessa looked up from the bowl. "How will they wager, I wonder? Will anyone attempt to rescue you?"

"Simiad had better..."

Tannessa shook her head, "According to Fillop, Simiad fights alongside Maldinado. That leaves Honcherub, and I know how many letters you sent to others before you wrote to your *dearest* friend in Third Circle; and all he sent in reply was enough gold to pay for one clean shave." She stood, "No, it occurs to me, Valun, you don't possess any friends. All of Delacroy travels to your beheading, yet they seem to have completely forgotten you exist."

Valun spat at her, "Leave me, wench."

"If I leave, you will truly be alone."

"Better than listening to your rhetoric."

Tannessa retrieved the bowl from the stone floor, "I am your only hope for rescue. Given the circumstances, I'd wager you have reason to pay me...let's say 5,000 gold pieces. In advance."

"I'll pay you nothing of the sort."

She held out her hand, "Then I'll take the razor from you."

Valun flinched from her, rubbing at his hairless chin, "You know I don't have any gold. They've taken everything from me."

"Write a letter to Troq. He is master of your manor, and still beholden to you. I will deliver the note myself. Tonight, in fact. If they condemn you in the morning, rest assured, I will pull you from the guillotine before the blade falls."

"How do I know you won't just keep the gold?"

Tannessa smiled, "Because Valun, I am not after your gold. I seek the allegiance of a magnate. A successful rescue means you are forever indebted to me."

"You are a *foul* woman."

"And *you* are a murderer. Do we have an accord?"

Valun sighed, "I'll need parchment."

Moments later, letter in hand, Tannessa climbed a foreboding and winding stone staircase toward the swad barracks above. The tower extended five levels above Fourth Circle; and the dungeon sank two levels below ground. Within minutes of reaching the first level, therefore, and after catching her breath, Tannessa dispatched a much sprier member of the order, commanding him to arouse the remaining swads from their bunks.

When she had gathered all of them together, Tannessa told the swads about the revolution's planned attack, "Maldinado walks freely about Fourth Circle. We must find him. More importantly, Morlac travels to Fourth Circle. We must warn him—or prevent an ambush if that is Maldinado's intentions. Adherent Shale will insist Morlac stay at the magnate's manor, so we must meet him there, if not before."

She separated them out and assigned tasks. Thus, when the swads finally left the tower, a legion of them traveled with Tannessa toward the manor. The rest of them took position in front of the still simmering Fourth Gate, determined to not let anyone through. Among those at her side, twenty-seven carried a flintlock rifle; Tannessa, too. They traveled in smoke and darkness.

As dawn approached, they encountered the horde of restless swads littering their pathway. Swads from the inner circles. They shared news of Morlac's arrival, but Tannessa cursed them, anyway, for impeding her progress. Adding to her misery, the residents of Fourth Circle emerged from their homes at sunrise, and the congestion in the street became an impassible blockade.

Phinx lifted the iron grate and climbed up into Fourth Gate. He wrapped the yellow-squared scarf around his mouth and over his nose to avoid breathing the smoke. His eyes burned. Beads of sweat formed on his forehead, and he could feel heat emanating from the stone walls like a furnace. A glow of firelight filled the cavern, allowing him a clear view of the wreckage. Mostly piles of ash and clumps of charred remains. Beams of timber jutted upward where a stage or shelving case once stood. If any of the typical taggle colors remained, they lay beneath blackness.

The taggle moved away from where the fire burned hottest which, from what he could tell, occurred closer to the Fourth Circle outlet than where he stood nearer to center of the cavern. His earlier fears of emerging within the heart of the blaze went unrealized, fortunately. He walked close to the edge, initially, but the heat coming off the stone forced him back to the middle where he traversed the simmering rubbish with relative ease, finding several open areas of uncharred dirt. Aside from the soot coating his clothing, and the general discomfort of the environment, Phinx found the path quite passable.

After learning about the fire, Phinx determined Fourth Gate offered the easiest method for the Sons and Daughters of Oblation to access the sewer system, offering them the ability to gather above ground, and disappear below without notice. While the residents of Third Circle were not likely to stand in resistance to the revolution, nothing prevented them from using their mouths to inform their fellow Delcreans about the sewers; and moving so many people into the network below necessitated they stand in groups and wait their turn before descending. Admittedly, he acted alone, for Maldinado and Edran remained in Fourth Circle enlisting supporters, a task to which they also entrusted to him, but Phinx was a taggle. He typically worked alone and usually followed his own advice.

Alone.

He thought of Jennaween. Their embrace on the guillotine. The embers at his feet proved that in the end, paintings burned. Scarves dwindled into tattered threads. Pathways closed. Only Jennaween subsisted. She had begun the journey with him, and he would end his journey with her.

He reached the giant, circular gateway leading to Third Circle. The area swirled with smoke, however, and darkness concealed his surroundings to the point he nearly ran face first into the gate. It remained closed, a gift from Fillop, no doubt; left during his flight from Second Circle. Phinx felt along the massive gate, his hand passing over the warm iron and the beveled marred heads of nails. Finally, he found the chain he sought and pulled.

Jennaween stood on the other side with a torch and with her sword drawn, "Phinx? I nearly killed you."

"Where is everyone?" Phinx pulled the scarf from his neck in search of fresh air.

"Not far," Jennaween sheathed her sword. "Inindu sent me ahead to see if we could get through the gate. I was just about to head back."

"I found a path. We can reach the sewers," Phinx noticed the magenta tattoo on her arm. "That's new."

"You don't know the half of it," Jennaween proceeded to tell him about Inindu and how she revealed herself, and how she had severed Mathay's head.

"Can't say as I'll miss the bastard." Phinx noticed the sky lightened with the approaching dawn, "Inindu. The Inindu? Do you trust her?"

"I trust she can defeat Morlac. I know the idea doesn't sound so ridiculous, anymore." She pointed to the mark on her arm, "And I guess I'm following her."

"Then I will follow you," Phinx stepped closer. "Jennaween, whatever happens, we fight this war together. I don't want any other lover. I only want you. I need you."

She did not resist his embrace, nor his kiss, "You taste like ash."

"And now your lips are black," Phinx grinned. "Take me to Inindu. We need to get everyone into the sewers."

A hazy dawn brought increased commotion not far from Denam's home. Shouts rang out from suddenly alert swads. Dispatched messengers attempted to navigate the congested street with their feet, but they could not outrun open mouths and impatient ears. Gasps of disbelief turned to urgent murmurs: Eight Overseers dead. Poisoned. Denam and his wife had confessed to worshiping the Sphere.

"Denam?"

"He worships the Sphere?"

"His poor wife. Denam probably forced her to worship the Sphere."

Maldinado positioned himself near the stream of dialogue. An assortment of scattered residents surrounded him in the street. Having recognized the tailor, they turned to hear his opinion on the latest developments. This shift in conversation garnered the attention of more eyes and ears. Maldinado did not miss the common, if unspoken, accusation in their narrow eyes, however. Only he rivaled Denam's popularity within Fourth Circle, and if the basket weaver worshiped the Sphere, then what about the tailor? Maldinado considered the moment, carefully. Any admission would result in his immediate capture. Although the warrior within him stood poised for the coming battle, age and maturity guided his decision to wait. Yes, the moment of attack drew near, but not then and not there.

"Morlac's judgment upon them," Maldinado's response brought a chorus of echoes.

He continued his journey, slowly moving through the mass of shoulders and limbs, working his way toward Denam's home. Familiarity brought engagement with nearly everyone he encountered, their eyes accusing him with equal amounts of vigor and desire, as though they wanted his head to fall alongside Valun's and Denam's. Their poorly concealed blood-lust left a sour taste in his mouth. The words he uttered tasted just as foul, however.

"Morlac's judgment upon them."

The Sphere's judgment on me.

Another commotion arose, this time with greater force than before. Anxious voices hurriedly turned angry and more elevated as people pushed and shoved their way forward. Maldinado skillfully wove between openings of arms and legs and bodies, enabling him to stand his ground despite the waves of dictated crowd flow. But the commotion persisted and grew until, finally, Maldinado encountered the reason. Denam and his wife walked amidst them, each bound and encircled by an escort of swads. The couple wore maldinado-robes: Denam's robe, red with yellow edging. Hers, monochromatic tan with woven designs in a matching thread; specially requested from the tailor. Though Maldinado had thought nothing of it at the time, he suddenly realized the meaning behind the unique design. He remembered every stitch: Nine interlocking circles on each lapel. Barely visible. Easily explained away as the nine circles of Delacroy. Yet, as she walked beside her husband, Maldinado understood. Denam and his wife never hid behind their masks. *Tasa Ro!* She wore the marks of the Sphere on her garment. Right there for anyone to see. They openly worshiped the Sphere, but Maldinado, in his blindness, saw only what he chose to see.

"May the Sphere be with us," they both shouted defiantly.

But no one dared return the salutation. Instead, the crowd attempted to drown out their words with a counter-chant, "Morlac's judgment upon you."

Again, they searched for their brothers and sisters in the crowd, but the Sons and Daughters of Oblation stayed hidden, "May the Sphere be with us."

"Morlac's judgment upon you," Maldinado's voice blended with the collective shout, but his heart journeyed with them. *And keep you in his light.*

The couple passed, leaving Maldinado to his task. He had failed to sway Lomax, but similar conversations with other residents had produced more favorable results. Fanzir, his oft victimized friend, would stand. Strade, the candle merchant. And someone new to Fourth Circle, Albie. The red-bearded, disillusioned pilgrim, and Strade's new apprentice, had apparently lost his aunt and uncle during the previous day's inquisition.

"I have no reason to follow Morlac," Albie had responded when Strade and Maldinado's approached him. "Delacroy is not what I expected."

"No, nothing is what it seems," Maldinado agreed. Though, he did not tell Albie about the illusion or about the dead beyond.

Dawn brought an end to these private meetings, however, so he moved into the street with a desire to make himself visible. His presence intimated order. Fourth Circle trusted him. Thus, when the moment of battle finally arrived, Maldinado had determined he must betray them.

Betray them, and then ask them to join his cause.

He prayed for thousands to respond. But he reserved his last hopes for Lomax.

Delacroy

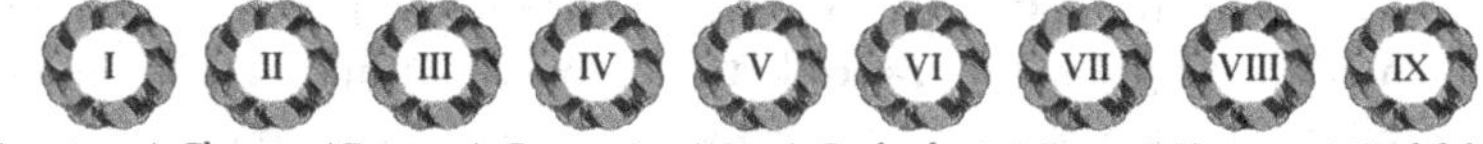

Troq and his servants flung open the door of the manor. Sunlight and smoke flooded into the entryway, revealing the ivory-eyed nascient and the bloodless image of a sphere carved into its bare chest. Its lifeless body hung bound to a makeshift wooden yoke, made from the splintered planks and legs of Magnate Boltmar's formal dining table, enabling the servants to carry the body in full display of the gathered swads who awoke from their miserable slumber with a start.

"Worship the Sphere!" Troq bellowed his assertion with enough force to draw everyone's attention, "Your god is dead."

Four servants, two for each limb, lifted the nascient by the yoke—lifted it high enough above their heads to keep its feet from dragging on the ground.

"Worship the Sphere," Troq restated. "Your god is dead."

He waited for any sign of attack, but the astonished army did not move. Heads turned and Morlac's worshipers gasped. Troq stepped forward. His moment had arrived. He led his servants out into the crowd.

A different crowd parted as Denam and his wife continued their march down the street, but Tannessa met them and her swads did not move. She listened to the report of his betrayal. How Denam murdered the overseers while they sat at his table. Then she reaffirmed the order to throw them into Fourth Circle's dungeon.

"Beware the basket weavers. Who would have guessed?" Tannessa spoke the warning to her swads, though she stared at Denam. "It seems you and Lomax shared much in common. Your rival also worshiped the Sphere." She laughed abruptly, as though burping, "He always wanted his baskets to catch the heads of the condemned. Imagine the applause when a lomax-basket catches your head…and his head fall into a denam-basket." Tannessa stepped to the side, her squad of Flints also making a pathway, "Throw both of them in with Lomax. You'll find his body in the cell next to Valun's."

She watched the couple pass with a mischievous lift in her lip. Tannessa determined to express her gratitude to the merchant upon her return to the dungeon. Denam's murderous act would result in the appointment of several new overseers, and though she possessed no political aspirations, others most certainly did. Many of her swad brothers and sisters, in fact. And such foolish ambition meant they would seek her favor with generous offerings of gold. *Gold.* She fondled the letter from Valun to Troq. Gold awaited her at the magnate's manor. More importantly: Leverage. A magnate beholden to her. Tannessa motioned for her swads to follow, and they promptly continued on their trek.

"What have you done?" A voice emerged from the crowd.

"Morlac is dead," Troq responded. "Sons and Daughters of Oblation, come forth. Reveal your true identity."

They could not hide from the Father of Oblation. Troq knew them. He, alone, knew his children. There, the woman with a concave chin. Whenever they had gathered in secret, she struggled to light her candle. The other Sons and Daughters of Oblation only saw her mask. He had seen her face.

Troq spoke directly to his Daughter, "Morlac is dead, daughter. May the Sphere be with you."

Trepidation turned to tears that welled and fell when she finally spoke, exhaling the words as though suddenly released from unseen chains, "And keep you in his light."

The man with a lick of hair stuck to his forehead.

The swad from Sixth Circle who wore his sister's ring around his neck.

Troq spoke to them all, "Morlac is dead. May the Sphere be with you."

They responded. They stepped forward and followed the Father of Oblation.

Troq no longer concerned himself with the presumed attack from those who worshiped Morlac, for they stood mortified, unable to comprehend the death of their god; unsure how to act. No, if any of them thought to attack him, they showed no signs. Indeed, only the Sons and Daughters of Oblation made any movement. Troq and his procession walked slowly through their midst, stopping frequently to draw out more followers. Surprisingly, news of what had occurred traveled even more slowly. Whispers went mostly unspoken or unheard. One swad unbuckled his sword and let it fall to the ground. Without a word, he started walking home.

Troq continued to parade the nascient before them, proclaiming the death of their god. But he mostly lied to them. He knew Morlac yet lived. Well, he assumed Morlac still lived since his illusion remained. Troq assumed many things about the god of another world but, admittedly, he knew little for certain. And he counted on Morlac knowing even less about him. Regardless, the ruse served Troq's purposes, well enough. In truth, the creature he paraded around was not Morlac. But their own god had convinced them otherwise, so the gathered residents of the city believed him dead.

And who among them would ever worship a dead god?

Tannessa heard Troq bellow to the crowd about the death of Morlac. She saw the nascient on display as though it somehow provided proof. And she laughed. Tannessa knew about the nascient. She knew *every* secret in Delacroy. Then she stopped laughing. As head of the magnate's manor, Troq controlled Valun's gold. But if the cook worshiped the Sphere...

She tore up her hard-earned letter and moved closer to the procession.

Troq never saw her. Tannessa pushed through the crowd and attacked, sending her sword up through his gut, curving upward into his chest. He felt the fire of the wound leap into his throat and shatter his vision.

"You just cost me 5,000 gold pieces," Tannessa shoved anew. "Morlac's judgment upon you."

"What?" Troq gurgled.

"And you still owed me for Beah, you bastard."

He fell away from her sword, barely aware of her words to the crowd, "Fools! Morlac never leaves his palace. He still lives. This creature only looks like him, but it most certainly was *never* Morlac."

Troq lay dying beside her exposed, bloated feet. He lay there, smiling. Tannessa represented the final ingredient he needed to complete the dish. His last meal, served, at last.

A necessary sacrifice.

His own life, forfeit.

He was the Father of Oblation. His Sons and Daughters would not stand idly. Indeed, they acted with haste. Hundreds of feet shuffled in the dirt around him, creating the vibrations of a revolution.

Troq coughed, "And that, Inindu, is how you kill a god."

He died without exhaling.

Beyond the illusion, in the land of the dead, a sphere of light left the rotting remains of Troq's fallen body. It rose above the heads of those below, hovering for a time. The Sphere fluttered. Grew larger. The Sons and Daughters had worshiped him openly, and more had followed. Their belief effectively transferred power from Morlac to the Sphere, and the Sphere drew this power to himself.

But Morlac still roamed this land, and the god of another world would surely consume the Sphere's light essence if he found him, so the Sphere searched the dead for a place to hide lest he find himself reborn and useless within Morlac's illusion. He searched for a warrior to protect his god.

Revolution

Delacroy

Certainty | Chastity | Fasting | Generosity | Joy | Orthodoxy | Peace | Honesty | Faithfulness

Shale awoke in darkness. Blindness. He felt rough fibers at his cheek and fingertips. A moist clump of food lingered on his tongue. Uneaten. Sweetened, tempting him to swallow. Instead, he involuntarily opened his jaw and pushed the remaining bits of the apricot confection, rank with soured saliva, out of his mouth. His arms, too, bent perforce at the elbow and heaved his listless body into a kneeling position. Shale wanted to lie back down. Instead, his legs raised him to his feet, and he began to walk, hands groping the darkness all around him.

He tried to breathe. He tried…to breathe…nothing.

Then Shale felt the other presence, "Who's there?"

"I am Morlac, pilgrim. I am your god."

"Where am I? Why can't I see you?"

"You passed beyond Ninth Circle."

"Dead?"

"Lifeless."

Nascient. Shale understood the implications. Morlac had turned him into one of the nascient, and then Morlac abducted his body. Desperately, he tried to breathe, "Please, my god, let me die."

"I have need of your body. I must return to the palace."

"Then go. Let me die. Why won't you let me die?"

Shale felt his forefinger bend fiercely backward as his hand unexpectedly struck the corner of an unknown smooth surface, but the resulting sensation of pain never materialized. He resisted further movement, longing to fall back to the ground, but Morlac forced him forward.

"I need your body, pilgrim," Morlac's presence dwarfed his own. "I fled the nascient when the servants attacked. I found your body in the darkness."

"You fled?"

"I am eternal, pilgrim, not immortal. Like you, I can die."

"How do you kill a god?"

"In this case, you kill the vessel and trap him inside his own illusion."

"But the nascient are already dead."

"More like erased. They think themselves a god. Me. Within the dream world, this illusion, the nascient represent me. They are alive, and they allow me to walk within the dream." Shale felt Morlac's presence lighten, slightly, as though lifted by a humorous thought, "Do you know why worshipers of the Sphere burn their dead? It keeps me from snatching their bodies. From keeping them alive. Well, alive in a sense. I prevent their life essence from rejoining the Sphere."

"It's true. You feed off the dead," Shale wanted to shudder, but his body would not respond. "The nascient…you weren't changing them. You fed off them."

"I've never fed off the nascient. I honor them above all others, granting them the favor and boon of my presence. For a moment, they are me. And they allow me to enter this illusion."

Shale's body grabbed the edge of a door, tracing it to the door frame and out into the expanse beyond. He vaguely recalled the manor where he died.

I've died before.

"The dead. I've died before. We're all dead. Everyone in Delacroy. I saw through the illusion. They tried to warn me. I saw…" *A door.* "I remember a different door. You opened a door to this world."

Morlac's presence felt closer, as though investigating, "You remember?"

No, Shale did not remember. But he knew it happened as certainly as he knew why it happened, "The dream world…this illusion." Shale leaned into Morlac's presence, merging with his god. There, he found a wealth of knowledge, memories, and motivations, "Death comes unexpectedly. Except in sleep. And you can see in the dream world. You can see them die when they sleep, so you search the dream world and measure their breaths. You hunt them down and snatch their light essence. You take them from the Sphere's world at the moment of their death. Fresh. Raw. Death. You harvest our souls."

Shale pulled away from Morlac, "The dead. All of this…we're dead. You wouldn't let us die. Wouldn't let us rejoin the Sphere. This is all an illusion meant to keep us worshiping you. Our worship…" He considered his previous question, "To kill a god, you must simply deny him worship. The more faithfully we served, the more we empowered you—this illusion you created. All the while, you contained our light essence."

Morlac's presence pressed against him as though enraged, "I *saved* you. You don't understand. The Sphere is dying."

"Because you're killing him. You're stealing his worshipers, weakening him. You keep our lights from rejoining the Sphere. You keep us from *his* light."

"I gave you favor and boon."

"You gave us the guillotine. You gave us death and torment. Over and over. Life. Death. You feed us lies and keep us trapped in this illusion. Why? How could you be so cruel?"

"When the Sphere is finally dead, you will understand."

"I understand everything, now. The Sphere cursed you, so you have cursed us."

Shale fought to maintain his suddenly dissolving conscience, "We are not your chosen. We are your victims."

"I am your god, pilgrim. You worship me with your sacrifice."

"I cannot worship a god who stole me from the light. You kept me from joining…joining…" Shale lost his train of thought as though it never existed. As though *he* never existed. Erased.

His lifeless body descended a stairwell, hands extended outward in blindness.

He was now Morlac in mind if not fully in body.

"Fire!" Tannessa ordered.

Flintlock rifles sparked and then smoked, sending lead balls into a group of combatants, killing swads and residents arbitrarily and without any real means of distinguishing friend from foe. They all looked like Delcreans to Tannessa. They wore Delcrean clothing: tymer-kurtas, yiddick-shawls, maldinado-robes, or kinu-scarves. Both sides of worshipers wore subdued tones of red, yellow, brown, or tan. So, she ordered the flints to fire into the bulk of the ruckus and trusted Morlac to sort things out.

But nothing she did made any difference. Mistrust seemingly raged through the streets, fueling the battle. Swad fought against swad until tymer-kurta's mingled with the dead. Fourth Circle residents funneled out of their homes and quickly turned against their neighbors, their maldinado-robes absorbing splatters of blood as they entered the street. Combatants used yiddick-shawls to strangle unsuspecting enemies from behind, and kinu-scarves wavered from the necks of swirling adversaries; or lay trampled in the dirt. Regardless of what they wore or didn't wear, or who they worshiped, a mass of sun-dried flesh and well-worn garments gathered in the street. And the street pulsed with the anger and fury of a revolution.

Many of the Sons and Daughters of Oblation, those whom Tannessa recognized when she first encountered Troq's procession, lay dead beside their white-haired leader. Selma, Myrtane, and Merrudi, too. In fact, most if not all the manor servants, those she knew, lay dead. Swads also littered the street. But the dead did not lie alone. The wounded squirmed like festering maggots, digging into the red dirt with claw-like fingers, crying out to whichever god they served.

Tannessa offered no assistance, "Fire!"

The battle spread throughout Fourth Circle, quickly reaching the nearby magnate's manor and barrier wall, but also migrating behind Tannessa toward Fourth Gate; and it stayed in constant flux, forcing combatants closer together to keep from tripping over the dead and wounded. Tannessa visibly saw the congestion move into homes; enemies struck one another with chairs and baskets and anything else they could lay hands on. Yearlings screamed all around her as mothers carried them out from hiding and away from their warring fathers. She watched as opportunistic thieves, most of whom Tannessa recognized, snuck along the perimeter of battle and into their neighbor's home, no doubt with intent to snatch what they had long coveted. And she saw cowards who slunk against stone pillars and wailed about their misfortune.

Tannessa knew she needed to bring an end to the growing fracas, or risk losing control of Fourth Circle, entirely. She knelt on her knees and pulled at the numerous bodies piled against, or otherwise covering, the nascient. The creature lay face down in the dirt, still bound to the wooden yoke. Yes, she knew about the nascient, but Tannessa didn't know how the magic worked. She needed the adherent, but she held no hope of finding Shale amid the chaos, if he still lived, so the task fell to her.

"Help me," she ordered.

Three swads knelt beside her and together they shifted the dead away from the nascient. They piled the bloody remains atop Troq, red staining his white hair and beard. Tannessa wiped sweat from her forehead and worked her sword under the rope strands still binding the nascient. The swads tossed the yoke aside and rolled the remains of the creature onto its back. Tannessa stared at the blind representation of her god, unsure how to proceed.

She slapped its face, "Wake up! Morlac, we need you. Do…whatever you do."

Tannessa lifted the nascient's arm and let it drop. Still lifeless.

"Tasa Ro!" She looked to the swads, "Pick him up. Get him to his feet."

The three swads positioned themselves around their fallen god. One of them, his knuckles bleeding after scraping them against the wooden yoke, several splinters noticeably lodged in the back of his hand, stood over the nascient to better grab under both armpits. He lifted the body high enough for the other two, one on either side, to get their head under an arm. Tannessa shooed away the swad with the bloody knuckles so she could get a good look at the nascient: Toes curled up under heels. Its head sat limply on sagging shoulders; mouth opened wide enough to reveal a folded tongue. She reached up and grabbed a handful of listless hair, pulling the head up and roughly centered.

She released her grip, "Morlac. Enter."

The head fell forward without any sign of a god-like indwelling.

"Alright," Tannessa relented. "We need to take it to Shale." She turned to the remaining swads, several of them engaged in battle, swinging fists, swords, or the butt of their flintlock rifles, "We need the adherent. Find him."

Simiad waited with apprehension in the stale sewers below Delacroy. He felt like an outsider amidst the taggles who gathered in a line at the base of a ladder leading up to the city. And for good reason. He wore a mud-toned maldinado-robe with tan lapels, oddly distinguishable, compared to the attire worn by the taggles, by its *lack* of bright colors or vibrant design. His beard reached down to his stomach and ballooned outward with descending thickness, whereas most of the taggle males kept short beards or chin beards; some shaved in such a manner as to create swirling designs on their face. He stood almost two feet taller than the average taggle, and he knew none of their names since these taggles did not perform in Second Circle. They were strangers. *Phinx and Jennaween.* He knew *their* names. But they had chosen another path through the sewers. They had all split into groups and traveled thru various tunnels, or stopped below a different entry point, so as to emerge all at once and throughout Fourth Circle.

Taggles. Residents of Second and Third Circle. Sons and Daughters of Oblation.

Magnate.

Someone tapped him on the elbow, "Care for a bottle?"

"Gladly," Simiad accepted the dusty bottle of warm ale, and drank the bitter brew with a twist of the head and a squint in his cheeks. He preferred the gripping tannins of a red wine. But alcohol was alcohol, and Simiad did not have any wine at his disposal, so he settled for the ale in his hand.

Several more bottles appeared and made their way along the line of taggles, "A toast before we die!"

They drank, and he drank. They shared that much in common.

The line shifted forward as taggles started climbing up the iron ladder. Simiad stood at least thirty spots back from the first climber: A taggle with light brown hair bound in tails on either side of her head. On one tail hung a blueish-green ribbon and on the other, a purple ribbon. She held a bottle of ale in her teeth for several rungs. Then, turning to the crowd while hanging from one arm, an arm proudly displaying a magenta tattoo, she raised the bottle and a final toast, "Let them have their gods. We have Inindu!" She drank the bottle empty and tossed it across the tunnel where it smashed against the stone wall.

She resumed climbing, but those who followed her also stopped and offered the same final toast. Simiad pulled on the light fabric of his left sleeve, revealing the same tattoo, hastily and painfully carved into his aging skin. It still ached. He let the sleeve fall and stepped forward in line. Within the span of a few days, he had offered his worship to Morlac, and then to the Sphere and, finally, Inindu.

She terrified him.

Simiad pushed aside the horrible images of Mathay wrapped in her hair and stepped forward in line.

Still, he found himself drawn to Inindu in a manner he never knew existed. She elicited emotions from the depths of his being—mostly fear—but also reverence, confidence, pride...and beauty. Inindu was beautiful. Not attractive, for Simiad still clung to his life of celibacy, but undeniably beautiful.

He stepped forward.

Sounds of battle overhead filtered into the sewer. Simiad took another step closer to the ladder and the city above. What would he discover? A swad standing over the dead, impaling victims as they stepped away from the grate? The silence of defeat? Cheers of victory? He stepped forward.

His duties as magnate demanded little. He spent most of his time longing for the pleasures and treasures of the other magnates, or drinking. Morlac never asked anything more of him, and Shale remained secluded in the palace. Servants delivered Simiad's food and left him bottles of wine, usually varieties of blackcurrant. He answered when beckoned by the other magnates. He accepted bribes. That described the entirety of his life.

Another bottle shattered. He stepped forward.

Morlac never asked for anything more from Simiad.

As for the Sphere: Unknown. Distant. Truly, the god of another world. How could he claim any power over Simiad's world? No, Simiad felt only indifference toward the god of legend. The god of fire. He stepped forward, five spots away from the ladder.

Inindu asked Simiad to follow. Demanded, actually. All the same, he *did* follow. She marked him as belonging to her—to the revolution. Physically marked him. She sent him into the sewers like a rat, and with a strange group of rats who wore brightly colored scarves and drank ale. She wanted more from him. *A creature with such power...* He believed her capable of defeating Morlac. Alone. Yes, she could defeat him alone, but Simiad didn't want her to fight alone. He desperately needed to share in the moment.

He stepped forward and grabbed the first iron rung; looked up at the ascending taggles and placed the bottle in his mouth; started to climb. His sleeves gathered near the elbows, revealing the magenta tattoo, and he suddenly understood the urge to raise a final toast. It spoke not of the battle above, but of the victory within. Feelings of elation exploded throughout his body, demanding he acknowledge the moment.

"Let them have their gods," Simiad bellowed, displaying a daffy grin, tenuously balanced while he hung by one arm. "We have Inindu!"

He drank the piss-flavored ale of the taggles and threw the bottle across the tunnel, as much from disgust as any celebration. It smashed with echoing force, shards of glass scattering in every direction, forcing the taggles still in line to guard their faces. Simiad noticed some of them even jumped. He gave a hardy laugh at the sight, and they cheered even more. Then he took hold of the next rung and climbed out of the sewer.

He emerged inside the courtyard of Boltmar's manor. Screams and shouts rose from somewhere over the structure. The battle still lingered in the street beyond. Smoke lightly tinted the daylight and gathered in the terrace. The taggles who had gone ahead of him motioned for Simiad to remain silent. He joined them where they huddled near the sewer grate. One of the taggles pointed a rust-laden finger across the empty courtyard toward the man who kept them hovered in silence. Simiad recognized him immediately: Shale.

The adherent moved slowly along one wall with his hands extended as though feeling the stone texture. He stopped every few steps and cocked an ear upward; or felt around with his outside arm. Then he moved forward. Simiad watched the odd behavior for several more minutes. Another taggle emerged and huddled. Then another. He realized they would soon fill the entire courtyard, held captive by the adherent while the battle raged.

"Adherent Shale," Simiad stood with confidence, navigating the alarmed taggles. "Does something bother you?"

"Who is there?"

The voice sounded congested or overly rugged, "Simiad. Second Circle magnate." As he closed the gap between them, he noticed the adherent's ivory-white eyes, "Forgive me, are you ill?"

"Simiad...yes, Simiad," Shale reached out with his hand. "Come closer, Simiad, I am struck blind. Lend me your shoulder."

Blind? Simiad motioned for the taggles to move out of the courtyard, "I am at your service, Adherent."

Shale touched Simiad's beard, clumsily following it up to his neck and then his shoulder. His touch felt cold and unsure, "Good. Yes, very good. I might have wandered for days if you hadn't come along. Guide me back to my palace. I must return, at once."

Simiad led Shale around the terrace at an even pace. Smoke swirled delicately under the veranda. Less than a hundred feet away, the taggles moved quietly through the manor doors.

"A revolution moves through Fourth Circle, Adherent," Simiad responded. "The journey may prove treacherous."

Shale turned to Simiad, placing both hands around his bearded face, "Simiad, listen to me. I am Morlac. I am your god. For now, I must dwell in Shale's body. He lends it to me as an act of worship. You must also worship me. Guide me to my palace and you will join me there. You will live forever with your god. This is your path, Simiad."

The adherent...or Morlac...whoever or whatever stood before him...this creature didn't blink. Simiad watched. Not a single blink. And he spoke without pausing to breathe. It sounded unnatural, and Simiad found himself taking deeper breaths as if to compensate.

"Your favor is upon me," Simiad continued in his walk. "I am honored above all others." He turned to the departing taggles and raised a fist. His sleeve slipped down to reveal the magenta tattoo. They returned the silent salute. He felt elated, realizing that after so many years of misery, his god had finally blessed him. She entrusted him with her greatest enemy, asking him to deliver Morlac into her hands. Simiad turned and led Morlac toward the manor, following the last taggle through the doorway, "Yes, I will deliver you safely, my god."

Edran trailed behind Denam and his wife, keeping his distance to avoid notice. He had managed to visit several more Sons and Daughters of Oblation before dawn, convincing them easily enough to join the revolution. That left him free to wait for the battle to begin, but when he saw Denam and his wife bound and led through the street, he decided idle boys make for poor soldiers, so he followed, intending to rescue them. He lacked a proper plan, however, so he waited and watched for an opportunity.

They moved remarkably fast through the uncrowded marketplace. In fact, Edran had rarely walked so freely through any portion of the city, but half of Fourth Circle remained blockaded in their homes due to the presence of Morlac's army which also rendered Fifth Gate largely impassible. But the army thinned considerably the further Edran walked toward the still burning Fourth Gate until only a legion of Fourth Circle swads, some of them carrying flintlock rifles, remained in the marketplace. They seemed oddly unconcerned with the battle taking place further down the street. Instead, they stood guard over several lomax-baskets, all of which overflowed with gold coins.

Denam and his wife maintained their defiant mantra, "May the Sphere be with us..."

"Morlac's judgment upon you," the swads standing watch over the gold spat in response.

Edran slowed his pace, allowing the distance between himself and the prisoners to stretch further. He estimated one resident for every five swads. Poor odds should he have reason to run. The crowds had offered concealment. The marketplace left him exposed. The boy sniffed and rubbed his nose. He shuffled his feet and then hopped a few times over a line he drew in the dirt with his foot. He jumped atop one of the bales of hay used to outline merchant spots along the perimeter. Edran sat for a time, allowing the swads to grow comfortable with his presence. He pretended to wait impatiently for the merchants to arrive and inquired about the apple cart three times.

"My master be sending me to get apples and asparagus," he told the swads. He asked them about the pile of gold pieces, and whether someone offered the coins as a gift for passerby, "'Tis a generous gift to be certain."

Eventually, the swads considered him part of the background, and he drifted further across the marketplace. Unnoticed. Unimportant. Forgotten. He reached the area surrounding Fourth Gate and made his way around the charred wreckage. Denam and his wife had disappeared, but Edran knew their destination: Fourth Circle dungeon. A plan formulated in his mind. He decided to wait and see if the escort of swads would return to the marketplace and the battle beyond after they secured the couple inside the dungeon. The revolution took precedence, he reasoned, likely pulling every swad away from the tower. He clung to this hope, but also conceded he may happen upon at least one guard once inside, so he resolved to snatch a sword or a flintlock rifle from the swad barracks prior to descending into the dungeon. Surely, no one slept at this hour—not with so much chaos and destruction taking place throughout Fourth Circle. Then, once he held a weapon, Edran felt confident he could deal with any swad he encountered. From there, find the key and complete the rescue.

Simple.

As he walked onward, Edran envisioned Troq preparing a feast in his honor, celebrating the boy's daring feat. A table filled with five different desserts and countless bread rolls. All his favorite dishes: Roast lamb and crushed cranberries. Buttermilk and boiled potatoes. The images made him hungry and Edran realized he had not eaten since before he and Maldinado and Phinx had entered Fourth Circle.

In the distance, Edran saw the escort of swads returning from the dungeon. He nearly jumped with excitement, counting to make sure they had all returned. Indeed, none of them lingered behind. Unfortunately, the area between Fourth Gate and the dungeons provided few places to hide, fewer homes, and only one reason for a boy to visit.

The guillotine.

Edran dutifully turned his attention away from the swads and pretended to investigate the denam-baskets gathered at the base of the platform. Delcreans encouraged yearlings to play on and around these platforms, allowing them to grow comfortable with the guillotines and severed heads and streams of blood until, eventually, all of it simply blended into the background. And so, too, did the taggle boy. Edran's ruse had worked perfectly. The swads passed without any concern given to the boy.

But Edran never saw them pass.

There, in one of the baskets, he beheld the severed head of his friend, Tilly.

He nearly missed it entirely. Bruised and decaying, her face hardly resembled the girl Edran had known——a portrait he abruptly struggled to recall. He only saw a painting with too little paint, and the shredded canvas beneath. Her sun-touched, brown hair piled in strands around her right ear. Dark eyebrows free of the immense anxiety she seemingly carried with every dish. Closed eyes. Closed mouth. Garish wound.

Edran collapsed to his knees. Broken.

Delacroy

Phinx followed Jennaween into the fray, joining the stream of colorfully attired taggles who rushed the street from seemingly every direction. All around him, the taggles roared with madness and swung fists with incredible fury, smashing faces like savages. Indeed, the battle in Fourth Circle resembled a street brawl. Fists and knives. Daggers and elbows. The taggles attacked anyone they encountered who did not otherwise display a magenta tattoo or wear taggle clothing. Phinx wielded a makeshift club and cracked skulls, arms, and knees without mercy. He wrapped his scarf around his assailant's throat and choked the life from him. Brandished a blade only to sheath it again under rib and chin. Jennaween flung herself at her enemies, driving their faces into the ground as they fell. She slit their throats. Grabbed a shoulder or handful of hair, pulled them downward, and drove a knee through their face.

Phinx and Jennaween and the taggles moved with grace and agility. Nevertheless, their coordinated assault resembled a brutal and fierce dance. They jumped and rolled and ducked—raising their fists to show the image of Inindu and howling with delight at every opportunity. They showed no concern for their physical well-being, flinging their bodies around whenever they found themselves without sword or club; some taggles made it a point to never grab a weapon. For her part, Jennaween content to step on toes and climb over shoulders. She kicked, and Phinx kicked, and together they turned to kick again.

When Phinx took a blow in the back from an unseen assailant, Jennaween stepped forward to punch his attacker in the nose. When an older, square-shouldered woman wrapped her arms around Jennaween's mid-section, Phinx rammed his club into the back of the woman's head. Each new attack left a mark, however: His knuckle bled after punching someone in the teeth. A sword struck the side of his leg, and his elbow throbbed after he used it to break a fall. Jennaween, too, showed visible damage: A bruise spanning eye to ear on the left side of her face. A nasty burn mark around her throat from where someone wrapped her with a yiddick-shawl. Her palm bloodied from a gash near her thumb.

In time, every taggle Phinx encountered or fought beside displayed similar signs of battle weariness. Splotches of blood marred bright orange trousers. Torn, purple sleeves hung from scraped or slit shoulders. Swollen hands held silver swords despite broken fingers; flecks of yellow, red, or gold paint still outlining shattered fingernails. As Phinx swung upward with his club, catching his foe under the chin, he couldn't help but wonder if they ever stood a chance of securing Fourth Circle. No matter how passionately he bit into the arm around his throat, ten more arms wrapped around his legs and arms.

Someone tossed Jennaween to the ground so hard she went sliding in the dirt for at least three more feet. Phinx turned to find a beast of a swad with a fist as wide as a mule's nose. He ducked under the intended blow but felt the wrath of his backhanded return. He landed beside Jennaween with a rolling flourish. Fortunately, their attacker never followed, content to strike at the next closest taggle.

Jennaween sat up, massaging her elbow, "I think we lost that fight."

"This is what I get for choosing you over my other lovers," Phinx rubbed at his jaw.

"I didn't tell you to follow me around."

Phinx got to his knees. Red dust coated the air all around them, kicked up by a thousand shuffling feet. He faced her, "Yes you did, you told me I had to choose a lover. I remember losing that battle, too."

"Yes, you did."

"You know, I wouldn't mind winning now and again."

"Then you should have chosen another lover."

Phinx stood to his feet and helped her up, "And risk waking up to your knife at my throat? Or in my back? No, thank you. I definitely made the right choice." He looked around at the chaos of revolution, "I don't see Inindu."

Jennaween lunged at a new foe, "She'll be here."

Phinx shrugged and followed her.

Tannessa carried the nascient on her own back. The swads previously serving as her escort had all fallen in battle once the taggles attacked, and she couldn't find any other Fourth Circle swads. She tried to command a few of the other swads from other circles to her side, demanding they lift the creature, but she held too little sway over them. They ignored her, focusing on the attack, instead. So, the task of transporting the dead god fell upon her wide and overly rounded shoulders.

The nascient stunk of death. Putrid, rotten death. Its skin felt cold in her hands and against her neck where the creature's nose lay buried in her hair. Tannessa's girth enabled her to balance the bulk of its weight around her shoulders, quite easily, but her shorter stature meant that a good portion of the creature's legs dragged along in the dirt. Every step proved a challenge, and after several feet she felt an ache stretching from her lower back to both her shoulders. Then the nascient suddenly slipped from her grasp. Tannessa fell forward, dirt mixing with the sweat that coated her face and hands. She turned herself over into a seated position, reached for the nascient's yiddick-shawl, and configured it into a makeshift gurney. She stood to her feet and started pulling Morlac's corpse.

She heard swords clashing all around her. Yells and shouts of rally rose above the wounded who groaned at her feet. She pushed through several combatants, three of whom proceeded to trip over the nascient's body. The strain in her fingers mounted until finally she had to rest. She leaned backward, swaying slightly, and then with inglorious flare, Tannessa sat upon the carved-up chest of her god. She sat there heaving, hands on her knees, staring at the face between her legs—specifically, his two ivory-white eyes. Before that moment, she had never paid much attention to the face of her god. She found his wan face calming, his features handsome.

A flintlock rifle fired.

The piercing burn of a lead ball lodged in Tannessa's throat, severing an artery. She reached up to inspect the wound with her hand even as she fell backward. She died, never knowing whether friend or foe had fired the rifle.

Maldinado stood helpless at the edge of battle, too old to fight. But sheer stubbornness kept him from fleeing. Making matters worse, no one attacked him. No one asked him to join in their respective assaults. Mostly, they ignored him and, honestly, he found their lack of attention oddly pleasing. Which absolutely infuriated him.

When he had fought for the Adow, Maldinado was young and agile and skilled. This revolution, however, required him to exchange pride for prudence. His hip prevented him from effectively engaging with even the most inept of foes. Any attempt by the tailor to swing a sword promised a corresponding and humiliating loss of balance followed by a mouthful of dirt. He imagined Hintor roaring with laughter at such a sight, and even he had to snicker at the thought.

When they captured Simiad and his swads in Fourth Gate, or later, when they rescued Lyshmee, Maldinado found it easy to believe himself the imposing warrior again. His mind remained vibrant. His will resolute. But neither affair required him to do anything more than speak atop a platform. He gave voice to the revolution, nothing more. Standing there, watching the taggles charge into the fray, Maldinado finally knew his role. He belonged on a platform, or in the shadows rallying support. Not in a battle. Such a useless and hasty death seemed to him a foolish and selfish act equivalent to falling upon his own sword.

So, he stood and watched and hated every minute.

Beyond the illusion, in the land of the dead, a sphere of light floated above Maldinado's decaying body. It studied him and found the warrior within, a familiar champion from an age before. The sphere descended and filled his body. Maldinado, still inside the illusion, felt the presence of the Sphere within. He closed his eyes, savoring the union. A tepid light appeared in the depths of his soul, and the vastness of all knowledge filled the cavernous void of his mind.

"Maldinado."

"You know my name?"

"Yes, my son, and you know my name."

"The Sphere."

"I watched you and Inindu enter the Kul. Do you recall?"

Maldinado felt a sudden kinship, "The blacksmith, Hiate. He watched us from the hill. He stood beside the Adow." Maldinado moved closer to the presence within, bathing in its radiating light. Then he merged with his god. An embrace like no other he had ever known. Finally, he understood, "Troq is dead. You knew he would die. He had to die. That's why you sent me here."

"I need your help. Will you join me, Maldinado?"

"Yes."

The light essence of Maldinado merged with that of the Sphere. The warrior and the tailor and a god. Intense emotion filled Maldinado's soul: Hatred. He despised Morlac. And sadness. Sorrow overwhelmed Maldinado as he thought about how the god of another world feasted on the dead.

He stole them from me.

Something else swept over Maldinado: Hope.

He opened his eyes, "I must find Inindu."

Revolution

Inindu

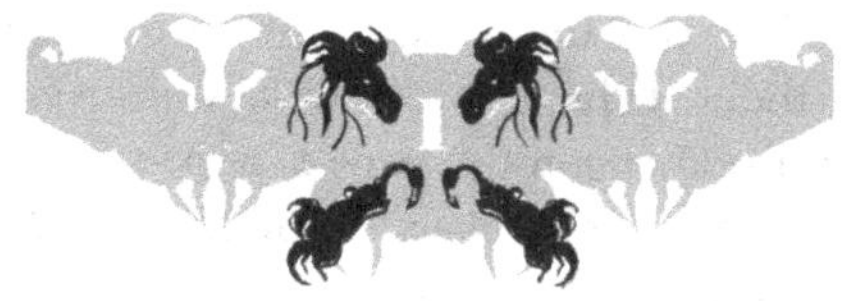

W e journey alone through smoke and shadow. Fourth Gate. Those who worship our beauty have slipped into the sewers. In general, we prefer to stay out of sewers but, admittedly even we cannot climb a ladder. They offered to stay with us, several of them initially refused to leave our side, but they would not have survived the fire and, well, we thought it harsh to knowingly lead them to certain death. We are not, after all, like our father—willing to manipulate the Sons and Daughters of Oblation for his own gain. Yet, we too, sent our worshipers into battle. Some will die. Does that make us like our father?

Ahead, we see the glow of fire outlining irregularly jagged and oddly angled shapes. The remains of the taggles' world. In these shadows, our newly revealed magenta color still looks black. We appear as nothing more than a mute and her horse. But we are more than we appear. We are a wraith mounted atop her dark dragon. A demon and her beast. We are Inindu in life or death, whether dream or illusion.

The air tastes like soot but remains cool against our skin. Ash swirls lightly. The glow of fire morphs into hundreds of patches of flame scattered across the entire width of Fourth Gate and extends ahead of us for a distance. We mostly navigate around the burning rubbish. When no other path exists, we walk on fire.

Yes, father, we can walk on fire.

The flames shift. Images of horses appear in the fire all around the cavern, horses that run as though a predator chases the herd. The horses run through the fire, and then become shadows along the walls and on the arched ceiling above us. Thousands of horses run in every direction. *We are controlling your illusion, Morlac.* We are a god, now. We are prone to do such things. Not surprising, really. We often shape our father's world, too.

The flames shift, and a tiny sphere appears on the wall above the shadow of a horse and a shadowed rider. The rider stretches forth her hair, reaching out to enwrap and absorb the sphere. *We like this game.* The flames shift, anew. The image of a warrior appears, sword raised against her attacker. *The Adow.* We stop walking and watch our sister battle an army of flames. She fights alone. Where is her First Etabli?

We stole him like you took Adarian from us. And he will die like Adarian, too. Our thoughts linger on Adarian, our lover. He, too, appears upon the cavern walls: Dying in the arms of a shadow figure of the Adow. The last time we saw him. Untouchable. Unreachable. Not ours. We wipe the memory from our thoughts and the shadows fade. Another horse and another rider appear in the flames. Ten of them. A dozen more. All of them run in the same direction. Flames of yellow and red and orange turn to pink and purple and magenta. And we know we are Inindu. We know we were once loved by Adarian.

We are the god of Morlac's world.

The god of gods.

Our father was right to fear us.

We gather the magenta-colored flames and form them into a large sphere. It hovers before us. It fills the circular cavern, liquid flames moving across the surface in waves that leap outward with seething desire. What burned moments prior, now only simmers. Fourth Gate burns no more.

We travel fast. We push the sphere of magenta fire before us. Our shadow dwarfs any other shadow upon the wall. All remaining timber, pottery, and piles of ash get swept into and consumed by the sphere. Purple and pink flames emerge from Fourth Gate like ribbons in the wind. The fire roars outward and upward, searing a large portion of the marketplace, burning anyone in the vicinity. Friend and foe.

We enter the battle, our hair mimicking the flames. It stretches forth and attacks in all directions, extending to wrap anyone wielding a sword. We gather the magenta flames from the sky and send them piercing through the street, burning a hole in the chest of anyone not brandishing the mark of Inindu. We gallop full speed through the street toward the bulk of Morlac's army, slaying hundreds with the force of a god, for we are a god.

This is how you destroy a world, Morlac. This is how you kill a god.

They stand in horror before us. We consume them. Several run away. We burn them. Their bodies litter the street. We trample them. Those who worship us raise their arms to display the mark of Inindu. We let them live, and they cheer with the joy of certain victory. Their god is revealed.

We are Inindu, father! Do you see us? Look upon us. We are . . .

Thirty flintlock rifles open fire.

Twelve lead balls hit their mark.

We fall.

Horse crumbles to chin and rolls—pinning and breaking the leg of our topi whose head slams into the red dirt of Delacroy. Our hair retreats from the attack, no longer slithering from mane or head. We feel pain in multiple parts of our body, horse and topi, and more pain comes with the fall…and each subsequent, limb-flailing bounce. We tumble without grace or beauty until finally we lay bleeding in the street.

Red.

We bleed red.

We hear a hush come over the suddenly stalled revolution. We see the magenta flames disappear. We taste dirt upon both of our tongues. And the blood on our lips. Mostly, we feel the sting of death. We are eternal, not immortal. Yet, the only pain we have ever felt was the loss of our Adarian. Heart pain. Emotional pain. Never physical agony. Never the certainty of death.

Adarian, our love, will you be waiting?

But we already know the answer. Adarian is with his Adow, serving her even in death. That is the most for which we can hope. A glimpse of our lover in the arms of another. We were created to kill, and to be feared. Our sister is the one everyone loves. Our own father loves her more than he loves us. Happiness is not ours.

We are Inindu.

Once, we were loved by Adarian.

(before)

Pockets of fire ravaged the surrounding battlefield, sending columns of black smoke skyward to blot out the sun. Adarian, hero of Ire, lay bleeding in the arms of his Adow even as Inindu watched from the shadows. While the Adow shed unchecked tears and wailed the mutterings of a heartbroken lover, Inindu stood resolute and without emotion. She watched and waited…and breathed. She matched the rhythm of her breathing to that of Adarian's final, wheezing gasps. The warrior's fingers, still clutching the golden hilt of his bloodied sword, slackened slightly. His head fell limp, and his eyes captured one last image. Inindu. A magenta demon cloaked in darkness. In the moment of his death, Adarian knew fear. Not fear of death, but fear of his scorned lover. Inindu snatched his soul—his light essence—inhaling the ethereal streams of yellow light with a single, deep draw of life-extending breath. She denied him the peace of rejoining the Sphere—preventing him from receiving the honor he had earned by giving his life for the Adow who mourned over his body.

Inindu held Adarian in her lungs and slipped away from the hellish scene. City and farms and forests blurred all around her as she traveled the land toward her cave home in the Nelic Mountains. When she arrived, Inindu opened her mouth and exhaled the essence of her lover—streams of yellow had now turned magenta. The kiss of a jealous lover. She wrapped Adarian's essence with her ever-moving hair, shimmering magenta waves that transformed into the shape of a body…his body. Inindu again felt the lover her sister had taken from her. What she remembered of him. The man she once knew. Slowly, within this follicle cocoon, the body solidified. New. Unbroken and undead. Hers alone. Strands of hair slid away to reveal Adarian. Then, he opened his eyes.

Inindu immediately embraced him, "Adarian, my love. You are mine, once more. We are together and she will never take you from me, again. I promise."

But Adarian drew back from his former lover, "No! I died. I wanted to die. What have you done?"

"I saved you."

"I felt his presence," Adarian looked at Inindu with disdain. "The Sphere. I felt his arms around me and then…nothing. You took him from me."

Inindu stepped closer, but Adarian withdrew, "My father embraced *you*? I've never felt his touch. You're the only one who ever loved me, Adarian. But even that displeased my father…" Horse and topi stood with heads held high, "What have I done? I found a way to save you. To save our love."

"How could you do this to me?" Horror flashed across Adarian's eyes.

"My love, we are…"

He fell to his knees, "Send me back. Let me die."

topi-Inindu bent to place a hand upon his head, intent on lifting his gaze, but he recoiled.

"No, let me die. I choose death, you…you…magenta mongrel. Yes, I see you for what you are. The truth of it all…so much hate and jealousy." Adarian turned his head away from her, "Please. Don't make me beg. Death surrounds you…it always has…the way your hair constantly moves about…no wonder your father has never embraced you. How could anyone love such a creature? How could I have been so blind as to think you beautiful? Please, let me die."

Anger welled up inside of Inindu such as she had never felt before. Her hair flailed wildly about her shoulders, whipping across her face with the ferocious energy of a dozen vipers uncoiling. She seemed to tower over the timorous remains of her one-time lover, looming over him as though passing judgment. Her sister had left him weak and lost and pathetic, and she hated—HATED—this version of him. How dare he spew such vile accusations. Blind? Blind! She hated Adarian. She hated him. She hated her father, and her sister, too. Yes, she hated the Adow. None of this should have ever happened. Adarian belonged to her. To *Inindu*.

Adarian continued to plea, "Please, let me die. Let me return to the Sphere."

The groveling fool infuriated Inindu. She had recaptured her lover— the only one to ever love her. How could he so unequivocally reject her? Inindu had lived so long without him. Yet, what version of him now remained. Who lay sniveling like a sickly child at her feet? Adarian. The blob of flesh at her feet was Adarian. His light essence. Once, he had made her feel alive with love and joy and the desperate intoxication of his metal-tinged, sweat laced, rugged scent...

"No," she finally replied, her newfound hatred for him momentarily damned. Inindu had created life. Indeed, for the first time ever, she had embraced life instead of death. But nothing remained of her Adarian. Her lover. This man deserved every ounce of whatever wrath she unleashed, "No, you will not die. You will suffer as I have suffered ever since the Adow stole you from me. You will understand the agony I have felt since losing...not you. I thought you were Adarian. But he is dead, now. You are something else. You are *someone* else."

Her hair seized him and encased him tightly as though she meant to strangle him. And perhaps she did, in a sense. Inindu suffocated whatever endured of her love for the man she had once embraced, and all that remained of his identity. Strands of hair thrust through his nose and streamed into his brain; strands that penetrated fluid and tissue and the shadows where memories lay. She ravaged his mind. She changed him, warping every remembrance to which he clung except one. She left one magenta image, so he would never forget her.

And then she cursed him.

Inindu gathered moths from across the land and fed them to him so he could no longer plead for death. Then she blinded him. If the fool could not see her beauty, let him see nothing.

"Yes," Inindu considered the creature she had created, "Now, I think you see what kind of life I can give you..." She thought for a moment before deciding on a new name, "...Morlac."

She left him in the cave and forgot about him. She fled from his memory until only the love of Adarian lingered in her heart. His green eyes. His confident embrace. His…all of him. Nothing of Morlac. She remembered everything about Adarian, and she loved him with every ounce of her majestic being.

Inindu left Morlac at the edge of death. Alive, but not without life. Helpless, but not without hope; for there, inside his head, several strands of Inindu's hair—like the severed fibers of a torn scarf—lay on the greater weave of his brain. The touch of Inindu remained. A hint of her power, and the knowledge of life and death. The death of Adarian. The birth of Morlac.

"'Tis a peculiar place to be taking a nap," Edran leans over and strokes the nose of our horse.

We cough weakly, "Where have you been?"

"I went to Fourth Circle dungeon to rescue Denam and his wife, but… I guess I be getting lost along the way," Edran lies in the dirt beside our horse and begins stroking the length of our mane. "Seems I be the bastard son of a binary god."

"And I'm your deranged older sister."

"The Sphere doesn't really care about us, does he? 'Tis only using us."

We close both our eyes, horse and topi, allowing the darkness of impending death to draw us downward, "No, Edran. Our father never loved us. He only loves the Adow."

"Tilly died. She be dead before I met her, of course. 'Tis the only way to enter Delacroy. I know that, but still…"

"You loved her."

Edran shrugs as though uncomfortable with such terms, "'Tis my friend, and Troq promised to be looking after her. Maybe. Maybe, I loved her. Yes, I loved her. A beheading 'tis no way to die."

"There is no good way to die." We try to shift away from the pain that invades our collective body, "I should know."

Our brother runs his dirty fingers through our mane, "What happens when you die?"

You meet Inindu. "I don't know."

"I do." We recognize the familiar voice of Maldinado, "Death means you have to spend eternity with your father. Imagine, every second of every day, year after year spent in the presence of the Sphere. Nowhere to run or hide. No means of escape. Eternity."

We lean into the cold darkness threatening to envelope us, "Maybe I'll die worshiping Morlac instead."

"Rumor has it you've become something of a god, yourself."

"Naturally, I was created to be worshiped."

Maldinado sits and places our topi's head into his lap. He caresses our face, "It may prove difficult to worship a dead god."

We open our eyes to find Maldinado—the warrior. Maldinado. The *warrior*. Young and healthy and…a warrior. His face is that of a younger man. His hair is black. His eyes are gray. Here is the same warrior who departed the Sphere's world, yet not the same.

"So Troq is dead?"

Edran sits up, "He's dead?"

Maldinado places his warm hand near our heart, the first of our wounds. We feel a searing pain as he pulls the lead ball from our chest with prying fingers that severely widens the hole. But as he removes his fingers the pain subsides. We feel the wound close. Completely healed. Then he moves to the next wound just below our rib cage.

"Yes, Troq is dead," Maldinado confirms. "Edran, watch, like this," he again digs into our flesh.

"Let me die."

"You don't want to die," Maldinado digs deeper.

"'Tis nothing I can do for her," Edran stares at our horse. "I'm not like you, and I don't ever want to be like you. Yer only saving her so you can use her again."

"As you stated earlier, boy, you are the bastard son of a binary god. That makes you *exactly* like me, and with the power to save your sister. So, don't sit there whining about who you like or don't like, do something!"

Soon enough, we have both the binary god and bastard son digging into our flesh. Pain. Healing.

"Let me die. Why won't you let me die?" *He refuses to let us die. Every time we try, our father saves us.*

"Inindu," Maldinado stops digging. "I will let *you* die when you finally let Adarian die."

"He's already dead."

"No, he isn't," Maldinado drives his fingers into another wound.

"He died in the arms of my sister, your beloved Adow. The hero of Ire. I should know. I was there."

"Inindu." Healing. "Adarian never died."

"No, he died. He died in her arms. How could you let him die in her arms?"

Plunging pain. "You said it yourself, I love your sister, as did Adarian. How could I dare deny them one final moment together?"

"That was *my* moment."

"No." Healing. "This is your moment, my daughter. A moment that you've clung to for several lifetimes. At any point, any day, you could have said a final farewell to the man you loved, but you refused to let him die. Instead, you left him cursed and alone. Only the dead keep him company, now. And you, of course. You haunt his thoughts for reasons he can no longer understand. You utterly terrify your one-time lover."

"Let me die. Why do you speak such nonsense? Why do you hate me, so much?"

"I don't hate you. I worship you. Your beauty overwhelms me."

"I'm dying, and you're making me nauseous."

"Do you really want to die? I mean, it's not my fault you're still alive. Die if you wish. I really have no choice in the matter."

"I don't understand anything you're saying."

But that's a lie. We do understand. We are death. Our name is Death. And Death cannot die.

Memories of Adarian return. Memories of Morlac. The lies we told give way to truth.

"I think you understand everything," Maldinado penetrates another wound.

We grimace. Yes, we understand, "You are life. I am death."

"The reason I avoid you," he withdraws his healing fingers. "I created you to destroy that which I have crafted. To bring an end to things. Tales and stories and lives. And you will even bring an end to me one day. When I look at you, Inindu, I see my own death." Maldinado places his bloody fingers on our topi's cheek, looking fully at us without flinching, "But that doesn't mean I don't love you. There is great beauty in death."

"Something I will never know."

"That's not true. Well, I mean death is violent and unexpected, and beheadings are certainly a bloody affair, but you must admit there is something poetic in the tragedy of it all. And more so in the release of a life. When we allow someone to finally pass beyond our grasp. When we free them, allowing them to rejoin the light. When they finally find peace."

"I hate you."

But that, too, is a lie. We hate what we must do. We hate the emotions that arise and flood our collective being. We hate everything about saying farewell, and worse, we realize what we have done to the man we loved.

We are Inindu. Once, we were loved by Adarian, but no longer. We are Death. Once, we clung to the idea of life, but no longer. Now, we lift ourselves into the sky. Horse and topi. We thrust ourselves from where we lie, in an instant, soaring away from a visibly stunned Maldinado and Edran. We heal ourselves, too, closing every remaining wound. We close *every* wound. Pain rips through us. Agony threatens to consume every thought.

"No!" We fall to the ground. Maldinado still embraces our topi. Edran, our horse. "I cursed him, father. I cursed him."

Our father holds our head against his chest, "If you still love him, you'll let him die. He's suffered enough."

"Yes, it's time."

"Edran," Maldinado shifts his attention. "I can see it in your eyes. I don't know how, or what happened, but I'm sorry about Tilly."

"'Tis her head I be finding in a basket." Edran grips our horse's mane, a little too sharply, "Why did you let her die?" We push his arm away.

"Edran, all of the other manor servants are dead. Troq is dead. I sent you and Tilly away in hopes you would survive the battle. It was the best I could do. But it's Morlac's illusion, not mine. I'm sorry, son. I don't expect you will ever forgive me, but please understand some sacrifices are necessary."

We must ask, "Was Adarian a necessary sacrifice?"

We find it strange speaking to Maldinado in this manner. We have only known Troq or Hiate, but there is no mistaking the presence of our father in the suddenly transformed warrior. Not that we mind the change— both changes. We never cared much for Troq, aside from his pipe, and the tailor version of Maldinado was borderline useless.

"Would it make you feel better if I said, 'yes'?"

"No," we admit. "There is nothing you can say that would make me feel better."

"Which is why we never talk."

"I talk to Hiate."

"You drink with Hiate," Maldinado counters. "There's a difference."

"Now that Troq is dead, I think I'll drink with Maldinado, too. Does that make you happy, father?"

"What? I don't get to be drinking with anyone?" Edran asks.

"You can drink with me," we offer. "We will drink to the memory of lost lovers and horrible fathers."

"Maldinado?" We see Phinx and Jennaween emerge from the crowd. They are bloodied and bruised and filled with despair and wonder and general confusion.

"Yes, it's me," Maldinado responds. "Though certainly a younger, stronger version of the tailor you knew."

"What happened," Jennaween points to the scorched dirt.

We shrug, "I was playing with fire. Speaking of which..."

The flints who shot us still stand a few yards away, mouths agape and rifles pointed downward. We summon the magenta flames, drawing heat from the ashes until we have enough to create fire. Then we separate the flames and send magenta strands searing through their bodies. The flints fall atop one another, burned and dead.

Then all the swads for as far as we can see suddenly drop their sword or rifle.

The taggles, finding themselves the surprising victors, quickly accommodate a decidedly hasty surrender.

Our topi mounts our horse, and we are joined together, once more. We are Inindu. We are Death. Our hair wavers in the air, hungry to devour more swads, but the battle is ended. Only one thing remains.

"What now?" Phinx asks.

"Now, we kill Morlac." *We allow Adarian to die.*

"Bow before your god," Simiad grandly announces. He makes his way through the crowd, leading an unfamiliar blind man. He brings him directly to us, "Bow before Morlac," he says. "I bring you Morlac." Simiad stops before us. He bows and silently motions toward his captive, "I bring you Morlac."

Yes, it is Morlac. Our Adarian. We have no doubt. We can feel his presence within the blind man. Our hair leaps outward and, in an instant, we wrap him with our hair. We feel the power of a god fight against his bonds, but there is no escape. And no more curses. And no more life. Only death awaits.

But we don't devour him. We cannot.

"How do I kill him, father? How can I just let him die?"

Maldinado looks directly into our eyes, "You simply say goodbye. Throw in something about always loving him, of course. Make it personal, that always helps. Then, I suppose, in your own way, you sort of, well, devour him. That's it. I mean, if that works for you."

We hate our father. But we sort of like this Maldinado version of him.

We look around at the world our Adarian created. Stone walls and stone homes. Red dirt and gray sky. The dead. His captives. His people. A thousand or more people standing in the street before us, and thousands more residing within the inner circles. Simiad. Phinx and Jennaween. The taggles, tru-born.

Our people, now. Worshipers of Inindu.

"'Tis the reason he couldn't save Tilly," Edran realizes with a painful tear. "She be destined to die with Morlac."

"If I kill Morlac, we all die don't we, father?"

"No," Maldinado shakes his head. "Not everyone."

Only those who already died.

The truth hits us with the force of a tree striking the ground, splintering every branch. We will survive. Maldinado and Edran will survive. The three of us entered Adarian's world through the Kul. But everyone else, including Troq, entered Delacroy while they slept. Adarian snatched them as they took their final, suspended breath. The land of the dead. That is why Hiate sent Maldinado. Our father needed the warrior so he could escape Adarian's world. He needed Maldinado's body.

If we kill Adarian, all those who died will *finally* cease to exist. Their light essence will rejoin the Sphere.

"What about the taggles?"

But we already know the answer. The tru-born were never born. Never dead. Those born in Delacroy do not exist beyond Adarian's illusion. We turn to Jennaween—she was the first to worship us as her god—and to Phinx, her lover. Must we now destroy them? Must we betray their belief? They don't exist, so why do we care? We shouldn't. But we do care. Lyshmee and Alanna emerge from the crowd to stand beside Jennaween and Phinx. This woman has sacrificed far more in the afterlife, we realize, than should ever be required of the living, let alone the dead. And the orphan girl—both will die, again. And Simiad. He presented this gift to us—delivered Adarian into our hand—never realizing it would seal his own fate. All of them will die their first...or their second death.

If we kill Adarian. If we let him die.

"What happens if I let him live?"

"Inindu, he has suffered enough. They all have. Let the dead pass beyond Ninth Circle."

Phinx and Jennaween are the first to understand the choice we must make. How easily we play with their lives—with their deaths. Others follow, comprehending at least enough to know they face imminent danger, and begin whispering as much to the person standing beside them. Their growing panic pales in comparison to the rage—no, hatred—building within the cocoon where we hold Adarian at the edge of his own death. How did he become so powerful? The energy he emits sends massive ripples through our hair, but he cannot escape our grasp. Unless...

Unless we free him from our bonds.

So, this is what it feels like to be a god?

Destroy one world to protect another. Spare one world and lose the other. Caring for someone is overrated. We are Inindu. We are Death. We are reminded of the magenta sphere of flame still hovering overhead… reminded of our power to create. No! We are Death.

But our father is Life.

"Maldinado." We smile with just an ounce of innocence, "Daddy, now that you're the big, strong warrior type, I was wondering if you might want to rescue these people?"

Revolution

The painter known as Phinx ate a cold meal of celery sticks dipped in brown mustard and strips of sourdough bread brushed with oil. He drank from a bottle of warm ale. Dressed in a wool tunic dyed black from a mixture of dirt, soot, and splattered blood, and wearing a red scarf around his neck which he constantly suspended from his teeth, Phinx stood with the hastily assembled plate of food in his hand. A neglected knife dangled on the edge of the plate while he studied his latest, and perhaps his last, work of art. He leaned forward, causing his wrung-out, shoulder-length hair to fall away from where he had tucked it behind his ears. Suddenly convinced of what he needed the painter shoved the plate onto a small table beside the canvas which already appeared cluttered to the point of collapsing. The careless placement sent the knife careening onto the red dirt floor of the marketplace in Fourth Circle.

Ignoring the utensil in favor of a brush, Phinx hastily mixed a pool of red and blue before adding more and more white, finally forming the wet magenta color he wanted. The painting depicted a horse standing serenely beside a pool of water. It stretched its head forward to better assist the topi who stroked its nose. Great green trees and lush undergrowth surrounded the pool. Under one of the trees, a familiar girl sat next to a tipped-over basket of apples. She gathered the red spheres into her apron, clumsily allowing them to fall off again on one side.

"'Tis be looking a lot like Tilly," Edran commented.

"Taggles protect their own," Phinx replied with a warm smile.

a taggle's painting

Inindu

We tell them they must enter the painting. We send messengers riding horses throughout Delacroy. We send Edran to rescue Denam and his wife, and Valun, too, if he chooses, but Valun refuses to follow the god of another world, so Edran leaves him in the dungeon. We send Phinx to find his mother and father, but he returns alone; they are dead. We send an invitation to everyone in Delacroy, but only a handful respond.

We gather in Fourth Circle. The end draws near.

Death approaches. Indeed, Death is here.

Phinx places his painting on the ground, and then he walks over to take Jennaween's hand. The first to worship us, the first to leave. Together they return to the canvas. Faithful to their god in life or death. No, more likely blinded by love. They foolishly think they will survive anything or, if nothing else, die in each other's arms. Well, we hope they do. They take a final step forward and the painting absorbs them—swallowing them completely. Several gasps arise from the crowd.

We turn to Maldinado who does his best to avoid our gaze. Our father has always possessed a taste for the dramatic. We approve.

Edran steps forward and stares at the painting, "'Tis still the same painting. I half expected to be finding them standing by the water. But the painting be unchanged. I guess I be hoping…"

We know what our brother hopes. A painting of Tilly. Another world. He thinks he can somehow keep her from death. But our brother must learn to say goodbye, just as we must learn. He must let Tilly die lest he, too, find himself fighting the warped and twisted version of his lover in a land of the dead.

I wouldn't wish that on anyone. I should know.

"They are safe," we assure our followers. "You will find them once you enter the painting. Who is next?"

In our hair, we hold Adarian. The end of this world. He struggles mightily, but we will not yield. Not this time. He will die, soon, along with any who remain.

"We will go," Lyshmee and Alanna step forward from the crowd, and then into the painting.

Simiad follows with a toast of wine and an unsure step.

None of them re-appear in the painting, and again we are forced to reassure those who await their turn. Harian goes next, giving a wink to Maldinado before she steps in. Soon afterward, Maldinado helps a woman with black teeth enter, but he does not enter himself.

Edran shrugs his shoulders, "Might as well..." He jumps, knees to chest, onto and into the painting as though jumping into a lake.

They each take their turn. Some without hesitation, some only after several prior attempts and with a great deal of coaxing. Old. Young. Taggles and Delcreans. A few swads and one magnate. Eventually, they all disappear into the painting, leaving only Maldinado...and those who came to witness the defilement. To these doubters we offer a final opportunity, but only five accept. The rest will die when I kill their captured god.

"I don't want to kill him, you know."

Maldinado moves to stand above the painting. He looks out at the city of Delacroy and the people who remain, and the bulbous patch in our hair where we contain Adarian. Finally, he looks at us with a tenderness we have never before seen in his eyes, "I know."

Maldinado steps into the painting and disappears.

We take a final look at the drab city of Delacroy. The world of Adarian. The city our lover created. With twisted amusement, we realize how much we despise his choice in decorations. Stone. Our sister likes stonework. We prefer nature. *Maybe we never really knew you, after all. Maybe it was us who stole you from my sister, if only for a time.* We consider the cocoon in our hair and the life within. *A simple goodbye, and then devour him, huh?*

No, he deserves more.

"I'm sorry, Adarian. I thought I could walk on water. Turns out, I can barely keep from drowning. Goodbye."

We enter the painting, even as we tighten our bonds of hair and, at last, allow Adarian to die.

Emerging from the illusion, we stand once more in our father's world.

Maldinado nods with resignation and a flash of empathy.

The dead surround us. Fallen. All of them. Released and allowed to die. Some of them—their light essence—rejoined the Sphere. Simiad. Denam and his wife. Lyshmee and Alanna. Harian and the woman with black teeth. Adarian, too. Those who remained in Delacroy, however, and those who died in battle, they are forever lost.

Lost because of choices we made.

"Where are we?" Jennaween still holds Phinx by the hand. Both taggles survey Fourth Circle as though for the first time, and with good reason for only the dead fill the circular street.

"'Tis the afterlife of the taggles to be certain," Edran kneels beside a fallen corpse. Troq's body.

Yes, our father kept his word. The taggles survived. Illusions now brought to life. All that remains of Adarian. The most beautiful portion of his imagination, every wonderful color. Yellow. Orange. Blue. Red. Green. Every glorious magenta tattoo, and one shredded silk scarf. Disgusting habit, really. But all of them are wholly alive.

Our topi mounts with a nod to Maldinado, "Thank you, father."

"You have an army of skilled assassins and cutthroats, schemers and thieves, spies and scoundrels who also happen to dance and paint and make music as easily as they make love. Whatever do you plan to do with such a lot, my daughter?"

"I think I'll start a revolution. It's about time someone liberated the taggles."

"A bit late to the party. I've already started that particular rebellion."

We smile, "The heralded Arms of the Sphere. I know."

"Do you, now. Well, don't let me keep you from the battle."

"And where will you go, father?"

Maldinado looks across the bodies until he finds our brother still kneeling beside Troq, "Edran and I must stay here for a time. Burn the dead and that sort of thing. Clean the place up a bit." He turns a curious eye toward the sky, "Find someone to help, I think. The girl will bring nothing but trouble, of course, but if we maybe happen across her body..." He flashes a wicked smile, "Well, what's the point of being a god if you can't raise the dead from time to time?"

We look between him and our brother, "But... What happened to *Say goodbye and devour him*? Doesn't Edran have to learn to let people die, too? Why does he get to keep his lover?"

Maldinado shrugs with obvious bemusement, "The truth of the matter? Tilly died by accident. In both worlds, actually. She'll likely die again. Several times more. Probably, she will cross the street and somehow manage to get run over by a tortoise. I would have already brought her back to life if not for Morlac snatching her from me. Klutz of a girl if ever I've seen one, but the boy, there, seems smitten by her."

"And what of my sister? The Adow seemed rather stricken by a certain warrior."

"Yes, Maldinado and I have a few things to discuss."

"Then I will leave you to your wretched life, and to the burning of the dead." We turn to the taggles, "Jennaween. Phinx. Gather the taggles. It is past time we leave this miserable city."

"When next we meet," Maldinado starts making his way toward Edran. "I'll buy you a drink."

"Make it several. And Edran, too."

"Edran, too," Maldinado agrees.

Several minutes later, after giving our brother a hug, even as he excitedly tells us all about how Maldinado has decided he is old enough to drink beer and broth, and ale, too, we finally depart Delacroy. Behind us, several hundred taggles follow. The last remnants of Adarian. Behind us, too, several thousand bodies litter the city. All that remains of the dead.

We are Inindu. We are Death. But this is our life.

Revolution

Morlac

The last moth exited Morlac's mouth. It fluttered around the tower looking for a place to land, but every inch of the stone wall was covered with black moths. It flew higher and higher, searching for even the tiniest of spaces. Below the moth, Morlac collapsed. His corpse withered and curled inward. The skin wrinkled and darkened, turning darker until every feature was void of color and definition. This darkness bled outward from the body, covering the tower floor. Thousands of moths took flight as the darkness climbed the tower walls and together with the last moth it flew upward and out of the tower.

A cloud of black moths then filled the sky, and the darkness stretched across dirt streets, breached doorways, and rose up and over the walls of Delacroy. Moths filled the mouths of any resident who screamed, and darkness absorbed any who stayed silent. The ruby palace fell into darkness. Ninth Circle and Eighth Circle fell into darkness. Delcreans ran in terror, crying out for Morlac to save them, but their god remained silent.

Near Fourth Gate, Valun paced the length of his dungeon cell, unaware of the approaching darkness. He considered the news Edran had brought: A revolution. Morlac dead. The Sphere's world. All lies. "This is a trial," he spoke loudly, feeling confident someone stood guard on the other side of the iron door. "I sent for Morlac. I asked him to judge me, and this is my trial. But I will not falter. I do not worship the Sphere. I worship Morlac. Do you hear me? I worship Morlac!"

The darkness crept in through hundreds of tiny, unnoticeable cracks between the red stone blocks which comprised the walls of his cell. It flowed like water over a crevice and grooves. When he spotted the darkness, Valun initially froze. When it moved closer, Valun backed away. He scrambled to his bed, lifting his feet even as darkness flooded the floor. He curled knees to chest and covered his head with both arms. He closed his eyes and prayed the horror was nothing more than a dream. An

illusion. But Valun only felt emptiness. Then nothing.
All Delacroy fell into a void.
Then moths consumed even the darkness.

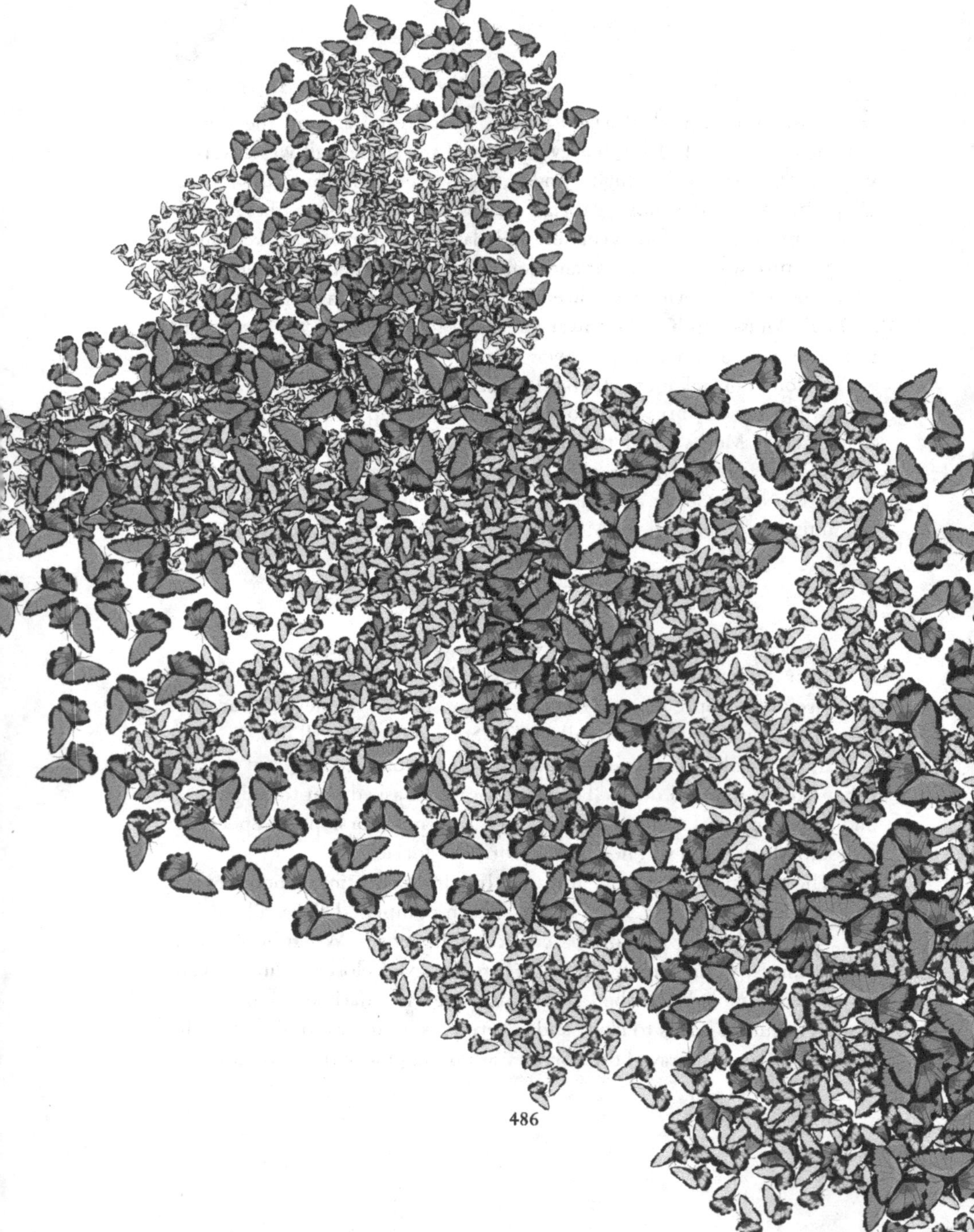

Author's Note:

The artwork depicted, described, and destroyed in these pages really does exist in the real world and has served to inspire creatives for hundreds of years. Whether you enjoy romanticism, cubism, chiaroscuro, impasto, neoclassicism, or some other art style, these works of beauty impact our lives and our culture in unexpected ways. To those who have created works like *Execution by Guillotine in Paris during the French Revolution* by Pierre-Antoine Demachy (see The Sorting); or *Les Grandes Baigneuses* by Pierre-Auguste Renoir (see Condemned); or *Wanderer above the Sea of Fog* by Caspar David Friedrich (see Severing); or *Les Sabines* by Jacques-Louis David (see Revolution); or *Inindu* by cover artist Eric Wilkerson—to you I say thank you for sharing your gifts with the world. To the performance artists who bring vast worlds to life; or to the authors who capture our imagination; or to those who produce sound or give us reason to dance— to you I say thank you for your vulnerability and honesty. To the unknown artists who choose everyday to continue the struggle—to you I say thank you for your courage and perseverance.

Art makes a difference.

Art matters.

But art does not exist without the artist. To these people I say thank you for giving a damn!

CHAD MICHAEL COX was only five years-old when his grandpa, a police officer known for crafting stories, handcuffed him and left him in a holding cell as punishment for ending a sentence with a preposition. He worked off his debt to society by diagramming sentences for his mother, and then was forced to accompany his father during visits to local bookstores—a tradition Chad sustains with his own (three) children.

Having grown up under such literary hardship, he continued to torment himself by studying Writing, Literature, and Publishing at Emerson College. If this wasn't bad enough, he married a girl and built her numerous bookshelves and together they accumulated a wonderfully large library and also five cats. Now, he tortures other people's children as a contract writer for Iowa Testing Programs at the University of Iowa.

GLOSSARY

5-RUBY | A common high-stakes game consisting of tossing boar tusks toward an outlined circle. Often played to pass the evening, or turn a profit.

ABRE | (ĂB-rāy) | City—Located near the western coast line.

Abre 10th | (ĂB-rāy) | Division of the Adowian Army. Journeyed to the Torment.

ADARIAN (city) | (ă-DĀR-Ē-n) | Major City—Known for its marble sculptures displayed throughout. Named after Adarian, hero of Ire.

Adarian 6th | (ă-DĀR-Ē-n) | Division of the Adowian Army. Fought in the Battle at Quel. Suffered complete annihilation three-days prior to the final assault on the city.

Adarian 8th | (ă-DĀR-Ē-n) | Division of the Adowian Army. Fought in the Battle at Quel. Generally considered brutes.

Adarian 11th | (ă-DĀR-Ē-n) | Division of the Adowian Army. Fought in the Battle at Quel. Strategists.

Adarian 29th | (ă-DĀR-Ē-n) | Division of the Adowian Army. Fought in the Battle at Quel. Known to capture and torture prisoners regardless of age or gender.

Adarian 41st | (ă-DĀR-Ē-n) | Division of the Adowian Army. An embarrassment to the city of Adarian. Gan, Overseer of Adarian, hasn't allowed the 41st to leave the city since they mistakenly shot a barrage of arrows into the ranks of the Yakur 3rd at the Battle of Ire.

Adarian 45th | (ă-DĀR-Ē-n) | Division of the Adowian Army. Fought in the Battle at Quel. The city of Adarian's most honored battle division. Journeyed to the Torment.

ADARIAN, HERO OF IRE | (ă-DĀR-Ē-n [hero of] Ĭ-r) | Deceased. First Etabli for she who served During the Completion of the Yellow Moon under the seal of the Sword with Crown on Hilt. He died in the Adow's arms; first to die in battle - first to die protecting the Adow. Revered. Also, the subject of many works of art; the majority of which portray him in the moment before his death.

ADELIC HON | (ă-DĔL-ĬK HĂHN) | A name from prophecy. Also, separately, nephew to Troq.

ADHERENT | Resident of Morlac's Palace. Messenger of Delacroy. When Morlac speaks, the Adherent listens, and then moves residents between circles according to those Morlac favors or those the god of another world no longer favors.

ADOW | (ă-DŎU) | A title passed down and used as name when referring to she who rules the known land. A queen-like figure. Born with the title of *Daughter of the Adow*, she who reigns assumes title and throne of the Adow upon the death of her mother. The Adow (the collective that is the singular) have ruled from the Completion of the Purple Moon to the current Dark Moon.

    [*also*] **Oracle** when speaking prophecies as given by the Sphere

ADOWIAN ARMY | (ă-DŎU-Ē-n) | General term for the warriors who assemble from across the land and follow the Adow into battle.

ADOWIAN BURIAL | (ă-DŎU-Ē-n) | See Glossary of Rituals and Traditions.

ADOWIAN DECREE | (ă-DŎU-Ē-n) | Formal decree issued by the Adow. Each decree is numbered and recorded for historical purposes.

ADOWIAN DECREE 1575 | (ă-DŎU-Ē-n) | "We seek the Five Arms of the Sphere. All who are able must journey to Dragon's Torment—to death or glory. An Adowian Burial awaits the one who finds the Five."

ADOWIAN GUARD *or* GUARD | (ă-DŎU-Ē-n) | Twenty warriors hand selected by the First Etabli to protect the Adow wherever she may wish to walk, rest, or ride. From these ranks will the Adow choose her (next) First Etabli.

ADOWIAN PROPHECY | (ă-DŎU-Ē-n) | Recorded prophecy as spoken by the Adow in her role as Oracle of the Sphere.

ADOWIAN SEAL | (ă-DŎU-Ē-n) | The chosen symbol of the reigning Adow, for most, variations of a crown.

AIYA | (Ī-yŭh) | Maidservant to the Adow.

AGATHA | (ĂG-ŭh-thŭ) | A pig owned by Magnate Boltmar.

ALBIE | (ăwl-BĒ) | A pilgrim on the road to Delacroy. Son of Murdin.

ALANNA | (Ā-lănŭh) | Resident of Second Circle. A yearling.

ANINE | (Ā-nēn) | Deceased. First Etabli for she who served During the Completion of the Purple Moon under the seal of the Hemming Tree above Crown.

ARMS OF THE SPHERE | Five figures from a prophecy spoken by the Adow: Madic Baltin, Pel F'rute, Sol Pedantic, Disen T'lade, and Adelic Hon. The prophecy serves as a quest to seek the five.

    [*also*] [**the**] **Five** when speaking in general terms.

    [*also*] [**the**] **Five Wolves** | Characters from a story as told by Troq to the Adow, and how she often refers to the Arms of the Sphere when ruminating on Adowian Decree 1575.

ATHOYEN | (ĂTH-O-YĪN) | Deceased. First Etabli for she who served During the Completion of the Green Moon under the seal of the Crowned Boar.

AUL | (ĂLL) | Deceased. First Etabli for she who served During the Shadow of the Purple Moon under the seal of the River Under Crown.

AURIFEROUS | (RŌ-fĕr-ŎS) | Resident of Fifth Circle. Goldsmith.

AYSON, OF QUEL | (Ā-sŭn) | First Etabli for she who served During the Completion of the Green Moon under the seal of the Crown between Swords.

[also] First Etabli for she who serves During the Dark Moon under the seal of the Tiger and Crown.

BALOR TREE | (BŎ-lōr) | A type of tree. The only kind found in the Torment. Easily identified by its shimmering black leaves.

BATTLE AT IRE | The last great war prior to the Battle at Quel. Revered as the location where Adarian, First Etabli, died protecting the Adow.

BATTLE AT MALI | A lesser battle before the Battle at Quel. A terrible loss for the Adowian Army.

BATTLE AT QUEL | General term used to describe a five-year battle between Yenen and the Adow; though it included multiple cities across a large portion of the known land, and ultimately ended with the destruction of Quel and the deaths of both Yenen and the Adow.

BATTLE AT STYCRAL | A lesser battle before the Battle at Quel. Here, Decrome beheaded the Rovet of the Stycral 12th.

BEAH *OR* **TAGGLE** | (BĒ-ŭh) | A taggle boy. Friend to DK Vel.

[*also*] **BEAH** | Second Gate taggle. Storyteller.

BEAUG | (boh-G) | Deceased. Master artisan. Sculptor of Adarian. Responsible for most if not all significant artwork across the known land.

BEGN PATTERN | (BĀN) | Pattern in 5-Ruby: Two tusks located anywhere outside of the circle, each pointing back toward the circle; the third tusk inside the circle pointing toward the Sphere.

BEGN RUBY | (BĀN) | Bottom left ruby in 5-Ruby.

BELLA *OR* **TAGGLE** | (BĔL-ă) | Eighth Gate Taggle.

BELLADONNA ROOT | In small doses, this powdery substance is Adarian's drug of choice. Typically poured into wine and ingested. Lethal in large doses.

BELUR | (bāy-LŪR) | Adarian resident. Daughter of Kanbis and Nataline. Niece of Maldinado

BIRATE *OR* **LITTLE BIRTY** | (bī-RĀT) | An aspiring topi warrior of the Adarian 45th eager for advancement. Short. Nickname: Little Birty.

birmly weed | (BĪRM-lē) | Made from the pistil of birmly weeds; often used as a yellow dye. It also crushes down to a piquant tasting white powder which cooks throughout Delacroy use to thicken a soup or gravy base.

<u>BLIND GOAT</u> | A yearling's game. Participants take turns wearing a blindfold and attempt to first retrieve a ribbon and then tie the ribbon around a tied-up goat. Prior to the attempt they are spun around, making the task all the more challenging as the participant struggles to maintain their balance.

> [*also*] **<u>BLIND GOAT</u>** [*Adarian 45th version*] Warriors of the Adarian 45th substitute knives for the prescribed ribbon. Once killed, the goat is cooked and served with a toast to the champion. Some participants will toss the knives, thus inviting the gathered audience to participate in the game at their own risk.

<u>BLOODGRASS</u> | Red-tipped grass that grows across the Adarian region. The bright red coloring gives the illusion of fresh blood; seemingly all that remains of the ghosts of warriors fallen in battle.

<u>BOLTMAR</u> | (**BŎLT-mŏwr**) | Magnate, Fourth Circle. Father of Valun. Secret lover of Remni.

<u>BONTLEVIER</u> | (**BŎN-T-lĕ-vēr**) | A pilgrim on the road to Delacroy. Brother of Murdin.

<u>BREAD AND STEW</u> | A tavern located in Lor.

<u>BRELINE</u> | (**BRĀ-LĒN**) | A Daughter of Oblation. Mother of Maldinado.

<u>BRENDT</u> *OR* **<u>TAGGLE</u>** | (**BRĔN**) | Fifth Gate Taggle.

<u>BRINK</u> *OR* **<u>LUCKY BASTARD</u>** | (**BRĒ-nk**) | The stout Banner Bearer of the Adarian 45th. Brother-in-law to Gan.

<u>BROKEN TUNNEL</u> | An unfinished tunnel in Yenul known for it's marketplace.

<u>B'TUL</u> | (**BĔ-tūl**) | Deceased. Former resident of Sixth Circle. Condemned and beheaded.

<u>CADUUM</u> | (**CĂH-DŌM**) | City—Entrance to Dragon's Torment. A city of wraiths and ceaseless wind. Originally built as a base camp when trade with the Rorne began.

<u>Caduum</u> [*1st*] | (**CĂH-DŌM**) | Division of the Adowian Army. Journeyed to the Torment. First division by default since they are the only division from Caduum to march with the Adow.

<u>CAIG</u> | (**CĀ-gh**) | A craftsman from the southern provinces, likely near the Tessel region.

<u>CAMEN</u> | (**CĀ-mĕn**) | Magnate, Eighth Circle.

<u>CATAREB</u> | (**CĂT-a-rĕb**) | City—Located near the center of the known land just northwest of Plenrid; conquered by Yenen prior to the *Battle at Quel*.

CHANCE | Inner-city of Adarian—Known for its colorful architecture, [*topi*] bone and skeletal sculptures, and rooftop marketplace. Place where Nataline resides.

CIDAL | (SY-dle) | Deceased. First Etabli for she who served During the Completion of the Green Moon under the seal of the Sun Rising Over Crown.

CIL | (SĬL) | Third month of the spheric calendar.

CINTYGE | (SĪN-TĬJ) | Deceased. First Etabli for she who served During the Completion of the Green Moon under the seal of the Crowned Swallow.

CHRONICLES OF YENUL [or other city] | A recording of the names of the topis who reside within the city; also, their profession.

CORRALEA *OR* **TAGGLE** | (COR-ă-LĒ) | Second Gate Taggle.

CYLEN TREE | (CĪ-lĕn) | A type of tree.

DADEN | (dāy-DĔN) | Adarian warrior.

DALLIC | (DĂWL-ĬK) | The term used for the dwelling place of taggles located beyond the city walls. Typically, a mud pit offering little more than a hut as shelter and an open grave where the dead gather. Every dallic is heavily guarded to prevent taggle newborns from going unmarked.

[*also*] **dallic** a small reed basket; a beggar's basket.

DALLIC RIVAC | (DĂWL-ĬK rī-VĂK) | A taggle chosen to continually repeat the taggle's prayer on behalf of those taggles living in that particular dallic. Highly respected by all taggles. Identified by the red paint on their face.

[*also*] **RIVAC** when speaking in general terms.

DARROL | (dār-RŎL) | Resident of Fourth Circle. A fetch-all for the Fourth Circle merchants. Mauled by a beast at some point in his life, perhaps as an infant.

DAUGHTER OF THE ADOW | (ă-DŎU) | See Adow.

DAUGHTERS OF OBLATION | Worshipers of the Sphere who have committed themselves to a life of service and to the ministry of the Fire. Often, caretakers of orphans.

DEAD [*the*] | Found in Morlac's World. Unmoving figures. Deteriorating forms.

DECROME | (DĀY-crŭm) | Rovet of the Adarian 45th. A flat-nosed warrior with overly long arms. Known more for his courage than his compassion.

DELACROY | (dĕllă-CRŎĪ) | City—The city of Morlac. Where Morlac lives and pilgrims journey, seeking an invitation to live within one of the Nine Circles.

> [*also*] **DELCREAN** when referencing residents of Delacroy

DELCREAN ROTGUT | A clear liquor distilled from potatoes and honey. A strong drink for even the most dedicated drunkards.

DELLA *OR* **TAGGLE** | (dĕl-LĂ) | A taggle girl with unusually white eyes and unblemished skin—healthy in appearance. Member of Uncle Taggle's adopted family. Commonly identified as DK Vel's first love.

DELLINA *OR* **TAGGLE** | (dĕl-LĬNĂ) | A taggle girl. Daughter of Della. DK Vel notes she had a slender frame, black hair, and a throaty voice.

DENAM | (dĕ-NŬN) | Resident of Fourth Circle. Basket merchant. Accused of selling baskets that fall apart within a month. Blessed with an ageless complexion.

> [*also*] **denam-basket** when referring to the baskets made by Denam.

DIATO *OR* **TAGGLE** | (DĬ-ăto) | Fifth Gate Taggle.

DISEN T'LADE | (DĬ-SĬN tŭh-LĀD) | A name from prophecy. Also, separately, cousin to Troq.

DISSEMINATION POLE | A visual decree displaying the sculpted wooden head of the condemned atop a long, ornately decorated pole. Carried like a trophy through the streets of Delacroy pronouncing an approaching beheading. A traditional precursor to the guillotine.

DK VEL *OR* **TAGGLE** | (D-K-vĕl) | A taggle boy. Storyteller.

DRAGON'S ORE | Consumable fuel source favored by Hiate for its ability to burn evenly and produce the concentrated heat required to forge metal objects. Mined from Dragon's Torment. Deep red in color before burning.

DRAGON'S TONGUE | Pass leading from Caduum into Dragon's Torment. Steep, but offers solid footing.

DRAGON'S TORMENT | Mountain range. Cursed dwelling place of Morlac.

> [*also*] **[the] Torment** *or* **[the] Dragon** when speaking in general terms.

DSAL TIGER | (DĬ-SŎL) | The figure of Dsal Tiger varies greatly depending upon the dallic where the taggle was born, ranging from Kiel where he is portrayed as white with black stripes, to Ire where he is described as being all black, more panther-like. In Caduum, Dsal Tiger is described as having two red eyes. His fur is white, and he has a single black stripe—a scar on his left side reaching from shoulder to hindquarters. In Adarian, Dsal Tiger is orange with black stripes and has a short tail and three white paws. No matter his physical appearance, however, Dsal Tiger is always depicted as a tragic figure and sardonic sage who never emerges the victor. Instead, his tales serve as warning that they may guide the listener to the Sphere. (Traditional tales may or may not include other characters such as rabbit, owl, wolf, or bear among other creatures.)

EDRAN *OR* **TAGGLE** | (ĔD-rĭn) | A taggle boy. Apprentice to Hiate, the blacksmith. Known for his red hair.

> [*also*] **EDRAN** | Apprentice to Troq, the cook, and servant of Boltmar, Fourth Circle Magnate.

ELE | (ĔL) | City—Located near the center of the known land just northwest of the *Lake of Seven Cities*; conquered by Yenen prior to the *Battle at Quel*.

ELSANE | (ĔL-SĀN) | Resident of Fourth Circle.

ENYURE | (ĕn-YĒR) | Deceased. First Etabli for she who served During the Completion of the Green Moon under the seal of the Two Crowns.

eodor sap | (Ā-dŏr) | Sap derived from a common tree found in the outer lands; often used as a green dye.

ERBOHN | (ĔR-bŏn) | Deceased. First Etabli for she who served During the Completion of the Red Moon under the seal of the Crown of Leaves.

ERIN, THE FIRST ETABLI | (ĔR-ĭn) | Deceased. Original First Etabli who served During the Completion of the Purple Moon under the seal of the Floating Crown Over Sphere.

ERIN'S FIRE | (ĔR-ĭn) | A flower with red pedals and a white center that floats on the water. Prevalent on *Lake Yenul*.

ERIN'S MAST | (ĔR-ĭn) | A shipping vessel.

ERISYTE | (ĔR-ĭ-SĪT) | Consort of Gan.

EROG | (ĔR-ŭg) | First month of the spheric calendar.

ESHION | (ĔSH-Ē-ŏn) | Rovet of the Stycral 14th.

ETIOLATING PHLOGISTON | (ē-tē-ŬH-lăt flŏ-JĬS-tŏn) | An ancient Delcrean tale about the mystic qualities of fire, though translations vary.

EXCHURE | (ĔKS-chĕr) | Magnate, Seventh Circle.

FAEL | (FĀY-ĕl) | Deceased. First Etabli for she who served During the Changing of the Blue Moon under the seal of the Crowned Warrior.

FANZIR | (FĂN-zēr) | Resident of Fourth Circle. Bookkeeper.

FATHER OF OBLATION | Worshiper of the Sphere who has committed himself to a life of service and to the ministry of the Fire. Head of the

Fire and leader of the Sons and Daughters of Oblation.

FAUNRIDE | (făhn-RĪD) | A member of the Adowian Guard. Succeeded Troq as chosen protector of the Daughter of the Adow.

FERYA | (fĕrh-Ā) | Deceased. First Etabli for she who served During the Completion of the Green Moon under the seal of the Hammer Striking Crown.

FILLOP | (PHĬLĬP) | Overseer of Second Circle.

FIRE OF THE SPHERE *or* [**the**] **FIRE** | A place of worship. Home to the Sons and Daughters of Oblation who tend to the fire that ever burns high above the city.

FIRST ASSASSIN | Mythical slayer of those who seek to ascend to godhood—those who dare challenge the Sphere. Whereas Morlac deploys many assassins, the Sphere has need of only one.

FIRST ETABLI | (Ē-tăb-LĒ) | Consort and Protector of The Adow.

FIRST TAGGLE | (t-ĂG-le) | The first tru-born of Delacroy. Created by Morlac. Builder of Delacroy.

FLATINE | (FLĀ-tēn) | Fourth month of the spheric calendar.

FLINT | A swad armed with a flintlock rifle.

FURMEC RO | (fîr-MĔK-rōh) | A vile curse rarely used, and never in polite company.

GALEAB | (gŭ-LĒB) | Honored Magnate, Ninth Circle.

GALINOR | (găl-ē-NŎR) | Considered a leader amongst the sorcerers.

GAN, OVERSEER OF ADARIAN | (GĂN) | Caretaker of Adarian. Powerful ruler-type, second only to the Adow in political power. Old, dreadfully old. Lover of Erisyte.

GAN-PI | (GĂN-PĪ) | An pimple-faced warrior of the Adarian 45th.

gefor | (gĕ-FĬR) | A chamber pot.

GIEEL | (GĪ-ĒL) | A character in *Misdeblue*, an ancient tale.

GILVAN | (gĭl-VŬN) | An Adowian Guard with straw colored hair and a missing front tooth.

GOD OF ANOTHER WORLD | Term used when referencing Morlac.

GOLD KEEPER | Designated collector of wagers at a beheading.

GOLEB | (GO-lĕ-b) | Resident of Adarian. DK Vel notes his rooftop served as the place where Dellina told a taggle's tale.

GOLESH | (GO-lĕ-sh) | City—Part of the seven islands that comprise the *Lake of Seven Cities.*

Golesh 13th | (GO-lĕ-sh) | Division of the Adowian Army. Part of the Adowian Army seeking the Arms of the Sphere in Dragon's Torment.

Golesh 41st | (GO-lĕ-sh) | Division of the Adowian Army. Journeyed to the Torment.

Golesh 47th | (GO-lě-sh) | Division of the Adowian Army. Journeyed to the Torment.

GUBYER | (GŬB-yr) | A traitor whom the Adarian 45th tracked down in Nelic Mountains.

HALCROMB | (hăl-KRŬM) | Grey-bearded warrior of the Adarian 45th. Father of Shamlon.

HARIAN | (HĚR-Ē-ĭn) | Resident of Fourth Circle. Cousin of Maldinado's long-deceased spouse.

HEALER | Someone skilled in mending wounds and comforting the sick.

HEMMING TREE | (hě-MĒ-n) | A type of tree.

Hemming Tree Forest | (hě-MĒ-n) | Geographic forested area located along the southwestern coast line.

HENRIT | (hĕn-RĬT) | Pilgrim possessing a black mole on his left ear.

HERALD | Learned speaker of words, often the only means by which a topi may hear, for example, an Adowian Decree.

hessup leaf | (HĔS-sŭp) | Pulled from the hessup tree found along the coastline. Often used as a blue dye.

HETHOR *OR* **TAGGLE** | (hĕth-OR) | Sixth Gate Taggle.

HIATE | (HĪ-āyt) | A red-bearded blacksmith. Resident of Caduum.

HINTOR | (HĬN-TOR) | A farmer from Plenrid. His friendship with Maldinado allows him to serve in the Adarian 45th.

HONCHERUB | (HŎN-chĕr-ŬB) | Magnate, Third Circle.

IG-POY | (ĬG-PŎĪ) | Deceased. First Etabli for she who served During the Changing of the Silver Moon under the seal of the Five Crowns.

ILION *OR* **TAGGLE** | (Ī-lēŏn) | A taggle. Member of Uncle Taggle's adopted family. Lover of Sanbi and, perhaps, father of Lay-I.

IRLOORE | (Ī-LŌ) | Deceased. First Etabli for she who served During the Completion of the Green Moon under the seal of the Crowned Rooster.

ININDU | (Ĭ-nĭn-DŌ) | A single creature comprised of topi and horse. The horse speaks, but the topi is mute. Sister of the Adow. Once, caretaker of the Daughter(s) of the Adow. Created by the Sphere at the beginning of time. Eternal. Jaded lover of Adarian, Hero of Ire.

> [*also*] **topi-Inindu** *or* **Inindu-horse** when referring to one portion of the creature that is Inindu.

> [*also*] **Inindu** when describing the personified myth of death or unexplained acts of horror.

IRE | (Ī-r) | Coastal City—Known for the *Battle of Ire*. Death place of Adarian, hero of Ire.

JANEEL *OR* **TAGGLE** | (jă-NĒL) | An old taggle woman. DK Vel describes her as a hunchback, and horribly scarred, but full of energy. He also notes she did not travel to the Torment.

JASPER| (jăs-PĬR) | Deceased. Former resident of Fourth Circle.

JETHROME | (JĔ-th-ROM) | Magnate, Fifth Circle

JENNAWEEN *OR* **TAGGLE** | (JĔN-ă-wēn) | Fourth Gate Taggle.

JIN *OR* **TAGGLE** | (JĬN) | A taggle woman. DK Vel notes her wide brown eyes sparkled and burned - indeed they conveyed vibrant emotions.

JOONE | (JŌ-nē) | Last month of the spheric calendar.

JOWL | (JŎWL) | Chosen by Morlac at the Nascence.

KALETINE | (kăl-ĕ-TĪN) | Adarian resident. Daughter of Kanbis and Nataline. Niece of Maldinado.

KANBIS | (kăn-BĬS) | Deceased. Former husband of Nataline.

KIEL | (KĪ-ĕl) | City—Located inland near the southern coast.

Kiel 2nd | (KĪ-ĕl) | Division of the Adowian Army. Journeyed to the Torment.

Kiel 9th | (KĪ-ĕl) | Division of the Adowian Army. Journeyed to the Torment.

KILAR | (KĪ-lăwr) | City—Part of the seven islands that comprise the *Lake of Seven Cities*.

KINU | (KĪ-nū) | Resident of Fourth Circle. Scarf weaver. Mother of Phinx.

    [*also*] **kinu-scarf** when referring to the scarves made by Kinu.

KIPLA *OR* **TAGGLE** | (K ĬP-lă) | Fifth Gate Taggle.

KOME | (ko-MĀ) | Post, Second Circle.

KOYO *OR* **MOTHER** | (coy-YO) | Gave birth to the taggles after an affair with Taggle, the cursed, producing the only male offspring of any First Etabli.

KUL | (KŬL) | A mystery.

LAKE OF SEVEN CITIES | A large lake containing seven island cities including Yenul where the Adow resides.

LAKE YENUL | A lake held above the cavernous entrance of Yenul by ancient magic. An ever active geyser erupts into and forms the underbelly of this lake.

    [*also*] **BLOOD LAKE** [*common*]

LAUS | (LŎWS) | Historical figure. Former Adherent of Delacroy.

LAY-I *OR* **TAGGLE** | (LĀY-Ī) | An unmarked taggle baby with red hair.

Born in secret and hidden from the dallic guards. Daughter of Sanbi and, perhaps, Ilion.

LEET SOCNO | (LĒT SŌK-nō) | A banner-like marriage token designed by the bride, and then placed over the couple's intertwined hands. After the ceremony, it is hung above the couple's bedroom door.

LEWHIT | (lū-HĬT) | Pilgrim in possession of a ram's horn.

light essence | A term for describing someone's soul.

LILTHIAN *OR* **TAGGLE** [AND HER THREE DAUGHTERS] | (LĬL-thē-ĂN) | Fifth Gate Taggles. Dancers [daughters]. Violinist [mother].

LIO | (LĒ-OH) | Deceased. First Etabli for she who served During the Completion of the Green Moon under the seal of the Crown over Crossed Swords.

LOMAX | (LO-măks) | Resident of Fourth Circle. Basket merchant. Husband to Muriel.

> [*also*] **lomax-basket** when referring to the baskets made by Lomax.

LOR | (lore) | City—Located near the edge of the known land.

LUCEN *OR* **TAGGLE** | (lew-CĔN) | A taggle boy. DK Vel notes the boy told stories with uncommon maturity and a surprisingly deep voice.

LULL | (LŬL) | City—Located near the western coast line; conquered by Yenen prior to the *Battle at Quel.*

Lull 28th | (LŬL) | Division of the Adowian Army. Journeyed to the Torment.

LYSHMEE *OR* **TAGGLE** | (lĭ-SH-mē) | A taggle girl.

> [*also*] **LYSHMEE** | The condemned. Resident of Second Circle.

MADAR | (MĀD-r) | A blood inheritance. Formal leaders of battle divisions. Detested cowards who quietly hide in their luxurious tents while Rovets lead their warriors into battle.

MADIC BALTIN | (mă-DĬK bal-TĬN) | A name from prophecy. Also, separately, brother of Troq.

MAGNATE | (MĂG-năyt) | The governing ruler of each circle as appointed by Morlac and passed down through bloodline; all except the chaste Magnates of Second Circle, least of the rulers, who ascend by selection process as determined by the previous Magnate.

MALDINADO | (MŬL-dŭh-năw-DOH) | Madar of the Adarian 45th. Friend of Hintor. Brother of Nataline. Son of Breline. Maldinado means *wrath of the Sphere.*

> [*also*] **MALDINADO** | The most prominent resident of Fourth Circle. If the roads of Delacroy end at Morlac's palace, they

begin at Maldinado's doorstep. Robe merchant. Residents throughout Delacroy wear his robes.

>[*also*] **maldinado-robe** when referring to the robes made by Maldinado.

MALI | (MĂW-lē) | City—Part of the seven islands that comprise the *Lake of Seven Cities*.

Mali 6th | (MĂW-lē) | Division of the Adowian Army. Journeyed to the Torment.

MARDTBREN | (MĂWR-T-brīn) | A farmer from Plenrid. Father of Hintor.

MATHAY | (MĂ-th-Ā) | A swad.

MENDELSOHN | (men-DŬL-sĕn) | Resident of Third Circle. Son of Tania.

MERRUDI | (MĔR-ū-DĒ) | Cook and servant of Boltmar, Fourth Circle Magnate. Reports to Troq.

MISDEBLUE | (MĬS-dŭh-blō) | An ancient tale about two anonymous lovers, Tenush and Gieel, filled with whimsical and witty dialogue; ultimately, a hopeful tale often recited and, on occasion, performed onstage.

MISTAN *OR* **TAGGLE** | (mĭ-ST-ăhn) | A taggle girl. Granddaughter of DK Vel.

MORLAC | (more-LĂK) | God of another world. A castoff disciple of the Sphere.

MORUNON | (MO-rū-NĪN) | Magnate, Sixth Circle.

MURAT | (MĔR-ăt) | Resident of Second Circle. Seamstress.

>[*also*] **murat-gown** when referring to the gowns made by Murat.

MURDIN | (MĔR-dĭn) | A pilgrim on the road to Delacroy. Father of Albie. Brother of Bontlevier.

MURIEL | (MĔR-Ē-ĕl) | Resident of Fourth Circle. Known for her black teeth. Wife to Lomax.

MYRTANE | (MĔR-TĀNĒ) | Cook and servant of Boltmar, Fourth Circle Magnate. Reports to Troq.

NARCH | (NĂR-sh) | Overseer of Fourth Circle.

NASCENCE | (NĂ-sŭhns) | A gathering of Delcreans to Ninth Circle during which time, Morlac selects one of them to join him and live in the Ruby Palace.

NASCIENT | (NĂ-sē-ŬHNT) | A mysterious creature created by Morlac.

NATALINE | (NĂ-tă-LĪN) | Adarian resident. Sister of Maldinado.

Daughter of Breline. Wife of Kanbis. (Deceased) Mother of Kaletine and Belur.

NATIEL | (NĂ-tēl) | Chosen by Morlac at the Nascence.

NEBON | (NĔH-bĭn) | Resident of Third Circle. Food merchant.

NELIC MOUNTAINS | (NĔH-lĭk) | Mountainous area separating Adarain and Tesa; the southern foot of Dragon's Torment.

NELIC STEMS | (NĔH-lĭk) | Flower found in the Nelic Mountains. Known for their smoke-like odor. A favorite of she who served as the third Adow.

NINE CIRCLES OF DELACROY | (dĕllă-CRŎĪ) | First Circle: Certainty. Second Circle: Chastity. Third Circle: Fasting. Fourth Circle: Generosity. Fifth Circle: Joy. Sixth Circle: Orthodoxy. Seventh Circle: Peace. Eighth Circle: Honesty. Ninth Circle: Faithfulness.

obian date | (o-BĒĬN) | Fruit of the obian tree.

OG | (ŎG) | A member of the Adowian Guard.

ORPHEUM | (or-FĒ-ŭm) | Deceased. Former Magnate, Ninth Circle.

outer lands | The horrific lands beyond Delacroy where a mysterious creature hunts and from which pilgrims flee.

OVDA | (ŭh-V-dŭh) | [short for *of the*] Troq's nickname for the Daughter *of the* Adow.

OVERSEER | Entrusted with the governance of a designated city, as appointed by the Adow.

    [*also*] **OVERSEER** | Keepers of Delcrean law. Top-ranked officer amongst the swads

PEEKS | (PĒ-ks) | Resident of Third Circle. Inspector of weights and measures.

PEL F'RUTE | (Pĕhl fŭh-RŌT) | A name from prophecy. Also, separately, brother of Troq.

PENREM *OR* **TAGGLE** | (pĕn-RĔM) | A taggle boy.

    [*also*] **PENREM** | The condemned. Resident of Eighth Circle.

PERINAH | (PĀR-ĭ-NĂW) | Resident of Second Circle.

PHAIN | (FĀN) | Pilgrim bearing three silver earrings in his left ear.

PHINX *OR* **TAGGLE** | (FĒ-nĭks) | Eighth Gate taggle. Painter.

PHIRE *OR* **TAGGLE** | (FĪ-r) | A taggle boy known to have traveled with DK Vel. Died with his hands tied, a captive on the road from Catareb.

PILGRIM | A follower of Morlac.

PLENRID | (pl-ĔN-RĬD) | City—Farm land. Hintor's home. Located near the center of the known land just northeast of Stycral; conquered by Yenen prior to the *Battle at Quel*.

POST | Carriers of messages for and from their respective Magnate.

PWAX | (fŭ-WĂCKS) | A member of the Adowian Guard.

QUEL | (qu-ĔL) | Destroyed City—Known for the *Battle at Quel*.

RAB | (RĂB) | Resident of Fourth Circle.

RAWLIS | (răw-LĬS) | Farmland settlement located in the outer lands.

RAYSHIN *OR* **TAGGLE** | (RĀ-shĭn) | Sixth Gate Taggle.

RECORDER OF DELACROY | Appointed keeper of lists recording residents of and movement within the Nine Circles of Delacroy.

REMNI | (RĔM-nē) | Post, Fourth Circle. Secret lover of Boltmar.

RHIL PATTERN | (r-ĬL) | Pattern in 5-Ruby: Two tusks located within the circle, each pointing toward the other; one tusk outside the circle and pointing away from the circle on the left, or Yowt and Begn, side.

RHIL RUBY | (r-ĬL) | Top right ruby in 5-Ruby.

RIN | (r-ĬN) | City—Part of the seven islands that comprise the *Lake of Seven Cities*.

Rin 9th | (r-ĬN) | Division of the Adowian Army. Fought in the Battle at Quel.

RISTAN | (r-ĬST-ăwn) | Overseer of Ninth Circle.

RORNE TRIBES *or* [the] **RORNE** | (ror-NĔ) | Mysterious native tribes inhabiting Dragon's Torment.

ROVET | (ro-VĔT) | A warrior who has proven himself in battle. Division leaders, but not the *formal* leaders of each unit. That title belongs to the otherwise detested Madars—a blood inheritance. While the Madars quietly hide in their luxurious tents, Rovets lead their warriors into battle.

RUTHEE *OR* **TAGGLE** | (rū-THĒ) | A taggle woman. Mother of five children. DK Vel notes she once gave him shelter, and further mentions her brother who survived the Torment only to die from a beating two days after his return, beaten by the same guard who carved into the ears of the youngest of Ruthee's children.

SAN RIENA | (SĂN RĒ-ĕnă) | City—Located in the outer lands.

SANBI *OR* **TAGGLE** | (săn-BĒ) | A taggle woman. Lover of Ilion. Mother of Lay-I.

SARKE | (SĂRK) | Chosen by Morlac at the Nascence.

sarlin root | (SĂR-lĭn) | A desert legume often used as a red dye.

SELMA | (SĔL-mŭ) | Cook and servant of Boltmar, Fourth Circle Magnate. Reports to Troq.

SELPHA | (SĔL-fŭ) | Deceased. Former resident of Sixth Circle.

Staged an unsuccessful attempt to rescue her husband, B'tul.

SCARLET | A prostitute.

SCHOLAR | Someone devoted to books and understanding the mysteries contained therein; also, recorders of prophecy as spoken by the Adow. Identified by their purple robes.

SHALE | (SHĀL) | Adherent of Delacroy.

SHAMLON | (SHĂM-lŭn) | Red-haired warrior of the Adarian 45th. Son of Halcromb.

SHARDELL | (SHĂR-dĕl) | Deceased. Painter who died young.

SILAR | (SĪ-lăr) | Name of the goat owned by Kaletine and Belur.

SIMIAD | (sĭ-MĒĂD) | Magnate, Second Circle. Disciple of Turnac. Least amongst his peers.

snarble extract | (SNĂR-bŭl) | Made from the anther of a snarble flower; often used as an orange dye, or smoked like tobacco.

SOL PEDANTIC | (sole pŭh-DĂN-TĬK) | A name from prophecy. Also, separately, uncle to Troq.

SOMERING | (sŏm-RĒN) | Appointed Recorder of Delacroy.

SONS OF OBLATION | Worshipers of the Sphere who have committed themselves to a life of service and to the ministry of the Fire.

SORCERER | A pompous sect of society given to vocal and frequent complaints. Good for amusing tricks, but generally useless in a battle. Identified by their black robes.

SORSE | (SORE-se) | Coastal City—Located along the southern coast.

SORTING TOWER | Spaced evenly around First Circle, eight large stone platforms serve as the focus of each annual Sorting, and as a platform from which the eight magnates announce those chosen to reside in Delacroy.

SOSIID | (so-SĒD) | Post, Eighth Circle.

SPHERE | (s-FĒR) | God.

SPHERE PATTERN | (s-FĒR) | Pattern in 5-Ruby: Two tusks pointing downward toward the Unern and Begn, one tusk pointing upward at the Sphere, all three tusks contained within the circle.

SPHERE RUBY | (s-FĒR) | Top ruby in 5-Ruby.

SPRINGS OF MIST | Geographic region located in upper northwest.

STRADE | (STRĀD) | Resident of Fourth Circle. Candle merchant.

STYCRAL | (STĪ-crŭl) | City—Located near the center of the known land just southwest of Plenrid; conquered by Yenen prior to the *Battle at Quel*.

Stycral 12th | (STĪ-crŭl) | Disgraced division of the Adowian Army.

Fought with Yenen against the Adow in the Battle at Quel.

Stycral 14th | (**STĪ-crŭl**) | Division of the Adowian Army. Journeyed to the Torment.

SUMATRAN | (**sū-MŎ-trĕn**) | Archaic name for tiger.

SWAD | (**sw-ĂD**) | Soldier.

SWORD OF THE SPHERE | Name given to the sword the Adow carries, yet never wields in battle.

tacia wood | (**TĀ-shē-ă**) | Made from tacia wood sawdust; often used as a purple dye.

TAGGLE | (**t-ĂG-le**) | A descendant of Taggle, the First Etabli who betrayed the Adow, identified by the scars given to all taggles—their pointed ears carved into and made round at the tip as they exit the womb. It's the mark of their bloodline, the curse given to them by the Adow because Taggle had an affair with Koyo, producing a male yearling. They're allowed to live because of their father, but their ears are a sign to all that their birth, their life, is not recognized by the Adow. They're not topis. They're taggles. Oddly, they are the keepers of story, great orators allowed to share their tales with everyone but the Adow–never the Adow, for although a select few are chosen to serve the Adow directly, they are forbidden to speak in her presence.

TAGGLE, THE CURSED *OR* **FATHER** | (**t-ĂG-le**) | Deceased. First Etabli for she who served During the Shadow of the Purple Moon under the seal of the Sword through Crown. He betrayed the Adow when he had an affair with Koyo, producing a male yearling. Father of the taggles.

> [*also*] **taggle** Artisans. Pure born of Delacroy and most favored by Morlac. Typically found within the city's gates selling their wares, dancing, painting, and telling fantastic tales. Available to perform darker and deadlier arts for a sizable fee.

TAGGLE'S PRAYER | (**t-ĂG-les**) | Tattooed markings on a taggle's knuckles which translates as follows: *Forgive our mother* [Koyo], *Remember our father* [Taggle, the cursed].

TAGGLE'S TALE | (**t-ĂG-les**) | An oral story as spoken, with minimal performance elements, by a taggle; often considered the only true value of a taggle. Few topis will dare tell a story in public for it is considered beneath them as proper members of society. Thus, and though the taggles serve as protectors of story, a taggle storyteller is not a position of honor.

TANIA | (**TĂ-nē-Ă**) | Resident of Third Circle. Mother of Mendelsohn.

TANNESSA | (TĂ-ně-SĂ) | A swad. Younger cousin of Lomax.

TASA RO | (t-ĂSĂ-roh) | A common curse muttered or shouted when someone feels perplexed, vexed, or otherwise finds the moment entirely out-of-sorts.

TENUSH | (tě-NŌSH) | A character in *Misdeblue*, an ancient tale.

TESA | (tě-SĂ) | City—Located near the edge of the known land.

Tesa 89th | (tě-SĂ) | Division of the Adowian Army. Journeyed to the Torment and wielded swords made by Hiate the blacksmith.

TESHA | (těsh-Ă) | Warrior in the Rin 9th. Wounded at the Battle at Quel.

Tessel Region | (tě-SĔL) | Located in the southern provinces of the outer lands.

TEYO | (TĀY-oh) | A member of the Adowian Guard.

THREE HORNS TAVERN | A tavern located in Yenul, its main decoration a full-sized bronze sculpture of a three horned ram. It is also the only structure in Yenul erected using timber.

TILLY | (tĭl-Ē) | Apprentice to Troq, the cook, and servant of Boltmar, Fourth Circle Magnate. Clumsy.

TOPI | (to-PĒ) | Those descended from the Adow.

TOPHER | (TOH-fur) | Resident of Second Circle. Robe merchant. Accused of selling "rags" rather than robes.

    [*also*] **topher-robe** when referring to the robes made by Topher.

TRETH *OR* **TAGGLE** | (TR-ěth) | [an] Uncle Taggle. DK Vel notes the Uncle lived in the Abre dallic and spoke slowly and with great patience, allowing the audience to absorb both the rhythm of his voice and the meaning of his words.

TROQ | (TR-ŎK) | Deceased. Former guardian of the Daughter of the Adow. A member of the Adowian Guard.

    [*also*] **TROQ** | Cook who oversees all kitchen prep and staff within the manor. Servant of Boltmar, Fourth Circle Magnate.

TRU-BORN | Those born within the walls of Delacroy. Taggles.

T'THAY | (TĂ-thā) | (former) Adherent of Delacroy.

TULOO *OR* **TAGGLE** | (tŭh-LŌ) | A taggle man. DK Vel notes the man told his story with minimal physical movement.

TURNAC | (tŭr-NĂK) | (former) Magnate, Second Circle.

TYMER | (TĪ-měr) | Resident of Seventh Circle. Kurta merchant. Tailor to the swads.

    [*also*] **tymer-kurta** when referring to the kurtas made by Tymer.

UNCLE TAGGLE | (t-ĂG-le) | Term given to the oldest living taggle within any given dallic.

UNERN PATTERN| (Ū-NRN) | Pattern in 5-Ruby: Two tusks located within the circle, each pointing toward the other; the third tusk pointing toward the Rhil and Unern rubies is also within the circle.

UNERN RUBY| (Ū-NRN) | Bottom right ruby in 5-Ruby.

UTINE | (Ū-TĬN) | Second month of the spheric calendar.

VALIN | (vā-LĬN) | A member of the Adowian Guard.

VALUN | (vă-LĔN) | Son of Boltmar, Magnate of Fourth Circle. Always clean shaven.

VITREC *OR* **TAGGLE** | (VĪ-trĕk) | A taggle boy.

      [*also*] **VITREC** | Fourth Gate taggle. Storyteller.

WAYLON *OR* **TAGGLE** | (wā-LĔN) | Second Gate taggle. Famed sculptor of the condemned.

wia fruit | (WĒ-ă) | Melon sized citrus fruit. Typically yellow in color; sometimes green-striped.

white box | A guard post located beneath Morlac's Ruby Palace. Attendants of the white box trade-off three hour shifts, ready to arose a full legion of servants should the Adherent have need of them.

WORSHIPER OF MORLAC | (more-LĂK) | A sect of topis who secretly worship the god of another world, actively seeking to kill the Adow who serves as the voice of the Sphere—a god they despise.

YAWEH | (YĂ-wē) | City—Part of the seven islands that comprise the *Lake of Seven Cities*.

YEARLING | (yēr-lēng) | A child topi.

YENEN| (YĔH-nĕn) | Rebel leader of the uprising at Quel. Formerly, a member of the Adowian Guard.

YENUL | (YĔH-nūl) | Royal City—Home to the Adow. Comprised of a series of extensive tunnels and enormous caverns located beneath the *Lake of Seven Cities*.

YERI | (YĔHR-ē) | Torch Keeper who runs the length of Delacroy each night to light the torches throughout the city, and again at dawn to douse the flames.

YIDDICK | (YĬD-dĕk) | Resident of Ninth Circle. Shawl merchant. Favored by Morlac.

      [*also*] **yiddick-shawl** when referring to the shawls made by Yiddick.

YLA | (Ē-lă) | A member of the Adowian Guard.

YLAF | (Ē-lŏf) | Deceased. First Etabli for she who served During the Completion of the Red Moon under the seal of the Broken Crown.

YOKUR | (YO-cure) | City—Part of the seven islands that comprise the *Lake of Seven Cities*.

Yokur 3rd | (YO-cure) | Division of the Adowian Army. Fought in the Battle at Ire. Mistakenly attacked by the Adarian 41st.

YOWT PATTERN| (y-ŎWT) | Pattern in 5-Ruby: All three tusks located within the circle; all of them must face the Yowt ruby.

YOWT RUBY| (y-ŎWT) | Top left ruby in 5-Ruby.

GLOSSARY OF RITUALS & TRADITIONS

ADARIAN GREETING RITUALS | Reserved for when the Adow visits Adarian. A test of the Adow. A rite of passage consisting of twenty-four greetings with five hours between each one. The greetings are precise in verbiage, dress, and ritual, and any slip of the tongue or gap in protocol brings perceived weakness upon the Adow. The rituals end with a masquerade and several ribbon dances that lead up to the Toast of Sark when all participants choose a partner to kiss before toasting the Adow's arrival.

> [*also*] **Greeting Feast** or **Tenth [other number] Greeting** when referring to a specific portion of the greeting rituals.

> [*also*] **[the] Toast of Sark** a popular alternative name since the Toast of Sark serves as the most popular and widely attended portion of the rituals.

ADDRESSING THE ADOW | It is tradition for a speaker to address the First Etabli unless the Adow initiates the discussion.

ADOW IN BATTLE | The Adow's sword, the Sword of the Sphere, remains sheathed. No Adow has ever used the sword. One of the Adow–the one who reigned during the time when Fael was First Etabli, whose seal was a Crowned Warrior–is known to have practiced swordplay in her early years. But even that Adow never drew her sword in battle, and most Adow are never taught such maneuvers. She may enter battle wearing ornamental armor or, as is more often the case, don a traditional white linen blouse with golden doublet and matching trousers. The Adow does not fight in battle, for she has an army, a royal guard, and a chosen protector to fight for her.

ADOW'S APPEARANCE | All Adow share a likeness to one another. It is how they are identified as chosen by the Sphere, confirmed as his chosen ruler.

ADOW'S JUDGMENT | (Occurring on the battlefield) Should the Sphere approve of the Adow's actions, and those of her warriors, light will emanate from her body and she will rise above the battle for all to see, signifying an end to the war; a symbol of either imminent judgment or pending victory for the warriors below.

ADOWIAN BURIAL | A burial ceremony attended by the Adow. Rare. Considered the highest of honors. Upon death, a funeral procession travels the land, stopping at every city for a five-day celebration of life before returning to Yenul where they burn the body in the Fire of the Sphere. Traditionally reserved only for the Adow, and for her First Etabli, only one other, Beaug, sculptor of Adarian, has received such an honor.

BEGGARS | Charity toward beggars in the form of food or token is considered honorable, and the greater honor when giving to the point of personal sacrifice as when someone gives bread to a beggar, and then must fast for lack of food.

BRANDING OF THE ADARIAN 45TH | Warriors of the Adarian 45th are branded as part of their initiation, leaving an unmistakable sphere upon their chest.

BROTH AND BEER | A favorite drink in the Caduum region. The broth, typically chicken flavored, is served in a bowl and consumed in whole prior to quickly drinking the goblet of beer in its entirety. A messy drink, most cannot complete both with a dry chin unless they dawdle which otherwise defeats the spirit of the quickly-gulped drink; or keep from retching afterward which speaks to the competitive nature of the drink. Considered a test of character. Rarely consumed alone.

CADUUM WRAITHS AND SCARS | Those who live in Caduum will greet strangers with a question, "Have you a scar?" In a city where wraiths often appear, residents prove they are real by displaying their scars—inflicted by self or happenstance, for in death all wounds are left behind with the body.

CHANCE—INNER-CITY OF ADARIAN | Once a place used to collect the dead and diseased, Gan, Overseer of Adarian, transformed the inner-city of Adarian into a colorful, exotically morbid, and risqué night destination. The bones of the dead serve as ornamental pieces. Full skeletons—posed unnaturally and often with mouths open in laughter—guard every doorway. Chance serves as Adarian's default celebration destination following a Final Cleansing, boasts a rooftop marketplace above countless taverns, and generally ignores questionable behavior whether of the lecherous or devious sort. Most scholars consider Chance ensnared in the struggle between the Sphere and Morlac, some of whom suggest it serves as Morlac's only connection to the land.

CHILD OF THE ADOW | Known as the Daughter of the Adow, this child serves as the only child of the Adow; a child gifted to the land by the Sphere, thereby granting the Adow a form of eternal life as spirit passes from mother to daughter with the former's death. Inindu once served as formal caretaker but now a chosen warrior looks after and guards the Daughter of the Adow.

[*also*] **Daughter of the Adow**

CHOOSING A FIRST ETABLI [ALSO] DEATH OF A FIRST ETABLI
Upon the death of a First Etabli his Adow will select one of the Adowian Guard to assume the role of both protector and consort. Once the Adow passes from one (old) body to the Daughter of the Adow's (new) body, she is able to, again, bear children with the First Etabli of her (prior) choosing serving as the father.

CLEANSING RITUAL | It is customary for those who worship the Sphere to undergo a cleansing on the fifth day of each month. This cleansing requires the worshiper to seek isolation so they may better focus their attention upon the Sphere.

CONDEMNING THE ADOW | Those who dare condemn the Adow while in her presence will quickly loose their head courtesy of the Adowian Guard. Their body will hang on display in the marketplace, and their name stricken from the Chronicles of Yenul [or other city].

CURSING OF THE BANNER BEARER | Adowian warriors are encouraged to openly mock, ridicule, or otherwise curse their division's banner bearer as it forces them to first find the lucky bastard and then follow them. In this manner, a heartily shouted and repulsive curse serves to unify and embolden a highly skilled division such as the Adarian 45th who, by all accounts, take great pride in their creative contumelies.

DEATH AND BURIAL | The body of a topi is burned in a ceremony conducted at the Fire of the Sphere. A taggle is dumped in a mass, open grave located within every dallic, denied the fire in one final curse.

DEATH OF A MADAR | As the only member of a battle division not required to fight in the actual battle, many a Rovet (or other warrior) has killed their respective Madar. These two titles, one earned with blood on the hands (Rovet) while the other (Madar) is passed down to those with shared blood, routinely cast diatribes at one another and seek alliances within the division—one through intimidation, one through manipulation. If the balance of power shifts toward the Madar, the Rovet is usually quick to take action and remove his only political threat within the ranks; thus placing a typically weaker heir into the role and better securing his grip upon the division.

DEATH OF A ROVET | (Occurring on the battlefield) The banner bearer moves the banner in a full circle five times.

DELCREAN BOW | A formal act of greeting between Delcreans. An act of humility, also, for the least favored resident initiates the bow, bringing forehead to forehead, upon which each resident displays a tattoo of circles indicating their place within the city. One who displays a four circle tattoo, for example, will wrap their hand around one with an eight circle tattoo, and bring the eight circle forehead toward the four circle forehead until they touch. In this manner, both parties acknowledge only the highly favored may approach the less favored; never the opposite. Note: Same-circle residents do not typically exchange such courtesies.

    [*also*] **[a taggle custom]** taggles bear no such tattoo

DELCREAN BRAIDS | A common hair style combining a single braid with a number of beads. Two beads signifies the wearer as a resident of Second Circle. Three beads, Third Circle. Etc.

EXCHANGE OF SWORDS | An Adarian tradition. Warriors exchange swords with a promise to exchange them again at battle's end. A promise to survive.

EXECUTIONS [DESIGNATED ROLES] | Three swads conduct the execution of the condemned, each with a specific role: 1. Orator 2. Executioner 3. Body Removal. Should the Executioner die during a rescue attempt, one of the other two swads will take up the responsibility.

FASTING RITUAL | It is customary for those who worship the Sphere to partake in a midday fast spanning five hours; and which occurs every fifth day.

FAVOR AND BOON | (bōn) | A common call and response salutation which intimates Morlac serves as the giver of such blessings.

    [*also*] **Morlac's Boon Upon Thee** serves as the formal variation; a call to which someone replies with equal formality or, more often, with the casual *favor and boon* response.

FIELDS OF BLOODGRASS | Grass fields near Adarian, each blade said to represent a drop of blood for every Adarian warrior who has died in battle.

FIRST CLEANSING | An observed isolation ritual conducted on a yearling's first birth celebration. The yearling is placed in the center of the attending family and friends, none of whom may embrace or touch or otherwise acknowledge the yearling's presence for five-minutes. After the ceremony, the yearling is celebrated as having survived their first cleansing.

FINAL CLEANSING | The burning of the dead conducted at the Fire of the Sphere. This topi ritual is then followed by a celebration of life for the departed.

FIRST ETABLI'S SHIELD | Display's an engraving of Erin, the First Etabli's head and torso.

FLOWER GIRLS AND BOYS | A selection of yearlings lead the procession as the condemned is led to the guillotine. They broadcast lily pedals, forcing the condemned to trample them.

GENERAL DISLIKE OF SCHOLARS AND SORCERERS | Honor is gained in battle and through service to the Adow. Those who seek an easier lifestyle, however, may choose to pursue scholarly studies or practice the craft of magic, but they will forever face public scorn, loathing, and ridicule. For some, it is worth the price, and well, they do have their moments of brilliance to ease the shame.

GUARDING THE ADOW | Twenty of the best warriors across the land are selected to serve in the Adowian Guard, and serve until death. The best of these warriors (typically) serves as First Etabli, as chosen by the Adow, and the next best warrior serves as guardian and caretaker of the Daughter of the Adow. The Adowian Guard work as a unit to scout, secure, and guard any area where the Adow may reside or travel; providing a constant sphere of protection. As for the First Etabli, he never leaves the Adow's side; similarly, the guardian and caretaker of the Daughter of the Adow never leaves her alone—both serve as a symbol of the ever-present Sphere, however, when the mother's spirit passes to the Daughter of the Adow the guardian and caretaker will remove himself from her side, thus allowing the First Etabli his rightful place beside the Adow.

INVITED TO LIVE IN NINTH CIRCLE | A sign of Morlac's favor. Worthy residents of Delacroy receive an invitation, thought reserved for the young, from the Adherent to move from their current circle to the much wealthier Ninth Circle.

KISSING OF GAUNTLETS | An Adarian warrior's tradition of kissing the back of their gauntlet in honor of their fallen brothers.

LEECHES | Commonly used by the healers to treat open wounds.

MADAR'S THRONE | Customarily made from silver.

MARK OF THE ADARIAN 45TH | Each warrior in the Adarian 45th boasts a circular mark burned into their chest; an act of initiation.

MARKING A TAGGLE | All descendent's of Taggle, the cursed, are marked at birth by removing the upper portion of the newborn's ears. To prevent a taggle from escaping the mark, therefore, each dallic is heavily guarded and every expectant mother closely watched.

MORLAC'S JUDGMENT | A rarely used legal appeal to Morlac asking him to review the case of a condemned Magnate.

MORLAC'S MARK | Circular tattoo placed on the forehead of Delcreans. The number of circles corresponds with the wearer's circle of residence within the city. In this sense, it serves as a circular key.

> [*also*] [**in greeting**] The resident with fewer circles upon their forehead initiates a customary greeting ritual, bringing the smaller number of circle(s) in contact with the larger number in an outward display of deference.

NASCENCE [FESTIVAL] | A gathering of Delcreans to Ninth Circle during which time, Morlac selects one of them to join him and live in the Ruby Palace.

ORACLE OF THE SPHERE | The Adow serves as voice of the Sphere. A group of scholars record her spoken prophecies.

ORPHANS | Battle comes with a cost and, as a result, many yearlings are left at or brought to, the steps of the Fire. These orphans are raised by the Daughters of Oblation.

Pass Beyond Ninth Circle | An expression of death indicating someone has died and no longer resides within the nine circles of Delacroy.

> [*also*] **join** [*the dead*] **at the bottom of the sea** which refers to the more common burial custom reserved for the less favored; those not invited to live in Ninth Circle.

PAY A TAGGLE | An act of faith and charity performed by Delcreans who seek personal gain. Pay a taggle, earn Morlac's favor. Earn Morlac's favor, move into a higher circle.

PRAYER RITUAL | It is customary for those who worship the Sphere to offer prayers five times each day: 1. A prayer of gratitude offered upon waking 2. A prayer for guidance offered after first meal 3. A prayer of silence offered at midday, listening rather than asking 4. A prayer advocating for others offered after the last meal *and* 5. A prayer of contemplation offered before sleep.

RED DEATH | Anonymous distributor of belladonna root known only by the mask they wear which is customarily red and without adornment. They attend every feast and festival in Adarian and are aggressively, if secretly, sought after by those in attendance. A simple exchange of gold for powder occurs, and then they disappear. Known as "Red Death" due to the lethal risk and symptoms associated with an overdose which cause the heart rate to rapidly increase before suddenly slowing and stopping; also a red rash seemingly bursts forth as though boiling atop the skin, and the victim further suffers from hallucinations and loss of balance.

> [*also*] [**the**] **mask of the Red Death**

RESCUING THE CONDEMNED | Every beheading promises a rescue attempt as a matter of tradition, to the point those who attend the execution place wagers on the success of such an occurrence. But the attempt always fails, usually led by members of Seventh Circle who hold an affinity for peace and maintain a general dislike for public executions.

SALUTATIONS | It is customary to greet a fellow topi with *May the Sphere be with you* which solicits a response of *And keep you in His light.*

SCHOLARLY ATTIRE | It is customary for a scholar to identify themselves as such by donning a purple robe.

SLEEPING TAGGLES | The taggles huddle together while sleeping with the eldest positioned in the middle of the circle of bodies and the youngest, or newest to join the circle, lying on the outermost perimeter of the circle. Newborns sleep at their mother's breast until they are old enough to endure the cold air that nighttime brings at which time they take their proper place within the circle. The taggles snuggle against or hug the body in front of them, and it is not unusual to find themselves embracing a cold body come morning.

[*also*] **taggle sleep circle**

SORCERER'S ATTIRE | It is customary for a sorcerer to identify themselves as such by donning a black robe.

SORTING | An annual ritual attended by pilgrims who seek entrance to the city of Delacroy. The sorting process refers to the drawing of names and the corresponding assignment of the chosen pilgrim to a specific circle within the city where they will then live and serve Morlac according to that circle's expression of worship.

SPEAKING TO THE ADOW | It is customary to address the First Etabli unless the Adow initiates the discussion.

TAGGLE GRAVESITE | Each dallic contains an open mass grave where taggle bodies are thrown when they die. Though it serves as a final destination it is rarely visited by those who still live, and never patrolled by dallic guards which has allowed more than one taggle to escape by hiding amongst the dead. Rarely covered, these mass graves harbor rotting flesh, ancient bones, and myriad diseases.

UNCLE TAGGLE | A term of respect given to an old taggle. Since few taggles see old age, they are considered remembered, or blessed, by the Sphere. A spoken blessing from Uncle Taggle, therefore, is considered good fortune.

WEDDING CEREMONY | The banner-like Leet Socno is designed by the bride, and then placed over the couple's interlocked hands. After the ceremony, the couple places the Leet Socno above their bedroom door.

WORSHIPING THE GOD OF ANOTHER WORLD | Those accused of worshiping the god of another world [Sphere] do not die alone. Behead the father, and also the son lest he go astray, in accordance with Delcrean laws.